"This second installment of the author's This Generation series continues the outlandish, yet compelling, story of powerful people attempting to bring about a New World Order via a revision of the Christian Gospel... It is, primarily, a fantastical thriller, drawing on the tropes of science fiction and mythology to ask questions about the fate of humanity that are moral as well as material. These are questions that will interest religious and secular readers alike, especially as technological advances bring us closer to knowledge that could reorient entire worldviews...

"A smartly written theological adventure from a dexterous student of biblical prophecy."

—*Kirkus Reviews*

"An audacious apocalyptic epic that fuses Christian myth and prophecy with science fiction elements... The story is powered by exceptional character development, an action-packed storyline, more than a few bombshell plot twists, and some mind-blowing speculation...

"The author has set the stage for some jaw-dropping, end-of-the-world-as-we-know-it action and adventure, and readers who have read the first two volumes will be anxious to get their hands on *Penance*, the third book in the series."

—*Blue Ink Review*

PENTECOST

THIS GENERATION SERIES: BOOK 2

PENTECOST

THIS GENERATION SERIES: BOOK 2

TC JOSEPH

ARCHWAY
PUBLISHING

Archway Publishing books may be ordered through booksellers or by contacting:

Archway Publishing
1663 Liberty Drive
Bloomington, IN 47403
www.archwaypublishing.com
1-(888)-242-5904

ISBN: 978-1-4808-1141-6 (sc)
ISBN: 978-1-4808-1142-3 (hc)
ISBN: 978-1-4808-1140-9 (e)

Library of Congress Control Number: 2014916528

Printed in the United States of America

Archway Publishing rev. date: 1/12/2015

For Mary Ellen,
and for the readers who have enjoyed the journey so far.

ACKNOWLEDGMENTS

I value my privacy and have joyously written under a pseudonym to preserve it! All in all I think it was a marvelous decision, but it is troubling when it comes to an acknowledgments page because it precludes me from thanking, by name, so many who have been instrumental in the production of this book. The failure to mention individuals is no reflection of the gratitude I feel. So I would like to offer a special thanks to the cadre of family and friends who read this novel in draft form. Each of your changes made this book better. Each word of encouragement was met with a grateful heart.

I also would like to thank the staff at Archway Publishing for taking a chance on me, for taking care of me, and for taking time to make this the best book series it could be.

AUTHOR'S NOTE
CATCHING UP

The *This Generation Series* is built on the premise that our generation has been the subject of prophetic writings from many traditions down through the ages. The series asks the questions

- What if these prophecies are right?
- What if these prophecies and visions are seeing the same events from different perspectives?
- What would it look like in the lives of three families if the visionaries are right?

In PRECIPICE, we looked at our cast of characters in 1969, 1979, and 1989. In PENTECOST, we catch up with them in 1999, 2009, and the present.

For those who have not read PRECIPICE, I encourage you to do so! But if you want to start the series with PENTECOST, here is a summary of what has occurred and a bit about the major characters.

The year 1969 introduces nineteen-year old orphaned heiress, Kimberly, and her older, manipulative half-brother, Benny, who is a Catholic priest with unbridled ambition. Kim is plagued by alien visitations and is convinced that only a pregnancy will thwart the aliens' plans for her. She takes matters into her own hands in an ill-advised visit to a backwater-Georgia bar, and pregnancy ensues. Not entirely thwarted, the aliens manipulate the DNA of her unborn son to enhance his intellect for their own nefarious purposes.

We are also introduced to main characters Fran and Sarah, seniors in a small Texas Bible school. On the eve of her wedding to Mack, Sarah is visited by an angel and told she will have a son who is destined for greatness.

Chris is a college football star with the chance to play professionally. He foregoes the opportunity in favor of the Catholic priesthood after his parents die mysteriously.

Throughout the year, there are periodic appearances of nefarious international financier Luciano Begliali, and a mysterious alien presence, the Lady, who alternately appears as an angel or a gray alien. She also acts as a spirit-guide to Benny. The futures of Benny, Kim, and Sarah are all affected by the Lady's actions.

In 1979, we meet Fran's husband, Tom, a missionary in Uganda, and their daughter, Gloria. Tom befriends Father Chris, who is also ministering to the war-torn nation. Their friendship is interrupted when Tom dies while Chris, Tom, and his family flee Uganda during the fall of Idi Amin's regime. Badly injured, Chris returns to Rome where he is given the assignment of working for Kim's brother, Benny. As the job begins, he is commissioned by the pope to spy on Benny, who has recently become a friend of Luciano Begliali. In this task, Chris is paired with Father Vinnie, a wisecracking old monk from Hoboken, New Jersey.

Back in the United States, we are introduced to Kim's sons Michael and Gabe. The intellectually enhanced nine-year-old Michael negotiates a $100 million, twenty-year loan to his uncle Benny. His intent is to protect his newfound half-brother, Gabe, from Benny's displeasure at the discovery of another heir to Kim's fortune. Benny puts the funds at Luciano Begliali's disposal in exchange for a Vatican appointment and a role in the development of the New World Order.

As the year progresses, Kim finds herself attracted to Father Chris, and the feeling is mutual. A devout priest, Chris will not break his vows, yet he longs for the comfort of a family in the wake of his parents' deaths. He and Kim agree they will have a platonic friendship and share in the rearing of Michael and Gabe.

Meanwhile, Fran and Gloria move back to Texas to start a life without Tom. Their affiliation with a Catholic priest causes discomfort in Sarah and her husband, Mack, who are among the first televangelists. Their nine-year-old son, Zack, who is in contact with the Lady and very adept at sowing seeds of doubt, convinces his father that Fran may have had an affair with Father Chris. The grief-stricken Fran lashes out against the accusation, resulting in a feud between her and Sarah.

Throughout 1979, the Lady influences all the children, appearing as an angel to Gloria and the representative of an advanced alien species to Zack. She also changes the DNA of Michael and Gabe to alleviate some of Benny's concerns about rivals to Kim's fortune.

The year 1989 takes place against the backdrop of the fall of the Berlin Wall. Now in college, Michael and Gabe are enjoying a raucous semester abroad. Their revelry is undermined as Gabe becomes addicted to drugs, and Michael has a horrific encounter with the Lady when he tries to lose his virginity. Chris barely saves Michael and Gabe's lives from an attempt by Benny to have them killed.

In the United States, Gloria has grown into a beautiful young woman who disavows her mother's Christian moral values. In college, she meets and falls in love with the weaselly Zack, who is now a marketing major with dreams of turning his father's televangelist ministry into a goldmine. Their relationship sets the feuding Fran and Sarah on edge. Sarah is also dealing with the antics of her mother, who has come to live with her following a personality-altering stroke.

The year 1989 ends at Thanksgiving when Gloria and Fran clash, Mack and Sarah commit a horrible faux pas on TV that will haunt their ministry, and Michael stuns his family with his intention to enter the Catholic priesthood.

In 1999, the characters all get to meet each other, and Benny's loan comes due—but I should let you read it for yourselves.

Enjoy the read!

TC
August 2014

1999

ONE

Michael's plane would soon land in Miami. He smiled at Gabe's idea to bring the family together for a cruise and wholeheartedly endorsed the idea of doing something special to honor Chris's twenty-fifth anniversary as a priest.

Chris was hoping to celebrate the time quietly and in prayer. He relented to the cruise only on the condition that it not be on the actual date of his anniversary and that no fuss be made. Michael knew Gabe had one surprise up his sleeve but didn't think Chris would mind.

Subtlety was never Gabe's strong suit. Michael was well aware that he had also planned the cruise to be a sort of bachelor party week for Michael before his ordination in the spring. Typical Gabe—he viewed the very notion of celibacy to be a fate worse than death.

Celibacy! The concept involved a renunciation of physical pleasure in the pursuit of spiritual purity. Well, there was nothing to renounce for Michael. His horrifying experience with the Lady in Amsterdam ten years earlier left him with a fear of intimacy. He had not so much as kissed a woman since, but he often wondered about it—about the joy of belonging to one woman, about whether he would be a good lover, about whether he would be a good partner, about whether he would be a good dad, but most of all, he wondered about the priesthood.

Over the past decade, the seminary had offered solace and protection against the memories of his otherworldly encounter with the Lady and a hedge against its recurrence. If he was in the seminary or at a lonely archaeological dig, the Lady was far away—never in his thoughts or dreams. But when he deviated from those two pursuits in favor of what would be considered normal relationships by the world, he felt her there, ready to burst into his reality. The mere threat of her reappearance served as an invisible fence, blocking him from finding love and herding him toward a solitary existence.

The life of a cleric wasn't all that bad. In fact, it would be fine if somewhere along the way he had acquired a strong faith or love of God, like Chris, but it had never happened. He had spent too much time with antiquities to believe there was an inherent superiority to Judeo-Christianity, and he seriously doubted he would ever find an emotional attachment to Christ or the Church. So what made this life livable? In a nutshell, the Church fed his passions for languages and the antiquities. It had a seat at the table of every major archaeological discovery, and there were many, although the bulk of them never saw the light of day in press reports or scholarly journals. The Church had used its considerable influence to silence some of the most amazing finds because they didn't fit a biblical account of ancient history. Strangely enough, science itself had been the Church's ally in the area of suppression. Evidence of a very ancient, very advanced global civilization on Earth didn't fit the conventional scientific paradigm, so more often than not, the sciences worked with the Church to deny and refute any evidence leaked to the public. If Michael wanted access to the most marvelous discoveries in his field, the Church was the answer. It had access to the ancient knowledge he was destined to bring to the world.

The archaeological opportunities were unparalleled, but Michael hadn't yet been ordained. He was years behind the men in his seminary class. They had been ordained and moved into ministry, but Michael hadn't made that final commitment. There was always an archaeological dig that he would administer for the Church. The urgency of the project invariably interfered with his studies, and that was just fine with him. Each delay offered him more time to find a compelling reason, other than archaeological access and fear of the Lady, to become a priest. Unfortunately, he had run out of time. His orders were to finish his studies and be ordained or leave the seminary. If he didn't become a priest this spring, he never would.

He weighed his options, wondering if the week with Gabe would shed any insight. Clearly Gabe's life wasn't an example to follow, but was there something there for Michael to learn? Would it be so bad to find a woman in the coming week? Not for some kind of vacuous sexual fling, but to have the opportunity to be attracted to a woman who was also attracted to him. A little flirting? A romantic kiss? If it felt right, maybe more. At least then he could make an informed decision to take his vows. And if he was lucky, if God really was there and wanted him in ministry, maybe he would finally hear the call.

The plane landed, and Michael ran from his gate to the luggage carousel and then to the taxi stand. If he wasn't careful, he could miss the ship's boarding time. As he advanced in the taxi line, he kept thinking, *Mom will* kill *me if I miss this boat!* He looked up just in time to see Chris heading to the end of the line. "Chris? Chris?" he called. It would be a lot easier to show up late if he was with Chris.

Chris had barely aged in the last decade. He still wore his hair a bit long, even though there was now an occasional gray hair. A few crow's feet at the eyes made him look more distinguished.

"Michael!" Chris called as he walked briskly up the line to hug the younger man. "We are seriously close to missing this boat. Your mother is going to kill us!"

Michael laughed. "If I have to helicopter out to the ship, I'll get there. First because we need a family vacation, and second because I want to see Gabe leading an aerobics class. I might not be able to contain myself."

"I always thought he would do something more substantive than become the activities director on a cruise ship," Chris conceded, "but he seems to have found his niche. What about you? Are you going to be ordained in the spring?"

"That's my intention," Michael said sternly. This was shaping up to be yet another of Chris's attempts to assess Michael's commitment to becoming a priest.

"Between you and me, Michael, it's a hard life," Chris said. "Are you really in love with Jesus? I mean enough to be married to Him?"

"I wouldn't say I'm in love with Him, but I understand what the Church teaches about Him, and I'm interested in helping to correct some of the things we got wrong over the years."

"Like what?" Chris asked with a look of displeasure. A cab pulled up. They hopped in and told the driver where they were going.

Michael drew a sharp breath. How could he explain the archaeological significance of Vatican secrets that he hoped to explore? "Chris,

I have worked on several different Vatican archaeological digs in the Middle East. It's a tremendous honor. You should see some of these ancient texts. They're astounding!"

"Will you be helping with the translations?"

"Yeah." Michael beamed. "And some of these things predate what we previously thought to be recorded history!"

"So, a five-thousand-year-old shopping list is going to correct our stand on Christ?"

"Maybe not directly, but it may change our views of biblical history. Chris, I'm not talking about shopping lists, trust me."

"So you're an archaeologist, Michael, but are you a priest? That's what I'm trying to determine."

"I will be, and I'll have the opportunity to find out what was really happening thousands of years ago on this planet."

They rode in silence to the terminal. Michael knew it wasn't the answer Chris wanted to hear.

Sunday was a busy day for all those in the cruise industry. On that day, cruise ships would dock in Miami to say good-bye to thousands of browned, satiated, and spoiled passengers. Then a rapid cleaning of the entire ship would precede the introduction of thousands of new passengers—pale, sun-deprived, and in need of some special attention. The special attention was what it was all about, especially when it came to the ladies. On an average week, Gabe, now the activities director on one of the new grand ships in the Caribbean, could count on about five different ladies to share his cabin. The pattern was always the same: pursue during morning activities, make vague sexual suggestions in the afternoon, bed them in the evening, and apologize for letting things get out of hand the next morning. It was a hard life, but somebody had to do it.

Since his stint at rehab, Gabe had been careful never to touch drugs again. Nonetheless, he still favored alcohol. His job was to create a party atmosphere, and he worked on a "booze cruise." The two went hand in hand. But Gabe was a highly functioning alcoholic. You would never know that his day started and ended with alcohol. He was fit—buff, in fact—with a great tan, bright smile, long hair, and glistening green eyes. He could bring even the most unwilling participant into the cruise activities. He had been gifted with the ability to read people, to know how to quickly gain their trust. He could have used this ability to take advantage of others, but he never did, with the exception of sex. But even in that circumstance, he saw himself as generous. He was fulfilling the beach-stud fantasies of most of the women he bedded.

This Sunday was different from most. At the terminal, waiting to board, were his mother, his brother, and Chris. None of them had ever been on one of his cruises, opting instead for yacht or sailing vacations. The cruise was Gabe's idea—to give Michael something like a bachelor party. Not that Michael would chase, especially with Mom and Chris around, but Gabe wanted him to have a reckless, sun-drenched week away from dusty old libraries, musty monasteries, and sandy archaeological pits.

To top it off, this was the year of Chris's twenty-fifth anniversary as a priest. Where would they all be without Chris's influence in their lives? It took a little bit of subterfuge and sneaking around in Chris's files, but Gabe had managed to find the address of the woman who was in Uganda with him in the early years of his priesthood. He was able to coordinate things so that Fran and her husband could bring a young-adult group from their church. He arranged to have the group's assigned dinner table next to his family's, and he couldn't wait to see the surprise on Chris's face when he saw her.

It was also an opportunity to reconnect. He and Michael had been inseparable for years, but there was little place for Gabe in Michael's world once he entered the seminary. To make matters worse, Michael had been a seminarian longer than almost anyone. Gabe wished Michael wouldn't go through with the ordination, but if he did, Gabe hoped for him to pastor a little church somewhere once he was ordained. Maybe with a more normal schedule and living in a rectory, Michael would be more accessible to him. He wondered if Michael knew how much he wished they could be closer.

David's church group sat in matching T-shirts, waiting to board the ship. Ten members of his young singles group accompanied him and Fran.

"I feel like a glorified chaperone," Fran whispered to David with a grin.

"It's more like a sorority house parent," David suggested.

"That makes me feel a lot better!" She laughed.

"Aw, they're good kids, and we'll have a great time. Besides, who would have thought that Zack and Gloria would agree to come along?" They had maintained a nice relationship with the couple, but every time they tried to do anything together, Sarah would find a way to come up with an alternate plan to pull the young couple back into her orbit.

"They're not here yet," Fran said, "and Sarah's pretty resourceful. I don't know how Gloria puts up with Sarah and Mack's constant meddling."

"I don't think she's happy, Fran. But to her credit, she loves her husband and is trying to make it work."

She floated the idea. "Maybe a baby would help ..."

"I don't think a baby is ever the solution to a rocky marriage. Babies add stress to a relationship. Hey, look to your right," he said surreptitiously.

To Fran's right, Danny sat staring at Tina as she read her Bible. Danny weighed all of 120 pounds and had large horn-rimmed glasses and a tendency to produce too much saliva, which pooled and stretched into little bands from his upper to lower teeth as he talked. By contrast, Tina was the church heartthrob. She had a radiant, full face and luxurious brown hair with bangs that framed her hazel eyes. Her figure was nothing short of voluptuous, and she was seriously saving herself for Mr. Right, not only in terms of keeping her virginity but dating in general. She refused to say yes to a date until she felt the Lord had placed the man in her life as a potential mate.

"It's cute, but it's sad," Fran said. "She's not going to fall for him. He's read too many novels where the knight wins the fair lady's hand."

"On a more selfish note, it kind of makes our chaperone role pretty easy, don't you think, my lovely missus?" David grinned and arched his eyebrows.

Just then they heard a chant rising from the crowd behind them. "Give me an R!"

"R!" yelled about a dozen people in wheelchairs, heading toward Fran and David, who could do nothing but look on in disbelief. The group continued to spell "Riverside." Of course, at the head of the parade were Sarah and Mack.

"Fran! What are you doing here?" Sarah asked in mock surprise.

"You know why we're here, Sarah. We've brought some of the young singles from our church."

"What a coincidence! We brought our challenged seniors," Sarah said, continuing the charade. Turning to Sandy, she said, "Mama, you remember Fran, Gloria's mother, don't you?"

Sandy shook her head with dismay at her daughter; she turned to Fran and said, "And they say *I'm* brain damaged!" Her tone softened as she said, "How are you, Fran?"

"I'm fine," Fran said with a smile. "How nice for you to get to go on a cruise."

"I'll say. Now if I can just find a way to cut loose from old iron girdle and shake my maracas!"

Kim sat at the other end of the terminal in the VIP section. She was the first one in her family to arrive. *Of course!* Michael was like the wind. He blew in and blew out. And Chris was Chris; their entire friendship was about varying availability. They had been careful to strictly respect his vows over the years, yet they were emotionally entwined. Each felt lighter and happier in the other's presence. That was enough for her.

In the background, the terminal speakers played Cher's "Believe." *Sing it, Cher!*

The years continued to be kind to Kim. She had kept her figure and added a little bit of dye to color the beginnings of gray hair. Her well-maintained face showed few signs of aging, amazing considering the day-to-day stresses of running a financial empire. She had her father's sense of when to buy and when to sell. Her cell phone rang. As she fished through her bag, she thought, *This better not be Michael or Chris calling to cancel!*

"Kim, it's John," said the president of Kim's holding company. She was training him to do more around the office. The business needed a clear succession plan, and it didn't look as if either of her boys was interested.

"John, what's up?" Kim asked curiously. She had left instructions not to bother her unless it was an emergency.

"I just wanted to say, 'Have a nice trip,' and to talk to you one more time about Enron stock."

"Don't go there, John. I'm telling you, I met with those guys. They're too full of themselves," she lectured. "I don't want to get involved. Hear me on this."

"I know you don't want to invest *your* money there," John said cautiously, "but I was hoping to get your approval to invest some of our pension funds in Enron. The pension fund isn't your money; it belongs to us employees."

"No!" Kim yelled into the phone, not so much to be difficult with John as to be heard above Cher. "I can't approve it, John. How could I, in good conscience, allow the employees to invest in a company I think will implode?"

"Okay," John said in a pacifying tone. "I just wanted to put it by you one more time."

"I appreciate your concern, John, but trust me. You'll be thanking me in a few years. Those guys are a phenomenon, but they don't have a sustainable business. I'll see you in a couple of weeks." She hung up, wishing one of her boys would go into the business.

"Ms. Martin?" an attractive redheaded woman wearing the standard cruise line navy blue suit, white blazer, and multicolored scarf asked.

"Yes?"

"I'm Clara, your VIP representative. I'll take you to your suite now."

"Thanks." Kim smiled weakly. *If those two stand me up, I'll kill them!*

The door to the lounge opened just as Kim and the rep were passing by. In poured Chris and Michael, who had clearly been in a dead run to get to the terminal on time.

"They're with me," Kim said with a dry smile to the rep. "They're cute but not very punctual."

The rep laughed as Kim hugged her guys. The rep then pushed through the crowded terminal, and the three dutifully followed as onlookers wondered who they were to merit such VIP treatment. The rep led them into an elevator at the far end of the terminal. Just as the elevator doors were closing, Kim noticed Chris was staring out at the crowd of people in the terminal.

"Fran?" Chris said softly.

The presidential suite was lavish and overdone as only a cruise line could do. Crystal chandeliers, wall sconces, and a baby grand piano appointed the sitting room with its facing crimson couches. The three bedrooms were decorated in bright Caribbean colors and gold-and-silver taffeta drapes.

Michael chuckled at the unrepentant gaudiness. "A little under-done," he chirped, "but I like it."

"It's a bit much, but we wanted three bedrooms, and this is what your brother booked," Kim said.

"The guy has definitely spent too much time in houses of ill re-pute," Michael added as Chris chuckled.

"Ah, the asexual musings of two vicars in sweet accord," Gabe pronounced as he entered the apartment. Michael and Chris ran to hug him, but they couldn't beat Kim.

"Hands off, fellas," she said. "Gabey can't come out and play until he gives his mommy a hug."

"Hi, Mom," Gabe said as he hugged her tightly. "So what do you think of my home away from home?"

"I haven't seen much of the ship yet. They kind of whisked us up here, but it seems beautiful."

Gabe conceded, "Look, I know it's gaudy, but that's true of cruise ships in general. This is a nice ship, though. It's one of the newest and biggest in the fleet."

"Maybe you could take us on a tour once you finish saying hello," Kim said.

"Sure," Gabe replied. He released his mom and held open his arms for a hug from Michael and Chris. "Hey, guys—"

"Michael, did you hear something?" Chris asked with studied nonchalance.

Michael chuckled softly and then joined the ruse. "Just a member of the crew looking for a tip. If we ignore him, he'll go away and pester someone else."

In a second, Michael was airborne as Gabe rushed first him and then Chris, knocking them into the facing sofas. Michael protested as he stood and hugged his brother hard.

After a while, Gabe said, "Ready for your tour, Mom?"

"Sure. Let's do it," Kim said as she took his arm.

Over his shoulder, Gabe said, "Clergy, follow us."

As they entered the hallway, Michael heard the porter taking another family to their suite.

"Here is your apartment, Reverend Jolean."

"Thanks, I appreciate your kindness," the reverend said.

"This should do nicely," the reverend's wife said to the porter. "After all, we're on vacation. I guess we can't have every convenience of home."

Behind them, an old woman in a wheelchair sat in the hallway with her caregiver, waiting to enter the room.

"It's not fair," the old lady complained to Kim. "Why should you have all the good-looking men on the ship?"

Kim smiled sweetly at her, bent toward her, and said softly, "I'm just lucky."

Michael thought it was all cute, until the old woman lightly slapped Gabe's butt and said, "This melon is just about ripe." Then he laughed hardily at the surprised look on Gabe's face. Chris rolled his eyes, covering his mouth to hide a laugh.

"I'll tell you a secret," Kim whispered. "He's my son."

"Well, it's just an old lady's opinion, but I think you should let him out to play every now and again." They all chuckled, except Gabe, who stood with a polite smile frozen on his face.

"He'll be teaching the morning aerobics classes. You should stop by," Kim said proudly and gave Gabe a mischievous wink. Michael and Chris snickered loudly, as did the woman's caregiver.

"I think I'll take you up on it." The woman grinned.

"Mama, get in here!" the reverend's wife yelled from inside the suite.

"The warden calls," the old lady said with a sigh and motioned with her hand for the caregiver to take her inside. "Nice meeting you. See you around."

"Nice meeting you too." Kim grinned.

As the door closed and they proceeded down the hallway, Gabe asked his mother in exasperation, "Why did you tell her I was teaching that class?"

"She'll balance out the young jiggly crowd, and I want Michael and Chris to remember the upside of celibacy." Kim laughed.

"Worked for me," Chris said as he high-fived Kim.

"Worked for me," Michael echoed.

Gabe shrugged and said, "I've had worse," to a chorus of laughter.

The cabin was small and had a tiny porthole for a window. Fran would have been happier with something a bit less cramped. She and David could afford it, but such accommodations would have been prohibitively expensive for the young singles group.

"Second thoughts?" David asked as they surveyed the small bathroom.

"Not really," Fran said. "When you think about it, how much time will we really spend in our cabin?"

David hugged her from behind and said softly, "Well, I was hoping for a little alone time."

There was a knock at the door. Fran opened it to reveal several of the young singles in their group.

"Come on, guys, we're about to set sail. Let's go on deck and say good-bye to Miami!"

"Knock on Gloria's door to see if she wants to join us," Fran said to Tina. To David, she said, "You'll have to unpack your stuff later." He shook his head and rolled his eyes.

Gloria met them in the hallway.

"Where's Zack?" Fran asked.

"He went to his parents' suite because he refuses to spend a week in the bowels of the ship," Gloria said with unbridled disdain. "Just a warning, Mom; he'll be a pain this whole trip. Nothing will be good enough for him while his parents are around."

"So hang out with us and have a good time," Fran offered. "Maybe he'll get tired of the wheelchair group they brought."

"It doesn't matter, Mom. Trust me, I'm happy to have some time without him—without the whole famn damily."

They walked in silence for a few seconds, when from behind them Danny spoke up, a little too loudly and a little too rehearsed. "They say a bon voyage kiss is good luck," he said as he stared at Tina.

"Not your lucky day, Danny," Tina said briskly as she pulled away from him and moved closer to Fran and Gloria. The older women laughed quietly.

Fran put her arm around Tina's shoulders and pulled her close. "Men," she said, "you can't live with them and—"

"You can't live with them," Gloria finished as the three smirked.

The group burst out of the stairwell onto the deck just as Kim and her family were coming down from an upper deck.

"Fran!" Chris cried as he ran to her. They hugged awkwardly as Fran pulled Gloria into it.

"Gloria!" Chris said, smiling. "You grew into a beautiful lady, sweetheart!"

"And you haven't aged a bit!" Gloria exclaimed.

"Kim, guys, look here!" Chris called to the group, who had pulled back to give him some space.

"Kim, this is Frannie and Gloria Ellis, the family from Africa."

"Oh well." Kim laughed. "We were going to surprise you at dinner. Gabe invited them in honor of your twenty-fifth anniversary."

Chris briefly hugged Gabe as Michael patted his back. Then he introduced Fran to Kim.

Fran hugged Kim and said, "You're the one who sent us the check. I don't know how I would have raised my daughter without your kindness."

Kim hugged her in return. "Don't even mention it. I'm happy to know things turned out well for you." Fran knew in an instant she could easily become friends with this woman. She introduced David to Chris and Kim.

Chris proudly said, "These two handsome men are Michael and Gabe. I wrote to you about them."

"I would know them anywhere from your descriptions." Fran

grinned. She hugged both guys, and Gloria followed suit. Fran couldn't help but notice the way Gloria looked into Michael's eyes, or the way Michael returned her stare. She looked at David with dismay.

Fran wasn't the only one to notice Michael and Gloria. Kim saw it as well. For years she had hoped and prayed Michael would either develop a passion for the priesthood or meet the one woman who would change his mind. If she never had met Chris, she would have dismissed out of hand the concept of love at first sight, but she knew she loved Chris the moment she saw him. Would it be that way for Michael as well? She took a second look at Gloria and drew a sharp breath when she saw her large diamond-studded wedding band.

Kim tried to get Gabe's attention, to see if he had noticed Michael's interaction with Gloria, but Gabe was staring intently at a young girl from the youth group.

"That's Tina," Fran said with a smile. "She's a great kid."

"I love Gabe," Kim said, "but he's trouble for young ladies."

"Tina will shut him down," Fran said with a confident smile.

The ship blew its whistle and moved slowly from the pier. The customary celebration began, and the deck turned into a New Year's Eve celebration. Everyone onboard waved and cheered. Couples hugged and kissed. David kissed Fran, Chris and Kim hugged, and Gabe kissed a surprised Tina. As they came out of their respective embraces, they watched aghast as Michael and Gloria shared a passionate kiss.

Fran made her way to Gloria and said, "Gloria! Look at the ocean!"

Chris followed her to move Michael out of the way.

Kim looked to David in shock. He wasn't looking at the couple but to the balconies above. She followed his gaze to a balcony where the woman in the wheelchair sat. With her were several others, but one in particular caught her attention. He was a thin man with hawkish looks and an expression of absolute rage. It sent a shiver up her spine.

David leaned into her to be heard above the crowd. "Gloria's husband," he said somberly.

"Bon voyage," Kim said. She sighed as the ship's whistle boomed.

TWO

It was a bitter-cold day in New York. Benny wore a wool cape over his clerical garb, but it barely dampened the chilling wind as he walked across the plaza to the entrance of the World Trade Center. Cold or not, it felt good to be in New York. He loved Rome, but every once in a while he longed to see the grandiose new construction of America. Antiquities were nice, but there was a pulsing of activity in the World Trade Center that made his heart race. New York was exciting, always fresh, always new.

He was a bit late. Luciano would no doubt be unhappy, but that was fine with Benny. Hadn't he spent the last ten years learning the intricacies of Islam for Luciano? Hadn't he come up with a way to use that religion to bring the world to its knees? Well, Kurtoglu had helped to be certain, and Luciano had been the project's mastermind, but Benny was the one who had worked his tail off! Thankfully that moron Chris had been happy to take on most of Benny's Vatican assignments. Benny's work would soon come to fruition. A pity for the World Trade Center, though. He loved these buildings. Too bad they had to go.

Benny walked casually into the massive open elevator car. To his surprise, Luciano was in the car, handsome and youthful as ever.

"Glad you could make it, friend," he said. "I was afraid you would be late, as is your custom."

A delicate hand interrupted the closing doors. In walked a businesswoman in her thirties. A blue dress adorned her slim frame. She carried a simple beauty, with a full head of short-cut hair. It was dark brown, nearly black, and shined in the lights of the elevator. Her brown eyes were meant to be hazel, and the result was a color that had a golden cast. They were deep pools of intelligence and grace. Her smile was brilliant as she made a brief apology for interrupting their ride.

The doors closed, and they began the long ascent to the sky lobby on the seventy-eighth floor. The woman nervously flicked her ID in her hand as the elevator ascended. Benny could make out the name Mary Ellen on the ID, but he couldn't read the last name. There was something about that girl that made him uncomfortable. He looked at Luciano and found him watching the woman as well.

Luciano rolled his eyes with displeasure and said to Benny in Italian, "*Lei sta pregando.*" "She's praying." He continued in Italian: "These Christians are everywhere!"

They exited at the sky lobby and took another elevator to continue their ascent to the restaurant.

"Such a pretty girl," Luciano said softly to Benny. "Too bad she has the scent of the Shepherd. Well, good luck to her. I have a feeling she'll need it."

They rode the second elevator to the top of the building where Luciano had reserved the entire restaurant, Wild Blue. As the elevator doors opened, Luciano and Benny were greeted by white-gloved staff who took their coats and ushered them into the dining room. At Luciano's entrance, those in attendance stood to applaud. The meeting was held to celebrate milestones that had been achieved in the twentieth century and to set the agenda for the ensuing years. The room contained only those initiated into the plans for a global government. They constituted a conspirator group of power elites, each a person of power and privilege, each someone to be reckoned with, at least in his or her mind. To Luciano, they were an efficient army of disposable parts, all lined up to do his bidding.

Benny proudly took his seat next to Luciano at the center of a dais. After wine was poured, Luciano stood to open the ceremony. "Ladies and gentlemen. It is a pleasure to welcome you to our meeting. After a wonderful meal, we will spend the evening updating you about the glorious results we have achieved. I will tell you now that we have much to celebrate. I'm sure you have all been following it in the press, but let me tell you from an insider's perspective that the move to the Euro went more smoothly than even I could have anticipated. Clearly, we have a lucky star looking over our shoulders." The room erupted in applause.

"I am informed that the staff is waiting to serve dinner. To them I say bring on the food!" Laughter from the crowd. "And to you I say welcome. At solemn occasions such as this, it is often customary to have an invocation. Although distinct people, we are all united at some quantum level. For that reason, I suggest to you that we continue the age-old tradition, but update it a bit. What do you say?" The crowd applauded. Few could resist Luciano's charm.

"Archbishop Cross, would you do the honors?"

Benny could not contain a grin of pride as he approached the microphone. Each member of the audience was easily as rich and powerful as his stepfather had been, and each looked anxiously toward him to inaugurate the evening. He had arrived! "We dedicate this meal to you, oh Spirit of the Universe, Father of Light. We seek the enlightenment that can come only from our oneness with each other and with the universe. We look to the day when mankind will be one in politics, one in action, and one in deed. We look to the creative moment when we will rise above our individual selves to join the Greater Consciousness where all needs will be met, and where we can live without want and without fear. Amen."

The meal was a sumptuous parade of small dishes: watercress salad, foie gras, stuffed Chilean sea bass with new potatoes, haricot vert, roast duck with an aromatic risotto, and a cheese platter before a rich marsala-infused mousse for dessert. French white and Italian red wines flowed freely.

Following the meal, Lucien Begliali addressed the sufficiently inebriated crowd. "Ladies and gentlemen, we are very close to the realization of our dream of a New World Order. You are among the few privileged people on Earth who will help to bring it about. And while we all have had our share of wine tonight, there are some sobering facts that need to be discussed. The first of these is sustainability. As you can see in the chart behind me, the world population has far exceeded the ability of our planet to sustain and nurture its inhabitants. Unless serious changes are made, by 2050 there will be too little oil, too little potable water, too little food, and too much pollution to enable the continuation of life on our dear Earth.

"We have commissioned an exhaustive study of the world's resources to arrive at a target population of Earth that will

- ensure the viability of life on this planet,
- enable the advancement of technological marvels at an accelerated pace, and
- provide a society where all are well fed; all have access to clean water; and all are valued and productive members of a thriving social order.

"That number, my dear friends, is five hundred million to one billion people."

The crowd gasped en masse at the thought. Benny studied their faces. Not one of them seemed as fazed by the implication of the statement as by the honor of being among the privileged few to inherit Earth.

"But how do we proceed? Do we run around killing those we believe to be undesirable? No, friends, that is not what I am proposing. We are not barbarians. There is only one answer; we must stop protecting the masses from themselves. We must let their petty jealousies and squabbles escalate. In a word, my friends, we must allow—even encourage—the masses to exterminate themselves." You could hear a pin drop in the room.

"With all due respect to my beloved colleague, Archbishop Cross, I would point out to you the obvious. Overpopulation, mindless superstition, and unbridled restraint are the hallmarks of Earth's religions. While there are many, such as the good archbishop here, who are willing to advance their faiths to a more scientifically proven quantum awareness, the bulk of humanity is mired in ancient beliefs of burning bushes, promised people, virgin births, substitutionary death, jihad, and ritual killings. These institutions need to change or die ... they will have no place in our new society." This time Benny mastered the urge to grin and wore instead a mask of grave concurrence.

"For the past ten years, Archbishop Cross has been studying the three Abrahamic religions. Curiously enough, all are gearing up for a final confrontation. The Jews believe their messiah will come to rescue an imperiled Israel. The fundamental Christians believe they are living in the age of Christ's return, where He will establish an oppressive theocratic government. Islam believes in a coming Mahdi, a messianic figure to war against the other religions and establish a worldwide caliphate. These factions, who account for a significant portion of Earth's population, are hell-bent on destroying each other.

"Left to their own devises, the existing tensions between the groups would foment to an Armageddon none of us desires. However, with some careful crafting, we can bring them what they all desire, but in a controlled manner. How do we do this? Simply by fulfilling their hearts' desires. What if we could find a man who we could promote as Mahdi to all of Islam, Christ to the Christians, and Messiah to the Jews? Each of the religions ascribes to this figure the political right to establish a theocracy. Such a man could rule the hearts and minds of this world. Under his spell, the world could be easily herded toward a new destiny. This new Messianic figure will work to combine the religions of the world, and then impose strict laws regarding childbearing. With only one child allowed per couple, we could reduce by half the world population within one generation. The enlightened would receive special dispensations to have more children, while the unenlightened population would continue to decline. No Armageddon, no nuclear conflagration, just the steady dismantling of the structures that have pushed our society to the brink. The joke of it all is that this messianic figure, of our own creation, will ultimately become the savior of humankind, just not as envisioned by the religious of the world." There was applause around the room.

"You are probably saying to yourselves, 'It all sounds good, but who is this messianic figure and how will he pull it off?'" Benny shook his head in long strokes to mimic the concern that Begliali had just mentioned. Almost on cue, the audience followed his lead and asked the question of themselves.

"Well, friends, it is a valid question, and the answer will knock your socks off. The fact of the matter is that a small membership within our group has been contacted by extraterrestrial life." Murmurs of disbelief filled the group.

At that moment, a brilliant flash of light shined next to Begliali. As the light dissipated, the Lady stood within their midst. Benny expected the Lady's appearance to frighten the group. He had anticipated fainting, gasps of fear, and screams of denial. Instead, he saw hypnotized awe. The Lady was working her magic on the crowd, aided by Luciano's free-flowing wine. The entire audience moved into a trance-like state, ready to accept unquestioningly the information she would present. Benny vowed to learn how to manipulate a crowd and applauded with total abandon her toothless attempt at a smile.

The Lady moved to the microphone and spoke. When using telepathy, her "voice" seemed velvety and full. But in Earth's nitrogen-rich atmosphere, her small lungs and tiny mouth produced a high-pitched, wheezing sound.

"Ladies and gentlemen," she began, "my remarks will be brief. Over many years, we have experimented with your genome. May I say you are a marvelous entanglement of contradictions, even at a genetic level?" The crowd laughed. "Your society's inclusion in a galactic federation of planets will be most appreciated." Again, the room swelled with applause.

"Over the years, we have learned that hybridization will not work. We have, however, found a way to combine our genetic code with the structure of human DNA to produce a viable individual that is entirely human and entirely alien. He will be a bridge between our civilizations and ease your transition to a cosmically conscious society. It has taken centuries of breeding, but I am pleased to tell you that at last we are ready to proceed. Once the new life form is born, we will take him to a place where he can be raised in a time-distortion field. In other words, he will grow to maturity along a human timeframe, but due to the wonders of space and time, we can accomplish this while a comparatively small time has passed on Earth.

"I want to express our desire to bring you peace, prosperity, and the companionship of other intelligent species in our galaxy." With a flash, the Lady was gone.

"Let it begin!" Begliali yelled. The crowd echoed him.

"Amen," Benny said into the microphone.

The presentation had gone so well; Luciano offered Benny a bit of a congratulatory leather-clad treat by the name of Bruno. The smell of leather had always turned him on. Cruising in New York was a good time, but now Benny had to kick Bruno out of the hotel room, put on his clerical garb, and get to the airport.

Bruno had been a great diversion. Maybe a little pudgy around the middle, but he had been just what the doctor ordered. Looking at the clock, he decided he had more than enough time to slowly wake Bruno.

THREE

I know what I saw, Gloria," Zack said bitterly as the couple dressed for dinner.

Gloria protested, flailing her arms in anger. "I don't even know what happened! He grabbed me and kissed me. I didn't ask him to. I had no idea it was going to happen!" She blushed, but not so much from embarrassment as from passion. Michael's eyes and so many of his mannerisms reminded her of Father Chris. She had almost forgotten how she crushed on Chris when she was young. Maybe she just missed the way things were when her father was alive. She didn't know the answers, but she knew that her heart melted when their lips touched.

"Are you telling me you didn't do anything to initiate it?

"Yes, Zack. That's what I'm telling you," she snapped. After a brief pause, she continued in a softer, more conciliatory tone. "I'm faithful to you. Michael is going to be ordained a Catholic priest in the spring, for crying out loud. Maybe he wanted one last kiss from a woman, and I happened to be standing there."

"Well, I have no choice but to believe you. But the priesthood means nothing to me. You remember those rumors about your mother and Father Chris." Zack stared at her smugly.

Gloria colored. "Those rumors had a lot more to do with your father's dirty imagination than my mother's actions. Chris was and is an honorable man."

"Who just happens to be here on a family vacation with a proxy wife and children."

Gloria threw her hands in the air and paced their tiny cabin.

"Enough, Zack! I'm not my mother's daughter; I'm your wife. You're not your father's son; you're my husband. Don't stay with your parents tonight. Stay with me. Just be my husband tonight."

Fran had just applied the finishing touches to her makeup when she heard a knock at the cabin door. There she found Tina in a beautiful dark green dress. It was a simple, summer knit that graciously accentuated the curves of her body. With it she wore a simple string of pearls and pearl earrings. The total look was stunning. The color of the dress made her hazel eyes appear to be a deep, mysterious green. The white pearls danced on her olive complexion. Her hair was pulled back on the right side of her head with a single comb that sported a white flower with dark green leaves.

"Is this dress too simple?" she asked Fran.

"No!" Fran exclaimed. "It's elegant. I think you look prettier than Princess Diana."

"I hope so. Fran, I feel so nervous."

"Sit down, Tina. Let's talk. You feel this way because of Gabe, right?"

She sat, collected her thoughts, and sighed. "I've never felt like this about a man."

"His mother tells me he can be trouble for young girls."

"I understand that, Fran. And you can trust me not to go against my principles or my faith. I've prayed about it since we left port, and I feel the Lord is in this."

"Men can be very deceitful when they're looking for a woman's affections. If this guy is a player, and I think he is, he'll know how to say all the right things, but there's only one thing he's after."

The sound of a toilet flush flooded the small cabin, and David exited in his boxer shorts, dress shirt, and knee-high black socks. At the sight of Tina, he jumped back into the bathroom and called out to Fran to bring his pants to him.

"Here's a teachable moment," Fran said with a smirk as she walked the pants over to David. "You can only trust men when you've got them by the pants."

A fully dressed David soon joined the laughing women. Tina asked him, "What if the Lord has brought this guy into my life, Pastor?"

"If the Father's hand is in it, at some point he will come to the Lord. You wouldn't want to be unequally yoked with a nonbeliever."

Fran added, "His mother has a strong faith and a good heart, and Father Chris is a man of God. I've known him for years. So it's not like Gabe has grown up around unbelievers. Maybe he's just sowing some wild oats."

"To me it looked like the brother, Michael, was goin' a-plantin' when we left port." David snickered.

"It was one kiss!" Fran said, more in defense of Gloria than Michael. "And he apologized repeatedly to Gloria afterward."

"Well, Gabe didn't apologize," Tina said, bringing the conversation back to her concerns. "I feel as if I want to spend the rest of my life with him. I've never felt like that before."

"I've never felt like that before," Gabe said to Michael as he sipped a scotch on the rocks in his family's suite. He shook his head at the apparent insanity of sudden feelings for a girl. It was totally out of character for him. Sudden lust? Oh, yes. Sudden infatuation? This was the first time it had happened to him, and it bowled him over.

"At least you didn't kiss a married woman," Michael said in self-disgust. He took a long drink from Gabe's glass.

"It was a mistake, Michael. Trust me, as long as I've known you, you've been the poster boy for purity. One kiss followed by twenty apologies doesn't make you a slut."

"Like you, you mean."

"Like me," Gabe agreed somberly. "That's why I find this girl so confusing. Normally I know within seconds if I want to have sex with a girl, and within a minute or two, I know if she'll have sex with me. It's not like that with this girl."

"So you kissed her because you *don't* want to have sex with her?" Michael grinned.

Gabe slapped him upside the head with a couch pillow and took his drink back. "No, Michael, I feel like I want to protect her—even if that means protecting her from me. I don't want to hurt her."

"Wow! I never thought I'd say this, Gabe, but I think you may have a conscience," Michael teased.

"Come on, Michael. I'm really confused about this."

"Let me give you my perspective. Not as a cleric, and certainly not as a stud, but as your brother. You're growing up, Gabe. The cruise business has allowed you to extend the freedom of college life until the age of thirty. But after a while, you long for something more permanent. Maybe this girl represents that kind of change in your heart."

Gabe heard the logic of Michael's assessment, and it sure did explain the feelings that he couldn't deny. "Could be. But it's not just a change in me. There is something about *her* that makes me want to choose a different lifestyle."

"Well, I think it's a positive sign. Just be careful not to hurt her. It's a little close to home, and you don't want to embarrass Chris."

Chris came out of his room in a clerical collar and a huff. "Yo! Stud-boy, put on a collar. We're remembering our vows tonight," he said tersely to Michael. Gabe watched as Michael lowered his head. Some things never changed. Neither of them dealt well with Chris's disapproval.

"Yeah, passion pucker!" Gabe said to Michael with a grin, hoping to alleviate the tension.

"It's not funny, Gabe," Chris said sternly. "Michael, get dressed in proper clerical attire for dinner."

"Aw, come on, Chris." Gabe took up Michael's defense, his tone tense but not defiant. "First of all, I find it really interesting not to be the one in trouble over misplaced affection. Secondly, and more importantly, it was just one kiss while everyone else was kissing the person next to him. Like New Year's Eve."

"I'm happy to hear you say that, Gabe," Kim said. She came out of her bedroom just as Chris was hustling Michael back to his room to change. "Because I won't stand by and let you hurt that nice church girl."

"You act like I'm not good enough for her," Gabe said defensively.

"No. *You* act like you're not good enough for her. Face it—you're a drunken playboy on a boat." The words hurt, but Gabe had long ago given up the pretense that his life was anything more than a series of alcoholic binges and sexual liaisons.

"Ship," Gabe corrected somberly, "but you're right about the rest of it." Now it was Gabe who stared at the floor, withering under a parental gaze of disappointment.

Kim's anger seemed to dissipate as her boy admitted his failings. She sat beside him and ruffled his hair. "Oh, honey. There is a beautiful, caring man inside you, but you've masked it behind years of bad behavior that has dulled your sensibilities."

"I want to change, Mom." Gabe paused for a moment. He hadn't expected to say the words. They came from somewhere deep within.

"It's just your nature to go against the grain, son. If only you could find a way to channel that part of your personality to something more productive. Let's face it, you're always going to be one who tries to rock the ship."

"Boat," he corrected with a sheepish grin.

"You know what I mean." She smiled.

"Yes. I do. But, Mom, what if she's 'the one'?"

"Then you have to count the cost. What would you give up to have a lifetime of love from a good woman?" Kim asked, patting his arm to punctuate her question.

Chris and Michael came out of Michael's bedroom. From behind, Chris tightened Michael's clerical collar again. "Come on, Chris," Michael whined. "You're choking me with this collar."

"Good. You'll remember it's there," Chris said sternly.

"So how do I look?" Michael asked Kim and Gabe to lighten the mood.

Gabe looked at his mother and said, "Dingy." The two laughed as Michael and Chris looked on, bemused.

After a brief toast to welcome the passengers, the ship's captain exited the dining room, leaving it in the incredibly capable hands of his staff. As Gabe had arranged it, Fran and David sat with their youth group at the table next to Kim's family. Kim had taken an instant liking to Fran, and through the appetizers, she and Fran talked incessantly.

"I have a great idea," Gabe said. "Why don't Michael and I trade places with Fran and David? That way you guys won't have to talk across tables all night."

"How selfless of you!" Chris said with a mocking look. David let out a hearty laugh.

"I'll leave that up to you and David, Fran," Kim said. "You're the chaperones. I'm just the mother of the wolf."

"What could it hurt?" David asked casually. "We're right here. Besides, Fran, you haven't seen Chris in years."

"I'm fine with it," Fran said as she stood to trade places with the boys.

Chris touched his collar while his eyes locked with Michael's. Less subtly, Kim looked at Gabe and pointed two fingers to her eyes in an I'm-watching-you motion. Michael nodded seriously at Chris to note that he understood. Gabe offered a devilish grin.

As Fran stood, Danny quickly moved to take her seat next to Tina. Gabe pulled the chair back and Danny fell to the floor as he attempted to sit. Gabe quickly helped him up, but in a way that emphasized his own strength.

"Whoops, buddy," Gabe said as he picked Danny up off the floor. Arms extended, holding Danny just so that his feet didn't touch the ground, Gabe looked sternly into his eyes, all the while asking very politely, "Are you okay?"

The ruckus brought the maître d' to the table. Of course the man knew Gabe. They had partied together on several occasions. "Can I be of assistance?"

"Charles," Gabe said in mock seriousness, still holding Danny off the floor, "this young man has taken quite a spill. I think you need to get him to the infirmary."

"I'm fine!" Danny protested as he tried to wiggle out of Gabe's grip.

"We care about the safety of our passengers on this cruise line," Gabe said. "It'll just take a couple of minutes for the doctor to check you out and say that you're fine. But this way, we'll know for sure."

"Come with me," Charles said to Danny, rolling his eyes at Gabe to indicate his irritation at being interrupted during the dinner service.

Kim sat with her head in her hand. "I apologize for that," she said as Fran and David took their seats.

"Sorry about all that," Gabe said as he took his place next to Tina.

"Not a problem," Tina said with a smile.

"Can I just say you look beautiful tonight?" he commented with a shy grin.

"You clean up pretty well yourself." Tina smiled.

The commotion of Danny's fall brought their attention to Kim's table, which was about thirty feet away. At their table were Zack and Gloria, and Meemaw and her caregiver. Directly behind them were the Riverside seniors.

"Look at that," Sarah said softly. "Fran found a way to sit with her priest friend."

Zack grinned broadly at the comment, but the grin froze to a mask of jealousy as Meemaw spoke. "I'll tell you," she said with a huge grin, looking in the direction of Kim's table. "Each of those boys is more handsome than the other. But the exercise instructor is my choice. It's like he decided to pick up the slack when the other two went celibate."

"Enough, Mama," Sarah said. "I think this family has had all the embarrassment we can handle in one day."

Mack opened his mouth to join in the fray but gulped at his wine instead.

"It was an innocent, platonic kiss, Sarah," Gloria said with a growl. "It's not like I was caught kicking a homeless woman for her jewels."

Sandy laughed and patted Gloria's hand. "Talk about being embarrassed! It was a long time before I could hold my head up." Then with a wry laugh, she said, "But it's more important that we focus on your indiscretions or mine, dear. That way Sarah can pretend to be the longsuffering saint of the family."

Tears came to Sarah's eyes. "It's been ten years, and still that's all I'm known for! Nobody will let me forget that horrible incident. I was set up, I tell you!"

She's right. No one will forget it, Zack thought. For ten years he had tried every marketing arrow in his quiver to help his father grow the ministry, but it always came back to that one incident. The clip had become a bit of a cult joke. Each year at Thanksgiving, the local news station hauled it out to the cheers and laughter of Houston. His mother was not only a pain in the butt; she had become a hindrance to his career.

"We know you were set up, dear," Mack comforted. "I don't appreciate your bringing that up, Gloria," he snapped.

"Hey, Dad," Zack said tersely, surprising even himself at feeling the need to come to his wife's defense. "Gloria and I work every day at that ministry. And every day we have to fight Houston's mental image of mother kicking that homeless lady. I know you're upset about the kiss. I was too, but Gloria explained it all to me. It was innocent. More importantly, it wasn't done in front of the most popular news team in our viewing audience. So let's just drop it, okay?"

Sarah gasped for breath at Zack's harsh words. Tears welled in her eyes as she pointedly waited to hear words of apology from her son.

Gloria grabbed Sarah's hand and kissed her cheek. "I apologize for bringing it up, Sarah. It was wrong of me."

"Thanks, Gloria," Sarah said, all the while looking at Zack. He stared back at her defiantly. An apology would never come.

As the evening progressed, the laughter from Kim's table grew. She and Chris were having a great time with Fran and David. So much time had passed, and yet Chris's memories of Tom were sharp and clear. He told funny stories about their adventures in Africa. They were fun tales that easily drew in David and Kim. At other junctures, Kim and Fran laughed about their inability to keep up with the lives of their adult children.

At the "kids' table," Gabe and Tina had long-since abandoned any pretense of interest in conversations other than their own. Danny had returned from the infirmary, judged fit to rejoin the group. He sat at the only open seat, putting him directly across the table from Michael. He refused to look toward Gabe and Tina and spent the night instead staring harshly at Michael. The others in the group didn't quite know what to make of a Catholic clergy at their table. Clearly Michael's presence was a dampening influence on the first dinner of their singles retreat.

Longing for a bit of fresh air, Michael excused himself and went on deck. The evening was young, and there was a lot of activity, but the ocean breeze and the rising moon offered an inviting alternative to the chatter of the dining room. Going to archeological digs and being the first in millennia to read thoughts that someone had scratched on a rock or a papyrus sheet thrilled him so much more than the mundane, went-to-the-gas-station conversations he encountered in society. He took a second to admire the rising moon's reflection on the dark sea.

"Beautiful, isn't it?" came a decidedly Texan drawl from behind him. Without turning, Michael knew it was Gloria's husband. *Would this day never end?*

"Yes. It is," Michael said calmly.

"Like my wife," Zack said slowly as he made his way to Michael's side in a menacing stride.

Michael would not be baited. "Listen. I don't know what happened when we left port. I've apologized to your wife, and I'd like to apologize to you."

As the two men stared at the moon, Zack leaned close to Michael's ear and spoke softly. "I can understand. My wife is a beautiful woman. You know what I mean. You've tasted her lips. But let me tell you what you'll never taste, what you'll never feel. The way she screams and clutches at your back when—"

Michael spun to face him. "Stop! I won't listen to this. Accept my apology or don't."

A look of rage came over Zack's face. He barely looked human, and it scared Michael, who took a step backward toward the door.

In one very quick motion, Zack was on him. He grabbed Michael's lapel and slammed him hard against the metal wall of the ship. His eyes blazed and his breath was hot in Michael's face. "What's the matter, Padre? Don't you want to hear about how I make her scream?" His full body weight pinned Michael to the wall.

All Michael could see were the flaming, almost inhuman eyes staring into his.

And then suddenly Zack was off him. Michael turned to see Zack flat against the deck. Gabe was on top of him, his forearm pressed hard against the man's throat. "Easy there, Preacher," Gabe said sternly. "I think we've had enough for one day."

Michael peeled himself off the wall and went to Gabe's side. "Let him go, Gabe. I started it with that stupid kiss."

"He wants me to let you go, Preacher," Gabe said softly. "Are you going to be a good boy if I do? Or would you rather I call security and have you put in a holding cell until our next port?"

"I'm fine now," Zack drawled. "I fell into a rage. I'm sorry."

"And I am truly sorry as well," Michael said.

Gabe helped Zack up. When Zack stood, Gabe grabbed his cheeks firmly and said, "It looks like I'm the only one here who's not sorry, Preacher. Don't touch my brother again, do you understand?"

"I understand," Zack said.

Gabe released his grip. Zack brushed himself off and went inside.

"Thanks," Michael said. "I suppose I deserved some of that. He had a right to be mad at me."

"I heard the trash he was talking, Michael. There was a weird sexual component to it. I've dealt with my share of angry husbands and boyfriends. And let me tell you, that wasn't normal."

"Yeah, well, it's over now. Thanks, bro. How did you find us, anyway?"

"I just happened to see Pastor Potty Mouth follow you out of the dining room. I figured I should check things out."

"So how long were you standing there?"

"Long enough to hear that the guy is definitely sick. One good thing came out of this evening, though."

"Yeah? What's that? I could use a little good news."

"I finally agree with your choice to go into the priesthood. You have to be celibate, Michael. I don't think the world is ready for the power of your love," Gabe said in mock awe.

Michael laughed.

"No. Think of it, Michael. If one kiss caused all of this trouble, all-out sex would probably open up a portal to another dimension or something. For the sake of us all, you *have* to keep that magic wand in its holster."

Michael wrapped one arm around his brother's shoulder. Gabe always knew how to make things right for him. "I've missed you, Gabe."

"Ditto, dude."

While Michael and Gabe were talking on deck, Zack made his way toward the dining room. Just before he entered the room, he heard the words "You're pathetic!" He turned to see his father.

"You're drunk," he replied in a monotone.

"I may have had too much wine, Zack, but I saw it all. Heard it all. What kind of man talks like that about his wife? It was weird, almost like you were coming on to that priest."

"You don't know what you're talking about," Zack said with disgust.

"I *do* know what I'm talking about," Mack said indignantly. "There's always been something harsh and off-center about you. For years, I have looked to see something of myself in you. It's not there. I've pretended all these years, but it's not there."

"Come on, Dad." Zack grinned the winning smile that had worked through the years with his father.

"I've tried to be a good father. God knows I love you, but something's not right here. Never has been." Mack put his hand firmly on Zack's shoulder, forcing his attention. "It's time I admit it. I've lied to myself, to your mother, to my parish, and to my viewers all these years."

"What are you talking about?"

"The ministry. All the promotions! Send money and I'll send you a cloth that I've blessed for your healing! I *know* you have been writing the testimonies we read on the air. I'm not that stupid. But I let it go. All these years I let it go. Do you see what we've become, Zack?"

Zack was annoyed at the need to deal with his drunken father on top of everything else that had transpired that day. He spoke sternly, "You need to go sleep it off, Dad. Everything will look different in the morning."

"You're half-right. I need to sleep it off, but things won't look different in the morning. I'm closing up the ministry when we get back home."

Zack gasped and his heart raced. Mack glared at him for a second and then stomped back into the dining room, leaving Zack's panicked mind to find a way to avoid this impending crisis.

A light twinkled on the eastern horizon as the sun sank into the western sea. Within that light, the Lady watched her prey, knowing their thoughts, feeling their passions and waiting for the right moment to put her plan into action.

She saw Zack as he opened the door to the ship's deck and gazed at the first star of the evening. He remembered a cruise years before when the light came to be with him. He wished it would come to his aid now. He took a seat on a portside bench and rubbed his forehead, as if doing so would tease forth a decision. What to do to keep the ministry afloat? He couldn't let his father throw away his dreams.

He bowed his head to pray, but his mind kept coming back to the angel—or alien, whatever she was. Maybe she was both. Maybe what other generations called "angels" we would call "aliens." She was an instrument of the Divine; that much he knew.

The ship rocked in a gentle, lulling motion as he fixed his attention to the light on the horizon. It grew larger as he prayed just under his breath, "Come on. Come on. I'm waiting."

The Lady next concentrated on Michael. After hours of tossing and turning, he had finally gotten to sleep. But his sleep was fitful. In a dream, a great light shined through his bedroom window. He felt adrift in the atmosphere as if he were floating.

"It's a dream," he told himself. "I have to wake up." He tried to move his legs and his arms. They would not respond to his commands. "Wake up," he said and then screamed to himself, but his mouth wasn't moving.

He smelled the salty air of the sea and heard the waves hitting the side of the ship. He was sure he had floated outside the ocean liner. It couldn't be. He tried to open his eyes. They wouldn't budge. *Wake up*!

The Lady moved to Gloria, who awakened in a sea of light. She felt weightless and free. This was very much like the recurring dream she had when she was in college. She loved those dreams. They always involved wild, abandoned passion with Zack. Maybe it was happening again.

"Come on," Zack said to the light as his body lifted from the deck of the ship.

Then the light flicked out, as if turned off by a switch, leaving an empty deck and the sound of waves against the hull of the ship.

The Lady smiled and went about her work.

The sex was animalistic, brutal, and savage. Gloria threw herself onto him and took the pleasure she longed to have. He responded in kind, and for a moment the two were one.

Michael looked down to see Gloria's beautiful face, but in its place was the Lady.

"You belong to me," she spat. "There will never be sex with another. If you don't desire me, then celibacy is the only answer."

Michael cringed in the same combination of disgust and fear he had felt in Amsterdam. He threw himself off her, and gravity immediately took hold of him, hurling him against the wall. He lay there and wept, praying to be relieved of this vision.

Gloria screamed as first she and then Zack climaxed in the weightlessness of the dream. She instantly fell into a deep sleep.

The Lady entered the room as Zack and Gloria's still bodies were lowered gently to the floor.

"Well done, Zack," the Lady complimented.

"I always try my best," Zack said breathlessly. His face broke into a smug grin.

"We will need some time alone with your wife to adjust the genome of the zygote. Some aspects of your DNA are missing crucial personality traits. Thankfully we can use material from another donor."

Zack wasn't heartless. He looked over at Gloria with concern. "I just hope this is the right thing."

"You were bred for this," the Lady cooed. "Your DNA has been carefully cultivated to react favorably with the DNA of our species. Your son will be a new species. He will bring peace to the world."

"And Gloria?"

"Most of her DNA will be removed from the zygote. We have tested her from her youth. The pH balance and some anomalies we generated in her womb will make it a safe place for the young embryo to develop. After three months, we will harvest it."

"And then you'll leave her alone?"

"She is of no further concern to us once we have taken the child."

"Thank you. And what about Michael?"

"We can assure you his passion for her is spent."

Chris awakened with a start. Something felt "wrong." He couldn't put his finger on it, but there was an evil feeling. Praying, he opened the door slightly to Kim's room. She slept soundly. He did the same for Michael's room but found the bed empty. Gabe snored on the couch where he had fallen asleep earlier.

"Father, show me what You will," he prayed as he went back to his bedroom to throw on a pair of sandals. He had a strong impression that he should go down to the ship's deck.

"Father, bless Michael. And help me find him." As Chris exited onto the deck, he was surprised to find David there. "David! Couldn't sleep either, huh?"

"I have a bad feeling, Chris. Like there's evil here."

He nodded. "That makes two of us."

"Well, God led us here for a reason," David said. "Let's pray."

The two men of God prayed for the grace and peace of the Lord to surround them. As they were praying, they saw a flash of light from the other side of the ship. When they made their way around the bulkhead to investigate, they saw Michael lying naked on the deck.

"Michael!" Chris yelled as he ran to him.

"Stay away! Stay away from me!" Michael screamed hysterically, looking over Chris's shoulder.

"Chris. He's panicking," David cautioned. "Maybe he's sleepwalking."

"Michael! Michael!" Chris yelled as he shook the man awake.

"Chris?" Michael said groggily. He felt the cold steel of the deck under him and sat up slowly. Looking around, he asked, "How did I get on deck?" Then looking down, he continued, "Naked?"

"I don't know," Chris said, as he quickly pulled off his shirt and gave it to Michael to wrap around himself. "I woke up and you weren't in your room. I felt the Spirit telling me you were in some kind of trouble, so I went looking for you."

Michael wrapped Chris's shirt around his waist. It covered his front but left some of his backside exposed. Seeing that, David contributed his own shirt to the cause. They walked briskly to the apartment.

"I think I just had one heck of a nightmare," Michael said to Chris.

"One that produced a flash of light that David and I saw?" Chris asked in disbelief.

"I don't know what you saw," Michael responded, still a bit confused. "I think I was having a nightmare and sleepwalking to boot. You guys found me and woke me up. Who knows, I could have walked off the ship in my sleep. I really should be thanking you."

"Well," David said, "we men of the cloth have to stick together."

Looking at Michael, Chris said, "Apparently some of us have more cloth than others."

Gabe woke early. There was a little kink in his neck from sleeping on the sofa, but otherwise he felt fantastic. He couldn't remember when he had enjoyed time with a woman more. Tina was witty and charming. She spoke in elegant sentences pointed with just the right amount of self-deprecation. Her smile beguiled him, and he honestly felt that he could spend the rest of his life looking into her eyes. More importantly, she didn't look down on him. She didn't treat him like he was a trophy to take back to her cabin, a photo to show the girls back home. She saw something more to him, and it made him want to be more for her. His spirit soared at the thought of seeing her again today. Seconds later he would feel pain that she would be gone at the end of the week. He whistled to himself as he made a pot of coffee.

Michael came stumbling out of his bedroom. "What drags you off the couch so early?" he asked groggily.

"That girl, Tina. I can't shake this feeling that she's someone special in my life."

"You mean, 'the one'?" Michael asked, making quote signs with two fingers, as his eyes grew wide.

Gabe grinned sheepishly. It was almost too weird for him to verbalize.

"Wow, dude. That's some heavy vibe coming from you," Michael said warily. "Are you thinking the L-word?" he asked, avoiding saying the word "love."

Gabe pursed his lips and his eyes got glassy. "Pretty weird, huh? I just met her."

"Not so much weird as neat," Michael said approvingly as he took a seat at the kitchen table.

"You think?"

"Yeah. I really do." Michael grinned for a moment and then asked, "So what's on the agenda for today?"

"Day at sea. I have an aerobics/dance class at ten. Tina is coming. Why don't you join in?"

Michael snapped his fingers and said, "Darn! I forgot to pack my leotard. I guess you'll have to go on without me."

"Come on, Michael. We wear shorts or bathing suits. I want you to see what I do."

"No. You want me to run interference with Danny so it doesn't get too uncomfortable for Tina."

Gabe shrugged. "That too. What do you say?"

"Oh, why not," Michael said helplessly.

"Good. But you have to wear more than Chris's shirt ..." He hoped Michael would talk about what was bothering him. Gabe suspected, and silently wished, that it would involve Michael not wanting to be a priest.

"You heard Chris and me coming into the suite last night?" Michael stared at him.

Gabe returned the stare. "Yep. But unlike Chris, I grew up with you. I've never known you to sleepwalk. What really happened?"

"Amsterdam."

"Ouch!" Gabe said as he put a hand to his head and looked on incredulously. After a while, he asked, "Same Lady?"

"Same."

Gabe shook his head. This was far out of his depth. The supernatural, the spiritual—they neither intrigued nor enticed him. He found them distasteful at best and downright frightening at worst. "That stuff scares the heck out of me," he said, taking the seat next to Michael.

"It's one of the reasons I have to wear a collar, Gabe. She doesn't bother me when I'm living like a hermit, reading ancient texts, and going to archeological digs in remote locations."

Well, there it is. It does involve this decision to become a priest. "Maybe you could go to a shrink or an exorcist or something."

"I don't know that it's psychological," Michael said. "You were there in Amsterdam."

"But I was way high, Michael. I remember it, but I can't say some of those memories weren't chemically induced."

"Really, Gabe? Think about what that building looked like at the beginning and then at the end of the evening."

Gabe thought about it and a chill went up his spine. "Okay ... so maybe it was real," he conceded. "But if it was real, then there must be some real kind of help you can get."

"Like an exorcist?"

Gabe couldn't believe he was having this discussion. "Well, maybe not an exorcist, but there's got to be somewhere you could go."

"Where are you planning to go?" Kim asked as she came sleepily out of her bedroom.

"Gabe wants me to exercise more," Michael covered. "I keep telling him there aren't gyms at archeological digs."

Gabe joined in. "I just think there's someplace he could go, Mom."

"So why don't you make up an exercise program he can do wherever he goes?" Kim asked Gabe, but her half-frown and manner of expression indicated she knew they had changed the subject upon her entrance.

"Good idea, Mom," Gabe said as he shrugged off her look and poured her a cup of coffee. "In fact, Michael said he's going to come to my aerobics class at ten this morning. Why don't you and Chris come too?"

"Chris will make me wear a collar." Michael chuckled. "I'll look like a Chippendale dancer in my swim trunks and collar."

"You could always wear your collar as a sweatband," Gabe offered.

Chris, soaked from his morning run, entered the suite drinking orange juice. "Nobody from this family is wearing a collar as a sweatband," he said with a grin.

Zack lay peacefully in bed as Gloria snuggled close. Suddenly she sprang up and ran to the bathroom. He heard her vomit ... lovely way to start the day. By the time she returned to the bedroom, he was nearly dressed.

"Aww. I was just about to snuggle next to you," she whined.

Zack grimaced thinking of the retching noises coming from her just moments before. "Sorry, but I want to get some breakfast and then talk to my father. He had a little too much wine last night and was talking crazy things."

"Like what?"

"Like he's not really doing God's work. Like he wants to close the ministry."

"But that ministry is his life. What would he be without it?" Gloria crawled back under the covers.

"I don't know. I need to see him. Maybe he'll forget all about it. Maybe it was the wine talking. But if not, we have a big problem."

"We'll find our way," she said to comfort him. "We're young. There are plenty of things we could do."

"Nothing that will pay like Dad's ministry. I won't stand by and let him throw away what he has worked all his life to build."

"Maybe he's getting tired, Zack. He could scale back a bit. David seems to really enjoy pastoring a smaller church."

"Oh, yes. David's 'Little Church with the Big Butt'!"

"Heart," she corrected with a grimace, "and don't knock it. All I'm saying is, he and Mom seem to be happy in their work. I'd love the same for your mother and father."

Zack stared down at his lovely wife. Something had changed last night. He could sense his child growing within her, and it thrilled him. But her? She liked that one little kiss from Michael. He knew it, and it disgusted him.

Barely mumbling that he would see her later, Zack left the cabin and headed toward the dining room to talk some sense into his father. Hopefully he could enlist his mother's aid in persuading him to keep the ministry.

"Good morning!" Zack cheerily said to his parents when he found them at their table.

"Good morning, son," Mack said happily.

Zack saw no traces of a hangover there. A hangover would have been a good place to start his lecture about how Mack had really gone overboard the night before.

"How are you feeling today, Dad?" he asked cautiously, trying to tease some admission from his father.

"I haven't felt this good in a long while." Mack smiled broadly.

"Do you remember what you said to me last night?" he asked incredulously.

"Of course I remember."

Sarah added, "Your dad has talked to me about it, and I agree that it might be time for us to retire. I could get used to cruising, to traveling in general. There are so many things we want to see."

"But, Mom! What about me?" Zack burst out. His sense of betrayal was palpable.

"You could go to work for one of the Christian television networks. I'm sure they'd be glad to have you," she suggested, but her voice had a stern overtone to it.

"I don't understand, Mom. You've always supported me."

"Listen, Zack. I've been trying to dig out of a hole ever since that incident in the parking lot. Everybody watches me to see if they can get another free show. I don't want to live under a microscope anymore." Her eyebrow arched as she issued the next directive. "And I don't want anyone to throw that incident in my face again—like your wife did last night."

There it was. Zack had backed Gloria last night, and now Sarah was retaliating. He knew in that instant that day-to-day life would be a lot nicer without them around, but why kill the golden calf as well? "Mom, Gloria apologized for that remark. She feels bad about saying it."

Sarah stared at her son, took a deep breath, and then delivered her harsh assessment. "I gave you my whole life, Zack. When you had an opportunity to defend me last night, you didn't." She wrung her hands from the anxiety of what she was saying, but her tone remained resolute. "It opened my eyes. Your father and I want to find each other again. The ministry has gotten in the way. You have gotten in the way."

Zack turned his gaze away. He was furious with her. He looked at his father for assistance.

Mack stared defiantly back at him, and then after a few seconds, he spoke. "It seems like a hard decision at first, son, but take some time to think about it. We all need to have some freedom—from the ministry and from each other. Don't you want the opportunity to go out into the world and make something of yourself? Try to grab hold of the sense of adventure inside you."

"What do you mean 'make something' of myself?" Zack nearly shrieked. This buffoon had no idea that Zack had made something of him! Couldn't his dad see that he had taken them every step of the way from that horrible electric piano program they used to produce when he was a child?

"I mean, be your own man, son. We love you to death, but it's time to cut the apron strings. Time to make a place for *yourself* in this world," Mack answered.

Zack was livid at their lack of understanding and the outrageous contention that *they* had built the ministry. But he was smart enough to know that an argument would not win the battle for him. He had to find a way to keep the ministry alive, not to mention its cash flow. "Dad," he said in a soft tone, "you make it sound like I haven't contributed to the ministry. I've poured my heart and soul into it. I did it for you and Mom."

"We know, sweetheart," Sarah said, her tone softening. "But we can't allow it anymore. If we don't move on, you'll one day find yourself in the same position I'm in with your grandmother. I know you love her, but she's suffocating me. Your dad and I would never want to put you in such a position."

"What about Meemaw?" Zack asked in disbelief. "What are you and Dad going to do with her while you're doing all this traveling?"

"It's time for your grandmother to enter a facility where they can take better care of her." Sarah's voice broke a bit at the admission. She reached out to touch Zack's hand, but he withdrew it.

"So you're going to just dispose of her because she's inconvenient?"

"We're not going to *dispose* of her," Sarah said in an annoyed tone. "We're going to let her enjoy herself with others her age who have similar interests. The other men and women the church brought on the cruise, for instance."

"So that's why you and Dad brought the group of disabled elderly? So Meemaw could meet them?"

"It's one of the reasons," Sarah said. "Now does that sound like we're *disposing* of her?"

"But, Mom, how could you?" Tears stung at Zack's eyes. These two buffoons were willing to cast him, Gloria, and Meemaw aside to fulfill some hackneyed touring fantasy!

Now Sarah exploded. "How could I *what,* Zack? Have a life of my own? Not be bound by an adult child? A senior child? An all-consuming ministry? How could I finally take some time for me ... to have a life?"

"I didn't realize you were that unhappy, Mom."

"I didn't either. But your father and I have been talking about it. Now that I'm actually away from that life, I've got to tell you, I rather die than go back to it."

"I'm sorry you feel that way," Zack said tersely and stomped off. He paused outside the dining room, waiting for her to follow. She didn't. Looking in, he saw them smiling and talking excitedly about their plans.

FOUR

It was a rainy January day in Rome. Gusts of wind smacked cold rain at Benny's face as he made his way across the courtyard to the brilliantly white stucco edifice of Casino Pio IV, headquarters of the Pontifical Academy of Sciences in the Papal Gardens. Members of the Academy are scientists from all around the world, of various faiths. *Eggheads! Just what I need on my first day back from New York!* Benny had never been to this beautiful building for two very good reasons. First, it was in the center of the Papal Gardens, where popes have been known to stroll. He preferred to be where his boss wasn't. Second, scientists inhabited it. No fun there! But Luciano wanted him to meet with these guys.

A secretary greeted Benny warmly and then escorted him to a conference room. He opened the door to see ten men crammed around the table. The old building was beautiful on the outside, but sections of it were carelessly converted to modern use. Plumbing and wiring ran up and down the walls of the conference room. No one would ever break through walls of such an historical edifice so plumbing and electrical routes were usually chosen to be as inconspicuous as possible—not so in this room. It was as if the plumbing was the focal point of some design that completely eluded Benny. He thought this space surely would have been designated as a utility closet if eggheads immune to aesthetic amenities didn't administer it. He immediately forgot most of their names after they were introduced to him—all but one.

There was a young visiting American scientist named Daniel Shanks. Benny found his longish hair and deep blue, intelligent eyes to be intriguing, not to mention that he was wearing jeans. The others were obviously British, German, Russian, and Chinese names. They looked like cartoon characters and among them had every fashion stereotype of a beleaguered scientist: unkempt, unwashed hair and pencils in the breast pockets of white oxford shirts were the order of the day. Apparently Daniel hadn't gotten the memo, and that was fine with Benny. Thankfully there was a seat next to the young American, and Benny took it.

"Archbishop," Dr. What*ever*-His-Name-Is (WEHNI) said to Benny, who was busy trying to tell Daniel how nice it was to see another American. "We asked Mr. Begliali to deliver you to us for a very specific purpose."

Daniel rolled his eyes at the phrase "deliver you to us." Benny giggled like a schoolgirl. The lights dimmed as the slide show began.

Dr. WEHNI continued. "What you are looking at, Your Eminence, is a photograph of a huge, perfectly round stone tablet. The photo was smuggled to us from contacts in Iraq. As you may know, the dictator of that country has a fascination with antiquities. He is convinced that he is of the line of King Nebuchadnezzar.

"The interesting thing about this stone is that it was found in a layer of dirt that hasn't been disturbed in the last twelve thousand years. Saddam Hussein, of course, believes it is from the days of Nebuchadnezzar, but the science dictates otherwise."

Wow! A really, really old stone!

"The writing on the stone is unfamiliar to us. The Iraqis believe it to be some kind of encryption, but we don't think so. We believe it is evidence of an advanced, preexisting civilization on Earth."

"I see," Benny said. He hoped they believed him. Mostly he was interested in lunch.

"To put this in terms that may be more familiar to you, we believe this presence may be what the Bible and Apocrypha referred to as 'The Watchers.' They come up a lot in the book of Enoch."

"But it is not just a Judeo-Christian tradition," the Chinese doctor to Benny's right explained. "Every culture on Earth has allusions to a prior time when humanity lived in the proximity and perhaps the protection of superior beings from the heavens. They were variously called angels, demons, and gods. To the modern mind, we would call them 'extraterrestrial biological entities,' or EBEs for short."

"This is all very exciting, gentlemen," Benny said impatiently as his stomach growled. "But I don't see what this has to do with me."

"Your nephew is a very gifted young man. His talents in the area of ancient languages are well documented. We will want him on our team as soon as he is ordained."

"He eats this stuff up," Benny said. "I'm sure he'll be happy to join you in this endeavor. But I still don't understand why you need me."

"Your nephew is a bit of a loose cannon in the scientific community. He prefers work in the field to the type of analytical work we do here. He eschews conventional archeological thought, and he seems intent on avoiding Church hierarchy. We believe he may find our offer undesirable. In short, we want to enlist your services as one who can control him."

"Ha!" Benny laughed. "Good luck with that one. The kid negotiated a deal with me when he was nine years old, and he won!" Benny realized that in some respect, he had just bragged about Michael. Those every-once-in-a-while moments of honest sentiment and goodwill toward his family bemused him.

"Nonetheless," Daniel said, his countenance suddenly more fierce. "We need you to deliver him to us."

"Well, getting him here won't be much of a problem once he knows what you're working on."

"No!" Dr. WEHNI said sternly. "He cannot know anything about the project until he has been assigned here. We can't run the risk of him telling even the smallest part of our plans."

"He won't tell anyone if you tell him not to. He's no more of a risk to your project than I am. How do you know I won't tell someone? Maybe even tell him?"

The screen flashed as the slide changed to reveal a very unflattering photo of Benny in bed with Bruno, the leather guy. It was followed by another ... then another ... and another.

"I understand," Benny said. "You can turn off your machine." He stood abruptly and left the building in a huff. The photos didn't embarrass him; he knew who he was. Rather, he was hurt and angry that Luciano would set him up this way.

The winter air seemed even colder on the walk to the restaurant where he was scheduled to meet Begliali for lunch. He made it to the restaurant with little time to spare. Luciano had his meal served the moment he was seated.

A plate of veal marsala, some freshly made pasta, and a bottle of wine were enough to take the chill off. Benny loved the food in Rome, and the Italian red wines were just fantastic. He ate ravenously. Luciano sat across from him eating a small calamari salad.

"I'm very disappointed in you, Luciano. Very disappointed," Benny said. "I've done everything you ever asked. Why did you let me be spoken to like that by a group of scientists? And don't tell me you don't know. There's no doubt in my mind you set up the entire Bruno thing."

"Well." Luciano grinned. "Not the entire Bruno thing. After all, you can lead a horse to water, but you can't make him drink."

Benny briefly wiped his mouth. Returning the napkin to his knee, he said, "Fine. I am responsible for my own actions, but why didn't you just come to me and tell me we need Michael on a project?"

"Don't be disappointed, my friend," Luciano said nonchalantly. "This happened for several reasons. First, may I say that you are a man devoted to the gratification of your selfish desires? I like that. Second, you are truly only loyal to yourself. I like that in a man too. But the fact of the matter is that the very reasons I like you are the ones that make me want to ensure your loyalty on occasion."

"You think I'm not loyal?" Benny asked with breathless exasperation, the palm of his right hand clutching at his heart.

"Of course you aren't!" Luciano chuckled. "It is one of your most endearing traits. Benito, very rarely do I sense in you the constraints of a conscience. This makes you one of my most respected associates. But there is always a pecking order."

"I'm not sure I understand," Benny said tersely.

"Our shared dreams for society have caused us to become friends. But we must always realize that, while we may be friends, we are not equals. Sometimes I believe you forget who is the boss."

"Not true, Luciano," Benny said, but in his heart he was terribly disappointed. He had begun to think of Luciano as a friend and co-conspirator rather than a boss. He took a long drink from his glass of wine. He was too hurt to say more. He was more than hurt. He felt anger growing inside him. Luciano's power play had the earmarks of his abusive stepfather. Stan had never understood Benny. He used him and berated him, just as Luciano had now done.

"Come now, Benny. No need to be coy with me when I can read you like a book. Don't be disappointed. We are still comrades in arms. But you must realize that I am the general and you are a sergeant."

"Sergeant!" Benny howled.

"And this is what I mean, Benito. What sergeant would ever speak to his general that way? This is but a small chastisement—a clearing of the air and the establishment of authority. Do you understand?"

"Yes, Luciano. I do," Benny said softly, eyes downcast. *Do* you *understand who you are dealing with, you surly dago?*

"Good, Benito. Well done. Did I ever tell you I own this restaurant?"

"No, sir. It is really lovely," Benny said, looking down at his plate. He refused to look at the restaurant or comment further on the surroundings.

"Would you like a tour of the kitchen?"

Benny felt petulant. Surely Luciano didn't think they would have some sort of friendly chat after he had hurt Benny so. "Well, actually, I have an appointment," Benny began.

"Ah. You are a slow learner, Benito," Luciano growled. "I know your calendar. You are free for another two hours yet. Follow me. I want to show you the kitchen."

"Since you put it that way, I think that I would love to see it," Benny said sarcastically.

In retrospect, Benny remembered very little of the tour. There were several stoves with burners glowing and men in white jackets and chef hats, just a few more of Luciano's servants. At the end, however, Luciano motioned for the head chef to leave him and Benny alone. Then they walked up to a large wooden door.

"This is my own personal freezer, Benito. This is where I keep the finest cuts of meat that find their way only to my table. In fact, only the head chef and I have keys." Luciano unlocked and opened the heavy door. A blast of freezing air assaulted them. He flipped a light switch to reveal a small room lined with stainless steel racks filled with frozen cuts of meat. In the center were full carcasses hanging on meat hooks.

"There's a lot of meat here," Benny said.

"I entertain a lot." Luciano smiled. "Did you enjoy the veal today?"

"Very much."

"Good, Benito. Good. There is just one more thing that I want to show you. It's over here in the corner." He led Benny to the back of the freezer where an animal hung loosely covered with white freezer paper. Luciano pulled the paper away with one quick tug to reveal the frozen carcass of a middle-aged man. The meat hook had been stabbed unceremoniously into his back. The frozen flesh took on a bluish tone, except for a section of the butt, which had been cut out.

"Oh, Luciano, what happened to him?"

Begliali shrugged dismissively. "He had the audacity to think I would repay a loan he made to our cause. Could you believe anyone would be so absurd?"

Benny thought of the $100 million loan Michael had negotiated with him. It was coming due this fall, and of course Benny had placed the money with Luciano. These thoughts and the unwelcome sensation that his veal hadn't been veal at all were too much for Benny. He stumbled, unable to take it all in. He steadied himself against the huge freezer door as fear transitioned to anger.

Luciano called his chauffer. "Something has disagreed with the archbishop," he said. "Could you see to it that he gets back to his office?" Luciano walked away without saying so much as good-bye.

Benny stewed about the incident upon returning to his office. He had to get Michael to roll over the loan, but first he needed to make sure Luciano would pay dearly if he ever dared hang Benny on a meat hook. Luciano had to know there would be a huge price to pay if he ever intended Benny Cross to be lunch for some other feckless fool! He locked himself in his office with a cassette recorder and laid out his involvement with Luciano and his understanding of Luciano's goals for a new world order.

After a full day at sea, the ship docked in Mexico. The cruise line offered a trek to Mayan ruins, a favorite among the passengers. For someone, like Michael, with an archeology background, the visit was bound to be both interesting and unfulfilling. He would likely be excited to see the ruins but frustrated to have only a few hours there. He reminded himself that this was trip about family and that he needed to keep archeology on the back burner. One hundred degrees with 90 percent humidity! The walk from the port to the Mayan ruins of Tulum wasn't so much hard as uncomfortable. No clerical garb on this junket, just plain old shorts and T-shirts that were soaked through within the first several hundred feet.

"Wow! This heat stinks!" Michael said.

"You kind of get used to it," Gabe answered. Clearly he was putting on a good face for Tina, who was walking with them.

Michael laughed. "Tell me you take this excursion every week!"

"Well, maybe not every week."

"I'm guessing the crew likes the peace and quiet when everyone leaves the boat," Michael said, purposefully drawing Gabe out to correct him.

"Ship."

"What?" Michael asked innocently, winking at Tina.

"Ship, Michael. It's a ship!"

"No ship! You mean it's not a boat?"

"You know it's not a boat."

"Not a-boat what?" Michael asked. "And when did you become Canadian?"

"Do you see what I have to put up with?" Gabe asked, smiling broadly at Tina, who laughed at the interplay between brothers.

The Mayan ruins were certainly impressive. The group climbed the stairs twenty-five feet up to the top of the Castillo pyramid. The entire complex stood on a cliff overlooking the Caribbean. The stark beauty of the temple was accentuated by a strong breeze coming off the ocean. The sky had clouded over, and it looked as if a storm was approaching. The distant sound of thunder pealed, giving the entire area an otherworldly sensation. Michael could imagine what Tulum had been like as a thriving city. His mind was pulled to that imaginary place, but he checked himself. After his weird dream, he wanted to ground himself securely in reality, lest he see the Lady again. He concentrated instead on the reactions of the other passengers to the ruins, first watching Mack and Sarah, who were nearby.

Mack exclaimed to Sarah. "This is like being in a movie!"

"I'm so happy we'll be traveling in our retirement," she said as she placed her arm around his waist. "There's so much to see."

"I'm happy we've found each other again, Sarah. Zack may not realize it, but closing the ministry is the best thing for all of us. I've done a lot of things I regret in the name of that ministry."

"We both have," she comforted.

"Well, there's a chance to try to set some of it straight. Fran," he said as he strode determinedly toward her, "I want to say something. The Lord has been working in my heart."

"Our hearts," Sarah said as she joined him, tears clouding her eyes.

"I ..." Mack started, and then, looking tenderly at Sarah, continued. "*We* have done some things in the name of our ministry that weren't of God. We didn't understand it then, but we understand it now. When I get back, I'm closing down the ministry. Sarah and I are going to retire. I wanted you to hear it from us first."

"I don't know what to say," Fran answered.

"I'm not done, Fran. We treated you horribly after Tom died. We ask your forgiveness."

"That happened years ago." She brushed an unexpected tear from her eye. "I'm just happy to have my friends back." At that point, she hugged both of them. Mack freed one hand and offered it to David in friendship as the women cried with each other. The thunder grew louder in the distance.

Over Mack's shoulder, Michael saw Zack staring at them harshly. Beside him, Gloria fell to her knees and vomited. Michael moved closer.

"Guys," David said, breaking up the reunion, "I think the kids need us."

The four ran to where Gloria was bent over, resting her hands on her knees.

"Sweetheart, are you all right?" Fran asked.

"I'm fine. I guess the heat and humidity finally got to me."

Fran seated her on a rock, while David went for some water.

"I think she's fine." Zack smiled. "Like she said, it was probably just the heat."

"Unless you two are finally planning on making us grandparents," Mack said jovially.

Zack snapped. "Wouldn't that be great, Dad? No job and a pregnant wife? That would make you happy?"

"Zack," Gloria called over to him, "not here. Not now. Let them do what they want; we'll be fine."

Zack stomped over to her, nudging Fran out of the way. "Your job is to be supportive of your husband," he hissed at her in hushed tones. "If you have nothing positive to say, then *shut up*!"

Returning with the water, David placed himself between the husband and wife. "Here, Gloria, drink some of this."

"We were in the middle of a discussion, David," Zack said sternly.

David said tersely, "I heard 'shut up.' That sounds more like abuse than discussion to me. Take a hike, Zack, and calm down."

"Trouble in paradise?" Michael said softly to Zack as he huffed past. Zack turned fiercely, only to find Gabe in his face.

"Move on, buddy," Gabe said.

"What a messed-up family," Michael said reflectively.

Gabe laughed in response. "Get a mirror, bro! We're not exactly *The Brady Bunch*."

The sky finally opened with a bright flash and a loud peal of thunder. The ship's passengers scurried to the edge of the ruins for the walk back to the port in the torrential rain.

When they reached the ship, Gabe walked Tina to her cabin and then went to his for a quick shower and change of clothes. Kim, Chris, and Michael headed to their suite. Typical of tropical weather, the storm was violent but quick. The sun came back out and had pretty much dried their clothes by the time they made it onboard. The heat, the hike, and the storm had made for a tough day, and each of them was ready for a shower and possibly a quick nap before dressing for dinner.

Kim slid her key in the door, pushed it open, and let out a yelp. She ran into the suite, with Michael and Chris following, and hugged her big brother. "Benny! What a wonderful surprise! How did you get here?"

"Well, I got to thinking that we're never all in the same place at the same time now that the boys have grown up. I got a little bit of time from my superiors, and here I am."

"Oh, Benny. I'm so happy." She hugged him again. "How long will you be staying?"

"Just tonight and tomorrow night. I jet back to Rome when the ship docks at Grand Cayman."

"Hi, boss," Chris, said, extending his hand.

Benny shook it warmly. "How are you, Chris? Things aren't the same in the office without you, you know."

"Hi, Uncle Benny," Michael said with a perfunctory hug and pat on the back.

"I hear great things about you, my boy. People in Rome laud your intellect, attention to detail, and abilities with ancient languages; I can assure you. You should visit us sometime."

Michael winced. He wasn't happy to be so visible to the Church hierarchy. And he certainly didn't like Benny keeping tabs on him. He shrugged off the comment. "I'm not much of a Rome type. I'd much rather be in the field on a dig somewhere."

"Nonsense!" Benny exclaimed. To Michael's surprise, Benny slapped his back warmly. "You haven't given it a chance. Stay with me a week, and I'll have you hooked."

Changing the subject, Michael asked, "So, Uncle Benny, where's your cabin?"

"Right here. I moved my stuff into the room on the left."

"That's *my* room," Michael complained.

"So you'll take the couch for a couple days," Kim said resolutely. "The important thing is that we're all here together. It really is a family vacation now."

A freshly showered Gabe entered the suite talking. "Hey, guys, guess what! I heard they brought some international diplomat onboard today. It's all hush-hush, but I know the first officer, and he said—"

"Hey, Gabe," Michael offered as he strode to the door. "I found that mirror you were talking about."

"What?"

From the living room, Benny called out, "Gabriel, come and give your uncle Benny a hug!"

Gabe stuck his finger in his mouth to make a gagging gesture.

"Come join the fun," Michael said with a sarcastic grin.

"Whatever you do, don't go close to the railing on deck while he's here," Gabe whispered.

"Hi, Benny," Gabe said as he extended his hand.

"When did you stop calling me 'uncle'?" Benny asked as he shook the younger man's hand.

"I never did. You told me not to when I was nine." Gabe snorted.

"Oh, well, forget that," Benny said with a dismissive wave of his hand. "You can call me Uncle now."

"'Benny' is just fine," Gabe said. Chris looked at Michael and shook his head. "So, Benny," Gabe continued, "how long will you be onboard?"

"Just tonight and tomorrow night."

"Where are you staying?"

"My room," Michael said, tilting his head and smiling in mock joy.

"Well, we still have a couple hours before dinner," Gabe said, raising his eyebrows. "Why don't you come have a drink with me. It'll give Mom and Benny a chance to spend some quality time together."

"Sounds good," Michael said. "Chris?

Chris jumped up. "I'm in. Let's go."

The three men chose a shaded table overlooking the deep blue water of the port, the steep, green-covered mountains in the background. Steel-drum music wafted in on the breeze. Their pensive looks seemed out of place in the bar on the sunbaked deck.

"So why do you think he showed up all of a sudden?" Gabe asked.

"He has a hundred million reasons to be here." Michael sighed.

"The loan! I forgot all about it," Gabe said as he gulped his drink.

Michael fiddled with his drink stirrer, remembering his first real confrontation with Benny.

"I've never really asked about this," Chris said. "It happened before I was in the family."

"When we were young, Benny wanted money from Mom, but he wasn't being nice to Gabe. So I asked Mom if she would let me negotiate with him. Long story short, he wanted a gift. Instead he got a twenty-year loan that comes due this fall."

"So at the age of nine you tried to buy protection for you and Gabe?" Chris asked.

Michael nodded and offered a wry smile. "Sort of. Twenty years seems like a long time when you're a kid. Here we are twenty years later, and Benny is much more dangerous."

"Well, are you going to roll over the loan?" Chris asked.

"I hadn't even thought about it," Michael answered. "God knows we don't need the money."

"But he hasn't been nice," Gabe said sternly.

"What?" Michael asked.

"He hasn't been nice, Michael!" Gabe's voice grew louder and his speech more emphatic. "He tried to kill us, for crying out loud! Take the money back. Make *him* squirm for once!"

"Gabe, you have no idea what a dangerous man your uncle can be," Chris cautioned.

"On the contrary, Chris, I have a very good idea what a dangerous man he is. He needs to be taught a lesson." Gabe stopped short. Michael followed his eyes to a very tanned young blonde in a tiny white bikini.

Chris rolled his eyes. "Guys, focus! Your uncle is involved with some of the most ruthless men in the world. I'd be willing to guess he no longer has access to that money."

"Which is why he shows up here all nicey-nice," Michael said.

"In other words," Gabe said, returning to the conversation, "we have him where we want him."

"He's too slippery, Gabe. You won't win if you two go head to head with him," Chris argued. "The man has no conscience. No morals."

"Gabe might have a point, though," Michael added. "There's no way I'm going to forgive the loan. I'm not going to reward his bad behavior."

"Michael," Chris said, "he's not a naughty child. He's more like a dangerous animal."

"Who can be tamed," Gabe said defiantly. Michael's eyes met his. Somewhere in the silent communication of brothers, they agreed to take on Benny.

"What are you two thinking?" Chris asked.

"At most, I'll roll over the loan, but only for a year at a time," Michael said.

"Then he'll have to let us alone for year at a time to get it renewed again," Gabe concurred.

Chris sighed. "I'll say this one more time. I think you two are playing with fire. If you don't need the money, let him have it."

"We appreciate the advice, Chris," Michael said, "but I think we can handle this."

Chris threw up his hands and slammed against the back of his chair in exasperation. For the next few moments, they sat silently, taking in the scenery.

Then Gabe said dejectedly, "So for the next two days, I just have to live with the fact that his presence puts a damper on the family vacation I planned for us."

"Big deal. I just got put out of my room. I don't even have a bed," Michael said.

"And I'm on vacation with the worst boss in the world," Chris added.

"Bartender!" Gabe sang out. "Another round, *please*!"

The drinks mellowed the guys, and the walk to dinner was somber for them as they followed behind Kim and Benny. There is nothing subtle about the décor of a cruise ship. At each outlandish chandelier, Benny would make a "tsk" sound as if the very sight of it disgusted him.

At one point in the walk, he changed positions to walk alongside Gabe and said softly, "Gabriel, this place is tacky, even for the son of a crack whore. You can do better than this." Then he resumed his place at Kim's side.

Gabe stared straight ahead.

Michael could see he was barely maintaining control. "Did he just say what I think he said?" Michael whispered.

"Uh huh," Gabe said through pursed lips, still looking straight ahead.

"Well, guess what?" Michael said softly. "That remark just cost him one hundred million dollars."

They entered the dining room. Chris tried to show Benny to their assigned table. Benny said, "Oh, thank you, Chris. But I'll be dining at the captain's table tonight."

"Well, at least stop by to meet our friends, Benny," Kim said. Then more softly, she said, "You have to see this girl who caught Gabe's fancy. I think he may actually settle down for this one." She chuckled with delight.

"I wouldn't miss it," Benny said.

Chris rolled his eyes as Kim excitedly told the table of her surprise to see her big brother in their cabin when they got back from the Mayan ruins. She explained that Benny was a man of no small authority in the Vatican and was Chris's boss.

"Must be nice having the boss on vacation with you," David teased.

"You have no idea," Chris said grimly.

"Oh, come on. He's not that bad!" Kim reproved. Then to Fran and David, she said, "Something about him drives Chris and the boys crazy. I know he has a lot of issues from when he grew up, but I love him. What can I say?"

"You've said enough." Chris smiled.

"Fine," Kim said frostily. She looked up and called to her approaching brother, "Benny, I want you to meet our friends Fran and David. Fran knew Chris in Africa."

Benny smiled and touched Fran's arm. "I don't think I could ever forget meeting you and your daughter at the airport. What a horrifying experience for you. You look well now, though."

"It was a tough go, but I'm fine. This is my husband, David."

"A pleasure to meet you, David." Benny smiled.

Kim smiled with pride as she discretely directed Benny's attention toward Tina, who again looked lovely in a sapphire-blue, off-the-shoulder gown.

"She really is quite beautiful, isn't she?" Benny asked.

"She is," Kim confirmed, "and she's a nice girl with a commitment to the Lord. What's more, she brings out the gentleman in Gabe. It's a pleasure to see."

"She's in our young-adult group," Fran said. "The guys all like her, but she's pretty aloof. With Gabe, it's different. I think they could have something special together."

"How wonderful for both of them," Benny said enthusiastically.

Kim took him to their table and introduced him around. Chris followed. Gabe and Michael said nothing as their uncle complimented Tina's dress. Chris thought Danny gloried in the old guy's neutralizing effect on Gabe and Michael.

"Archbishop," Danny said, "it's a pleasure to have you grace our table. Maybe tomorrow night you could eat with us?"

Benny jumped at the opportunity. Michael stared wide-eyed at Chris.

At his table, Zack fumed as his parents enjoyed each other's company. Gloria ate insatiably beside him. You would never guess she had been throwing her guts up all over Mexico just a few hours earlier. Meemaw sat with a bit of butter slowly sliding down the left side of her face. God, he hated all of them tonight! None of them realized what the future could hold. He had to find a way to take charge. Sometimes he thought he was the only sentient being in his entire godforsaken family.

He ran a napkin over Meemaw's cheek. She smiled at him lovingly and said, "Thanks, sweetheart."

Well, maybe Meemaw's okay. At least she couldn't get too much in the way. He looked at his wife. Beautiful she was, but in some ways so vapid. There she sat, the brooding incubator, shoveling food into her mouth. *She won't even begin to think she could be pregnant until she misses a period in about three weeks. How could she live through morning sickness and cravings yet not suspect she might be pregnant?* "Slow down, honey," he said softly with a grin. "It looks almost like you're eating for two."

"Fat chance," she said, not even acknowledging the possibility. On the few occasions when she managed to get pregnant, her body aborted the child well before the third month.

"It will happen for you one day, Gloria," Sarah said. "And when it does, you will be so happy."

"For a short while," Mack said. "Then there will be days when all you can hear is crying and all you can smell are dirty diapers."

"Mack!" Sarah giggled. "It wasn't that bad. In fact, I thought it was a joy." Sarah smiled at her son.

Zack wasn't too much in the mood to be nice to his parents, but he grinned at their remarks as if he found them adorable. In reality, he had come to the conclusion that they were as disposable as diapers—and just as full.

FIVE

The wind blew fiercely that evening as Vinnie made his way to the papal apartments. While he and the pope were friends, the extreme differences in their political status rarely allowed him to be invited to dine with the pontiff. That was fine with Vinnie. He wasn't a big fan of Eastern European food. Give him a plate of pasta and a shaving of hard Parmesan cheese any day.

He passed the Swiss Guard at the entrance to the apartments and was escorted to the small, less formal dining room. There the pope sat wearing a simple white cassock—practically loungewear for a pope.

"What? No sweat pants? Thanks for goin' all out for me, boss!" Vinnie mock-chided.

"Ah, Vinnie, you don't know how nice it is *not* to have someone blowing smoke up my butt."

"Can't say as I do. When you are on the Franciscan end of the totem pole, you think maybe a puff or two of smoke would be nice every now and again."

The pontiff laughed heartily. One of the house staff brought in a bottle of red wine, pouring a bit for each man.

"So who's joining us?" Vinnie asked as he looked at the empty place setting.

"Father Morton, from New York."

"You're kidding! I haven't seen him for years. I read his last book, though. Pretty dicey stuff, I got to tell you."

Father Micah Morton was an enigma. Years before, he had taken a strong stance against the incursion of evil into the Church. At a point, the day-to-day strain got to him. He asked for, and received from a previous pope, the right to remain a priest but to function in a lay capacity in the media. Since then he had written several books taking to task the insidious forces at work in the Church universal. This made him a controversial and polarizing figure, particularly with his former order, the Jesuits.

"He does us a great service, bringing to light the agenda followed by the less faithful of our numbers," the pope said, taking a sip of wine.

"And can I tell you? He's a pretty good pinochle player too." Vinnie cackled.

The pope stared at him, not sure of what to make of the comment.

Vinnie shrugged. "It's a card game. In Hoboken, where we don't have the Alps to ski down, we play card games every once in a while to pass the time."

"Oh," the pope commented as a grin framed his face and his light-blue eyes danced in the opportunity to be teased by an old pal. "Any news from Chris? What's going on with my favorite archbishop?"

"Funny you should mention that. Chris is on a cruise in the Caribbean with Kim and the boys. So I've been hanging a little closer to Benny, just to make sure he's not plotting to blow up the world or somethin'. Anyway, I just happened to see travel plans he had jotted down on a pad at his desk."

"In his locked office?" the pope asked.

Vinnie answered with a wink. "It was an amazing thing, Holiness. I just jiggled his office door a little, and it opened."

"I'm sure," the pope said, rolling his eyes. "Let me guess. When you opened the door, a gust of wind blew the notepad off his desk ..."

"That's a pretty good scenario. Let's go with it. You know, you came up with that pretty quick!"

The pope shrugged. "I grew up evading communism."

"So here's the deal. Benny met his sister's ship in Mexico. He'll be staying with them while at sea. He has plans to fly back home after the ship docks in Grand Cayman."

"So Chris's vacation is ruined," the pontiff said.

"Yeah. I can just see the look on Chris's face when big old Benny shows up in a Speedo and tells Chris to apply the suntan lotion." Vinnie paused and then chuckled at the thought.

The Swiss Guard admitted Father Morton as the two joked about the misfortune of their friend.

"Micah!" the pope said warmly.

"Holiness," Micah said with a hint of an Irish brogue even after years in New York. He hugged the Holy Father, and then looking at Vinnie, said, "I guess heaven doesn't want this one, so you got him."

"Yeah, yeah, yeah, Micah. I see your wit hasn't gotten any sharper." Vinnie hugged his old friend.

As Micah hugged the brittle old priest, he asked, "Seriously, Vinnie, how old are you now? A hundred twenty?"

"But then again, you're not lookin' so young yourself, Micah. I guess it's true what they say: only the good die young."

"That doesn't bode well for any of us, now does it, my friends?" the pontiff enjoined.

"He's right," Vinnie said.

"Of course he's infallible," Micah retorted.

The three men moved to the table, and wine was poured for Micah. As the first course was served, the conversation turned serious.

"Vinnie," the pope said, "Micah is here to discuss a new project. It will be explosive."

"What's it about?" Vinnie asked. "I'm surprised someone hasn't killed you after your last book."

"That book was fiction," Micah said. "This new one will name names and tell truths that no one ever suspected would see the light of day. It's an exposé that deals with the New World Order's designs to take over the Church."

Vinnie whistled softly. The implications of bringing this to light were staggering. First and foremost, it would tick off some very powerful men and women. Second, it would set their plans back by a matter of years as they spent their time fending off the watchful eyes of conspiracy theorists. But third, it would bring the entire Church under suspicion.

"My sentiments exactly," the pope said in response to Vinnie's whistle. "This is going to hurt our Church. It will mean a purging of our ranks. It is something I was loath to do prior to the fall of communism, but now I fear it must be done."

"People will criticize you for allowing them to get this far," Vinnie said.

"History may not favor me, but the truth is I believe the Lord led me to bring down communism. I couldn't do that while at the same time purging our ranks. We needed to present a strong, unified front in the face of the communist manifesto."

"You don't have to convince me. I was here, remember?" Vinnie responded.

"You were. And that's why I want you to work with Micah. Tell him everything you know. Name names. Give dates, times, and places, Vinnie."

"That's a death sentence!" Vinnie spat.

"It may well be," Micah said gravely. "I don't expect to survive this book."

"Nonetheless, I want you to tell Micah everything you know about Benny Cross," the pontiff said gravely.

"My pleasure, but most of what I know came from Chris. He's a young guy, Holiness. I don't want to put him on anyone's death list."

"It's a most fortuitous time," the pope said. "Benny is in the Caribbean. If Micah writes that he met with an unnamed person at the Vatican on these dates, then Benny will know it couldn't have been Chris."

"So you set me up," Vinnie said dismally.

"Not exactly the hardest thing to do," Micah joked.

"No, Vinnie," the pope said somberly. "I'm giving you the opportunity to continue your distinguished service into your twilight years. I'm also trying to protect young Chris."

"Well, I never had a kid, but Chris comes darn close," Vinnie answered. "I have a Savior who said there's no greater love than to lay down your life for a friend. In the long run, it's what I'm called to do. What we're all called to do.

"I hope you're at least going to serve some port wine after dinner, considering what you just laid out here," Vinnie complained.

"I think we can do that for you, dear friend," the pope answered.

While his friend Vinnie was having a glass of port, Chris was relaxing on deck with a good book. Occasionally he would take a quick dip in the pool to cool down, and then he would return to the deck chair and his book. So far, Benny hadn't bothered much with him today. That alone was a blessing.

Kim joined him, sitting on the chair beside him with a stack of contracts. Chris had asked her to leave the work at home, but she responded by saying there was a lot of pressure when running a business.

"Where's your brother?" he asked casually.

"He went looking for the boys. I think Gabe is just wrapping up a class, and then he has the afternoon free. I'm guessing we'll see the three of them here at the pool within half an hour."

Chris lowered his sunglasses and spoke in a conspiratorial tone. "I think you mean the four of them," he said, motioning across the pool to where Tina was spreading towels out on several chairs.

"Chris, I have to tell you I just adore that girl. I try really hard to stay out of the boys' personal decisions, but part of me wants to just go over there and propose to her for Gabe."

"Propose? They just met!"

"You know as well as anyone that love at first sight can happen." She stared at him over her sunglasses.

He met her gaze. "Yes. I do. I also know Gabe isn't even one week away from his playboy lifestyle. Let's see what next week brings. She'll be back in Texas, and he'll be flirting with a new group of passengers."

She tossed down the contract she had been reviewing. "Don't be so cynical! Give Gabe a little more credit than that," Kim said as she returned the contracts to her bag.

"I'm not picking on Gabe, but if anyone stands to get hurt, it's that lovely girl across the pool." Almost as if on cue, Tina looked up and waved at Kim and Chris. The two smiled broadly and waved back.

A worried-looking Gabe and a bemused Michael entered the pool area. Gabe scanned the area until he saw Tina. He smiled broadly and went to her. Michael followed.

Gabe spoke briefly to Tina, who motioned to Kim and Chris across the pool. Gabe beelined toward them. "Mom," he said tersely, "you have to do something about your brother!"

Chris laughed at the incredible understatement.

"He just wants to spend time with his nephews, Gabe."

"All my life he told me I'm not really his nephew, and now he's going to embarrass me."

"How is he going to embarrass you?" Kim demanded in a motherly tone.

By this time Benny had made it to Michael's side and was removing his robe to reveal a European-cut Speedo. Michael grinned at his family as his uncle's stomach fell low enough to nearly cover the red Speedo. For all intents and purposes, Benny looked naked.

"I see," Kim said, trying not to laugh. "It's a European thing, Gabe. He's not *trying* to embarrass you."

"Mom, I want him to stay away from me. I just want to know how much it will hurt your feelings if I tell him that."

"A lot, Gabe," she said sternly. "He's here trying to get close to us again, and I want you to honor that. I think you, your brother—and you, Chris—haven't been very nice about his being here. He leaves tomorrow, so just suck it up for the rest of the day. Will you do that for me?"

"Fine," Gabe said flatly, "but I'm not rubbing suntan lotion on him."

"Way to stand your ground, Gabe," Chris teased.

"Chris!" Kim barked. "I'm talking to you too."

Chris stared intently in a rare display of displeasure with her. "Kim, I deal with Benny every day. I'm not about to have you tell me how to react *to* him, *with* him, or *around* him," he said quietly but firmly.

"Fine," Kim said coldly as she gathered her things to stomp off. "I'm going to spend the afternoon with my brother."

"Her devotion to him is going to get one of us killed," Gabe said to Chris after she left.

"She's just trying to find the best in him," Chris said, clearly wishing he had been a bit more tactful in his dealings with her.

"What do you guys want?" Michael asked as he made his way to their side of the pool.

"Nothing, why?" Gabe asked.

"Mom said you wanted to see me."

Across the pool, Kim sat to one side of Tina, Benny on the other.

"You've got to admit it, she's good." Chris chuckled. "Your mom just put the three of us in a time-out."

Gabe watched as his mother kept Tina and Benny engaged in conversation. Benny glanced over to Gabe and winked.

"Could be worse," Chris said, returning to his book. "You could work for him every day."

The morning sickness had passed, and Gloria felt fine. Deep in her heart she considered the fact that she might be pregnant, but that awful dream kept coming to mind. Could it be that alien abductions actually happen? She found it hard to fathom, yet the dream was so vivid. And the sickness was certainly no dream.

Zack was at a crafting exhibition with his parents, no doubt trying to talk them out of closing the ministry. She had agreed to meet her mother on deck for a little sun.

She stood before the mirror in her bathing suit. It felt tight. She would swear her hips had spread, and her waist felt thick. Her breasts pushed at the confines of the suit. All signs of pregnancy, but one that is further along than a couple days.

She pulled on her cover-up, more than a little bit concerned it hadn't been a dream after all. Her mind fell back to how she met Zack. She had always thought that drunkenness had brought about the weightless dream of their first passion. Now she wondered. It was just too much to ponder. These things happen in novels and television shows, not in real life. She was letting her mind get carried away.

But she had been through her monthly cycle just before they boarded. How could she look like this? She had heard of women who didn't discover they were with child until later in the pregnancy. Could it be that she had her cycle but was pregnant anyway?

She pulled up the cover-up to look at her waist again. *You've got to believe something, girl, because your body is changing—and fast.*

After a time, Kim went to the other side of the pool to make things right with her guys.

Seizing the opportunity, Benny looked after his sister as she headed to the boys. "My heart goes out to my poor sister," he said to Tina.

"Really? Why?"

"She has loved Gabe like her own son from the moment she adopted him, but she can't make up for his genetic heritage. His birthmother was a hopeless addict, you know."

"I had no idea," Tina said softly. "I didn't even know Gabe was adopted."

"Yes. And I'm afraid his birthmother's weakness has carried over to Gabe. He's been in and out of rehab."

"He told me he had some trouble with drugs when he was younger," Tina said somberly as she put a towel over her thighs, which were turning red in the bright sun.

"Younger as in last week is what he meant to say. Oh, it's not so much the hard stuff anymore. I'd say he is more an alcoholic than a drug addict. He drinks to get through the day. Drugs are more for partying."

"I haven't seen him drunk," Tina said defensively. She stood and changed the angle of her chair to line up with the sun, putting some distance between herself and Benny.

"Of course you have, dear. He's drunk right now. I venture to say you haven't ever seen him sober." Benny aligned his chair with hers, closing the gap. "Like I said, he drinks to get through the day. He needs alcohol to behave normally. It's the same old addiction, just a different drug," Benny said sorrowfully.

"Oh, the poor thing." Tina sighed. "He needs a good program and some time with the Lord."

"And the love of a good woman?" Benny chuckled and gave her arm a condescending pat. "Oh, my dear, let me save you from needless heartache. You are the flavor of the week. When this ship docks on Sunday, it gets ready for the next group of passengers. And so does Gabe."

"So you're saying he's some kind of drunken playboy? I don't believe it. He's been a perfect gentleman with me," she pronounced defensively.

"Oh, dear, I don't mean to imply anything untoward regarding you. You wear your virtue like a beautiful gown." *Polyester, no doubt.* "It is easily seen by all, but let me ask you something."

"Okay," she said warily.

"Imagine you are a drunken playboy, partying your life away with your mother's considerable wealth. Then imagine she shows up for vacation with the rest of your family who, it just so happens, has given themselves wholly to the Lord. What would you do to save face? To make it look like you're interested in settling down with someone? To keep mommy's money flowing?"

"I ... uh ... I don't know what to say," she fumbled.

As she blinked away tears, Benny knew the seeds of doubt had taken root. "It's a lot to hear, dear. I'm just telling you so you don't get your heart broken. If you're having a nice week with the attentions of a handsome, rich playboy, by all means continue to enjoy it. Go with it! But don't start painting mental pictures of a home with a white picket fence. That's just not who Gabe is."

"Well, thanks for your concern." Tina attempted a smile.

"Don't think of it. I'm going to get a Coke. Can I get you one?"

"No thanks," she said distractedly.

Well, so much for Frankie and Annette. Benny smiled as he headed to the bar.

As the day proceeded, Gabe was beside himself. All he knew was that Tina had spent some time with Benny and now she was acting coldly toward him. Hot, thirsty, and aggravated, he asked the server to bring him a cold beer.

"Do you drink all the time?" Tina asked.

"Well, not all the time," Gabe joked. "It gets a bit messy when I'm in the shower."

She didn't laugh.

Gabe sighed. "So I'm guessing dear old Uncle Benny told you I had a drug problem when I was in college."

"Well, did you?" she demanded.

"Yes, but I haven't touched drugs since I came out of rehab," he said defensively.

"Have you substituted the drugs with sex and alcohol?"

"No!" Gabe said angrily. "You can't believe a word that Benny says, Tina, trust me. Michael, can you help me out here?"

"Tina," Michael said deliberately, "Benny is one of the meanest, most dangerous men I've ever met. He and the truth are seldom friends, and he's had it in for Gabe since the day he entered our family."

Tina wasn't impressed. She turned to Gabe. "Well, your uncle told me you were adopted. That's more information than you cared to offer about your past."

"Tina, do me a favor. Don't listen to the man," Gabe pleaded. "He doesn't want me to be happy. And he can see you make me happy."

"I'll hang in there and make my own decisions," Tina said, but Gabe could see Benny had poisoned the well of her affections.

"Gabe," Michael said, "give me your beer. I'll drink it before I go."

"Where are you going?"

"I need to have 'the conversation' with Benny, and now is as good a time as any. He's got me fired up." Michael started to leave and then turned back toward the couple to say, "And Tina, Gabe is the most loving and loyal person I've ever known. And *that's* the truth. Now it's time for me to go talk to the liar."

"Yeah, well stay away from the railings," Gabe cautioned.

"He's over there at the bar. I'll give him the bad news in a crowd. He won't tarnish his image by doing something now," Michael said with a furrowed brow. "Later is when I'll have to worry. To be on the safe side, can I sleep in your quarters tonight?"

"You got it," Gabe said seriously.

As Michael approached the bar, he caught the end of a conversation Benny was having with Danny. "All I'm saying is that you can't be sure you don't like something until you've tried it," Benny said as he pushed a piña colada toward the boy.

Danny tasted it gingerly. "Wow! I had no idea. This tastes great," he said with a huge grin.

"See, my boy? Life is too short to clam up and deny yourself the bounty of the Lord's blessings," Benny said as he tapped Danny's hand.

Michael was disgusted at the corruption of the boy. "I hate to interrupt this conversation," Michael said sternly, "but I have to talk to you, Benny. Danny, can you give me a few minutes with my uncle?"

"Uh, sure." Danny made a pained expression and sulked away.

"Well, that was rude, Michael," Benny began.

"Spare me the indignation, Benny," Michael said with a frown as he lowered his face to the older man's. "You and I both know what you're trying to do with the boy."

"Oh, so it's acrimony today, is it, Michael?" Benny asked, matching Michael's tone. "I don't know why I try with you."

"Benny, let's just make this short and sweet," Michael snapped. "I won't extend the loan when it comes due in October."

"Oh, Michael," Benny said in mock offense, "you think I came here because of the loan? Trust me, it was the furthest thing from my mind. I'm here to try to reconnect, that's all."

"Well, since we've reconnected," Michael said sarcastically, "I'm telling you I won't roll over the loan."

"And why may I ask?" Benny asked with a snarl.

"One word, Benny: Germany." He walked away, leaving Benny to ponder how much Michael knew about his attempt on their lives ten years before.

Gloria tired of the fashion magazine. She self-consciously placed it over her expanding midsection and closed her eyes. The DJ had just begun playing songs, and the sun seemed to caress her body. Soon she drifted off to sleep and dreamed.

"We will need time to manipulate the zygote." Gloria heard the words clearly as she strained to open her eyes to see who was speaking. Cold, clammy fingers held her still while someone examined her there. She opened her mouth to scream but couldn't.

As the thing examined her, Zack stood near, telling her everything was going to be fine. He was her husband! How could he let them do this to her? How could he watch it?

She struggled and thrashed, kicking at the things that held her. She drew a deep breath and let out a huge scream.

Walking back from his confrontation with Benny, Michael passed as Gloria's own scream awakened her. He rushed to her and held her quaking body.

"Oh, my God," she cried, "it was all real! I know it! The Lady ... all of it was real!"

Michael held her closely as she gave voice to his own worst fear. "I was there too," he whispered in barely coherent words as tears filled his eyes.

She pushed him away and cried at the implications. "No ... no!" she screamed.

The scream was very loud and could be heard above the music. All chatter around the pool stopped, and everyone's attention was drawn to the beautiful blonde who was crying and yelling at the handsome young man.

Fran, Chris, and Kim rushed to Gloria. Michael moved to the back of the crowd forming around her.

Gabe came up behind him and asked, "What was that all about?"

"She saw the Lady too," Michael said eerily. "Gloria was there. I remember her being there."

Gabe put his arm around his brother's shoulders. There was nothing he could say.

Micah arrived to find Vinnie sitting in Benny's office.

"How did you get keys to his office?" he asked.

"Keys are kind of old-school in Hoboken, if you get my drift," Vinnie said.

Micah grinned. "So what have you got?"

"Well, for one thing, we can tell his public files from his private files pretty easily. Chris has the normal Church stuff in impeccable order. I love the kid, but he can be a bit anal that way. Unlike Benito Cross, who can be a bit anal in another way." Vinnie shook his head.

"Rumors and innuendo, Vinnie. I need proof of everything going into this book. I've hinted at all of it in fiction, but I want this book to document places and events."

"Well, here's something that might interest you then," Vinnie said, handing him photos of Benny's exploits with Bruno in New York.

"Charming," Micah said, as he produced a small camera to take pictures of the photos.

"Son of a gun!" Vinnie said. "I always knew, but now I have proof."

"What is it?"

"This is the address of a man in Germany. He was killed in his apartment the night the wall fell in Berlin. Kim's boys were going to college on an exchange program. Someone drugged them and tried to kill them. Chris and I got there just in time." Vinnie waved the address card. "Michael heard their attackers talking to this guy about someone they called 'the bishop.'"

"And Michael thinks this 'bishop' was Benny?"

"He always thought so, but we never really knew—until this. What's the likelihood that Benny would have this guy's address and not be the bishop they referred to?"

Micah photographed the address and said, "When we're through with his office, I want you to tell me the Germany story in full, Vinnie, every detail you can remember."

"Sure. What I'm looking for is something to tie him to Luciano and the Illuminati. And I'm guessing it's in this cabinet. It's got a padlock as well as the cabinet's locking mechanism."

"But how will we access that information?" Micah asked with a knowing smile.

"Sometimes you can jiggle a lock open, if you have the right equipment. I'm warning you, Micah, it's probably not very ethical."

"Neither is taking over the world, Vinnie."

"Good point." Vinnie produced his lock-pick kit and knelt painfully in front of the cabinet. Within a matter of seconds he removed the padlock. The cabinet lock was tougher. It was an ancient piece of furniture, and the tumblers didn't move easily. "Have you ever seen *The Music Man*?"

"Sure, several years ago. Why?"

"Because my legs are killing me, and this lock is tough. We're gonna play *The Music Man:* 'Pick a Little, Talk a Little.'" He rose painfully from his knees.

"Isn't one of the lines in that song, 'Cheap, cheap, cheap, cheap, cheap, cheap, cheap, cheap'?"

"Yeah." Vinnie grinned and shook his head. "They don't write 'em like that anymore!"

"Do you mind if I take a stab at that lock?" Micah asked as he knelt before the cabinet.

"Fine with me, but I think lock picking is more of an Italian art," Vinnie said as he plopped into a chair and rubbed his knees.

"You forget I'm Irish, Vinnie. In my youth, I found my way around locked liquor cabinets, I'll have you know."

"I don't believe that," Vinnie said, handing over the lock-pick set.

"Would you believe I did a turn in the MI6?" Micah asked as the lock sprang open.

"A spy I would believe," Vinnie said. "Let's see what we have in here ..." He joined Micah at the cabinet to review its contents.

Inside they found a treasure trove of information. There was a long report authored by Benny and issued to Luciano. It detailed a manner in which they could infiltrate Islam. The report noted that a carefully manipulated, radicalized form of Islam could provide the Illuminati with unwitting ground troops to bring down national boundaries. Combined with the group's control of the Catholic Church, they could move the world to a synthesis of Christianity and Islam—a new world religion to meet the needs of a new world order.

Vinnie said, "I knew he was an evil guy, but this stuff is worse than anything I had imagined." He rifled through the information. "It's amazing he didn't hide this stuff better!"

"Not when you think about it, " Micah corrected. "The Swiss Guard secures this building, and most days Father Chris sits outside this office. This is Benny's comfort zone. He has made the same mistake as every known conspirator down through the ages. He has kept trophies of his work in a place where he feels personally secure. If you had spent any time in MI6, you would know this is precisely the place to look."

"Well, excuse me Agent 007," Vinnie chirped. "I guess I'm just your beautiful assistant!"

Micah rolled his eyes in response.

They read for a large part of the morning, proceeding methodically drawer by drawer through the cabinet. Micah photographed the documents, and Vinnie gingerly replaced them in the same haphazard order in which he found them.

"These documents will put Archbishop Cross seriously at risk," Micah said. "Benny's handlers would kill him if they knew he had kept copies of these reports."

"I know. Let's just hope they kill him before he kills me." As Vinnie opened the bottom drawer of the cabinet, he said, "This could be interesting."

He removed Benny's small cassette tape player, set it on the desk, and pressed play. Benny's voice filled the office. "This is Archbishop Benjamin Cross. I leave this tape to be played for the media in the event of my untimely death. I have over the past two decades been in the service of Luciano Begliali to bring about a one-world dictatorial government on Earth. I must say upfront that I believe in the cause of world peace and the nullification of Christian exclusivism to attain that goal. I do not make this tape to explain or to seek forgiveness for my actions. I make it only because today Luciano threatened my life."

SIX

Tina and Gabe did not talk a lot during dinner. Doubts had been placed in Tina's heart, and Gabe had already begun to form justifications that their relationship wouldn't work out. *She's just another girl. There'll be a new one next week. I don't know what I was thinking.* Yet there was something about her—the warmth of her smile, her genuineness—that left him enrapt with her.

Benny held court at the table with tales of his life in Rome. He spoke at length about his culinary adventures in the Eternal City. He had obviously had too much to drink by the time dinner began. Danny, his sidekick, could barely sit up straight from his first-ever bout with the bottle. The others in the group of young adults listened to every detail. None had ever been around a Catholic archbishop. They were charmed by the gleam in his eye and his carefully constructed images of Rome's beauty.

"Of course, all the beauty of my beloved Rome can't replace the joy of being able to spend time with my nephews," he said with a smile.

Gabe picked up his head at that remark and glanced over at Michael, who could barely withhold a grimace.

Benny left a pregnant pause for them to respond in kind.

After what seemed like a millennium, Benny said, "Well, they're too emotionally bound to make a public declaration of their love for their old uncle, but when we're alone, we are the best of buddies. I can assure you." He took a long sip of his wine and looked lovingly toward Michael. "When Michael here was but a young boy, he convinced his mother to donate a very large sum of money for me to use in helping the poor. The money is gone, but the changes made in the lives of the unfortunate live on to this day."

"Gone?" Gabe mouthed to Michael, who raised a curious eyebrow.

"In fact," Benny continued as he raised his glass, "I want all of you to join me in a toast. To the best nephews in the world! I love you guys like you are my own sons."

All eyes were on the brothers. "Wow, now I feel like I've suffered parental abuse," Michael said with a wry smile.

Gabe stiffened in his seat when Benny spoke the toast. Then he colored when Tina looked at him, confused by his reaction.

"Listen, folks," Gabe said. "The truth is there was no charitable donation. Michael made a *loan* to Benny, that's all."

Benny jumped up. "How dare you call me a liar! You weren't there. You don't know what transpired between your brother and me."

"Are you talking about the night I made the loan to you?" Michael asked indignantly.

"You've cut me to the quick!" Benny yelled loud enough for Kim to hear at her table. He threw down his napkin and stomped out of the dining room.

Kim went to the boys to see what they had done.

They rose from the table to intercept her. "Come on, Mom," Michael said in soft tones as he and his brother met her in a little huddle between the tables.

"Mom, he's just super dramatic," Gabe said. "He was telling a story, but he got some of the facts wrong. I corrected him, and he stormed out."

"Well," Kim said sheepishly, "that does sound like your uncle Benny. But, Gabe, do you always have to be right? You know Uncle Benny is sensitive that way. Couldn't you have gotten through the dinner without contradicting him, even if he had his facts screwed up?"

"He was kind of sticking up for me, Mom," Michael said.

"I'm sure he was," Kim said with annoyance. "You two always covered for each other. It's endearing, but only to a point."

"Mom, here's the deal," Gabe began. "In a toast, Benny thanked us for our charity in front of everyone."

Kim interrupted. "Well, I can see how you would have to defend yourselves against that sort of accusation," she said sarcastically.

Michael jumped in. "He was thanking me for *giving* him $100 million twenty years ago. Do you remember when you let me negotiate that loan?"

"The loan! I had completely forgotten about it," Kim said as if the agreement was inconsequential. "I pretty much wrote that off once Benny took the money."

"In the toast, he said he had given all the money to charity. It's his way of saying he doesn't want to pay it back."

"Well, Uncle Benny's never exactly been frugal," Kim said dismissively. "Why don't you just forgive the loan then?" she asked matter-of-factly.

Gabe shook his head at the suggestion, and Michael explained. "No, Mom, he made a deal. He has to honor it. Let him borrow it from his wealthy friend, Luciano. Let him agree to pay $100 a month. He'll never pay it all back, but at least he'll have tried."

"You sound like your grandfather," Kim mused.

"Not only that, Mom," Gabe added, "but doesn't it bother you that he is suddenly seeking family time only in the year the loan is due?"

"And to top it off," Michael said, "I gave him the loan to make sure he treated Gabe well—and we both know he hasn't. Uncle Benny is still giving him grief."

"How?" Kim asked.

"Like painting me out to be a hopeless drunk and philanderer to Tina."

"Well, you are a bit of a drunken philanderer, honey," Kim said in a tone that only a mother could muster.

"But he's not hopeless." Michael smirked at his brother.

"None of this is the point," Gabe said resolutely. "For once I found a woman I could love for the rest of my life. Benny decides to butt in, and now she's turned cold toward me."

"Listen, Mom," Michael continued, "I know he's your only brother, but let's face facts. He didn't come here to get closer with us; he came to get out of repaying the loan. And to top it off, I think he purposefully sabotaged Gabe's relationship. He knows that if Gabe settles down, you'll want to bring him into the business. Then Gabe the usurper would be sitting on a pile of cash that Benny has always thought he could get someday."

Kim drew a sharp breath at the realization. "I'm sorry, boys. I always want to see the best in your uncle. My father made his life pretty miserable. I guess I feel like I owe him. There's a kernel of niceness there, and I still want to reach it. But he has to know we can see through it when he's using us."

"Can *we*?" Michael asked indignantly.

"I admit I'm blind when it comes to my brother, Michael. Just like the two of you. But let me just say if you had come to me with your thoughts earlier, rather than try to protect me, I would have remembered the loan and put two and two together. Instead, you left me twisting in the breeze."

"Did this just become our fault again?" Gabe asked. "Michael, we should have quit while we were ahead."

Kim smiled broadly. "You two were never really ahead, sweetheart. Mothers have certain privileges. Go finish your dinner. And Gabe?"

"Yeah?"

"Positive attitude and actions on your part will undermine anything negative Benny has said about you to Tina. She wants to believe in you. Give her time."

"Thanks, Mom." Gabe smiled.

Kim kissed her boys on the cheek and returned to her table.

Zack was plying his parents with wine. In the breast pocket of his suit was a fax. His lawyer had prepared a simple document that would announce his parents' retirement and their transfer of all authority in the ministry to him. His thinking was that if he could get them drunk enough, they would sign without even knowing it. He would fax the signed agreement to his lawyer, who could easily file the appropriate forms, and the ministry would be his by the time the ship docked in Miami.

He rose with glass in hand and said to his parents, "I've been hardheaded in not wanting you guys to retire, but I've changed my mind. I see the joy on your faces, and I know you're making the right decision." He paused to let it sink in and then smiled broadly. "I want to offer my apologies and a toast. To a wonderful future in your retirement."

"Here, here," Gloria said as she reached for her wine.

Turning toward her, Zack reflexively knocked the wine glass out of her hand. It spilled to the floor, but not before soaking the front of her dress. "Oh, sweetheart," he said tenderly, "I'm so sorry. I don't know what happened. I was just turning toward you and—"

"It's okay, honey," Gloria said as she dabbed with a napkin at the spreading red stain on the front of her dress. "It was an accident. I think I need to go change, though."

He sighed. "Probably. Again, sweetheart, I'm so sorry." He sighed with relief that he had protected the fetus. "Do you want me to go with you?"

"No. Stay here with your family. I think you guys need this time together." She turned to Mack and Sarah, taking their hands in hers. "Mom and Dad, I want to join Zack in saying congratulations. You've worked hard all your lives. I think it's great that you're going to take a little time for yourselves."

"Thanks, dear," Sarah said. "Your support means a lot to me. We may not have always agreed on things, but I do think of you as my daughter, and I value your opinion."

"Ditto from me," Mack said warmly. "Now go change that wet dress."

Gloria kissed them on her way out.

"Shall we?" Zack raised his glass again.

Benny fumed in the hallway outside the dining room. Where was Kim? Or Chris? Hadn't they seen how angry he was? He relished the opportunity to tell Kim what insolent brats she had raised. How dare they contradict him like that in front of people!

He made his way quietly to the door of the dining room. Kim was talking to them, no doubt telling them she didn't want to see such rudeness again. Good. Chris seemed to be enjoying himself at his table. No comfort coming from him! *Oh, here it is, Kim is done with the boys ... now she'll have to deal with me. By the time I'm done, she'll be giving me another hundred million! But wait. She returned to her table!*

He'd had enough for one day. He would have to confront her there.

From his seat, Michael had a view of the door, but Gabe did not. Michael saw Benny sweeping into the room in a fury, caught Gabe's attention, and said, "Act two."

Benny swept red-faced to Kim's side. "Kimberly," he demanded, "a word with you."

Kim turned to him and said sharply, "If the word is 'loan,' Benny, I told you years ago it was Michael's call. You have to deal with him. And you might start by being polite. They're not kids anymore. They're grown men."

Gabe was leaning back in his chair to hear their conversation and then repeating it to Michael. "Well, at least Mom admits we're not kids anymore," he added to the play-by-play commentary.

"She meant that for Benny. We'll always be kids in her eyes." Michael grinned.

"Kim, I came here with one thing in mind, and that was to get closer to you and the boys again," Benny protested, his face turning a deep red.

"And I want that too, Benny," Kim said with nonchalance. "But we've all grown and changed. We have to learn about each other again." Kim turned to her dessert and ate.

"Well, I don't know how we'll do that when your sons accuse me of wanting nothing more than an extension on the loan," Benny snarked.

"Prove them wrong, Benny. Be nice to them. Show some interest in their lives—and I don't mean warning Tina off Gabe." She paused briefly with a raised eyebrow. "Show them some real support."

"So now you're saying this is all my fault?" he demanded.

Chris instinctively moved to calm Benny down before he went into a full-blown hissy fit. Kim raised her hand in a silent gesture, telling him to do nothing.

David and Fran purposefully busied themselves with their desserts.

"Nobody's pointing fingers, Benny. We're adults who don't agree on everything, and we won't come to any meeting of the minds without calm discussion." She turned in her chair to face him. "No rhetoric, no sarcasm, no tantrums. If you want to talk, I'll be happy to—after I've had my dessert. If you want to yell ... well, I'm not available for that."

Benny let out an involuntary huff, like a lead soap opera actress who has been unjustly accused of a crime. He turned on his heels and stomped out of the dining room.

"I guess he wanted to yell," Chris said with a bemused smile.

"Is this what he's like in Rome?" David asked.

"No." Chris grinned. "Some days he's bad."

As Gabe and Michael laughed at Chris's joke, it was now obvious to Kim's entire table that they had been listening.

"All right, show's over," Kim said, shaking her head.

At the boys' table, a drunken Danny said loudly, "Isn't anybody going to go after him to see if he's okay? He's a man of God, for crying out loud!" He stumbled out of the room after his new friend.

"Act three ... and ... curtain," Michael said.

"Coming through!" the tubby archbishop barked at Gloria as she made her way back into the dining room. She stepped aside and tried to catch his eye with a smile. He would have none of it.

"Hi, Gloria," Danny said as he stumbled past her. She smiled and said hello in return, but he had already gone into the hallway. *What a strange night!*

As she went past her mother's table, she waved. They all waved in return. She wished she could stop and talk but didn't want Zack to see her with Michael's family.

Gloria was astonished at how drunk her in-laws had gotten in the short time it took her to change her dress. Zack looked just a bit tipsy, but Mack and Sarah's eyes had a half-lidded look, and they were laughing at everything Zack said. She was a little concerned as she had never seen them drunk, but it heartened her to see their warmth as the three of them reminisced. Meemaw wasn't faring so well. She was just about asleep in her wheelchair.

Her caregiver nudged at the old lady. "Gloria's here."

"Oh, good. I have to get to bed, honey, but I wanted to make sure you were all right first."

"Oh," Gloria cooed, "that's so sweet. I'm fine, Meemaw, you go have a restful sleep." She kissed the old dear on the cheek, and the caregiver began to wheel her away.

"Wait," Zack called. He smiled as he bent to kiss his grandmother. To Gloria, he said, "I was wondering if you would help get Meemaw ready for bed." Gloria had a confused look on her face as her husband hugged her. While in the hug, he whispered, "I think I'm resolving years of conflict with my parents. Do you mind letting me talk with them alone?"

Gloria hugged her husband hard. She would do anything to put this impasse behind them. "Of course I don't mind.

"Come on, Meemaw," Gloria said sweetly. "I could rub your back for a while if you like." They left the table and headed toward the door.

"Let's stop to say hello to the handsome guys and your family on the way out."

They stopped by Kim's table, and Gloria told them the story of the spilled wine.

Sandy said, "It's bedtime for this old lady, but I thought some of you handsome fellas might give a nice old gal a goodnight kiss, something to dream about," she said with a smile as she tapped at her cheek with a gnarled finger.

The guys grinned, and each in turn kissed her cheek. Michael was last. He caught Gloria's eyes as he bent to kiss the old lady. In his eyes she saw a horrible truth.

He was there! He knows!

Danny followed the old cleric on deck. Passing through a darkened section near the bow, Benny slowed to allow him to catch up.

"Your Reverence, I just want to tell you I thought it was horrible how they treated you. After all, you're a man of God."

In seconds the beast within Benny had the boy pinned to the deck, where he had his way with the young man.

Scant minutes later, as he was preparing to leave the sobbing boy, he said, "I like you, Danny, so I'm going to let you live. If you ever breathe a word of this to anyone, I'll know. And when you least suspect it, I'll come out of the shadows and have my way with you again, only it won't end on such a pleasant note. Do you understand me?"

Danny whimpered and nodded as he pulled up his pants. Benny

grabbed him by the hair, got close to his face, and said, "Do you understand me, Danny? Yes or no."

"Yes!" Danny spat.

Benny yanked on his hair. "Yes what?" he demanded.

"Yes, Eminence," Danny whined.

Benny turned his back on the boy and went to the suite to shower, and a faint grin pulled at the corners of his mouth.

As the water of the shower hit him, Benny felt the Lady trying to break through to his consciousness. Every time he offered someone up to her, as he had Danny earlier, her presence in him grew stronger, her call more intense. She called to him now. He could tell it would be a call to action. This night wasn't over yet, not by a long shot.

"What a lovely sacrifice you made to me tonight," she purred. "Of course it would have been made perfect if you had dispatched the boy."

"It's too confined a community," Benny explained, a bit hurt. "I couldn't afford to have him go missing right before I left the ship. Especially when everyone at the table saw him follow after me."

"No need to be defensive, little one. You have a perfect opportunity to make it up to me this evening, not with one sacrifice but two. I will lead you to where you will find the sheep for slaughter. Will you follow me, little one?"

"Yes, my Lady. I will follow."

Zack and his parents had lingered in the dining room until they were the last guests. The three had been reliving memories, laughing at their foibles, and enjoying their successes all over again. Zack kept pouring the wine, although he had decided long before to merely sip his.

"This has been so nice," Sarah purred. "We haven't laughed like this for such a long time. I guess it was the pressures of the ministry, but somewhere along the way we forgot to laugh at ourselves. What a shame!"

"There's plenty of time to make up for it, my dear," Mack said, a grin of pleasure frozen on his face. "This is the first day of the rest of our lives. You know what I'm thinking? I'm thinking I'd like to retire in the Caribbean. What do you think?"

"Well, how about part of the year, Mack?" Sarah offered, her eyes mere slits from too much wine. "A big part of me belongs to the Republic of Texas. I don't want to leave her forever."

"Understood," Mack slurred. "As soon as we get home, we'll get Meemaw settled and close things down. Then we can come back and look for a place."

"I can take care of Meemaw and shut down the ministry for you," Zack offered. "You and Mom could get a hotel room in Grand Cayman tomorrow when we land. Why not start your dream now?"

"I don't know," Sarah said with the deliberate concentration of one who has had too much to drink.

"Sounds like a fine idea to me, son," Mack said with a grin. "Come on, Sarah, it would only be for a week or so." Mack petted her arm. "We could scope it out, maybe find a place, and then go back home for a retirement party."

"He's got a point, Mom. If you guys go back and get into your routine, you'll let your dream steep on the back burner. But if you come home with a plan, you'll follow through."

"Yeah, but I've got to tell the church elders what we're doing," Mack said with sudden clarity.

"Write them a note," Zack said with a grin. He motioned for the server, who agreed to find them a pen and paper.

"Okay, Dad. You're a little bit tipsy, but you don't want that to show in your letter," Zack cautioned. "Why don't you let me help you?" Zack quoted from his lawyer's fax. "Just say this: 'After a lot of thought and prayer, Sarah and I have decided to retire from ministry effective immediately. We have decided to stay on in the Cayman Islands for a bit. Until we return, we give to our son, Zack, full power of attorney in our personal affairs and the affairs of our ministry.'"

Mack dutifully wrote all his son dictated. Then he and Sarah signed. Zack folded it and placed it in his pocket as the three of them left the dining room.

Gabe decided there was time for a stroll along the deck as he made his way back to his quarters. His attention was taken by a single, gut-wrenching sob to his right. He turned to see Danny climbing onto the ship's railing. Adrenalin took over as he rushed to the boy and pulled him from the railings in one fell swoop.

A startled Danny turned to see who had foiled his plan, and he cried. "I wish to God I had never met you and your family!"

Gabe held him, not wanting to take the chance that Danny would succeed in a second attempt to jump from the rails. "Danny, you have to trust me. You'll get over this crush you have on Tina. I don't know a lot of things, but I know about crushes on girls."

"It's not Tina," Danny sobbed.

"Benny?" Gabe asked cautiously. At the mention of Benny's name, Danny's body stiffened in horror.

"What did he do to you?" Gabe demanded, even though he had a sickening idea.

"Nothing!" Danny said.

"Let me guess," Gabe said. "He threatened to kill you if you told."

Danny cringed at Gabe's words, providing all the assent needed. Gabe felt incredible compassion for the young man, and he wanted nothing more than to see Benny off the ship. He held Danny at arm's length and looked directly into his eyes. "Listen to me, Danny. Benny is a horrible man. He's able to deliver on his threat, but once he's gone tomorrow, you'll be fine because you'll be just a memory to him. For now, though, we need to keep you safe. Let me take you to the infirmary. I have friends on the security team; I can have them post a guard for the night."

"O-okay," Danny sobbed.

Gabe put his arm around the boy and gently led him to the infirmary.

Zack and his parents strolled along the deck. Sarah and Mack were still drunk, but the night air had a bit of a sobering effect. A twinge of conscience fell on Zack. He loved his parents, but they were standing in the way of his future—his destiny.

"Well hello there!" someone called from a deck chair in the darkness.

The man from the deck chair strolled toward them into the glow of the lights from the ship's interior. They recognized him as the archbishop who had joined the cruise in Mexico.

Sarah and Mack both greeted the aging cleric, their faces frozen in contented grins and half-lidded eyes.

"Nice evening, isn't it?" Mack asked happily.

"It sure is," Benny said with a smile. At that moment, Zack's vision doubled. It was as if he was seeing the archbishop and the Lady at the same time. She seemed to be urging him on to his designated task. Instinctively he knew she had sent this priest to help him.

"Isn't it beautiful on deck tonight?" Sarah asked.

"It's like being on the edge of eternity," Benny said as he drew in a deep breath of the sea air. "If you look into the distance, you can barely see another ship on the horizon," Benny said. As they leaned over the rail to look, he quickly picked up a deck chair and smashed it on their heads. It wasn't enough to knock them out, but they were fazed.

"Don't just stand there, help me!" Benny commanded a frozen Zack. They lifted the partially conscious bodies and flung them overboard in a matter of seconds.

Zack collapsed on the deck as the weight of his actions overwhelmed him. Benny helped him up.

"I'm the only one who knows what you have done," Benny said to him. "I don't need much to ensure it stays that way."

Zack's eyes widened as it dawned on him that he had traded one form of bondage for another that would be much worse.

"First, I'll need a slight 10 percent of your offerings each week. I'll set up a Swiss bank account for you to use."

Zack stared in disbelief as he received his instructions.

"Secondly, I'll send you an outline of the concepts you will preach. We are building a global church, one the Lady can be proud of. We're dispensing of archaic ideas such as sin and salvation," Benny continued, and Zack listened like a man in a trance.

In Gabe's quarters, he and Michael had passed a fitful night once Gabe had gotten Michael alone to tell him of his encounter with Danny. The doctor at the infirmary noted that Danny was traumatized but showed no significant physical injuries. Danny refused to say a word to any of them, and the cruise line encouraged his silence. With no statement from Danny and no witnesses, Gabe and Michael had no evidence against their uncle. As with their near-death experiences in Germany, they were left with nothing but strong suspicions.

"Did you sleep much?" Michael asked as he heard Gabe moving in his bed.

"A little. I'm just so anxious to get Benny off this ship. It's all I could think about all night."

"He certainly has a way of making life difficult." Michael yawned and wiped at his sleepy eyes.

Gabe threw a pillow at his brother. "Understatement of the decade! The man is straight-out evil. Never have I been so happy to be adopted."

Ignoring the obvious call to return the pillow to its owner, Michael turned somber. "Promise me something, Gabe."

"What?"

"Say it's genetic. Say I end up like Benny. Will you promise to kill me?"

"Trust me, Michael. I'd know by now if you were like Benny. You're nothing like him. You're Mom through and through."

Michael offered a weak smile.

Benny left the ship early that morning. Zack was up early as well, telling everyone of his parents' decision to retire in the Caribbean. He explained that they had left the ship at first light to start the adventure of their lifetimes.

"Why didn't they tell us?" Gloria asked in disbelief as she held the sobbing Meemaw.

"They were afraid they would change their minds if confronted with tears like this," Zack offered as he hugged them both and squeezed out some tears of his own.

"I just don't understand how they could do this!" Meemaw shrieked.

"Don't worry about a thing, Meemaw," Zack comforted. "Gloria and I will take care of you. We'll take care of everything."

The time on the cruise after Grand Cayman passed quickly. Everyone seemed to be content to enjoy the Caribbean sun.

Fran and David enjoyed themselves and spent most of their time with Kim and Chris. Fran and Kim had developed a nice friendship, and Fran was happy to see Chris again. David enjoyed himself but was worried about Danny. It was clear he would require professional help.

Gabe and Tina continued to enjoy each other, but Benny's words had done their damage. As they got closer to Miami, Gabe spoke much of what they could do to continue the relationship, but Tina surprised him. She gave him her Bible and told him to study the Gospel of John. She explained that Christ was her first love and that she needed to spend her life with someone who loved Him as well.

Once Tina and his family had left the ship, Gabe felt more alone and adrift than ever. He poured himself a stiff drink and started his tasks in readying the ship for its next group of passengers.

SEVEN

Benny couldn't put his finger on it, but something was different in his office. There was no defining piece of evidence that led him to this conclusion, but things didn't "feel" right. Items on his desk were where he left them to be sure, but they looked as if they had been placed there more neatly than he would have left them. The contents of his cabinets were unchanged, yet his files seemed just a bit more orderly than he remembered them. Nothing obvious, just a constant niggling, small mental nudges that everything was somehow askew. He heard whistling in the outer office as Vinnie came to water the plants. He couldn't put two and two together yet, but if someone had been nosing around in his stuff, it was probably that hobo from Hoboken.

"Vinnie?" he called from his office.

"Oh, I didn't see you there," the old monk said cheerfully. "Chris comes home tomorrow. I thought I'd pretty up the plants a bit."

"You didn't happen to go into my office while I was away, did you?"

"No, you never gave me a key," Vinnie said. "What's the matter? Did one of your plants die?"

"No, they're okay. They could use some watering though."

"Sure thing. They probably need it. The heat in this building is too dry. They're my babies, you know. I hate to lose a plant. If you want to give me a key, I'd be happy to—"

"No." Benny cut him off, thinking Vinnie was a bit talkative for an innocent man. "No thanks, Vinnie. I have papers in here that are too important to His Holiness. We'll just have to rely on God's grace to care for these plants when I'm out of the office."

"Whatever you say. I just want to be a good and faithful servant. I'm not getting any younger, you know. When I stand before the Lord, I want Him to say I was faithful."

Benny smiled as if he concurred. *You'll be standing before Him sooner than you think if I find out you've been going through my stuff!* "Vinnie, how about letting me buy you lunch today?"

Vinnie had to steady his hand. He nearly dropped the watering can.

He's guilty of something ... but I have the only key to this office and to my files.

Vinnie smiled. "That would be wonderful, but I'm already meeting someone for lunch. Can I take a rain check?"

"Sure you can, friend," Benny said, as Vinnie stared at him with a blank expression.

"Yeah. Maybe when Chris gets back, we can all go, and he can tell us about his cruise," Vinnie rambled. "I've never been on a cruise. I don't think I could stand all that water. I'm not such a swimmer, you know. I think I'd spend the whole trip hanging onto something and praying the ship doesn't sink."

"Or that someone doesn't throw you overboard." Benny grinned. "It happens more than most people think, you know. And the cruise lines cover it up to avoid bad publicity." Benny shrugged dismissively. "Of course it doesn't have to be on a ship. You would be amazed at how many people die each year just falling down the stairs. Particularly old people ... with gout."

Benny was sure Vinnie had understood the threat. But did that mean he had been in Benny's office? Curiosity got the better of him.

He decided to follow the old monk to his lunch engagement. The winter air was moist and the wind carried a strong bite. Benny cursed the man's slow gait. *I could get frostbite in the time it takes that old fool to get down the block!*

Finally Vinnie stopped by a water fountain in the square, where he met a stately fellow wearing a long, tailored, gray-tweed coat. It looked decidedly expensive.

Who could that be? Benny wondered as he watched from a nearby storefront. When the two left the fountain, they passed directly in front of the store. Benny got a good look at the fellow as he heard Vinnie say, "I'm telling you, Micah, he suspects something."

Micah ... Micah. Benny knew the face from somewhere. It would come to him.

Zack fiddled with his microphone as the choir sang a rousing tune. It was his first time to preach as the new pastor of Riverside. The church board was shocked when he produced the letter signed by Mack and Sarah. Nonetheless, they were quick to grasp that Zack was the best hope for continuity—for keeping the ministry alive. Predictably, they voted unanimously to welcome Zack as the new head of Riverside's ministry.

Zack looked out over his new flock singing joyfully with the choir. Soon they would sink their spoiled posteriors into the deep red-velvet cushions Zack had ordered for every pew in the cavernous sanctuary. As the tune ended, he had one last chance to gaze at the huge, rotating globe he commissioned to replace the old map of the United States. His blue eyes flashed, and he maintained a perpetual smile. All he had to do to keep the money flowing was keep this group comfortable and well entertained.

As the congregation sank into the new cushions with a collective sigh, he began. "We could stand here and talk about sin all day, but what's the point? We've been delivered from the consequences of sin. God is in the process of reshaping each of us. We are moving from glory to glory as we discover the nature of God living within us."

He paused to stare intently into the crowd. "Do you know what happens if you drive down the freeway looking only into the rear-view mirror? You crash before you get very far. God has given each of us a shiny new car, but when we concentrate on the old sin nature, we're looking only in the rear-view mirror. We've been set free of that reality. We live in God now."

He paused for dramatic effect and looked up to heaven. A slow grin dawned on his face as if he were receiving fresh revelation from above. "We need to get behind that wheel and *move,* and I don't mean at fifty-five miles an hour, either. There are no speed limits on God's highway. We're going to get in our cars and speed down the road to our destinies in the Lord." It was like a huge pep rally. His voice grew louder with each sentence.

"My parents have done a great job with Riverside. Now it's time for us to take what they have given us and go to the next level. They've given you a fine car, and now Gloria and I are going to teach you how to drive it." A few in the crowd shouted amen, and Zack screamed, "All I can say is this. Hang on, folks, because you ain't seen nothin' yet!"

The church applauded long and hard, barely noticing that they hadn't so much as opened their Bibles during the service. The changes made to the camera angles and lighting were subtle, but they made a significant impact on the TV broadcast. Zack looked as if he lived inside an otherworldly glow. The camera caught his smile and every twinkle of his eye. And when it came time for the collection, the members in the church dug in deep. Donations from TV viewers rose dramatically as well.

After the service, Zack and Gloria posed for photos with Meemaw. Viewers were enamored with the idea that Zack and Gloria were caring for Sarah's mother. For her part, Meemaw was more docile than usual, thanks to Zack's changes in her medication. He also had dispensed with the constant caregiver in favor of a motorized wheelchair and aids who came in the morning and evening.

As they were shutting down the auditorium, Zack took a hard look at his church. He was made for this ministry, and this ministry was made for him. If only his parents hadn't tried to stand in the way of God's will, they could have participated in his joy.

Back at the mansion, Gloria had gotten out of her Sunday dress and into a pair of jeans. They were nearly too tight to button. And she got through the service by holding her breath in a dress that had always been a bit big on her. She was pregnant and she knew it, even though the result of the home pregnancy test was negative. The result only fed her suspicion that she carried no normal child. *Of course it was negative! It tested for a human fetus!*

They had only been home from the cruise for a little more than a week, which meant she couldn't be more than a couple weeks' pregnant. But all the changes in her body made it seem as if she were two or three months along. The morning sickness was beginning to abate, but her hips had spread and a baby bump had appeared.

She lay on a bed that a week before had been her in-laws'. Not much more of the abduction memories had resurfaced after the dream she'd had on deck. But fragments were there—just beyond her grasp. She closed her eyes and slowed her breathing. Her eyes were closed, but she was still looking to see if images of that night could somehow present themselves.

She drifted to a light sleep, during which most memories of that evening were recovered. She woke an hour later, her pillow wet with tears. There was no doubt. She had been used as part of some sick experiment, and Zack was a part of it. *Damn you!* she screamed at him in her mind but then considered how illogical it all sounded. Could she really *believe* her husband, the man she loved, would work with aliens to produce some weird space baby in her? It was too crazy. She couldn't bring herself to say it aloud, let alone confront Zack about it. She let out a loud moan and sob. Maybe what she really needed was a psychiatrist. But if it was all in her mind, what was causing the physical changes? No. Something was alive inside her, and she didn't believe it was human. Something had to be done!

She never really had the faith of her parents, but she had their strength of character. She knew how to make a decision and follow through on it. And she had made her decision. She refused to be an incubator for the thing growing inside her. That very thought brought a wave of nausea, and she ran to the bathroom to vomit.

Whatever she had been given, it was wearing off. And she was livid. She had seen enough. Zack was going to have to tell her how to get in touch with Sarah and Mack. She needed to know her daughter was safe.

She abandoned her wheelchair, walked gingerly with her cane to the foyer of the great house, found a chair, and waited for him. When the front door finally opened, he came into the house with a carefree smile.

"Zack!" she said sharply, "we have to talk. I need answers. What did you do with your parents?"

The smile never left her grandson's face, but his eyes grew sinister, deeply menacing. "I helped them find the rest they were longing for."

"Get them on the phone. I need to talk to them," Sandy demanded.

"I can't do that, Meemaw."

"But I want to see them. Talk to them. I need to know they're okay!" she shrieked.

"You can't do that, Meemaw," Zack replied sternly.

"Then I'll call the police," she threatened, pounding her hand on the arm of the chair.

In a second he was in her face, his nose touching hers. "No ... you ... won't," he snarled. "I would be more than happy to send you to be with them, old woman. But I need you right now."

"As a prop for your ministry!" she yelled back at him.

"Whatever you want to call it." He wagged his index finger in her face and lectured sternly. "Here are the rules. If you play the game, you'll live out a nice end to your life. If you don't, you'll lose privileges—like eating, for example. You'll waste away, Meemaw. And the entire world will share my grief at how sharply you've started to decline. The choice is yours, old woman."

Sandy had a million things on the tip of her tongue, but she held them. It was the first use of a filter since the stroke. She had to be smart. She had to get away from this monster. But for now, she had to play his game. "Fine, Zack, you win."

"Thanks, Meemaw," he said with a kiss to her cheek. "But just to make sure you know I mean business, I'm going to take away your cane and wheelchair privileges for the afternoon. If you want something more comfortable than this straight-back chair, I'm afraid you'll have to crawl for it." He made his way to his study in the north wing of the house, twirling her cane—and whistling.

As Sandy cried softly, Gloria quietly descended the stairs. Putting one finger to her lips, she motioned for the old woman to be quiet. She then helped Sandy stand and walked with her to the couch in the nearby sitting room. Though they spoke nothing, the tears in their eyes bound the two women. They would have to look out for each other.

"Hi, babe," David said as he walked into the TV room. Fran sat reading a book, the TV on mute.

"How did it go?"

"Danny's going to be okay, but he's got some problems. The psychiatrist said he's suffering from some sort of traumatic stress. Judging by the ship's medical records, he thinks Danny may have been sodomized."

"Oh, David!" Fran said in horror, putting the book down. She stood and put her arms around his waist. She pulled him close, and he returned her hug.

"Danny refuses to talk about it, and it's hindering his progress. I spoke with him tonight and explained that whatever happened, he bears no shame. He's a victim."

"Do you think it helped?"

"No such luck, but he asked me to do something odd. He asked me to get in touch with Gabe and ask him if it's safe."

"What could that mean?"

"Who knows?" David shrugged. "The ship's doctor says Gabe all but carried Danny into the infirmary that night. Maybe Gabe knows what happened."

"Are you going to call him?"

"I already placed a message with the cruise line asking Gabe to get in touch with me. I want to try to schedule a conference call at the mental facility so Danny can talk to Gabe in the presence of the psychiatrist." He put his head on her shoulder. She caressed his cheek.

"David, it sounds like Gabe knows what happened. And I would be willing to bet the farm it has to do with Benny Cross. God help Chris! He has to deal with that petty little man every day."

"If he were just a petty little man, it wouldn't be so bad. We could be talking sexual assault here, Frannie. It's a criminal offense."

Fran turned up the volume on the TV as the Riverside church show was just beginning. "Speaking of criminal offense. Something isn't right about the way Sarah and Mack just faded into the sunset."

"Isn't right in what way?" David asked cautiously. He had been harboring suspicions that he didn't want to admit aloud.

"They weren't irresponsible. They gave their lives to that ministry. They may have retired, but I can't believe they would have walked away."

"You're speaking about them in the past tense," David commented.

Tears burned Fran's eyes. "David, what if Zack did something to them?"

"We don't know that anything untoward happened," David offered, as much to quell his own fears as those of his wife.

"But you feel it too, David. I know you do."

He sighed. "I feel that it's not exactly what Zack has told us, but that doesn't mean there was foul play."

"Well, what then?" she asked, rubbing her forehead.

David paced the room, searching his mind for a reasonable explanation. "Maybe he had some evidence of financial impropriety, for example. He could have told them they could either retire in the Caribbean and leave the ministry to him or face exposure at home."

She took a deep breath and mulled it over. "Actually, that sounds more like Zack," she agreed. "I feel a little bit better with a scenario like that ... but not a lot."

"You don't think he would physically hurt Gloria, do you?" David asked cautiously.

"He never has to my knowledge." Fran offered with little conviction.

"Do you think he's emotionally abusive?"

"In a word, yes. He's a spoiled brat who still throws tantrums when he doesn't get his own way."

"Gloria's a pretty tough cookie in her own right," David ventured.

"And spoiled." Fran grinned. "Go ahead and say it. Two spoiled children trying to find a life together."

"It's too bad she couldn't have met Michael when they were both younger," David mused. "There was an instant chemistry there. You can't deny it."

"I think he would have been a nice catch, but then my baby would have an uncle Benny who just may be a sexual predator."

"Man!" David sighed. "My life was so simple before I met you."

Fran grinned.

The phone rang and David pounced on it. "Hello? Gabe! Thanks for returning my call."

"David. I'm surprised by your call. Is everything okay? How's Tina?"

"Tina's fine. You know, you could call her to find out how she's doing."

"Not yet, David. She gave me her Bible and said something about being unequally yoked. I started to read it but didn't get too far out of the Garden of Eden."

"Let me give you a pointer," David said. "Try to read the Gospel of John. It's toward the back of the Bible. If you have questions or want to discuss anything, you can call me."

"Thanks, David." Gabe sighed. "I really appreciate it. I think Tina and I could have something together, but I would be doing her and me a disservice if I just give lip service to her beliefs."

"That's honorable. Read John, and then let's talk about it, okay?"

"Okay. So why did you call?"

"We're at an impasse in Danny's treatment. His therapist thinks he needs to talk about his trauma, but Danny refuses. He asked me to call you to find out 'if it's safe.'"

"Phew, David. That's a tough one. Here's my answer. Anything that stays within the confidence of the client-patient relationship or your relationship with Danny as his pastor is safe. If the police were involved, I think Danny could be in danger."

"From the ship's medical records, it looks like the boy was sodomized," David said with disgust.

"David, Benny Cross is a twisted and dangerous individual. And I'm telling this to you as someone who has been in his crosshairs. It's safe for Danny to talk to get better, but his life will be in danger if he tells the police or the press."

David grunted with disgust. "Do you think you could convince him it's safe to talk to us?"

"Sure. How do you want to go about it?"

"I was hoping for a conference call among you, me, Danny, and his doctor. When is your next port of call?"

"We leave Miami in about an hour. Tomorrow we're at sea, but I can do a ship-to-shore call with you if you'd like."

"That would be wonderful, Gabe. I can't tell you how much I appreciate it. How about two o'clock tomorrow? The doctor will be at the facility, and I can meet him and Danny there." He gave Gabe the number, and the call ended shortly after.

Gloria looked intently at her reflection as she applied her makeup. She looked tired and drawn. There were circles under her eyes. She wasn't sure how much she could do to counteract the effects of her pregnancy, but she had to try. Zack had arranged an interview for them with the largest newspaper in the area.

As Zack entered the room, he said, "Now don't fret too much, darlin'. You look beautiful."

"Do you think so? I feel out of sorts today, and I think it shows."

He caressed her shoulders, kissed the top of her head, and said, "You always look beautiful to me, and you're going to look beautiful to that reporter as well. Now get a move on; we have a photo shoot scheduled in the church in fifteen minutes."

The interview was a revelation to Gloria. She saw how easily Zack manipulated the reporter. He discussed his plans for church expansion and treated her as an equal partner in all the discussions. They worked as a couple, and she found it exhilarating. At that moment, she knew she could be very good in this role. It was so different to be at the center of the ministry than the daughter-in-law of the pastor. The respect and attention were like a balm.

The only problem was the thing growing inside her. If it were gone, life could be so nice. Zack was courteous and giving with her now that he didn't feel the need to prove himself. They could be a wonderful team. And in time, maybe they could have a child of their own. But the thing inside her wasn't a child. It was an abomination.

She didn't believe in abortion. Their church took a strong stance against the termination of pregnancies. But what if the child wasn't human? Would it be a sin to squash the insect thing growing inside her? To her mind it would be no worse than killing a yeast infection.

She wanted to scream from fear and torment. For all she knew it was a hysterical pregnancy. After all, the home pregnancy test had been negative. But they're designed to test for *human* babies. All doubt was gone as the baby kicked for the first time. She buried her head in her pillow and screamed again and again as she acquiesced to this new reality and a plan to take care of it.

"Danny? Are you there?" Gabe's voice rang out from the speakerphone.

David and the doctor had said hello into the speakerphone, but Danny had not.

"I'm here." His voice cracked with emotion.

"Listen, buddy, you had a run-in with a real bad guy, but you need to understand that it is safe for you to talk about it to your doctor or to David. You'll be able to get better and move on with your life. Do you know what they say?"

"No." Danny shifted in his chair.

"The best revenge is to live a good life. Work with these guys, Danny. Let them help you. Then go out there and lead a great life. You can do it. I know you can."

"He won't kill me?" Danny asked tentatively as he wrung his hands.

"You're not going to the press or the police, right? All you're doing is trying to live your life. Don't let him win, buddy."

"Okay," Danny said with a sad chuckle and a sigh of relief. His entire body relaxed for the first time since the incident on deck. "I want to get better, Gabe. I'll talk about what happened."

"Do it!" Gabe coached.

"I will," Danny replied, already sounding more animated. After a pause, he added, "There's something else, Gabe. You've been really nice to me, and I wasn't so nice to you ..."

"Don't even worry about that, sport. Your plans were dashed and your feelings were hurt. For what it's worth, I had no ill intent toward you. I just was a little bit blindsided myself."

"Tina will do that to a guy," Danny commiserated with his first grin since that terrible evening.

"Well, I'm not sure we were right for each other anyway. The unequally yoked thing and all."

"Don't say that, Gabe!" Danny chided. "The reason I was upset was that you two fit like a glove. You'll make a wonderful couple. And you'll love being in a relationship with Jesus if you give it a chance."

"Hey, Danny, you're quite a man. If Jesus could make me half as good as you, I might just give Him a shot," Gabe comforted.

"Do it!" Danny said, echoing Gabe's earlier encouragement.

"So you're going to talk to these guys? Let them get you better?"

"Yeah. I'll talk to them. I'll get better, and I'll dance at your wedding."

"You bet. If I can find my way through this," Gabe said.

"You will."

"Thanks, Danny. I appreciate it."

After hanging up with Danny, Gabe saw the Bible and the bottle of scotch on the table. He looked at the Bible and said, "Maybe later, John." Then he poured a stiff drink and got ready for his "date."

Gloria tied the bandana around her head; her grandmother would have called it a babushka. She wore no makeup, a pair of jeans, and a nondescript white T-shirt. Now all she had to do was get out of the house without Zack seeing her. It shouldn't be hard. He had just left for a breakfast meeting.

From the top of the stairs, she could hear Meemaw's wheelchair whirring on the ground floor below. Gloria hadn't planned on her being up and about so early. She decided to come down the stairs slowly, nonchalantly. Meemaw continued on to the fruit bowl in the dining room. Gloria descended a few more stairs, and she could see the old woman peeling a banana.

As if feeling her stare, Meemaw looked back at her just as the front door unlocked and Zack entered to retrieve his forgotten notes for the meeting. Gloria's eyes locked with Meemaw's in a desperate plea for help. Meemaw pushed herself unsteadily up on the chair and let herself fall. The breath exploded out of her as she hit the floor. Zack ran to the dining room to see what had happened. As he knelt over his grandmother, Gloria slipped out of the house.

She parked her car a block away from the abortion clinic and then walked slowly toward its entrance. She had always taken such a stand against abortion. She cried softly as she thought of how much she would love to have a baby. But not this one, not this thing growing inside her.

She put her head down and stared at her feet as she passed anti-abortion protesters on the block. Her hand pushed away pamphlets and cards they tried to hand her. This day was hard enough. The last thing she needed was to read literature she herself had handed out only weeks before.

She heard her name. Soft at first, and then louder as she passed a news van. "Oh God, no," she mouthed silently as tears formed. But there was no mistaking it; the local reporter had recognized her. Dragging a half-prepared cameraman behind her, the reporter ran after Gloria.

"Gloria Jolean! Gloria Jolean! Is that you?" the reporter yelled. Several protesters grew silent to watch the impending confrontation.

Not knowing what else to do, Gloria stopped and pulled the scarf from her head in resignation. As her luxurious blonde hair fell into place, the cameraman moved in for a close-up. She heard murmuring from the crowd that had formed. Her heart raced as she thought of the implications to Zack, their marriage, and their ministry.

"Gloria, I'm Maria Esteban, Channel Five Live at Five. You look as if you aren't here to protest abortions."

Gloria's mind raced in a panic until it found a course of action. "I'm not, Maria," Gloria stated boldly as she launched forth with a lie she hoped would be believed. She stared defiantly into the camera. "I'm here to evaluate the efforts of the protesters. For years, I have taken part in it, pushing pamphlets at distraught girls as they try to find the fast way out of some trouble they've gotten into."

"And what have you found?"

"Well, I had hoped to do more—until you blew my cover. But what I have found so far is a lack of the feeling of love." Real tears fell down her cheeks as she sensed the ruse was working. She looked for all the world like a woman filled with compassion for others. "These girls need our love, not intimidation. I think if the Christian protesters could exude more warmth and more love, we could be a lot more persuasive." She picked up the pace of her speech, mimicking Zack's pattern when he preached. "We need to love the girls who come here in fear and desperation. We need to show them God cares for them, that *we* care for them."

"Well, you heard it here first," Maria said into the camera. "Houston's new televangelist darling isn't just wearing nice jewelry and offering platitudes. She's on the streets where the action is, and she has some harsh criticisms for her fellow Christians. A brave woman indeed." Maria smiled at the camera for ten seconds, and then snarled and yelled, "cut" to the cameraman. As she was arguing with him, Gloria slipped away through the protesters and ran toward her car.

"Could this day go more wrong?" she asked herself as she ran.

Zack took the phone call from the producer of Live at Five asking for a comment about his wife's brave efforts at the abortion clinic. He bluffed his way through the interview by declaring his love and support for his wife. Then he turned on the TV and watched as his fury mounted. He drove home in a rage, slamming the front door as he entered the house.

Gloria was waiting for him at the door.

He strode quickly to her and took her head in both hands. "What have you done?" he screamed as he looked at the defiance in her eyes.

"Nothing!" she spat as she wrestled away from him. "As you obviously have seen, I was interrupted by that stupid reporter."

"Why? Why would you do it?"

"Stop it! Just stop it, Zack!" she screamed as she pounded his chest with her fists. "Stop lying to me! Please, *please* just tell me the *truth*!"

As if blinders had lifted, Zack suddenly felt the pain of the only woman he had ever loved. He reached out and gently wiped a tear from her cheek. "All right," he said in a barely audible tone as he took her hand and led her from the foyer to the living room.

She sat on the couch. He sat beside her, holding her hand as she sobbed.

He asked, "What do you know?"

"I think I remember the Lady ..." She cringed at the memory, as if saying it aloud made it more real.

Zack winced. They had told him she wouldn't remember. He wiped a tear from his own eye and drew a deep breath. "Our baby—and it is at least partly our DNA—has been developed through selective breeding for decades, maybe centuries. He'll be a true cross between alien and human DNA. He'll bring peace to this planet and move it into a galactic federation. I know it sounds weird, all *Star Trek* and everything, but it's true." His voice trailed off to uncharacteristic silence.

"I have vague memories of the, for lack of a better word, 'conception.'" She wrung her hands. Her face looked as if it would break into cascading tears as she asked, "Why did you play me for a pawn, Zack? Did you think I wouldn't put it all together when I gave birth to a lizard or insect or whatever they are?"

"You aren't supposed to give birth. There is a critical period of three months when he needs to be in your womb. Then they'll take him and raise him somewhere. I was hoping you would never have to know."

"And you went along with it?" she spat contemptuously. Her shoulders heaved and tears flowed freely.

"You might have noticed they don't seek our approval," he said weakly as he put his arm around her slumped shoulders. "It's not like they offered a choice. They told me you wouldn't remember, Gloria. I never expected it to hurt you." Now it was Zack who appeared to cry.

Tentatively, Gloria reached out to comfort him. She kissed him softly. He turned to her and they held each other close.

But as his wife held him, Zack could barely suppress a grin.

The news report about Gloria made an impact on the entire community. She was branded a hero, someone who had found the proper balance between the pro-life stance and recognition of the turmoil of mothers seeking abortion. Soon she was speaking at churches and women's groups throughout the area, advocating love and tenderness toward women seeking to terminate a pregnancy.

Her message of love without recrimination worked well into the new message of Riverside Church, and Zack was enormously proud of her. As the ministry gave Zack and Gloria something to share and nurture, their relationship improved. Gloria felt very much like Zack's partner, and Zack had found new affection and respect for her.

For her part, Gloria vowed she would never forget the compassion shown to her by Meemaw. She vowed to make the old woman's last days on Earth happy and to give her a warm, loving environment.

And the money kept rolling in.

EIGHT

Michael woke early at the old seminary in the hills of Georgia. His accommodations were sparse, designed that way to aid the aesthetic of emptying one's self so the Holy Spirit may enter. It was May, the month of ordinations, and the rising sun cast a rosy glow about the little cinderblock room.

Today he would became a priest. His emotions were mixed. Somehow the day felt anticlimactic. The others in the ordination class were younger, and they had the vigor and innocence of young brides. For Michael, his marriage to the Church seemed to be the next logical step, more of a promotion than a life-changing event.

He wondered about other options. Would he have been happier as a husband and father? Gloria. He thought about his unexpected attraction to her. He had never felt like that about a woman. He could easily see himself by her side. He smiled for a brief second before his reverie dissolved into the image of the Lady. He fought an involuntary shiver.

It was always this way. She forced her way into his conscious mind any time he so much as considered a life other than the priesthood. Prior to today, she hadn't made an appearance in his life since the cruise. But then again, since the cruise, he had lived a monastic existence.

Michael might have been confused about a lot of things, but one thing was certain. His only relief from the Lady was in the Church. He may not have found Chris's devotion to Christ, but he knew beyond a doubt that the Church was his salvation from this toothless, pale apparition—and that would be reason enough to be ordained.

"You probably need a psychiatrist more than an ordination," he said aloud to the empty room. But there was his work. He was passionate about antiquities, and the Church had offered him tremendous opportunities for research. He would never gain such access as a layperson. True enough, his mother's fortune had greased the skids in any event, but his commitment to the priesthood opened doors that otherwise would have been closed to him. When it came to work that fulfilled him and made him happy, the Church provided the best opportunities. As for the pastoral side of it, he found he was actually pretty good at it. He was friendly and truly enjoyed people. His incredible adroitness at languages made him accessible to the flock wherever he went.

As for a love of God—of Jesus? Well, somehow that all eluded him. He recognized the historical Jesus as a wonderful teacher and definitely inspired of God. He understood all the doctrine about His substitutionary death for the sins of humanity. Yet he also understood the doctrine of so many ancient religions from the ruins he had studied. Each thought they had the full picture, only to have that picture revised, usually by a conquering invader. His studies had shown him that mankind needs a connection to something otherworldly. It was a driving force in any culture he studied. And whether people realized it or not, it was a driving force in the cultures of the present age. In his estimation, Western culture had been greatly influenced by the self-sacrifice embodied in the stories of Jesus. He would be happy to perpetuate the good that such beliefs had wrought.

So there he was. He looked in the mirror at the passionate archeologist and linguist who wanted to do good for others and for civilization. Maybe he would never be canonized as a saint, but he would make this role work. He would be good at it, and he would help others along the way. Hopefully that would be enough.

The cathedral in Atlanta was the site of the ordination. Michael and his fellow candidates were dressed in white robes. Each wore a white diagonal stole that went from his right shoulder to his left hip, the sign of a deacon. At the ceremony, the stole would be exchanged for one worn around the neck, the sign of a priest. Only five men from this location would be ordained. They would travel in a van to Atlanta, where they would join ten other candidates for the ceremony.

Looking out the van's window as they approached the cathedral, Michael saw his brother pacing up and down the street. He laughed to himself. The whole idea of becoming a priest was so foreign to Gabe.

Gabe ran to the van as it pulled up to the curb. The deacons descended one by one as family members took photos. As soon as Michael appeared, Gabe ran to hug him and then pulled him to the other side of the van, away from the families and cameras.

"Michael, I have something for you," Gabe said in a hushed tone, looking around to be sure that no one was listening.

"Not now, dude," Michael cautioned in a hushed tone. "I can't take a gift right now."

"It's not a gift," Gabe said as he pressed his car keys into his brother's hand. Michael looked at the keys as Gabe said, "If at any time you decide this isn't for you, walk out and drive away. Nobody will think any less of you."

Michael understood the gesture and pocketed the keys to make his brother feel better. He smiled at Gabe and asked, "Where are Mom and Chris?"

"I wanted to bring my own car for obvious reasons," Gabe answered. "We left at the same time, but you know how I drive."

"Yeah." Michael chuckled. "You view speed postings as suggestions, not rules."

"They're probably here by now." Gabe grinned. "Michael, I'm serious about the keys. Do what *you* want to do. If it's the archeology, we can build a wing on a university of your choosing."

"Or I could just join a cruise line," Michael said with a smirk.

"You could join me, and we could build our own cruise line," Gabe offered.

"This isn't only about me, is it tough guy?" Michael asked somberly.

"I don't want to lose you, Michael. Once you're married to the Church—"

"I'll still be your brother and best friend. Holy Orders won't change a thing, Gabe. You will always disgust me." Michael smiled.

"Oh yeah?" Gabe asked with a smile. "I think maybe there's time for me to kick your butt one last time before you become a priest." He quickly put Michael into a headlock.

"And plenty of time after," Michael said when he heard the click and whine of a camera. The boys looked up to see their mother and Chris.

"Well, some things never change," Kim said with a smile. Embarrassed, they let go of each other. "First picture in your ordination album," Kim said with a grin. "And if you continue to misbehave, you're going to have the silliest album in your class."

"You look great, Michael," Chris said. "Don't be offended, but I have to ask you. Are you sure this is what you want?"

"I'm sure," Michael said.

"No reservations?"

"None," Michael answered, pretending Chris meant hotel reservations so it wouldn't really be a lie.

"You remember my car?" Gabe interrupted.

"Red Ferrari." Michael smiled.

"Yo! Ferrari," Chris said to Gabe. "Let's give your mom a moment alone with her baby boy."

They each hugged Michael, holding him close for just a second.

"I thought this would be easier for me," Kim said after Gabe and Chris left. "After all, I know the drill. I remember Benny's ordination, every detail. But you're not Benny. You're the precious little boy who brought meaning to my life." She couldn't continue; the tears rocked her convulsively.

Michael held his mother for a few moments, until the tears subsided. "I don't think there's ever been a better mom," he said. "I can't thank you enough for all you've been to me. Not just a mother, but a friend and confidant. None of that changes, Mom."

"I know," she said, pulling herself away from him. "It's just a big day for a mom, you know?"

"I know."

Then she pressed the spare keys to her Bentley into his hand. "If you have any doubts, any at all, just get in the car and drive away."

Michael burst out laughing and said, "I'll put these right next to Gabe's Ferrari keys. Doesn't anyone in this family drive a Ford?"

The organ music had started to peal out from the cathedral, and the bells rang from the steeple, echoing in the streets for blocks. Kim ran to get ahead of the procession and made it to Gabe's side in the pew only about five steps ahead of the line of celebrants. The candidates walked slowly down the aisle on a white floor covering, much as a bride at her wedding. They filled the first row of the cathedral. Following them were the priests, including Chris, who proceeded to the altar and formed a semicircle around the marble table.

Once the candidates were seated, a roll was called. Upon hearing his name, each candidate replied, "Present," and walked to the altar. Once there, the bishop enquired and received testimony that each candidate had received proper education and was worthy of the priesthood.

At the end of the enquiry, the bishop said, "We rely on the help of the Lord God and our Savior Jesus Christ, and we choose these men, our brothers, for priesthood."

"Thanks be to God," said the assembled crowd, which then broke into applause for the candidates.

Following that, the bishop enquired of each candidate if he was willing to faithfully serve Christ and the Church. Each candidate replied that he was. He then took the bishop's hands into his and pledged his obedience to the Church and his religious superiors, specifically the ordaining bishop.

The same thing occurred for each candidate, and Michael was last. Everyone had heard the back and forth for each candidate, so they knew what to expect when Michael finally got his chance, but after Michael had his enquiry with the bishop, there was a pause, followed by a quick shuffling on the altar.

From the sacristy, Archbishop Benjamin Cross appeared in full regalia. He swept to the bishop's side and grasped Michael's hands.

The cathedral was silent as everyone wondered about the break in the normal course of the service. Michael mirrored the alarmed look on Chris's face. He heard Gabe say, "Chris, can you stop this?" The comment would have barely been audible under normal circumstances, but it reverberated in the silent cathedral. Chris slowly, almost imperceptibly moved his head from side to side.

The onus was on Michael now. If he took this vow of obedience to

Benny, it would effectively make Benny his superior. If he refused, it all ended here. His life would change forever. He looked into Benny's eyes, pleading. But in return he saw a smug smile, his recompense for not renewing the loan.

The crowd waited in silence. Michael felt the car keys in his pocket. How hard would it be to start over? Maybe there was something else he could do in life. Benny squeezed his hands, and immediately Michael saw the Lady. She was what waited for him if he decided to chuck it all and walk away. It was her or Benny, and the clock was ticking.

Slowly, nearly inaudibly, Michael made the promise of obedience to the most wicked man he had ever known, who then blessed his hands with holy oils.

The bishop introduced Benny to the crowd and spoke of how honored he was to share the altar with a Vatican representative. He also explained to the crowd that Michael was nearly speechless at his uncle's surprise.

Following the Litany of Saints, the candidates rose and walked to the altar. There, in turn, the bishop laid his hands on the head of each man and asked the Holy Spirit to fill each and convey upon him the sacrament of Holy Orders. The other priests on the altar followed his lead and prayed over each candidate.

When Chris got to Michael, he whispered, "It'll be okay, Michael."

Michael kissed Chris's hands once the older man had finished his prayer. And then Benny stepped up to pray for him. For the sake of the crowd, Benny made a show of praying for his nephew. Michael, whose back was to the congregation, made no such show.

"I bless you, my beloved nephew, in the name of the Father, Son, and Holy Spirit."

"Like you've ever prayed to any of them," Michael said derisively.

"There, there," Benny whispered condescendingly, "remember your vows."

"Here's another one," Michael said. "You'll live to regret this, Benny."

Benny bent to kiss his nephew's cheek as Kim took what must have been her two hundredth photo of the event. He whispered, "I have one hundred million reasons to believe you're wrong, Michael."

Michael only barely held it together through the congratulations and photos that followed the service. Leave it to Benny to ruin this for him! Finally it was time for him to fold his vestments and leave the cathedral.

He found Gabe waiting. His brother hugged him, held him for a second, and said, "I'm so sorry, Michael." Michael hugged Gabe hard.

Chris was next to exit the cathedral. "Where's your mother?" he asked.

"She convinced Benny to come stay with us at the house," Gabe said. "They took the Bentley. And just so you know, she's not too happy with our attitudes."

"She never is when Benny comes to town." Chris groaned.

Gabe drove the crowded Ferrari slowly, an outward exhibit of an inner desire not to be around Benny.

"So I'm guessing this is over the money?" Gabe asked his brother.

"Yes," Michael said, and then related to them his conversation with Benny during the ceremony.

"Are you going to give it to him?" Gabe asked sullenly.

"I don't know. I hate to, but he's my superior now." Michael winced at the thought of it.

"First of all, he's your boss. Trust me, Benny Cross is *nobody's* superior." Gabe snorted.

"You don't need the money," Chris said. "And trust me, you don't need Benny at you all the time. I say give him the money and hope he leaves you alone."

"What? Are you crazy?" Gabe shrieked.

"We need to talk, boys. You know your uncle is a very dangerous man. He is involved with the most powerful, and might I add *satanic* people on Earth. Nothing is beneath him. His *only* good trait is that he loves your mother, and believe it or not, he loves you guys too."

"Yeah, he showed us his love in Germany ten years ago," Gabe spat.

"He has a point, Gabe," Michael said. "His love for Mom, and whatever he feels about us, may be my only way to survive this with my sanity intact."

"He wants you to care for him, Michael, and he's even softening in his attitude about you, Gabe," Chris added.

"I'm not buying it," Gabe said. "Any of it. There are times I think

I could find a nice life with Tina, but this Christianity baloney drives me crazy."

"It's not baloney, Gabe," Chris said tersely. "Did you read the Gospel of John like she and David asked you to?"

"I never seem to be able to get around to it," Gabe said in frustration as he moved the car to the passing lane.

"That's kind of a weak answer," Michael said. "It's not like you, Gabe. If you want something, you go get it. Why won't you at least consider reading the Bible if it means you can have the life you want?"

"Don't take this the wrong way, Michael, but it's this. All of this!" Gabe waved his arms in frustration, barely attending to the steering wheel. "Benny, the loan, your odd reasons for being a priest—it's all weird and hurtful … and hopeless."

There was silence in the car. Peach orchards and tobacco fields dotted the landscape, and small, rounded clouds drifted through the deep blue sky.

Michael finally spoke. "First of all, Gabe, we're all different. I know I have some issues, but they shouldn't influence your life. We're not alike in a lot of ways."

Chris said to Michael, "At some point, I want to revisit this problem of yours that only you and Gabe seem to understand. But for now, let's help your brother. Gabe, Benny is a bad guy even though he wears a clerical collar. There are a few bad apples in every bunch."

Gabe hit the steering wheel with the palms of his hands at the magnitude of Chris's understatement.

Chris continued more emphatically. "But there are a lot of good apples too. Christianity has produced the most incredible examples of selfless love society has ever seen. Jesus is real, and He'll live in your heart if you let Him. There's nothing better, Gabe. *Nothing.* And He loves you enough that He's put a beautiful, God-fearing woman in your path. Would you throw away the chance at eternal salvation and marital bliss because Benny's a jerk, and you don't think your brother and I are happy? That's crazy."

"He's got a point, Gabe," Michael added. "You and Tina are made for each other."

"And for the record," Chris continued, patting Gabe's arm to make his point, "it's wonderful to serve the Living God. I can't tell you the joy

I have when I spend time with Him. Do you remember Father Vinnie? He's the happiest man I know. He distributes sandwiches to the poor and waters our office plants, yet he has influenced the lives of more people than anyone could ever know. And it is all because he is in love with the Savior of the world. And I'll tell you something else, Gabe. When he goes to sleep at night, he sleeps in peace—and he doesn't need a glass of liquor to find it."

There was more silence as everyone thought about what Chris had just said. Finally, Gabe grinned and broke the ice with feigned stupidity, "So are you two saying I should read the Gospel of John?"

"Chris," Michael asked, "if I kill him, will you absolve my sin?"

"Yes!"

"Benny!" Michael roared as he entered the mansion. "What was that all about today?"

Benny stood in the doorway of the library, a beautiful wood-paneled room with two-story bookcases and a loft. The fireplace was lighted. On any other day, the room would be beckoning.

"Michael, we need to discuss this like adults," Benny cautioned.

"Well, here's an adult comment for you: I'm calling the loan!"

Michael, Gabe, and Chris followed Benny into the library. Chris closed the doors to keep the meeting out of Kim's hearing.

"Don't be silly, Michael," Benny said with a soft tone and a smug voice. "I'm your superior. You don't want to take that tone with me."

Gabe moved to the bar and poured himself a glass of scotch.

"Shut up, Benny!" Michael shrieked. "Don't pull that attitude with me. I'm not your subordinate."

"You are according to the vows you took," Benny said sternly as he sat on the oversized leather couch. "Sit down, Michael. I have to talk to you about something."

"Are you listening to me, Benny?" Michael yelled. "I won't let you get away with this. In anticipation of ordination, a month ago I signed a document with Gabe. From now on, any financial decisions that were under my jurisdiction must be approved by both of us. You might be my superior, but in the final analysis, you have to deal with Gabe and me."

"Salute!" Gabe said to Benny as he raised his glass.

The library doors flew open to reveal a saddened, angry Kim. "I've heard all I'm going to hear!" she barked. "I'm so disappointed with all of you!" She tossed a check to Benny. "There. I'm *giving* this to you. Pay back Michael's loan and keep the rest."

Turning to the boys, she said angrily, "You two know how much money this family has. You never should have put your own uncle in this position."

"But, Mom," Michael protested, "there's stuff you don't know. Uncle Benny—"

"Stop it, Michael! Here's what I *do know.* I won't have this anymore. Not in my family, and *definitely* not in my home. Do you understand me?"

"Yes," Michael said like a chastened schoolboy.

"Mom," Gabe began to intercede from the bar, where he was pouring his second glass of scotch.

"Not a word out of you, mister," she said sternly as she stomped toward the bar. "It's time for you to grow up, Gabe. And today Mommy is taking your bottle." She snatched the glass and decanter from his hands and stomped out of the library and up the stairs. The men heard the door to her bedroom suite slam shut.

Michael threw himself on the couch, aggravated at how badly things had turned out. Nobody spoke. The only sound in the room was the sound of Gabe opening a fresh fifth of scotch.

Benny reached into the breast pocket of his jacket and pulled out an envelope. He gently laid it on Michael's lap. "Your new assignment," he said quietly.

Michael read the letter with trembling hands. He was told to report in one month to the Vatican's science academy where he would be working to translate relics found in a highly secretive archeological dig. It was a dream assignment for him. If he could have chosen it, he couldn't have asked for more. His hands shook and tears welled in his eyes. Gabe and Chris drew close to see what had made him tremble.

"Benny," Michael said, "there are no words. This is the best assignment a guy like me could ask for. I thought I would have to work for ten years before I could even be considered for such a position."

"The position was open, and they know of your work. Apparently you are very talented at what you do, Michael. But I had to find a way to get you to Rome."

"I guess asking me would have been out of the question?" Michael asked softly.

"Would you have given it any credence? Or would you have just been suspicious?"

"I would have wondered about your motives," Michael conceded.

Benny spoke with quiet resignation. "To be candid, Michael, I also had other motives. The money is gone. I invested it badly and lost it. I was hoping if I helped you out, you could help me out. But it appears your mother has bridged the trust gap for us."

Chris took the letter from Michael and gasped as he read it. "This is quite an honor, Michael. And it sure would be nice to have you close by." He passed the letter to Gabe.

"Great!" Gabe exclaimed sarcastically as he read the letter. "Now I have more family *in* the Vatican than *out* of the Vatican. Maybe I should just become a priest."

"No!" the three clerics in the room shouted simultaneously.

"The Church has trouble enough!" Benny said.

It was the opening volley in Micah's attempt to reveal corruption in the Vatican. The Jesuits had been highly effective in their smear campaign against him over the years. The only venue willing to deal with him in an extended interview about his forthcoming book was a three-hour midnight radio show occasioned by insomniacs and conspiracy theorists. Still, it was a start, and Micah needed to build interest in the book if the exposé was to have any chance to shine light on the darkness encroaching on the Holy City. He sat anxiously opposite the show's host as the opening music came to a close.

"This is Art Knell, and you're listening to Sea to Sea, the largest late-night talk radio program in America. Tonight we have a very special guest, Father Micah Morton, exorcist, former spy, priest, and author. Father Morton, it is a pleasure to have you on the show. How are you doing?"

"I'm fine, Art. In fact, for a man my age, I'd say I'm doing very well."

"Father, I read some of your works in preparation for this show, and I've got to tell you: you hint at some pretty incredible stuff going on behind the walls of the Vatican."

"All of it fiction, of course, Art. Until now."

"That's an intriguing statement. But let's get everyone caught up before we go into your current project. In one of your more controversial novels, you portray a satanic ritual that supposedly opened the Vatican to the Prince of Darkness. That was all fiction, wasn't it?"

"In fact, Art, I wish it was. I changed some of the names and circumstances to fit the novel, but the basic facts are correct. There was a ritual performed simultaneously here in the United States and in the Vatican. The purpose of that ritual was to seat Lucifer as the power behind the throne in the Vatican."

"Are you saying, Father, that the pope is controlled by Satan?"

"Far from it, Art. He is, in some very real respects, a prisoner of the Vatican. Imagine being a spiritual man who loves the Lord, but you're surrounded by men who prefer to place their trust in Lucifer and his minions. Every step the Holy Father takes, every conversation he has can place him in mortal danger."

An exaggerated expression of shock and incredulity passed Art's face. "Do you mean to tell me you think these men would actually attempt to kill the pope?" he thundered with the sensationalist intonation of an infomercial host.

"It's happened before, Art, and in recent history."

"Are you talking about this pope's predecessor?"

"Indeed I am. He reigned only one month, but he stepped on many toes during that time."

Art whistled at the gravity of the statement. "So how has this pope managed to stay alive all these years without being one of them—or at least not giving in to them?"

The more animated the host became, the more Micah adopted a calm, professional tone. He *had* to control the interview. "The answer is simple. He focused his energies outward, toward the democratization of the former Soviet republics. In the process, he became a darling of the world. After one failed assassination attempt, they let him alone."

"But, Father, there are those who would say the Holy Father bears some responsibility if he knows about the corruption and allows it to continue."

"The Holy Father is a man of great principle, Art. But early in his reign, he realized he had a grievous choice to make. He could either direct his efforts to help free millions and millions of people from the shackles of communism, or he could die in office trying to fight the inevitable evil that has come upon the Church."

"The inevitable evil. That's a phrase filled with meaning. There has been a rumor for years that the actual third secret of Fatima predicts a time when the Church hierarchy will be overcome with evil, does it not?"

"Well, you're touching on a tough subject for me. As you know from your research, I was present when Pope John XXIII opened the third secret, but I swore an oath never to reveal its contents. I have taken a vow, and I regret it, because the secret was meant for the world, but nonetheless I have taken a vow."

"That puts you in an odd position, doesn't it, Father? You believe heaven sent this message to mankind, but you have taken a sacred vow not to disclose it."

"That is where fiction has become my friend."

"Because you can release the information under the guise of fiction."

"Yes, while at the same time communicating to the world some very important information they were meant to hear."

"Such as the prediction that there will be evil in the Vatican, like you portrayed in your novel *Hurricane Home*?"

"Exactly."

"Well, Father, in that novel, there's an evil pope."

"Yes. There is. Do you know there was a man, St. Malachy—an Irish saint, I may add with a bit of Irish pride—this saint had a vision of all the succeeding popes from his time until the end of the papacy. There is a little bit of confusion about the last pope, but either the next pope or the one after him will be the final pope."

"So you're saying we're on the cusp of something very significant."

"The third secret is not fifty years away. It's not thirty years away. Within the next decade or two, everything that was predicted will come to light."

"There are wild rumors about what was predicted, Father. I know you were sworn to secrecy, but you could tell me if I'm close to the truth or not, couldn't you?"

"We could try it, Art. What have you heard?"

"For one, I heard that it will be a time of great catastrophes: earthquakes of untold proportions, horrible tsunamis that make it seem as if the oceans have literally come out of their basins."

"I wouldn't argue with those statements," Micah offered cautiously.

"I've heard the United States will be destroyed in a nuclear exchange with Russia."

Micah shrugged. "I haven't any knowledge of such an event being predicted at Fatima."

"Okay. Well, we touched on it earlier. Some say Fatima predicts the Vatican will be overcome with evil and there will be a great apostasy."

Micah hinted at affirmation. "Go on."

"Well, as you know, we deal with a lot of paranormal activity on this show. UFOs and the like. And it strikes me as odd that the Vatican has spent so much money, and has committed even more, to the building of huge telescopes. Does this apostasy have something to do with aliens, Father?"

"The Bible tells us Satan can disguise himself as a creature of light. What would happen to this world if it met up with a more advanced being from outer space?"

"We would begin to question our specialness in the universe, and maybe our concepts of God," Art replied.

"Interesting, isn't it? But what if the beings were extra-dimensional?"

"Father, if we met up with something or someone who could purposefully navigate through dimensions beyond the four we're accustomed to, we would find such a being to be godlike."

"Even if that extra-dimensional being was Lucifer?" Micah asked with an Irish lilt.

"This is very interesting, but as you can tell from the music in the background, we're up against a hard break. Will you come back for the next segment? Maybe we can answer some caller questions."

"I'd be delighted."

During the break, Micah was able to get Art to agree to go into more detail about the upcoming book. Micah checked his notes as the commercial ended.

"And we're back on the air. This is Sea to Sea, America's largest late-night talk show. I'm your host, Art Knell, and I have a very special guest with me this evening. He is Father Micah Morton, former exorcist and Vatican official. He is now an author of nine books, most of them fiction. But within that fiction, he gives us tantalizing views into the inner workings of the Vatican. Tell us about your latest work, Father."

'Well, that's why I'm here with you, Art. I'm working on a different kind of book at the moment."

"Different in what way?"

"Well, primarily because it is not fiction. In this book, I will reveal some startling information—facts, dates, photographed documents—all of which prove the corruption that has taken over the administration of the Vatican."

"Wow, Father. The implications are staggering. If you really could expose them—"

Micah interrupted. "Then maybe we could stop them. Or at least slow them down, Art."

"I would imagine that just saying this on the air will put you in grave danger. Aren't you afraid of these men?"

"It does put me in danger. But I'm not afraid."

"But these men could kill you, Father," Art said somberly, with unfeigned concern.

"And send me into the arms of my Savior. T'would be a pleasure. You see, I have nothing to lose but one thing."

"What is that?"

"The chance to tell the truth to the world."

Benny turned off the radio in disgust. Now he knew who Vinnie had met that day in Rome. Father Micah Morton! He made his way to Kim's refrigerator to snack ... and plan.

NINE

The sunset was beautiful. Another warm Texas spring had begun. Gloria sat out behind the mansion with a cup of decaffeinated coffee, waiting for the night to come. She had a feeling they would come for her baby—their baby—tonight.

After the abortion attempt, Zack had tried hard to make her a full partner in this endeavor. He explained that this was a race of beings from outside our solar system. They told him Earth was in serious trouble, poised to self-destruct from any number of hazards—pollution, the failure of the ozone layer, nuclear warfare, unsustainable energy, and overpopulation. The decks were stacked against the human race. But the aliens had overcome these same problems and gone on to establish a galaxy-wide federation of sentient species, many of whom were helped by aliens in the same way that they now wanted to help Earth.

Although she had resisted at first, she believed what Zack had told her. Of course it helped that this information was confirmed in a very vivid dream of the handsome angel she had met in Africa. He explained that the aliens had been working for ages to bring about the right genetic matrix to allow the implantation and germination of their seed. He showed her that the child she carried was, in effect, two beings at once. He would have the entire genetic code of the alien race and the entire genetic code of the human race, making him simultaneously fully human and fully alien. Most importantly, the angel made her feel at peace about the whole endeavor. In fact, he made her feel blessed and privileged to be part of such a historic undertaking.

Zack joined her on the veranda. "Penny for your thoughts?"

"I'd love to see this little fellow. Will he know who we are someday when he starts his ministry?"

"I don't know, and I'm not sure it will be a ministry in the traditional sense. All I know is that he will lead Earth to solve its problems and join the other sentient races in our galaxy. I don't know how he'll do it."

"Zack, how does this square with Christianity?" She had pondered it frequently. In some very real way, it didn't matter. The child growing inside her was real, regardless of how it fit into her belief structure.

"I've thought about it a lot. The first thing I had to get comfortable with was this: These guys are real. Not figments of my imagination. Not demons. Real flesh-and-blood beings from another world," Zack said with a shrug.

"Have you ever asked the aliens about Jesus?" she asked, hoping to reconcile her current situation to Christian thought.

"They say He was, in the truest sense, a son of God. However, their concept of God is a bit more space-oriented. In their view, God created Jesus as a light-bearer to the world. The aliens say they have seen Jesus in many forms. He came as a light-bearer to each of the civilizations that are now part of their federation."

"So He is still the son of the creator, sent to Earth to die for our sins?"

"More likely to show us how to get out of a sin mentality. I kind of think Calvary may have been the biggest mistake mankind ever made. We snuffed out the messenger."

"But, Zack, what about all the teachings that say He died for us ... for our sins?"

"A guilty conscience on the part of the people who didn't realize who He was," Zack offered.

"Fully God and fully human?" she asked.

"A lot like the little bundle you're carrying. That little guy's going to save the world, Gloria, and we're part of it." He put his arm around her shoulder, and she nestled her head on his. And they waited.

Benny had left early the previous day.

Michael sat outside with a glass of wine and the newspaper. He heard an occasional grunt or cheer from the tennis court, where Chris and Gabe had faced off. Both would claim victory. The only way to know who really won one of their matches was to actually be there and decide for yourself.

He chuckled. What a nice family. Even Benny had come through. Dare he say it? He felt ... blessed. He wished he had Chris's strong, simple faith, but Michael was a man of science. He believed in the role Christianity had played in society. He believed in the Church. And he told himself that deep down, he believed in the Messiah as well. He just wished there was a little more scientific evidence for him to go on. Maybe this new assignment would prove not only to be interesting but would provide the final points his logical mind needed to throw himself into the arms of Jesus as Lord. He hoped for that. He loved the idea of being in love with Jesus—if only he could get there.

Kim joined him, bringing the late edition of the newspaper. "Are they still at it?" she asked, nodding toward the tennis court.

"You know how they are." Michael chuckled. "The best either will settle for is a draw."

"I'll never understand the male preoccupation with winning."

"Hah!" Michael laughed. "You're the most competitive of all of us!"

"I am not," she said with more force than conviction. "And I won't have you sit there and talk badly about me. I'm your mother."

"Who just won by playing the mother card?" He laughed as she swatted him with the paper. A headline caught his eye. "Can I see that?" he asked, motioning to the paper.

"Sure," she said, handing it to him. He read the article as a curiosity.

Associated Press. New York, New York. May 17, 1999.

Priest Found Dead in New York Apartment

Father Micah Morton, an author of several books on a wide range of subjects, was found dead this afternoon. Morton was found in the stairwell of his apartment building, where he apparently died from a fall. Police stated that his apartment had been ransacked. They believe Father Morton interrupted a burglary, and then fell down the stairs trying to get away from the intruder. There were no marks on his body to indicate a confrontation with the intruder had occurred.

Father Morton was a controversial figure. His writings, mostly fiction, were believed by many to be thinly veiled exposés of corruption within the inner workings of the Catholic Church. Conspiracy theorists believe he was murdered after a recent interview on Sea to Sea, an all-night talk show that deals primarily in pseudoscience and the paranormal. In his interview, he stated that his next work would not be fiction but a documented evidential record of, among other things, a satanic attempt to take control of the Vatican. Neither his computer nor his work papers were found in the ransacked apartment.

Vatican representatives have announced their sadness at the news of Father Morton's death.

As Michael finished reading the article, he heard the returning tennis champs.

"I won," Gabe said boastfully as he and Chris approached.

"Absolutely not true," Chris said with a smile. "I beat you fair and square."

"Well, I can see someone didn't take a vow of truthfulness." Gabe grinned as he went into the house to get a soda.

"Let me guess. You played until neither of you won," Kim said.

"Yes," Chris said. "But I outplayed him. His soft living is slowing him down!"

Gabe handed him a soda. "*If* you outplayed me, then it was only because I was taking it easy on you. Let's face it; you're not young anymore. A heart attack on the family tennis courts would be messy."

"Actually, Gabe, not that messy," Michael said. "Now that I'm a priest, I could bury him in the flower garden. Nobody would have to know." Chris lightly bounced his tennis racket on Michael's head.

Gabe broke up the fun. "I'm going to get a shower and turn in. I need my beauty sleep, you know. Just thought that, as the only sexually active member of the family, I would explain that to you three."

Kim swatted him with the newspaper as he kissed her good night.

"Well, here goes nothing," Gabe said to himself as he crawled into his bed and opened Tina's Bible.

"In the beginning was the Word, and the Word was with God, and the Word was God. He was with God in the beginning. Through him all things were made ...

"Wow," he said to himself, "pretty dramatic. Powerful writing." When Tina had asked him to read the Gospel of John, he was sure he would encounter a laundry list of "Thou shalt nots," most of which he had either done or was in the process of doing. He never expected this type of universal perspective. It seemed like a viewpoint that transcended time and space. Who had a viewpoint like that, other than God?

Something tugged at his heart. He felt it. Was this what if felt like to be in communication with God? "God, if you are real, please reveal Yourself to me as I read these words." Thus began one of the longest, most beautiful nights of Gabe's life. He read on.

"He was in the world, and though the world was made through him, the world did not recognize him. He came to that which was his own, but his own did not receive him. Yet to all who did receive him, to those who believed in his name, he gave the right to become children of God—children born not of natural descent nor of human decision nor a husband's will, but born of God."

The text spoke to Gabe. He had been born to vastly different circumstances than those in which he was raised. Yet Kim and Michael took him into their family. In every sense that mattered, he was Kim's child. He understood the power of someone caring enough to pluck you out of a bad environment only to place you in the bosom of a loving family.

So this was why Jesus came to Earth. This was why people loved Him so much. The more he read, the more he realized his entire life had led to this day. Through Kim and Michael, he had been shown over and over the kind of love the Lord has for His people. Jesus came to make us the adopted children of God.

For a brief instant, a horrifying image passed before Gabe's eyes. He saw himself turning away from Kim. How could he ever be so rude to someone who had spent her life to make his better? No sooner had he thought this than another image passed quickly in front of him. It was a beaten and bloody Jesus. His eyes were so full of love, but Gabe knew he had turned his back on Him.

"Oh, dear God," Gabe said to himself as tears stung at his eyes. "I have been so ignorant that I spurned the love You tried to show me. Please forgive me."

He continued to read.

Darkness had fallen in Texas, and the couple continued to watch the sky, both hoping and fearing they would see the lights of an alien ship approaching.

"There," Zack said.

"Where?"

"Over to the right." He pointed toward the horizon.

Gloria saw a star that seemed to be growing. Slowly at first, and then within seconds, it had become a glowing orb above their home. Fear enveloped her for a second, but it was quickly replaced by a feeling of extreme calm, a feeling that she was going home. The child within her stirred as if he knew his time had come. She took Zack's hand in hers as light surrounded them. With a flash the light was gone, and so were Zack and Gloria. The craft then accelerated upward at a frightening pace until it looked just like another star in the sky. Then it traveled to the east.

"Welcome," the Lady said to Gloria.

She tried to be strong, but she felt her legs grow weak, as if she was about to faint. She leaned heavily on Zack.

"Perhaps I should reveal myself in a form you will more readily understand," the Lady said in a peaceful voice. Light radiated out of her until her form could no longer be discerned through the brightness. Then as the light faded, there stood a handsome man. Gloria immediately recognized him as the angel she had seen as a child in Africa.

"It was you all those years ago?" Gloria asked as her strength returned.

"Yes," the angel answered. "I have many different forms from your perspective. Simply stated, my race can inhabit more dimensions than the four your species swims through. Any way you see me is really a four-dimensional depiction of a higher reality. Therefore, different aspects of my being can appear as different types in four dimensions."

Gloria thought she understood, at least as much as a "four-dimensional entity" could. She looked over at Zack, whose mouth was locked in a perpetual grin. "So you can take the form you choose?"

"Something like that," the angel answered. "However, each form is distinctly reminiscent of my personality in higher dimensions. What that means is this. Although I appear as different people to your awareness, each is uniquely me."

"Amazing," Gloria said, but inwardly she recoiled a bit. She couldn't possibly relate the odorous old bug lady to this shining, handsome angel. As she thought about it, her pulse raced, and a claustrophobic terror encroached upon her. But then the angel touched her head, and she was overcome with liquid calmness. In milliseconds she sat like Zack, a grinning, willing pupil.

"To your mind it may well be amazing. To my mind, it's just how I am." He smiled tenderly at her. "So now can you begin to imagine the difficulty we have had in engineering a hybrid of our two species? We had to find a way to develop a person sufficiently four-dimensional to live happily in your limited space, all the while inhabiting a higher dimensional consciousness."

"And that's what you've done with the child I'm carrying?" Gloria asked in an entranced monotone.

"Long ago we determined that certain parts of the human genome can be adapted to accept our nature. But the requisite changes could not possibly be performed within one generation. Through selective breeding, we have combined traits over centuries until we finally arrived at a generation of viable candidates to bear the hybrid. *This generation.*"

"So you have been involved in my genetic heritage?"

"With certain limitations. In actuality, you have not so much been bred as a progenitor of the hybrid as much as its incubator."

Although made calm by the angel, she was fully aware. She knew her natural instinct would be to rage against the notion of being treated like a lab rat. However, within the confines of this dreamlike state, it somehow made sense. "Does this child have any of *my* DNA?" she asked with a hint of sorrow.

"Enough to make him acceptable to your womb. Your womb has been altered to produce amniotic fluid with a pH level that would kill any Earth child, but is necessary for the early gestation of the hybrid."

"So whose DNA does my baby have?" she asked, surprising even herself at motherly feelings toward the child that had seemed so alien to her just hours before.

"It is comprised of a delicate balance of your husband's DNA, along with that of another human, as well as those aspects of your DNA necessary to allow gestation. To that we have added a third rung of nucleotides taken from the DNA of our leader. So you see, this child will be very human, but very much multidimensional as well."

"What will he look like?"

"A handsome human male. He will have a multidimensional power to draw men and women to himself. People will long for his countenance. Mystics of your world refer to this as the 'Christ-consciousness' because your Jesus was uniquely multidimensional as well. But He was too inhuman and frightened those around Him—so much that they took His life. That will not happen with this child. He will be loved and revered by all humankind."

"Sounds like the Antichrist," Gloria said with a nervous chuckle.

"There is no such thing, my dear. Only christs. This one will succeed where others have failed. Now if you will be so kind as to lie on this table, our scientists will get you started while I attend to other business."

The angel left the room as Gloria lay down on a metal table that appeared out of the wall. Zack stood at her side, holding her hand. The technician, who looked like the Hollywood version of a gray alien, worked silently as he made a laser incision into Gloria's abdomen. Within seconds, the fetus was harvested and handed over to another who placed it into a waiting incubator. As they began to wheel it out of the room, Gloria said, "Oh please! Please can I see him?"

The alien removed the child from its incubator and held it out for Gloria to see. In its stage of development, it was still very small and looked more like an animal than a child. Gloria was at first repulsed, but then intrigued as he moved his little hands. There was a light around him, a brightness that reminded her of old paintings where saints were shown with halos.

"Oh," she cooed, "he's so tiny. Is he safe?"

"Absolutely safe," the angel said as he reentered the room. "Our species is born young and grows in its mother's pouch, much like the marsupials of Earth. As a hybrid, this child needed to spend time in a human womb but now has to feed from us. He will be placed in this incubator machine, where he will be fed strong nutrients to accelerate his growth."

"But who will love him? He needs a mother," Gloria cried.

"The universe is this child's parent. We honored your request to see him, but your human instinct to bond is too strong. We will remove this memory before you return to your lives."

"Will I be able to have other children?" Gloria asked.

"The genetic changes made in you have made your womb a hostile environment for a purely human child. I'm afraid you will not be able to carry another child," the angel said. "But take heart, this is the most special child ever to have entered humanity."

Michael had been sound asleep when a bright light awakened him. He tried to move, to yell for help, but was paralyzed. His body lifted slowly from the bed but then accelerated though the walls of the house and into the spacecraft outside.

As the light faded, he found himself standing before the Lady in his underwear.

"You really should wear pajamas to bed." She smirked at him as a small string of saliva dripped from the corner of her tiny mouth. He felt the lust in her that had ruined his life. His blood ran cold.

The Lady waved her frail arm, and part of the wall became a screen on which Michael witnessed the child's birth. He was overcome with sorrow for Gloria. A doorway opened in the wall, and a small gray alien pushed the incubator toward Michael.

"I haven't put your spilled seed to waste, little one." The Lady grinned at her unwilling cohort.

Michael looked into the incubator at the hybrid child. He looked so frail and pale. His body was curled, and his face had that slight reptilian look of an undeveloped fetus.

"This child is mine?" he asked in incredulous horror, rage flashing over his face.

"Well, to be fair, only partly. Our species carries a much more detailed DNA structure." The Lady's pointed face showed an air of superiority in its expression. "In order to achieve the perfect blend of human and alien, we needed to extract DNA from several of your species to match against the amino acids of our species."

Anger overtook Michael. "Don't get technical with me! Did you use my semen to build this creature?"

"Bits," she answered with her toothless grin. "He also belongs to Gloria and Zack, with a third strand of DNA from our leader."

Michael felt his pulse racing as his head throbbed with each heartbeat. "So you have used us!" he screamed. His breath grew shallow and rapid as adrenaline took over his body. Michael charged the alien beast but was stopped by the simple raising of her hand. She touched his forehead to calm him. His breathing regulated.

"Did Zack and Gloria appear to be upset with the arrangement?" the Lady asked softly.

"No, but I know how you can manipulate people. For all I know, they aren't even here, and you are using visions to manipulate me."

"Come," the Lady said, motioning with one very long finger. She led him through the doorway, where she instantly became the angel again. Zack lay unconscious on a table. Gloria was awake but groggy. She looked up to see Michael with the angel.

"Michael, isn't it wonderful?" she slurred. "This child will bring peace to Earth and help us take our place with other civilizations in the galaxy."

He cried softly as he stroked her hair. She was too manipulated by the Lady to see that they had all been terribly used. Just before she fell asleep, she said in a barely audible voice, "I love you, Michael."

"I love you too," he whispered.

"Does she seem to be unhappy about this?" the angel asked.

"No," Michael said grudgingly. "But why did you put me through years of mental abuse to accomplish this?"

"Another of your line was chosen. His semen was readily available, but his DNA was inferior and would not form base pairs with ours. We had to find a suitable substitute. That was you."

"So you terrorized me and robbed me of natural human relationships?"

"Would you have complied willingly?"

Michael moaned dismally and then opened his mouth to speak. He wanted to say that, given a rational argument and his choice of a sexual partner, he might have consented. But deep down inside, he knew he wouldn't have. Something about this felt dire, evil, and disrespectful to the very species they claimed to be saving.

"Make me forget," Michael demanded. "Let me be like them. Don't let me remember this!"

"Your service is not yet complete, my young friend. You must remember some things." The angel transformed into the skeletal form of the Lady and said, "I am the only partner you will ever have. If I allow you to forget this salient fact, you may not complete your part in this mystery."

Fear gripped Michael at the thought of continuing involvement with these beasts. *Yea, though I walk through the valley of the shadow of death* ... the words struck his mind like a firebrand. He could pray about it. After all, he was a priest. He had studied all about prayer. He closed his eyes and slowly, deliberately said The Lord's Prayer.

Gabe had gotten far in the Gospel of John. With each action, each utterance, the person of the God-Man, Jesus, leapt off the page. "When it was almost time for the Jewish Passover, Jesus went up to Jerusalem. In the temple courts he found people selling cattle, sheep and doves, and others sitting at tables exchanging money. So he made a whip out of cords, and drove all from the temple courts, both sheep and cattle; he scattered the coins of the moneychangers and overturned their tables. To those who sold doves, he said, 'Get these out of here! Stop turning my Father's house into a market!' His disciples remembered that it is written, 'Zeal for your house will consume me.'"

This image of Jesus was compelling to Gabe. He had always thought of Jesus as sort of emaciated and wimpy. That's the impression he got from famous works of art. In fact, in some of those pieces, He looked downright effeminate. But this Jesus was a powerful man, who took after the leaders of His day. He didn't back down; He confronted evil with power and zeal.

"Wow, Jesus. You were more of a superhero than the milquetoast I've always seen in pictures," Gabe commented.

He rubbed his eyes and read on. "For God so loved the world the he gave his one and only Son, that whoever believes in him shall not perish but have eternal life. For God did not send his Son into the world to condemn the world, but to save the world through him.

"Whoever believes in him is not condemned, but whoever does not believe stands condemned already because they have not believed in the name of God's one and only Son."

"That's it?" Gabe said to himself as he read. "No list of things I have to do every day? No walking on my knees to some shrine? All I have to do is believe that Jesus was sent by the Father to save me from my sins?

"Do not let your hearts be troubled. You believe in God, believe also in me. My Father's house has many rooms; if that were not so, would I have told you that I am going there to prepare a place for you? And if I go and prepare a place for you, I will come back and take you to be with me."

Gabe started to breathe heavily. The words were piercing and fast. It was almost as if he could feel Jesus' urgency. He knew He was going to the cross, but He had so much He wanted to say to the apostles, His friends.

"I will not leave you as orphans; I will come to you. Before long, the world will not see me anymore, but you will see me. Because I live, you also will live. On that day you will realize that I am in my Father, and you are in me, and I am in you."

He knew what was about to happen in this story, but he had never read Jesus' actual words before. Somewhere along the way, he had fallen in love with the Man about to be crucified.

He read on as far as he could. He put the Bible down and sobbed openly when he got to the part about the crucifixion. "When Jesus saw his mother there, and the disciple whom he loved standing nearby, he said to her, 'Woman, here is your son,' and to the disciple, 'Here is your mother.' From that time on, this disciple took her into his own home.

"Oh, Jesus. You did this for me! I am so sorry for my sins. I want it to be like you said: the Father in You and You in me. I want to give my life to You, Lord. Please send your Spirit."

The Spirit was strong in Chris's suite. He had started the evening praying for Gabe, but he had felt an extremely urgent need to pray for Michael instead. He had long ago left his couch and fallen to his knees before the Lord. He prayed fervently with the deep longing that comes from a true intercessor. He turned his heart, mind, and spirit over to the Lord on Michael's behalf.

As he cried out to the Lord in his heart, the Spirit prompted him to sing, "The Light of Christ has come into the world." As the hymn poured from him, his hands found the eighth chapter of the Gospel of John. "When Jesus spoke again to the people, he said, 'I am the light of the world. Whoever follows me will never walk in darkness, but will have the light of life.'"

Michael could no longer feel the Lady's hot breath on him. He opened his right eye just a crack and saw her leaving the room. He opened both eyes and continued to pray. The room went dark, and then the darkness turned into utter blackness.

He awoke with a start. The dream had seemed so real. "Oh, God," he said aloud. "Did I just have a dream where I told Gloria I loved her, and we had a baby together?" It was clear to Michael he had fallen for her—a married woman! The Lady clearly represented the sin of his desires. Gloria was the object of that sin, as was the hooker in Amsterdam.

"Freud would have a field day with this one," he said to the empty room, with a grin that he had finally figured it out. He put on his robe and headed to the kitchen. He was hungry and needed to think.

A flash of light left Zack and Gloria sleeping in their bed. Gloria felt Zack's warmth and cuddled next to him. "I love you," she said in her sleep to a man whose face was not her husband's.

"Though the doors were locked, Jesus came and stood among them and said, 'Peace be with you.' Then he said to Thomas, 'Put your finger here; see my hands. Reach out your hand and put it into my side. Stop doubting and believe.'

"Thomas said to him, 'My Lord and my God!'

"Then Jesus told him, 'Because you have seen me, you have believed; blessed are those who have not seen and yet have believed.'"

Gabe put the Bible down. In a few short hours, his life had changed. He could feel that he was a new creation in Jesus. He had never imagined it would be like this. He was exhausted and elated. And hungry. He headed to the kitchen for a midnight snack. As he rounded the corner, he saw Michael seated at the table nursing a hot chocolate.

"Hey, Father, my brother." Gabe grinned.

"Hey," Michael replied.

"What's got you up?"

"Weird dream about the Lady again." Michael smiled just a bit.

"Again? Michael, you need to see somebody about this."

"No, Gabe, I think I figured it out. I think I've always known I wanted to be a priest. The Lady is a psychological device I must have invented to keep me away from the lure of sex." Michael parroted the most recent bit of programming from the Lady.

"Wow! Talk about the power of the mind, huh?" Gabe said as he heated some milk for himself.

"I just feel so relieved to have finally figured it out. Now that I know for sure I was meant to be a priest, I don't think I'll dream about her anymore."

"So you're saying your mind met its objective and no longer has need of this construct we've been calling the Lady?" Gabe asked, taking stock of and frowning at his own verbal acuity.

Michael chuckled at Gabe's expression. "Yes, exactly! I'm not mentally ill; I'm a priest!"

Gabe flashed his brother a devilish grin. "Not mutually exclusive terms. Have you met our uncle Benny?"

"Point well taken." Michael returned Gabe's grin. "In fact, it could well be that my distrust of Benny made me suspicious of my desire to become a priest. If there had been no Benny, there probably would have been no Lady."

Gabe chuckled. "You don't have to convince me that Benny is the kind of stuff nightmares are made of."

"What are you boys doing up?" Chris asked as he entered the kitchen. "That looks good. Gabe, warm up some milk for me too, will you?"

"Just talking a little bit," Michael said. "I've had an epiphany. I always wanted the priesthood, Chris, from my earliest days. I just didn't realize it until now."

"Thank you, Benny," Gabe interrupted as he looked longingly at his near-warm milk before pouring another cup of cold milk into the pan.

"I'm really happy to hear that, Michael. The Spirit has had me praying strongly for you two boys all night."

"That would make sense," Michael said. "I was having this weird dream where I figured it all out. The important thing is that I'm really happy about where I am in my life."

"That's wonderful to hear, honey," Kim said as she entered the room. "But it's three thirty in the morning."

"It's not like I called a family meeting, Mom. I was here having some cocoa, then Gabe came, and then Chris."

"Actually, that sounds good. Gabe, add some milk for me, honey."

Gabe looked at the pan. The milk was just starting to steam.

"Ah." Gabe sighed. "Michael, can I interest you in a second cup? Because I don't want to get these three almost done and then you ask for another."

"I'm fine." Michael waved him off.

"So why are *you* up, Mom?" Gabe asked.

"The pitter patter of little feet on the stairs." She smiled.

"Gabe and I did this all the time when we were little. You never heard us," Michael challenged.

"Every time, boys. I heard you every time!" Kim laughed at the memories. "When I heard you two, I would sneak downstairs to make sure everything was okay. And by the way, I heard every conversation."

"No!" the boys both screamed.

"I know you kissed Jenny Griffiths when you were eleven," Kim mused toward Michael.

"Jenny Griffiths!" Michael cackled. "I had forgotten all about her."

"And then there was Wendy Abrams," Kim said in reference to Gabe's early loss of his virginity.

"Point made, Mom, you heard us creeping down the stairs," Gabe said defensively. "No need for a litany of conquests."

"So Michael finally figured out he wants to be a priest, which is good because he just became one," Kim said with a bit of good-natured sarcasm. "Let me guess why you're awake. You finally figured out you want to be a drunken lothario."

"Exact opposite," Gabe grinned with pride. "I gave my life to Jesus tonight!"

"What?" Michael chirped.

"The Gospel of John became alive to me tonight. I started reading it just so I could tell Tina that I did, but then I realized who Jesus was—and is—and I knew I couldn't live my life without Him."

Chris crossed to the stove to give the younger man a hug. "I have prayed for this to happen for you for such a long time. I am so happy, son."

"And thanks for the prayers," Gabe said.

Kim was next to hug him, but she was a lot more cautious. "You know, Gabe, this is a big step. There's a lot about your life that—"

Gabe finished her sentence. "That Jesus doesn't want me to do anymore. I know, Mom. I'm fine with it. I could be crazy happy being in love with Jesus and Tina. And if God wills it, our kids."

"Wow. And I could be your kids' priest-uncle, who comes to steal their money," Michael grinned.

"Shut up and give me a hug, Father," Gabe said to his brother.

"So tell us all about it," Chris said.

"Before you do, Gabe," Michael said, "I've changed my mind. I'm going to need more hot chocolate."

Gabe growled and ruffled Michael's hair.

"Have you told Tina yet?" Kim asked.

"It's late. I figured I would wait until morning."

Finally, all the hot chocolates were made. Gabe had just served everyone when the wall phone rang.

"Probably Tina calling him," Kim said. "They have that kind of connection."

Grinning at her comment, Gabe answered it in a sexy voice. "Hello." Then he was silent for a moment.

"Chris," he said with a confused look, "Someone from the Vatican for you. Says the pope is trying to reach you."

"The pope?" Chris asked, looking at his watch. He took the phone, "Hello, Holiness. How can I be of service?"

The family watched quietly, wondering what was happening. Chris slid to the kitchen floor. Crying, he thanked the pope for calling him and hung up.

"Father Vinnie is dead," he blurted out as his voice cracked. The family drew around him, knowing how Vinnie had been a father figure to Chris.

They brought him to the table. Kim wiped the tears from his eyes. Michael rubbed his shoulders. Chris couldn't tell the family the rest of the pontiff's message: he suspected Benny had poisoned Vinnie.

TEN

Chris couldn't remember a time when he had been less happy. Vinnie had requested a private funeral, just him and the Lord. The pope himself said the funeral Mass. Chris had asked the Holy Father to concelebrate, but he was denied. It was Vinnie's wish to have a closed casket and a funeral with nobody in attendance.

Life was tough for Chris in the wake of Vinnie's departure. He busied himself at first with helping Michael get situated in Rome. But Michael was so good at adapting to new cultures that Chris could only be of help at the very beginning. They had a standing arrangement to have dinner together every Wednesday. It was great to have Michael nearby, but his work was bound by secrecy. In some hard-to-define way, Chris felt like he was losing Michael.

Chris had taken to getting up even earlier in the morning, and cutting his run short by a little. He used the extra time to make sandwich runs to Vinnie's church of the poor. They had come to rely on Vinnie's charity and counsel. Chris hated to deprive them of the little they had.

As for Benny, he seemed unusually quiet and condescendingly kind, even smug.

"I must confess, Eminence, you have impressed me," Begliali said to Benny.

"Only because you underestimated me to begin with," Benny said with a smile and just the right amount of indignation.

"Indeed I did, old friend. But I won't in the future. You have earned the privilege of being one of my closest confidants. Your ability to manipulate people and situations is of great value to me. And your absolute disregard for the sanctity of human life is an added bonus."

"Those are wonderful compliments, Luciano," Benny said, "but they are hollow if not backed by some show of your support."

"I have been thinking a lot of your situation, my friend. I believe this uncooperative pope has thwarted your upward progression. Until now, it was important to my purposes that he remain in power until the Soviet Union was dismantled."

"If only I could get closer to the seat of power," Benny said. "An aging, ailing pope relies heavily on his staff. In the right position, I could effectively neutralize him while leaving a figurehead the world adores."

"I love the way your mind works, Benito. I may be able to use my influence with the Curia to promote your cause."

Michael quickly acclimated to Rome with Chris's help. He felt sad for Chris in the wake of Father Vinnie's death. He saw the loneliness in Chris and the depressed way he went through his days. Michael could only imagine the tedious monotony of being Benny's assistant. Before, Chris had been able to manage it through Vinnie's paternal counsel and sense of humor.

The new assignment was not as Michael had envisioned it. There were no laboratories or libraries where troves of archeologists worked to tease out the secrets of past civilizations. He was instead seated at a desk in a tiny office. Yet their work had to be important, judging by the high level of security strictly enforced in the facility. Each employee was carefully searched upon entering and exiting the area. No visitors were allowed. Speaking with coworkers, beyond the normal "excuse me" or "I'll be away from my desk" was frowned upon. It seemed that many people each worked on a bit of the project, but only those in control knew the project in its entirety. The less people spoke to one another, the less able they were to pull together all the pieces of the puzzle.

In theory, Michael understood the procedure, but it made for long days. He might as well have been a monk in a cloister. As for his work, it was not exactly inspiring. He had been given some pre-Sumerian tablets to try to interpret. It didn't take him long to realize that, although the symbols were different, the language itself was very much like its Sumerian descendent. The text detailed the daily life of a village in Mesopotamia. His bosses seemed pleased, in fact infatuated, with his work. Others in the group were now using his template for the translation of this language. The amazing thing about all of this was that civilization was not believed to exist twelve thousand years ago, and yet here was a record of day-to-day life in what appears to have been a city. Michael dreamed of being involved with an archeological team that would go to the area to dig for more clues about this ancient society. But, even though he had been the one to discover the key to translating these writings, he was still bottom man on the totem pole. He hoped there still would be discoveries to be made when his turn finally came to go to the actual site.

There was a slight knock at the door of his tiny office as the project director, Kurt Waldenbaum said, "A word with you, Father?"

"Please, come in. Have a seat," Michael said in German to the renowned archeologist and physicist.

"Your German is without accent," Kurt said as he took the small chair in front of Michael's desk. "I saw in your biography that you speak a list of languages with no discernible accent. That is quite a gift."

Michael grinned at the compliment and the opportunity to actually *speak* to someone in this sterile environment. "I have always loved language. You can really understand a people when you grasp how they choose to describe daily events. A simple example would be in Texas, where they say 'I'm fixin' to do such and such.' They are more contemplative about their days. In New York, nobody's 'fixin" to do anything; they're just doing it. The thought isn't important; it's the action that counts."

"And your thoughts on the society you are examining?" Kurt asked as if testing Michael.

Michael drew a deep breath and gathered his thoughts. "The little I have seen strikes me as a bit odd in the way they speak to their daily lives," he said with some reservation. Then he noticed the sparkle of excitement in Kurt's eyes and believed Kurt may actually accept his unusual theories about the patterns he noticed. "There are phrases I have translated as being, 'I went quickly into the wilderness,' but the verbs and phrasing could just as well have been a modern person casually saying, 'I flew to the jungle.'"

Kurt stared at Michael intently, as if willing him to continue along his line of reasoning. "As you may be aware, I am not only an archeologist but a physicist. I find these writings to be unlike others I have seen in archeological sites," Kurt said cautiously.

"Yes, sir. I am aware of your incredible academic record."

"You have a rather distinguished record yourself, Father. For that reason, I have come to ask your opinion on a particular text." He showed a photocopy of the tablet to Michael. "One of our other workers here translated it as follows: 'I went to the well wherefrom we draw life. The center point of activity.'"

"Yes. I can see that," Michael commented with a shrug.

"But it is very idiomatic. If you were to translate it literally, Father, how would it read?"

"I went to the dark hole where we draw power. The zero point of energy," Michael translated.

"How would you read this if you were a physicist, Father—if you didn't presume this ancient culture to be scientifically unsophisticated?"

"I could read it to mean they may have found a way to tap into zero-point-energy, that place on a subatomic scale where matter pops in and out of existence," Michael conjectured as a huge grin spread across his face. Even the possibility of the existence of such a society on Earth thrilled him.

"Brilliant!" Kurt exclaimed.

"But, Herr Doctor, with all due respect, what is the likelihood of a prior civilization that was so technologically advanced?"

"Brace yourself, Father. Your security clearance is about to be elevated. Follow me."

Michael followed Kurt through large baroque double doors that had been secured with a biometric monitor. Kurt placed his hand on a plate and the doors opened for him. Once inside, they passed through screeners where nonplussed Swiss Guard soldiers scanned them to ensure they brought no outside substances. After a series of beeps, the guardsman removed a pen from Michael's pocket and placed it on a shelf. The two men were then ushered to an elevator and escorted twenty stories below the surface into a high-tech laboratory. Everything was bright white and stainless steel. It was clear that they tried to keep the environment as pristine as possible.

Kurt led Michael through a row of computers, their screens moving frantically. Finally, they came to a room with a large circular glass enclosure at its center. In the middle of the enclosure was a table on which a golden disc spun furiously as it was continuously struck by short bursts from a series of lasers housed in a canopy above it. Michael didn't know what to make of the rotating golden disc or the lightening-like flashes.

"Can you guess what you're seeing?" Kurt asked his curious guest.

"No, I can't," Michael answered, "but it feels like I'm inside a CD player."

A surprised laugh escaped Kurt's lips, brightening his otherwise stern demeanor. "You are closer to the truth than you could ever imagine!" He led Michael to a computer terminal and with a few keystrokes pulled up photos of an archeological dig in the desert.

"These photos were taken at a site not far from ancient Babylon. When Saddam Hussein began to reclaim the old city, he fell upon a treasure trove of artifacts, one of which was a rather mundane-looking clay disc. On the disc were markings that were clearly not Sumerian." He lowered his voice to a conspiratorial tone. "Through some very curious means, the artifact fell into our possession at the close of the Gulf War. It was acquired as a museum piece, but the markings were intriguing to our group of scientists because they hinted at a previously unknown civilization."

Michael looked intently at the markings on the disc. It was the same language he had been translating for the past few weeks. "I recognize the language." He chuckled.

"No doubt," Kurt continued. "We had a sense the disc either wasn't solid or contained an inner chamber as its mass seemed inappropriate. Using x-ray analysis, we found there was indeed a smaller disc inside and a hidden locking mechanism. When we finally found a way to unlock the device, we found inside the golden disc you see spinning in front of you."

"So you actually found a super-sized CD!" Michael beamed.

"It would appear we have." Kurt nodded with an ear-to-ear grin.

"After years of analysis, we were able to determine that it contained laser-encoded messages. We then had to figure out how to get at the computer encoding. It is very interesting. Their method of compacting data is far superior to what we currently have—or had, until the invention of the laser interface you see here."

"And the computers outside?"

"Downloading amazing amounts of information, the bulk of which seems to be textual. There are also what appear to be graphic images, but we have yet to find the algorithms to unlock them. We imagine there is some sort of instruction manual contained in the data feeds, but until you cracked the code, we have been unable to translate even the texts."

"But you showed me a photo of a tablet with the text on it," Michael said, confused.

"The tablet was created in this lab as a suitable cover. We are most probably sitting on the purloined repository of knowledge from an ancient, advanced civilization. We needed a cover story, including photos of artifacts, to obscure the truth while we learn what this disc is trying to tell us."

"Unbelievable!" Michael exclaimed. He raked his hands through his hair and shook his head at the possibilities. "So I've been working on the greatest archeological find of the ages, and I didn't even realize it!"

"Michael, your work has enabled us to program a template that translates the code first to Sumerian and then to English. Unfortunately, the ancient language and its Sumerian descendent have significant differences when taken over a broad body of information. Also, the language appears to be highly idiomatic and filled with allegory and metaphor, as if the information was 'dumbed down' to make it more understandable by a less-developed civilization. No computer can figure this out. We need talented men like you to reach through the alphabet and the allegory to the truths in the background."

Michael fairly salivated at the challenge. He moved about with uncontainable nervous energy, pacing about the room and unable to contain the broad grin dancing across his face. It was always his dream to solve the puzzles of a heretofore-unknown ancient civilization. The feelings of pride and scholarship offered by such an endeavor drove him. But add to it the thoughts that the ancient civilization was more advanced than ours and that the unearthed information could bring about concrete concepts to advance humankind. It was too much to take in. *Nothing could be better than this!* He was speechless.

"Ach, I was right when I sensed in you a kindred spirit, my friend. I smile like that every day I am here. When I saw your work, I knew we had to have you with us. That is why we contacted your uncle to see if he might convince you to work with us."

Michael broke into hysterical laughter. Kurt just looked at him. "It's nothing," Michael said, wiping a tear from his eye. "You have to know my uncle to get the humor. Suffice it to say he led me to believe it was he who contacted you."

"So you thought your position here was a gift from your uncle?"

"So to speak." Michael laughed.

"We must be clear about something, Michael. Your uncle knows nothing of this project. To him, indeed to almost all of the Vatican, this is a place where we page through dusty old manuscripts, like medieval monks. It's part of the cover, and you must maintain it, regardless of your love for your uncle."

An unexpected chuckle burst from Michael. "Not to worry, Kurt. Trust me, I am totally thrilled to work on this project, and I'll keep its secrets. As for my uncle, you might be overstating it a bit to characterize our relationship with the word 'love.'"

Kurt sighed. "What a relief, Michael. A man like your uncle is predisposed to use secrets to his own benefit."

"Not to worry. I've seen Benny for who he is since I was nine years old. I know how to keep him at bay."

"At bay?" Kurt enquired after the expression that was unknown to him.

"It's an idiom. It means to keep him away from me." With that, the two men simultaneously recognized the full weight of the task ahead of them. The idioms of an entire unknown culture awaited them.

"I need to talk to Gloria," Meemaw said weakly from her hospital bed. She knew her time was near, that the stress of not knowing what happened to Sarah and Mack had finally taken its toll on her stroke-weakened body. Her organs were beginning to fail, system after system shutting down in preparation for her final moments on Earth. She was on oxygen in an intensive care room—only one visitor at a time. Zack heeded his grandmother's request and went to the waiting room to get Gloria.

"I'm here, Meemaw," Gloria said as she entered the room. She tenderly took Sandy's hand in hers.

"I have to tell you that I'm sorry for some of the things I said and did after the stroke." A solitary tear formed in Sandy's right eye and rolled down her cheek.

"Don't worry about those things, Meemaw. You couldn't help yourself," Gloria reassured as she gently wiped the tear away.

Sandy fought back more tears to continue. She had to be strong—to say everything that needed to be said. But she was so tired. She wished more than anything to be able to close her eyes and not open them again until Jesus awakened her. "A stroke isn't that easy. I knew I was behaving strangely, but there was no filter in my brain. And there's something else. Some of it was calculated."

"I don't understand, Meemaw." Gloria petted her hair.

"I thought Mack and Sarah had turned too materialistic. They lost their calling somewhere along the way. Sometimes I did things to try to point out to them how far afield they had gone. I deliberately played the crazy lady when they got high-falutin' at their dinner parties." The heart monitor beeped faster behind her, highlighting the urgency of her words. Her voice faltered. "But I never wanted them dead." She cried now. Long, hard sobs.

Gloria bent over the bed to cradle her as she comforted. "Meemaw, they're not dead. They're living it up in the Caribbean. Just yesterday Zack told me he got a letter from them."

Taking a deep breath, Sandy regained her composure. "Did you see the letter?" she asked suspiciously.

"Well, no."

"That's because there wasn't one. You can't write letters from the grave!" The exclamation brought a fresh round of tears and a sudden round of coughing. "They never would have abandoned me without so much as a good-bye. Sarah was my little girl. I may have been a trial to her in the end, but she would never have gone this long without contacting me." Meemaw cried in long wails for the daughter she had lost.

"Meemaw, you're not strong enough to cry like this, dear. Try to be calm, okay?" Gloria urged through tears of her own.

Sandy calmed herself a bit. The girl was right. She didn't have long on this Earth, and she needed to make her last breaths count. "Gloria. I don't have proof, but I think Zack killed his parents to get hold of the ministry."

"Oh, Meemaw! Those are huge accusations. Maybe your mind is playing tricks on you."

Sandy pushed herself up in the bed to make a final stand. "No, Gloria!" she pleaded as she caressed the younger woman's face. "I may *sound* crazy, but I'm not. I can see through situations with amazing clarity. For instance, when I threw myself on the floor to cover for you, I think you were trying to sneak out to have an abortion. There was something wrong with that baby, and you knew it. I don't know what you didn't like about it; maybe Zack wasn't the father. But in my heart, I think it was more than that. I don't think you could dispose of a child ... but something inhuman? Well that's a different story."

Gloria's gasp of amazement and sudden tears told Sandy she had been right. She grabbed the girl's hand with both of hers and held it as firmly as she could. "I'm not judging you, dear. I felt that evil growing inside you, and then a few weeks ago, it just left. Am I right, girl?"

"It's not what you think about the baby. I was wrong about it too. He was a gift, but I didn't understand it. Now he's gone." Gloria wiped at the mascara-stained tears on her own cheeks.

Meemaw reached up with a frail hand to comfort the younger woman. "I don't mean to cause you hurt, Gloria, but I want to warn you. There is something hard, calculating, and mean-spirited about my grandson. I'm happy to die before he gets the chance to kill me. His parents weren't so lucky." Sandy could only hope the words would hit home. At least enough to get the girl to take a hard look at her husband.

Gloria kissed her cheek. "I'll be okay, Meemaw. Don't worry about me. I promise you. I'll be fine."

"Good," Meemaw said in a far-away voice. The conversation had drained the last of her strength. She was so tired! She fell asleep holding

Gloria's hand. When she awoke, it was the hand of Jesus. He hugged her and took her to the waiting arms of her daughter.

Chris knocked on Michael's apartment door for several minutes and then decided to use his own key to enter. The two were supposed to meet at a restaurant two hours ago. Chris waited at the restaurant, assuming something had detained Michael. As the hour grew later, he began to worry.

He flipped on the lights to see that the once-orderly place was a shambles. Texts were open everywhere. Reams of printed text from Michael's computer were on the desk, couch, and kitchen table. For a brief second, Chris thought it was vandalism but quickly realized the signs that Michael was deep into a research project. No doubt Michael had forgotten about their dinner. Nonetheless, Chris needed to talk to him. He went back to his own apartment to make some sandwiches and then headed back to Michael's place to wait.

While Chris couldn't compete with Michael's intellect and could never hope to understand his fields of expertise, he looked through the volumes strewn around the apartment. A lot of the texts were about the composition of language, common types used in the creation of idiomatic expression and the interpretation of ancient Sumerian texts. But the volume of information printed from the Internet was decidedly different. Theories about the lost civilization of Atlantis. Tales of the Annunaki, an ancient race of gods that supposedly made contact with the ancient Sumerians. Nibiru, the planet of the crossing. Chris flipped through the papers as he ate his sandwich. It all seemed very bizarre to him. Somewhere, Michael had drifted from hard science to the pseudoscience of Internet conspiracy theorists. What could the connection possibly be? Had Michael lost his way, or was something more going on?

The apartment door opened slowly. Chris heard Michael yell in Italian, "Don't move. I have a gun!"

"You do not!" Chris laughed as he replied in English from the living room.

Breathing a sigh of relief, Michael went inside. "Oh man, Chris! You scared me to death!"

"Good, because you scared me to death when you didn't show up for dinner," Chris answered with a forgiving grin.

"That was tonight? Oh, Chris, I'm sorry. I've been knee deep in this project."

"I could tell," Chris said with a sweeping gesture to the messy apartment. "Did you eat?"

"I didn't get the chance."

Chris took a hard look at the younger priest. He had lost weight, and there were dark circles under his eyes.

"Michael, I'm sure the Annunaki will wait long enough for you to grab a meal and get some sleep," Chris said as he headed to the fridge to get Michael's sandwich.

"How much have you read?"

"The language formation texts are a bit hard for me, but the Internet articles ..." He placed the sandwich and soda in front of Michael. "Why would you be looking at that stuff, Michael?"

"I don't know. Maybe I just find it to be interesting. Kind of fun," Michael said defensively as he dug into the sandwich.

Chris sighed as he sat down opposite Michael. Why play twenty questions? "Michael, my guess is you think you've stumbled upon evidence of a previous civilization. It's the only thing that could tie all this together."

Michael smiled in delight. Chris was drawn back to a memory of Michael as a child, waiting to present Chris with the apartment that he, his brother, and mother had prepared for him. The beautiful expression on the angelic face of that precious little boy—anticipation, pride, the longing to share himself. Chris had his answer in Michael's smile.

"Michael, just be careful to guard your faith," Chris cautioned. "A lot of really bright men have been caught up in ideas that appear to disprove their beliefs only to find they had thrown away the greater treasure."

"Point well taken," Michael said a bit too dismissively for Chris.

"So are you going to tell me about it?"

Michael chewed on his last bite of sandwich and washed it down with a drink of soda. "Only that it's truly fascinating, Chris." He beamed. "I never dreamed I would be part of such a monumental project."

"So for once in his life, Benny done good." Chris chuckled.

"Well, it appears the facts were a little different than presented by Benny. He didn't so much arrange the position as deliver the letter."

Chris laughed heartily. "And of course there was the $100 million shipping and handling fee."

Michael laughed as well. "I like hanging out with you, Chris. I apologize again for missing our dinner."

"That's not all you've missed, Michael. Gabe's been trying to get hold of you for days. Finally he asked me to tell you he's coming to Rome next week. He said he has something important to discuss with us."

"I think I hear wedding bells in the air," Michael chimed. "What about Mom? Is she coming?"

"No." Chris laughed. "She said the ordination nearly did her in. The thought of the three of us together on Benny's turf made her want to stay at home and pray."

The meeting was brief, and the Curia members were to the point. The pontiff's advanced age was taking a toll on his reign. The young priest who served as camerlengo was a nice man, but with the pope's waning strength, the Church required much more of a presence in that role. Their suggestion was to place Benny Cross in the role, as a cardinal.

The jackals are closing in for the kill, the pope thought. But he had more than a few surprises up his sleeve, the first of which was to comply with their request.

"Gentlemen, I too have noticed the falter in my step and the shaking of my hands. I welcome your suggestion. As for Archbishop Cross, his reputation for administrative skills has been forged on the sweaty brow of Father Chris Altenbrook. I would bring Cross on to assist me only if Father Chris is moved along with the would-be cardinal to be my camerlengo."

Not a man objected to the pope's request. He smiled like a benevolent old grandfather as they in turn kissed his ring and left. When they were all gone, he laughed like a wise old man who had bested young fools. They planned to use Cross to neutralize him! Well, those tables could be turned in a matter of moments.

Now for the distasteful act of welcoming Cross! He summoned Benny, and within minutes the oaf was seated before him.

"You wish to see me, Holiness?" Benny asked.

"Yes. Archbishop, many years ago I dangled a carrot in front of you. I took a wait-and-see approach about making you a prince of the Church. I have waited and seen. In short, I believe it is time that you be made a cardinal."

"Oh, Holiness, I can't thank you enough for this great privilege. I want you to know I won't disappoint you. Even with the new title, I will go about my duties with my customary humility, charity, and grace."

Why do I always want to cuss when this man speaks? The pontiff quieted his inner dialogue to continue the conversation. "Oh, my faithful young cardinal, you will not be performing in your present capacity. The Curia has made it known to me that with my age has come a lessening of my vigor. I require an assistant, a faithful lieutenant."

"Holiness, it will be a pleasure to assist you in your duties." Benny smiled profusely.

The pope stared at the man across his desk, wincing at the Cheshire cat smile. "There is more. I have become very fond of your assistant, Father Chris. I will require that he become my camerlengo. What are your thoughts?"

Benny gasped. "With all due respect, Holiness, I don't know that there is a clear enough definition of duties. For instance, would Chris report to me or to you?"

"To me," the pope said, barely containing a smile.

"That would effectively leave me without support staff," Benny complained.

"Then again, Chris is so competent he'll probably do your job as well as his own … as has been the case for many a year now." The pontiff's eyes sparkled as he watched the proposal dawn on Benny.

"But, Holiness, I don't find this to be in the least acceptable," Cross said with exasperation that betrayed his underlying disdain for the pope.

"Perhaps I didn't explain it well," the pope said as he lowered the boom. "Chris will be my assistant, confidant, and camerlengo. You will be promoted to cardinal as a bit of a prop. Your duties will include certain ceremonial appearances on my behalf. Beyond that, your existence should not be very taxing." The pope's grin broadened to a full-blown smile.

"And if I take exception?" Benny challenged.

"Then Chris will come to work for me anyway, you will not be a made cardinal, and I will leave you to the task of actually performing the job you already have," the pope said sharply. He could sense Benny's fury.

"I will need time to think about my response, Holiness." Cross snorted.

"Take all the time you need, as long as I have your response within thirty seconds." The pope drummed his fingers on his desk to mark the time.

Benny blanched. "With consideration, Holiness, I accept your offer," he said through clenched teeth.

"Wonderful. I will begin the process of making you a cardinal. Have a good day."

"You as well, Holiness." Benny kissed the papal ring and walked to the door.

"Oh, Cardinal Cross," the pope called as Benny's hand touched the doorknob, "I trust that you will go about your new position with something greater than your *customary* humility, charity, and grace."

"Yes, Holiness," Benny said sullenly as the pope returned to reading.

The amount of data on the huge spinning disc was enormous. It was daunting. To make matters worse, there was a strong indication that this culture used letters as their symbols for numbers. In this language, it was perfectly acceptable to write something like "A A, B," meaning "one plus one equals two." A lot of what had appeared at first to be gibberish could lend itself to some very precise science, including mathematical equations that appeared on the surface to answer physicists' quests for a unified field theory. The implications were staggering.

They had just scratched the surface, but there were some tantalizing clues in the data. This culture appeared not to have developed on Earth but rather somewhere in the constellation of Orion. The more startling of the revelations was the indication that these beings had manipulated the genetics of Earth life to produce an intelligent species—humans. What would the Church do with such data? Lock it up, along with all the potential scientific advances that could benefit the entire world? If this race had actually found a way to access zero-point energy, this knowledge could be used to feed the entire globe. The Church could effectively put an end to most of the physical hardships of the world, but it would require huge changes in its dogma.

The details were sketchy because the data was just so voluminous, but it appeared that this race believed in a "being of light," who created the universe. Parallels would have to be drawn between their supreme being and the Yahweh/Allah of the Abrahamic religions. The ancients also had a belief in the power of positive thinking, focusing on proven science that matter can be affected at the quantum level by an individual's thoughts. This power could manifest itself in great good or great evil, depending on the mindset projected by civilization.

The stumbling block, of course, would be Jesus. The Greek of the New Testament was an incredibly precise language. There was no denying texts in which Jesus proclaimed, "I am *the* Way, *the* Truth, and *the* Light." The only way to undo some of this would be to find earlier texts in which an indefinite article was used. He could then be quoted as saying, "I am a way, a truth, and a light." It would make all the difference in the world to find an ancient text replete with such subtle changes, just enough to present Christ as merely one alternative view of the universal force. If this could be accomplished, the Church could bring the entire world together under the auspices of the ancient religion of our creators. And, more important in Michael's estimation, the Church would be able to go public with their information and use the ancient technologies to heal the problems of the world. There had to be a way to break the Jesus myth for the benefit of all humanity.

Michael knew the answer. He would have to carefully forge earlier Greek gospels with those subtle changes, but the forgeries would have to be good enough to pass the scrutiny of Catholic and Protestant scholars, as well as modern archeologists. As if he didn't have enough to do, Michael was going through the most ancient manuscripts to find those places where subtle changes could be introduced to change the meaning, just enough.

Everything about this task caused him discomfort. As an archeologist and someone who had studied ancient texts all his life, the very idea of forging an antiquity was anathema. He never thought he would find himself in such a position. But so many people could be helped; so much suffering could be alleviated if he just participated in a little white lie. When boiled down to its essence, Jesus had commanded His Church to "Feed my sheep." If this could be pulled off, the entire world would be fed and educated as to its place in the universe. Surely even Jesus would applaud.

There was also sadness. He had longed for a simple faith like the one shared by Chris, his mother, and now Gabe. But that was lost to him now that he knew the truth, and while the truth might set the world free, it would come as a crushing reality to his family. He glanced down at his watch. He was already late to meet Chris and Gabe at the restaurant.

"Gabe's going to kill me," he muttered as he ran for the elevator to take him up to ground level.

At the restaurant, Chris and Gabe waited for Michael. Chris explained to Gabe that Michael was immersed in a new project. Gabe smiled throughout Chris's recollection of the pile of information strewn about Michael's apartment. Michael had been passionate about pretend archeological finds when they were kids. Gabe could imagine well the diligence his brother would apply to the real thing.

As the talk of Michael wound down, Gabe moved on to the topic of his mother's redecoration of the family estate. "Oh, Chris, before I forget, Mom needs an answer from you about your suite."

"I already told her it doesn't need to be redone," Chris said, rolling his eyes.

"Oh, you silly man!" Gabe chuckled. "Mom's redecorating is her way of tending to her family, even though we're all gone." Of course there was more to it than that. His mother was a complex woman and a strategic thinker. As the only one at home, Gabe was privy to some of the hidden aspects of her project. In the midst of the restoration, she was installing underground bunkers, dried food, a separate water supply; you name it—a survivalist's dream in the wake of a coming Y2K crisis.

"I know." Chris chuckled. "And I appreciate it. I really do. But there are more productive things to do with her time."

"I'll let *you* have that conversation with her! As for me, I'm lucky. I pushed all decorating decisions to Tina. She and Mom are going to redo my—our—space while I'm here."

"Your mom really needs a girlfriend with shared interests. You don't suppose Tina would work with her on my rooms, do you?" Chris raised a single plaintiff eyebrow.

"To tell you the truth, I think they would both love it, but you're going to have to lay down some rules. Otherwise, you'll come home to more lace and flowers than any man could want. As always, Benny being the exception," Gabe offered with a mischievous grin.

"Fine. I'll talk to her tomorrow morning. Maybe I'll get Tina in on the conversation, and we can brainstorm," Chris said.

Gabe sighed. "That would be a welcome relief. Benny had an architect draw up some plans and sent in an interior decorator. It kind of hurt Mom's feelings."

"Haven't you just become the Sensitive Man of the Nineties?" Chris teased.

"It's the kinder, gentler Gabe. What can I say?" He smiled.

"Say you're not too ticked off at me," Michael said as he approached the table.

Gabe took one look at his brother and felt bad for him. Chris hadn't been exaggerating. He looked like he was about to faint from fatigue.

"Couldn't happen, brother," Gabe said as he hugged Michael. He held him in the hug and said softly, "You look bad, Michael. Don't work yourself into a hospital bed, okay?"

"Okay," Michael said softly. "So what were you guys talking about?"

"Mom's redecorating project," Gabe said as they took their seats. A waiter rushed a menu to Michael.

"Oh man!" Michael exclaimed as he wiped at his forehead. "She sent me some swatches and color samples. I never got back to her."

"So she tells me," Gabe said sternly.

"You're in good company, Michael. I haven't gotten back to her either," Chris droned.

"And what about you, Gabe? Don't tell me you rushed to get your selections to her," Michael said.

"Actually, she and Tina are doing my space this week while I'm away."

"You don't suppose—" Michael began.

"Chris asked the same thing. We'll call them tomorrow with your color selections, and remember to be thankful to Mom. I know it's a pain to us, but she's doing it *for* us."

Michael looked somberly at Chris. "Sensitivity training from Gabe! Could I have gotten *that* bad?"

"No." Chris grinned. "It's the gentrification of Gabriel. Next year at this time, he'll be wearing an apron and trying new recipes with your mom and Tina."

"Actually, I might. That sounds kind of nice to me," Gabe said defensively.

"And it's great for Mom," Michael said.

"True," Chris agreed, "but you didn't fly all this way to get our decorating choices or to talk about recipes, Gabe. What's your big news?"

"As if we didn't know," Michael rolled his eyes. "When's the wedding?"

"We're planning a small ceremony when everyone is together during the holidays," Gabe grinned. "But that's not why I'm here." In a return to patterns he and Michael had built in childhood, he was creating suspense, dangling his news in front of them. Of course Michael would do his best *not* to take the bait.

"The gnocchi here are very good," Michael said as he pondered the menu, moving the conversation to the mundane.

"So you're not the least bit curious as to why I'm here?" Gabe asked.

"Don't be silly. I'm just happy to have you here," Michael said, batting his eyelashes. "Chris, have you ever eaten the polenta dish? It sounds really good."

"Over the years, I've eaten just about everything on this menu," Chris said, grinning at the game afoot. "And I have to tell you, I haven't been disappointed yet."

Gabe easily saw through their feigned nonchalance. He dangled another carrot. "I received my final check from the cruise line. I'm no longer an ambassador of fun."

"I'm liking the frutta di mare," Michael said, looking at the menu with the clear pretense of not being interested in Gabe's news.

Chris could see Gabe's frustration was building. "Okay. I'll bite. Gabe, what did you come here to tell us?"

As Gabe began to speak, Michael said, "Can you hold that thought? I have to go to the men's room."

Chris raised his eyebrow at the younger priest as Gabe laughed and placed a strong arm on his shoulder to prevent him from standing.

"Sorry. Force of habit." Michael smiled. "I'm dying to hear your news, Gabe."

"I've been accepted at Dallas Theological Seminary. In the new year, I'll be starting classes to become a preacher."

"Wow," Michael said, sounding supportive, despite a slight wince. "So you'll be moving to Dallas?"

"Actually, no. They've just opened up a campus in Georgia. I'm thinking we can live at home, and I'll take as many classes there as possible. There might be a semester or two in Dallas, but mostly we'll be in Georgia." Gabe couldn't contain a grin of joy. Finally his life had a purpose.

"I'll be honest with you, Gabe," Chris said. "I would have loved it if you could have found some of the beauty of Catholicism. Having said that, I guess your mother would have been suicidal at having yet another priest in the family."

"Chris, the Lord put Tina in my life. I'm meant to be married and have children. And I don't mean any disrespect, but if there are many more Bennys in the Church, I think I wouldn't work too well in it."

"Points well taken," Chris said. "Welcome to the ministry, Gabe. You'll find it to be the most frustrating and rewarding of professions. But in the long run, bringing people to Jesus and then tending His sheep is a wonderful way to spend your life. And I'm excited for your mom that you'll be living in Georgia."

"Thanks, Chris. I really appreciate it." Gabe stared at his brother. "Michael, you're awfully quiet."

"I just don't want you to get your hopes up too much, Gabe. It's a hard life. And there's always the chance some archeologist could find something that changes our perception of who Jesus was."

"I care less about who He was than who He is, Michael," Gabe said, looking incredulously across the table to Chris.

"Then I'm happy for you." Michael smiled awkwardly. "And in case I haven't said it enough, I love Tina. I'm excited to have a sister, and hopefully a brood of nieces and nephews."

"Well, I'm not as young as Tina. We'll probably try to have children right away."

"I can't wait," Michael said in earnest. "I can see Baby Michael right now."

"You mean Baby Chris," Chris challenged.

"Actually, I was thinking if I have girls, I would name them Chrissie and Michele. And if I have a boy, I'll name him Benjamin," Gabe joked.

There was an awkward silence around the table as the three of them thought about telling Gabe's news to Benny.

"How do you think he'll take it?" Gabe finally asked.

"Just tell him you're going to be a minister," Michael said. "He'll be fine with that, but I'd let him find out later that you will be living in the family mansion."

Gabe nodded at Michael's last quip as he set his wine glass on the table. The evening had been full of joviality and camaraderie, yet he couldn't help but sense some uneasiness about his brother. Michael didn't seem to be himself.

His attention shifted to the brightly festooned uniform of a Swiss Guardsman as he marched across the restaurant to their table. He strode to Chris and said, "*Monsignore*, His Holiness has requested that I bring you to him immediately."

"Oh, okay," Chris blurted in surprise. Turning to Gabe and Michael, he said, "I'll catch up with you guys later; just leave me a message where you'll be."

"I'm advised that your meeting will take you well into the evening," the guardsman offered. Chris raised a questioning eyebrow to the boys and followed the soldier out of the restaurant.

"You summoned me, Holiness?" Chris asked tentatively as he was shown in to the pope's office.

"Indeed I did, Chris," the pope said, motioning for Chris to sit opposite him on white loveseats near the windows overlooking the

Papal Gardens. "I wanted to speak to you about a slight reshuffling of the deck here in my offices. The Curia has proposed that I take on a sort of assistant, and they have recommended Archbishop Cross."

"Closing in for the kill, Holiness?" Chris asked with concern, Vinnie's death close to mind.

"More like having someone in my offices to neutralize my message. They tried to convince me to slow down a bit, let Cross do some of the heavy lifting."

Chris chuckled at the idea of Benny actually working. "Of course you rejected their suggestion, Holiness."

"On the contrary, Chris, I agreed to their suggestion, and I have agreed to make him a cardinal."

Chris was baffled and shocked that the pope would actually concede to such a request. Yet his training and vows obligated him to accept the decision. In his heart, he cried out "Why?" From his mouth, he spoke hesitantly with downcast eyes, "Yes, Holiness."

"Chris, you have been loyal to me for years. I value your friendship and your counsel. Please feel free to speak your mind."

"Why let the fox into the hen house?" Chris asked as he stood, walked to the windows, and peered into the garden he used to tend with Vinnie.

"To put him on a tighter leash," the pontiff answered. "Chris, the Lord will not be mocked."

Chris turned to the pope with a wry smile. "In other words, you've trapped them in the trap they laid for you."

"I fought communism from my youth, Chris. I am very accustomed to the chess moves of the impure of heart. But there is more. You will be relieved of your position as Cross's assistant."

A burst of happiness came over Chris. Years ago, he had found the task to be a huge burden, but in time he learned to thank the Lord for it and had gotten used to it. These few words of the pope had loosened the burden, and he couldn't believe how light he felt. "Oh, Holiness. I can't thank you enough for relieving me of that post."

"There's more, Chris. As a condition of my agreeing to elevate Archbishop Cross, I told the Curia I must have you as my camerlengo."

"Oh, Holiness, with all due respect, I don't believe I possess the subtle diplomacy required for that position."

"I don't want a diplomat, Chris. I want a man of faith and strength who will not be compromised. I want a man who will speak the truth with love rather than juggle appointments and tell me what he thinks I want to hear."

"You are resolute in this decision?" Chris asked.

The pope slapped his own knee. "That I am!"

"Then I graciously accept. However, if I am to be forthright, I think you moved me as protection against the horror you have admitted to the innermost chambers of the Vatican."

The pope laughed loudly. "I have, young Christopher. And you will not only cover my back, you will be the leash with which I administer Cardinal Cross."

"I beg your pardon?"

"I have explained to the cardinal-to-be that for all intents and purposes, he will be reporting to me through you. It was a condition he had to accept in order to become a prince of the Church. But you will need to be very careful, my son."

"You don't have to tell me, Holiness. I remember how things turned out for Cardinal Bilbo."

"Bilbo was an evil man playing an evil game with someone who was only slightly more of a monster than he was. That is not the case with you, Chris. You wear the armor of God and the indwelling of the Holy Spirit. These have kept you safe from his machinations for many years, and will continue to do so in the future."

A tear came to Chris's eye. "I can't help but wish you had made this decision months ago. Maybe we could have averted Vinnie's death."

The pope smiled warmly at Chris. "Your first act as camerlengo will be to accompany me to the cloister. Vinnie used to go there to hear confessions. Perhaps you would like to take up his task in the future."

Chris smiled and nodded. It would feel good to carry on Vinnie's legacy. He and the pope chatted like close friends during the limousine ride to the cloister but assumed more formal demeanors upon their arrival. The pope left to visit with the head of the cloister while Chris headed directly to the confessional.

There were three tiny boxes about the size of telephone booths. Chris sat in the middle box. He prayed he would be faithful in providing absolution. On either side of him were small windows covered with gauze. Each had a sliding door, so that when Chris opened the window, he would see through the gauze a vague figure that would then begin to confess.

When he had calmed his mind from the events of the day, and found the appropriate focus, he slid open the panel to his right.

A voice filtered through from the other side. It instantly sounded familiar to him. "Bless me, Father, for I have sinned. I haven't been to confessions since before my funeral."

"Vinnie!" Chris screamed as he exited the confessional. Vinnie had exited as well. Chris grabbed the old monk and hugged him fiercely.

"Easy, there, fella," Vinnie complained. "Any hug longer than five seconds is a venial sin!"

"You faked your own death?" Chris asked.

"It seemed like the thing to do when Cross came to my apartment with some soup. Do you really think I'm stupid enough to eat chicken soup from the hand of Benny Cross? Come on; give me a little credit here!" Vinnie raised both hands and looked toward heaven. "Besides, he didn't even care enough to kill me with homemade soup! He brought me stuff from the can. Do you know how much salt is in that stuff? I've got gout, you know."

ELEVEN

It was the evening of December 27, 1999. The world awaited the dawn of the new millennium in four short days. The news was filled with reports of potential worldwide problems if enough hadn't been done to correct the dating convention in computer codes underlying most systems—the Y2K scare. Students of Bible prophecy wondered if the Lord would wrap up everything before the year 2000 arrived.

On the Martin estate in Georgia, a small group of family and friends gathered in the small chapel on the property. It was lighted with a thousand candles that Kim had had placed in huge candelabras everywhere. At the altar stood Gabe, looking unusually handsome in black tie and tails. Next to him, his best man, Michael, wore a long, flowing black cassock. On the altar, David stood to perform the ceremony in black tie. Beside him, Chris stood ready to provide the sermon, dressed in a black cassock and a white stole.

There was muffled nervous chatter as those present awaited Tina's march down the aisle. Kim sat in the front seat dressed in a formal, navy-blue gown with one large white satin rose on its left shoulder. She invited Fran to sit with her, considering all their men were on the altar. Fran looked beautiful in a green gown with a white and green bolero jacket.

"It was a great idea to do the wedding by candlelight," Fran whispered to Kim.

"I agree," Kim added. "The glow of the candles is *so* romantic!"

"I was talking about how young I look in dim light." Fran grinned.

"I hear you." Kim chuckled.

Behind them sat Gloria, looking more beautiful than ever. The donations to the ministry were large, and with the extra cash came an exorbitant clothing, hair, and makeup budget. A quartet of chamber musicians began to play the wedding march. Tina's childhood friend, Gayle, entered the chapel wearing a sapphire-blue satin gown with long, white gloves. She carried a single white rose.

Tina strode down the aisle on the arm of her widowed father. She looked ravishing. Given the black-tie theme of the wedding, she had chosen a dress that looked much like a satin evening gown, with a slight bustle and train. Her veil was simple lace on a tiara. Wearing long white gloves that reached past her elbows, she carried a simple bouquet of white lilies with an occasional blue orchid.

Michael grabbed Gabe's arm as she started down the aisle. "She's beautiful, Gabe."

Gabe wiped a tear from his eye as he agreed with his brother. Chris and David smiled broadly at the sight of her. Kim furiously wiped tears from her eyes. Fran placed an arm around her new friend. She thought back to her marriage to Tom. It seemed so long ago and far away at this point, yet there was a dull ache to rest her head on his shoulder one more time. As she looked from the bride to the altar, she saw Chris was looking at her as if he knew what she was thinking and gave her a quick smile.

As Tina took her place next to Gabe, Michael and Gayle took their respective places on either side of the couple.

David began the ceremony. "Dearly beloved, we are gathered here to witness the joining of this man and woman in holy matrimony ..."

Candles were the only light in the cave-like, windowless room in Kurtoglu's Turkish estate. In the years since he had taught Benny, Kurtoglu's life had changed greatly at the hands of Luciano Begliali. He had taken up a political career in his native Turkey and had risen to prominence as a political leader who favored his country's return to its Islamic roots. Attaturk had compromised the glory of the Ottoman Empire in his desire to westernize. Once the great Islamic successor to the Eastern Roman Empire, the Ottoman Empire died with World War I. Attaturk sought the favor of the

Western conquerors. He moved away from Sharia law, emancipated women, and even changed to a Western alphabet, all in a quest to become "modern." Kurtoglu believed Attaturk only succeeded in turning this once-great empire into a sniveling sycophant of the emerging European Union. Turkey had been one of the first nations to apply for membership, yet its application was continually delayed. The Europeans saw them as a strategic partner in the Middle East, but too barbarous, too ... Islamic ... to integrate into a Europe for Europeans.

Kurtoglu's party advocated a return to greatness. He was determined to return Turkey to a truly Islamic state that would lead a new caliphate. By the time he was done, he would restore the Ottoman Empire. All that was required was patience, and the arrival of Mahdi.

Over the years, Son of Wolf had learned to appreciate the tenacity and visceral meanness of Cardinal Cross. And Kurtoglu had grown less mystic than pragmatic. He would happily work with a Christian papist to bring about the new caliphate.

In the candlelight, imams prayed in Arabic. Incense filled the room with a thick, sweet-smelling smoke.

Benny leaned into Son of Wolf and whispered, "Here we go. This will knock their socks off!"

As the imams chanted, a bright pinpoint of light appeared in the center of them. It began to grow and take shape. Soon it looked like a light-being about the size of a young boy. It danced to their chanting, drawing near to first one and then another. Whenever it encountered one of the imams, he was forced to the floor from the sheer power of the light. The religious leaders were at once too terrorized and too intrigued to stop. They continued chanting their prayers to Allah, and the being, thought by them to be a jinn of some sort, danced wildly among them.

Kurtoglu and Cross knelt on the floor with their faces to the ground. Every once in a while, Benny would steal a peek at the flabbergasted imams. His heart thrilled to see their instant submission to the hologram sent by the Lady. *Let the fun begin!*

The apparition performed its version of a whirling dervish as the imams grew louder and more ecstatic in their prayers. Kurtoglu and Cross kept their heads down. The cardinal had briefed him on what to expect. Despite the briefing, Kurtoglu felt his upbringing and millennia of Islamic hope building within him when he saw the imams' delight in this being.

After an hour of frenetic dance, the light diminished, revealing a smaller form within. The being stood perfectly still and the prayers ceased. In the terrible silence that ensued, the light grew dimmer until there stood a boy who appeared to be about ten years of age.

"We look ahead to a new century, a new millennium," Chris said during his sermon, "and when I look at the faces of Gabe and Tina, and imagine the little ones to come, I am overwhelmed by a sense of hope and passion for the new age dawning in our family. I see a brilliant future for these two, and for those of us who have been lucky enough to share in their lives."

As Chris spoke, Gloria drew a sharp breath. Something in her spirit flashed like an alarm. *He has come back to Earth.* Her son was somewhere on Earth at this moment. For better or worse, this child—her child—would change the world. An involuntary gasp escaped her lips. Her pregnancy had been real enough at the time, but the memories had faded with the help of alien machinations and, over time, were subsumed by the more realistic cares of day-to-day life. But now, surrounded by the soft glow of candlelight, her arms ached to hold her child just once.

Bathed in the glow of candlelight, the boy finally spoke. Pointing to Kurtoglu, he said, "You will be my father on Earth." The child left the circle of imams and went to the side of Son of Wolf, who stood to receive his new charge.

Benny rose to get a good look at the boy. He was strikingly handsome and had the bearing of royalty. Something about the child was at once arresting and commanding. He reached out to touch the boy's dark, curly hair, but his hand froze in midair. Suddenly his legs went weak, and he fell forward to the floor. Kurtoglu fell as well.

As the two men looked up at the boy from the floor, he smiled and said softly, "You may worship me."

In the golden glow of the candles, the child's blue eyes consumed Benny. He had seen these eyes before. Just as an invisible hand forced his head to the floor in worship, Benny recognized the eyes. They looked just like Michael's.

2009

TWELVE

"You would not believe your eyes if ten thousand fireflies ..." The Owl City song was on the radio again. Kim knew very well what would come next.

"Turn it up, Mimi," eight-year-old Michele cried from the backseat.

"Yes. Turn it up, Mimi," followed cries from her seven-year-old brother, Chris.

For the next three minutes, the three of them sang together. The kids were caught up in the lyrics—Michele in the beauty of so many fireflies, Chris in the idea of making the world turn S-L-O-W-L-Y.

In a flash, the last decade swam through Kim's mind. She couldn't imagine life without those two precious little packages in the backseat. Their arrivals were later than planned. Gabe and Tina had tried to get pregnant immediately after the wedding, but it wasn't the Lord's plan. It took two full years of fertility clinic visits, and more than a little teasing from Michael and Chris that Gabe needed to go to school to learn how to "get the job done." But in time, Kim became a grandmother. She was delighted that her first grandchild was a girl. Surrounded by men all her adult life until Tina came into the family, she was positively joyous at the thought of having little girl toys around the house.

After graduating, Gabe worked as associate pastor at different small churches in Georgia but finally found his true passion in the care of underprivileged youth and writing about end times Bible prophecies. His books were able to simply convey difficult concepts and found a large Evangelical readership. From the proceeds of his writing, he and Tina ran a group of Christian orphanages. All of this brought tremendous joy to Kim, because it allowed them to live at the estate with her.

She had spent years in love with a man whose life was dedicated to the Lord; so she learned to busy herself, first as a mother to the boys, and then as a force with which to be reckoned in the business world. But the role of doting grandmother was best of all.

They managed to live easily together, although Kim had decided early on that if she needed to, she would move into Joseph's old house at the edge of the property to give them privacy. The need never arose. The estate was large enough to handle all of them very comfortably, and given their busy lives, Gabe and Tina appreciated the stability a live-in grandmother brought to the kids' lives. Kim had found very capable executives for her company and was easily able to manage things from her home office while the kids were in school.

She had just picked them up from school, and they were heading back home. Tina would be home shortly after. Gabe was in Rome. It was the most recent of many trips there. His relationship with Michael required work, and Michael was too consumed with never-ending projects to put in the time. So, periodically, Gabe forced a visit.

Kim knew there was more to it. Gabe was convinced they were living in the end times, a contention specifically refuted by Michael. Chris believed Gabe may well be correct in his assumptions but had been a bit of an outlier from the time he embraced that eschatology in Africa with Tom Ellis. Of course, as brothers are wont to do, Michael resisted Gabe's entreaties. Thankfully they still enjoyed each other's company, so the visits weren't contentious.

Michael sat at dinner in Rome with Gabe and Chris, willing his face muscles not to show how little credence he gave to Gabe's belief that the world's clock was ticking toward a certain, knowable, and predicted future. He was happy for Gabe's success, but his books only furthered the religious bigotry Michael would one day have to fight once the contents of the disc became known. He had tremendous love for his brother, but facts were facts. Unfortunately, his reticence only compelled Gabe to push harder.

"Think about it, Michael," Gabe said after a sip of his soda. "When Israel became a nation again, God started to move all the other players in place. Even the biblically predicted enemies of Israel align with today's Islamic states."

"Gabe, listen to me. I'm the expert on ancient texts. All the Bible says is that ancient Israel didn't get along with its neighbors—and still doesn't. There is so much allegory and flat-out myth buried into those accounts that they're only good as pointers to proper moral conduct. You have to understand that. I applaud your passion, and I see the good work you are doing, but these ideas of a coming tribulation and an antichrist? They got old about two weeks after *The Omen* hit the streets."

"But, Michael, how do you explain that Israel became a nation again?" Gabe asked.

Michael's annoyance started to find its way into his tone of voice. "A bad call on the part of the British? Compassion from the United States following Hitler's atrocities? All real, Gabe. *Real* emotions and *real* decisions made by *real* men. No God waved some magic wand to produce the state of Israel. Trust me on that."

Gabe's tone matched his brother's. "No offense, Michael, but why would I trust you on that? You live out your 'faith' in a dungeon laboratory doing God-knows-what."

"Everybody take a step back and take a deep breath," Chris counseled.

Michael smiled for the break in the conversation and happily changed the subject. "Show me pictures of the best-looking kids in the world."

"Thought you'd never ask," the proud father responded. "The kids asked me to give one of these to each of you." In each photo, the kids were blowing kisses ... her in a Disney princess nightgown, him in dinosaur pajamas. Michele had dark-brown hair with luminous auburn highlights and green eyes, like her father. Little Chris was fairer. His hair was light brown in the winter and a deep golden color in the summer.

"I think they're just beautiful." Chris beamed. "I could look at this picture for hours."

Michael teased. "Whatever they taught you in fertility class, it worked. The kids are gorgeous."

"But then again," Chris corrected, "Tina's a lovely woman. You could probably mate a chimpanzee with her and get a good-looking kid."

"I thought we had." Michael laughed.

In Ankara, Turkey, Kurtoglu rushed to return to his office. Life as the recently elected prime minister of his country was intensely busy as he worked diligently to return Turkey to the sanity of Sharia law.

"Mr. Prime Minister," his secretary called as he breezed past, "your son is waiting in your office."

"Thank you," Kurtoglu said briskly as he sailed past his secretary. He had secured the role of prime minister a few short months before by running on a pro-Islam platform promising to bring back the glories of the Ottoman Empire. Son of Wolf was acutely aware that his current success, as well as the success of any future political endeavors, was the direct result of his relationship with his son. From the moment the boy came into his care, Kurtoglu's fortunes increased geometrically. He was now the wealthiest man in Turkey and not so far behind any individual member of the Saudi royal family in terms of his personal fortune.

But it was more than the power and wealth the boy generated. Kurtoglu was constantly amazed at the prowess and strength of this being who had become his charge. He was beyond genius, incredibly handsome, and wonderfully athletic. No matter where he went, men and women alike adored him. He exhausted tutor after tutor, as if he were able to reach into their minds and take from them their field of expertise. He aged a little more quickly than the average child. By all appearances, the man was approximately twenty-five years of age, with a swarthy complexion, dark curly hair, and eyes that shined like the sun.

"Isa!" Kurtoglu said with delight as he entered the office. The boy had chosen the name Mehmet Isa Kurtoglu, meaning Mohammed Jesus Son of Wolf. While known to many by his first name, Isa had become a name that he used with family and close friends. "What brings you from university, my son?"

The handsome young man grinned with unbridled pride. "I have exhausted the knowledge at that institution. In fact, I believe I have learned all I can in our country. I will soon be ready to be made one of your cabinet ministers."

The news struck Kurtoglu as strange. Isa had never before shown much of an interest in politics—at least not an interest in any visible role. His presence in Kurtoglu's day-to-day decisions easily made him the power behind the throne, as Kurtoglu was powerless to do anything but obey this god/son of his. Still, Son of Wolf had hoped at least to be the face of power in the eyes of his fellow Turks.

"When will you be ready, my son? I have only begun my reign. There is much to do, and I have yet to consolidate my powerbase," he gently protested.

Isa waved his hand dismissively. "I'm all the power base you need, my father. There is but a bit of knowledge I must obtain before I take over Turkey. I have spoken with Uncle Luciano, who will procure for me an internship of sorts at the Vatican. I will be working for your friend Cardinal Cross."

"He is a very dangerous man, my son. I would urge you to be constantly on guard around him."

Isa laughed derisively. "I am quite sure he poses no threat to me. I must get into the Western religious mindset. It's time for me to examine the work he has done for Uncle Luciano and to absorb all the knowledge he has gained."

"Has the cardinal been told you will work with him?" Kurtoglu asked cautiously.

"Uncle Luciano is taking care of it right now."

As much as Kurtoglu loved his son and disliked Cross, he couldn't help but feel a hint of compassion for the cardinal—and relief that Isa would not be taking control of Turkey for the moment.

At the papal offices, Chris went about his duties as secretary to the new pope. When the former pope died in the mid-part of the first decade in the new century, Chris was convinced his service in Rome had come to an end. In fact, Benny had told him as much. Considering the time Benny had spent in personal appearances on the pope's behalf, he was convinced that he was destined to be the next pope. But even someone as studied in intrigue as Benny couldn't anticipate the power of the Holy Spirit in the papal selection process.

Luciano had sufficiently bribed the cardinals who could be influenced, and they formed a faction that stood for Benny. Nonetheless, many of the older Western European cardinals took the stand that they would rather die than see an American pope. After all, hadn't we just had a Slavic pope? Where would the indignity end? This group stood behind Bruno di Pasquale, a sinister-looking little Italian cardinal who had been involved in the banking scandals of the 1980s. The factions within the College of Cardinals broke into long debate. Then almost on a whim, someone nominated the bookish president of the Pontifical Biblical Commission, longtime friend of the recently deceased pope. Many of those voting cast their ballot for this unassuming man to show their displeasure with Benny or Bruno, never suspecting he actually would be elected. But when the votes were counted, the world had a new pope.

As the previous pope's friend, the new pope valued the service Chris had provided, and he understood the wisdom of keeping Benny on a short leash. He set up his government with a new camerlengo, an old friend he trusted with his life, but he made Chris the papal secretary. In effect, both men provided the services Chris had previously performed. Benny retained his former position, but the new pope's health and vigor meant he had few obligations and a virtually nonexistent job.

For Chris, it was a welcome relief. He enjoyed Father Hans Kreutzer, the new camerlengo, and his reduced schedule allowed him the time to enjoy life a bit, particularly in time spent with Gabe's kids.

"I have your schedule for the day, Holiness," Chris said cheerily as he handed the pontiff a cover sheet of daily appointments attached to a binder of briefing notes for each meeting.

"Thank you, Chris," the pontiff said brightly. "Would you do me the honor of sitting with me a few moments?"

"It would be my pleasure, Holiness."

The pope began tenuously. "I am told you know much about the eschatology espoused by the American Protestants."

"Yes, Holiness," Chris said quietly. His viewpoint that the world was spinning into the end times predicted by the Bible flew in the face of an allegorical view of Scripture popular within the Church since the time of St. Augustine. He braced himself for a tough conversation.

The pope looked at Chris with a twinkle in his eye, as if he were about to divulge a great secret. "Relax, Chris. I've spent my life studying Scripture, and current events have persuaded me that some of Augustine's arguments may have proven over time not to be sound."

Chris returned the pope's gaze. "Particularly as they relate to Israel, Holiness."

"Exactly," the pope said with a twinkle in his eye. "The belief that the promises given to Israel were transferred to the Church was a concept that fit Augustine's worldview. But now, against all odds, Israel has been reborn, just as the prophets foretold. In the past, the Vatican has chosen to see this as a political event, unrelated to the will of God, but the miracle of Israel's rebirth has occurred against *all* odds."

"Exactly, Holiness."

"I don't have to tell you that my hold over the College of Cardinals is precarious at best, Chris. For me to come out and disavow St. Augustine, I would be overturning centuries of Catholic belief. Nonetheless, I feel compelled to follow this line of study. If we are indeed in the days predicted of old, I fear the vast majority of the Vatican will choose an unfortunate path. But what of the billion Catholics who are insulated from the Vatican's court of intrigue? Don't they deserve to be made ready to meet their Savior?" The pope waved his arms, unable to contain the joy of even thinking about seeing Jesus face to face.

"Yes, Holiness," Chris said with a tear in his eye. "They do indeed."

"Then we have a task before us." The pope pressed his intercom buzzer, and Hans entered.

"Hans, it would appear that our new friend, Chris, agrees with us."

Hans smiled broadly at Chris.

"From now on, I am asking you to take on the full responsibilities of camerlengo as well as secretary. Chris will further study this eschatological view and make suggestions as to how we can adapt the catechism and liturgy to prepare our members to meet the Lord."

"But, Holy Father, the Curia," Chris began to say.

The pope cut him off. "The Curia will not burden itself with items so mundane as the readings selected for Mass. They view me as a biblical egghead, and they're more than happy to let me putter with Scripture," the pope said to the chuckles of Chris and Hans.

The pope continued with a grin. "That view will help me prepare our sheep right under their noses. They will be happy to leave biblical and liturgical changes to me while they plot their New World Order."

The men exchanged glances. In the confines of this office, it was a foregone conclusion that the planet was rushing inexorably toward world government. The wealth, power, and political might of the world's elite were too strong to be challenged. If these indeed were the end times, there would be no stopping their preordained rise to power. Those facts didn't stop the pope from trying to hand them a hollow victory.

Chris smiled at the logic. "So, Holiness, while they're building a larger sheep pen, we'll rescue the flock from them."

"Absolutely!" The pontiff laughed. "But we have to make the most of the time we have, gentlemen. If St. Malachy's prophecies are correct, I may well be the last legitimately elected pope in history. We have a great burden and little time to turn a huge ship."

"Holiness, I have told you of my family situation. You know Gabe is a Protestant minister who has written several popular books on the subject. May I approach him for information?"

"Be my guest, Chris. I suspect his familial loyalty is just what we need to stay under the radar."

"That is fortunate, Holiness, because Gabe is in Rome right now."

"Then by all means, Chris, bring him to visit. I think you and I are about to have an old-time Bible study with your adopted son."

Gabe had mixed emotions about Chris's request. He knew he had to accede to it, but it bothered him. There was a feeling of being summoned by the pontiff … not something he found too palatable. Yet he trusted Chris.

"So the pope wants me to kind of do a class on Protestant eschatology?" Gabe asked, dumbfounded by the request.

Chris shrugged in a "can-you-believe-it?" expression and then grinned broadly. "Listen, just like you and me he senses we may be heading into the end times. But he wasn't raised in the culture or influence of the American Protestants."

"He has so much at his disposal, Chris. Why does he need me?" Gabe asked uncomfortably.

"Every move he makes is watched. Do you think he can just call up Billy Graham and set up a meeting without the whole world knowing about it?"

"So what if the whole world knows?"

"Gabe, sit down. I'm going to tell you some things I've never told anyone before."

Gabe braced himself as Chris drew a deep breath and then said, "The pope is a strong man of God, but the most powerful members of the Curia, the guys who run the Vatican, well, that's a different story. In almost any way you could imagine, the pope really is their prisoner."

"But he's an autocrat," Gabe countered with little vehemence. He had heard rumors in Protestant circles about corruption in the Vatican. Out of defense and love of both Chris and Michael, he never gave serious consideration to the rumors, but in the back of his mind, there was always Benny. Were there more like him trying to overtake the Vatican?

"The Curia is hell-bent on the formation of a New World Order. They'll kill any pope who gets in their way."

Gabe whistled as he pondered the gravity of Chris's revelation. Even though he had heard as much before, hearing it from an insider's perspective—from someone he loved and trusted as much as Chris—lent stunning clarity to the situation. "So if the pope publicly renounced centuries of thought that began with Augustine in favor of a more restrictive and less inclusive reading of Scripture—"

Chris finished the thought. "He would never live long enough to make such an announcement."

"Wow!" Gabe exclaimed. "Do you mean to tell me this place is *that* corrupt?"

Chris breathed deeply, and his face colored as if he were trying to hold back strong emotion. He put one hand on Gabe's shoulder, looked him squarely in the eye, and said, "It's not just the Curia or the Vatican, Gabe. It's everywhere. These people have infiltrated every government, every corporation. My father found some secret information about the

US government and never lived to tell anyone about it." Chris winced thinking about it.

Gabe had no words, only a physical response to the pain in Chris's eyes. He grabbed the older man and hugged him hard. He never knew Chris had waged a lonely, personal battle against an implacable evil since he was a teenager. How much must it have hurt to carry that kind of pain in silence all these years? Finally, he said, "Do you want to talk about it?"

Chris pushed away and brushed a tear from his eye. "I'm okay, but I'll say this, Gabe. These people are everywhere, and they're dangerous. They can and *have* taken out presidents and popes."

Gabe sat slowly as he thought about the implications. He had to help Chris and the pope. He would do anything for Chris. But what would be the cost? He asked Chris what he could bring to the table. "So what does the pope want to hear from me?"

"The bad guys are so busy building their kingdom that they have little interest in the devotional life of the rank-and-file Catholic. We want to tweak the readings at Mass and suggested sermons to educate the Church's body of believers—right under the Curia's noses. They think Bible prophecy is pathetic fiction anyway. They couldn't care less if the worldwide Church suddenly starts to spend weeks studying the letters to the Thessalonians."

In the bowels of the earth, far below Chris and Gabe, Michael sat as the head of his group in the secret Vatican science facility reviewing notes with his staff. If they were right, the disc's body of knowledge was more than a compilation of science and literature from a now-dead advanced civilization. There was a subtext that lent itself to fascinating studies of the nature of matter and the universe. If Michael was right, the Ancients had literally mastered inter-dimensional travel. In their universe, Mars was no farther away than Paris. Michael had found it strange at first, but the more he worked with the scientists, the more he understood that the things we call spiritual are really extra-dimensional. Covert Vatican science operations, in conjunction with some trustworthy scientists in Geneva, had used his findings to achieve near instantaneous transportation of molecules to and from Mars. This technology would work on Earth as well. At some point in the future, people would simply walk into an elevator-sized room and exit wherever they chose. Of course only the Church's control of the technology could ensure that it would be used strictly for peaceful purposes.

But now he had to adjust his thinking all over again. There were compelling patterns in the way information was organized on the ancient disc, structure he had not previously perceived. The latest thinking from Michael's group was that the information was holographic in nature. In other words, the text was not only linear but also three-dimensional.

"How long would it take us to develop the right program to read the data in three dimensions?" Michael asked Kurt Waldenbaum, who now worked for him.

Kurt offered with the slightest trace of a German accent. "The volume of data would be enormous. Fortunately, the Vatican is in possession of one of the world's most powerful supercomputers."

"Yes, but will the boys downstairs give us unfettered access to it?" Michael asked, referring to a group of techies who carefully guarded their time on the computer.

"I think the answer to that question is to involve them more intimately with the project." Kurt stared at Michael, indicating that the subject should be discussed outside the larger group. After a few moments, Michael dismissed the staff but asked Kurt to stay.

Michael understood well that they needed the use of the supercomputer. But supercomputers need supercomputer programmers. A small group of experts with little skin in the game were bound to be a security threat. They had to protect this information at all costs.

"Kurt, those computer jockeys don't have the clearance or the discretion we need on this project. Is there a way to ensure their compliance with our rules of secrecy?"

Kurt thought a second before gravely saying, "For years, various governmental agencies throughout the world have had great success with wiping clean the memories of former agents. I have contacts—"

"But we can't keep these guys here twenty-four-seven," Michael countered.

"We may not need to," Kurt said with a barely perceptible grin. He continued in a conspiratorial tone. "We could create in them alternate personalities that could literally be switched off whenever they leave the facility."

"Kind of like Manchurian Candidate technology?" Michael asked, going back to sci-fi movies of his youth.

"Yes," Kurt said gravely, "but creation of the alternate personality requires about a week of rigorous physical training in a drug-induced state." Kurt's knowledgeable look betrayed his euphemistic use of terms.

"And by rigorous physical training, you mean …?" Michael asked cautiously.

"Inflicting sufficient pain and fear to cause a fragmentation of the psyche."

Michael winced at the thought of torturing these men for a solid week. This decision put him in a very uncomfortable position. How could he forego the opportunity to bring such incredible knowledge to light? But the knowledge could be dangerous in the wrong hands; it had to be protected. If a compromised programmer sold the information to any government or rogue organization, the rest of the world could be put seriously at risk. Michael didn't know for sure, but he assumed the creators of the disc had suffered their demise in just this way. He wasn't about to make the same mistake … yet his mind ached at the thought of doing harm to the programmers. His only hope was for them to bear momentary pain with no lasting scars. He asked, "Will they remember the—how did you phrase it—the 'rigorous physical training' once the process is complete?"

"No, sir. It will be lost to them for the most part. The alternate personality will retain some of the fear, however, as a motivator."

Michael took comfort from the fact that they would have no memories of their conditioning, but he needed to know the lasting effects. "What are the effects to the main personality?"

"There is usually a deadening affect. They will be less humorous, less amorous, and less excitable. With this particular group of computer-nerds, I submit to you that the aftereffects will be hardly noticeable," Kurt answered callously.

"So, then," Michael summed it up, "if we are to unlock the secrets of the universe, we'll have to make five guys uncomfortable for a week, a week that they won't even remember." He drew a deep breath and continued in a grim tone of resignation. "Considering the potential benefits to the whole world, it's a trade we have to make. Is that what you're saying?"

"I would think, Father," Kurt said with a satisfied grin.

"Then do it," Michael said with hesitation, hoping he wouldn't live to regret it.

"There will be several million dollars in costs, for the drugs and the instruments to be used in the physical regimen," Kurt said. "Given the nature of the project, it would be unwise to requisition the equipment through traditional channels ..."

"I have access to funds," Michael said decisively. "How much will you need?"

"Ten million dollars should cover everything we need, as well as ensure the silence of our vendors."

"Fine." Michael rubbed his forehead as if he could wipe away the responsibility for the decision. "Where do we stand on the manuscript?"

"As you know, the curing process should be nearly complete by now. The fibers used in the document will pass any carbon-fourteen test as being true to the first century CE. Everything will be ready for you to discover the manuscript within the next few months."

"Fantastic!" Michael exclaimed. "Well done, Kurt."

As Kurt left the conference room, Michael battled his conscience. But the thoughts were outweighed by the chance to finally definitively see into the most awesome time capsule ever found. And if administered correctly, the disc's information could usher in a new golden age for the planet.

"My father speaks highly of you," Isa Kurtoglu said through a smile to Benny.

Benny was instantly mesmerized by the charm and handsomeness of the young man. He knew without a doubt he would do whatever the man wanted. "Your father and I are old friends." Benny drooled. "I was there when you were presented to him."

"I remember," Isa said. "The Lady wanted a ceremony the imams would never forget."

"I think she achieved her purposes." Benny felt himself getting lost in those eyes. The conversation continued. He knew he was participating in the banter, but his brain was somewhere else. He felt the young man probing his brain. Then he lost all sense of time and space as Isa led his mind down the most graphic fantasy he could ever imagine. In the fantasy, this beautiful young man from the stars pleasured him over and over. Benny was helpless to do anything but moan aloud.

Benny became suddenly aware of his surroundings. Young Isa was still talking to him as if nothing had happened, but somehow Benny knew the young man had been present in the fantasy. Using a handkerchief to wipe the sweat from his brow, Benny did his best to pick up the conversation. "How long do you envision staying with us?"

"I am a quick study," Isa said. "I don't think I should need to be here more than a couple of months."

"Wonderful," Benny said looking into the crystal blue eyes. Let me show you where you will sit." Benny led the man into the hallway.

Gabe was exceedingly nervous. He had the chance to bring the message of Christ's imminent return to the pope ... *the pope*, for crying out loud! How strange would it be if the pope himself espoused an eschatological view that not even all American Protestants embraced! On the other hand, Gabe could blow it with a poor presentation, or improper execution. The stakes felt enormous.

"Will you relax?" Chris commented as they walked down the ornate hallway toward the papal offices.

"I can't, Chris. This is unnerving," Gabe complained as he raked his hand through his thick hair.

"Listen. He's a very nice man, and he's eager to hear what you have to say. There's not even a chance it will be contentious."

"That's good to hear," Gabe said. He paused for a moment before voicing a fresh concern. "He's not going to throw a bunch of Latin terms at me, is he? Like *incubus succubus est*?"

"Certainly not those words." Chris laughed. "I promise to interpret any Latin, on the rare chance he uses any. You have to remember that the pope is also a polished statesman. His congeniality, kind nature, and understanding of the world are all going to surprise you."

As they got to the door of the papal offices, Gabe pulled up short. "Do I look okay? Is my tie straight?"

"You look fine, even without Tina here to dress you." Chris winked.

At that moment, Benny led an incredibly handsome young man into the hallway.

"Gabe, what are you doing here?" Benny asked with surprise. Gabe looked to Chris to answer.

"His Holiness heard Gabe was in town and asked to meet him," Chris said with a sheepish grin. "I guess I talk about Gabe's kids a lot."

"Well, let's hope His Holiness isn't disappointed," Benny said smugly.

Gabe had no time to react to Benny's put-down. He nearly felt faint in Isa's presence. It was as if the man was totally evil, yet there was something about him ... the eyes! His eyes reminded Gabe of Michael's.

"He won't be disappointed," Chris said distractedly as he stared uncomfortably at Isa. "Hi. I'm Father Chris," he said as he hesitantly extended his hand.

"Isa Kurtoglu," the young man said as he took Chris's hand.

"I'm sorry," Benny said entirely to Isa. "I should have introduced you. Chris acts as a sort of secretary to the pope, and he is an old friend of my family. And this is my sister's ward, Gabriel."

Gabe shook his head and frowned. "Neither of us likes to admit it, but I'm his nephew."

"Isa will be my intern for the next few months," Benny said proudly. "His father is the prime minister of Turkey. Sort of a diplomatic internship."

"I am sure the cardinal will prove to be a most excellent teacher," Isa said solicitously.

Gabe opened his mouth to speak, but Chris cut him off. "I'm sure he will. It's always an honor to entertain foreign dignitaries."

"Well, we must be off," Benny said, ushering Isa down the hallway.

"Must be," Gabe agreed, scowling at his erstwhile uncle.

There was no time to ponder the strangeness of the encounter. Chris opened the door to the pope's suite of offices and ushered him in.

Gabe wanted to gasp as he entered the expansive papal office. The ornate murals and antique furniture conveyed a sense of agelessness that was hard to find in the New World. This office had been in use for centuries and swam with the memories, foils, and victories of countless men through the ages.

The pope was not seated behind his desk but on one of two facing couches near a bank of windows overlooking the Papal Gardens. Winter sunlight danced through the windows to flood the room in a golden glow.

"Ah, Chris," the pope said as he stood to greet his guest. From the perspective of protocol, this was a high honor, and the pontiff's way of signifying that the visit was to be viewed as an informal gathering of friends.

"Holy Father, it is a pleasure to meet you," Gabe said.

The pope extended his hand. "And I am honored you have accepted my request for a meeting," he said. "Please sit. We are here as friends and brothers in Christ. Let's forgo all protocol," he said with a wink. "It's very boring, you know."

Gabe instantly liked the self-deprecating man of God. He and Chris sat opposite the aging patriarch, not knowing exactly how to begin.

"It is a pleasure to meet the father of those beautiful children Chris brags about," the pope said with a warm smile.

"They're a handful, but we love them dearly." Gabe smiled.

"It's nice to see so much good can come from a family that produced Cardinal Cross," the pope said with a smirk. It caught Gabe and Chris totally off guard, and they laughed heartily.

The pope continued, "Please see me as a friend, fellows. I think you may find I have many similar views to yours." The pontiff pressed a buzzer and a tray of coffee and pastries was immediately brought into the room.

"So how do we begin?" the pope asked with a sip of his coffee. "Let's give the proper accolades to St. Augustine for the very many good things he brought to Christianity, but let's assume he may have been remiss in his viewpoint that biblical prophecies should be viewed allegorically."

"That's a very good place to start, Holiness," Chris said. "In his day, the Church was the sanctioned religion of the state. Rulers were wary of an eschatological view in which Jesus comes to eliminate earthly governments."

"And if I may," Gabe interjected, "in his day, it didn't look as if Israel would ever be formed again as a nation."

"An excellent point as well," the pontiff said. "Augustine drew some very logical conclusions considering his worldview, but now we have the benefit of hindsight, do we not? Israel is indeed a nation again, and the human condition is still as pitiful as ever. Evil is afoot in this world, gentlemen, and it is easily seen from the unique perspective of my office.

"So then how do we explain the seventy weeks of years described in Daniel 9?" the pope asked, referring to Daniel's prophecy that only 70 weeks of years, 490 years, remained in God's dealings with Israel. "Surely more than 490 years has passed since the prophecy was given."

The question played to Gabe's field of expertise, and he rose to the occasion. "Sir, the answer to that question lies in the very same chapter. Daniel tells us that after sixty-nine weeks of years, the Messiah will be cut off—killed—but not for His own sake. We were told in a forthright manner that Jesus would be executed for our sakes after sixty-nine weeks had passed. Then there are, if you will bear with me, parentheses of sorts. The time clock stops to allow for the Church Age, the Age of Grace, while the Messiah prepares His bride. But for Israel—and remember that Daniel's prophecy speaks specifically to Israel—there are seven years left to be fulfilled."

"And you call those seven years the tribulation period," the pope said, "as described by St. John?"

"Exactly, Holiness," Chris said.

"With the understanding that it refers to a specific period of time covered by a peace treaty in the Middle East," Gabe lectured. "The second half of that period is when war, persecution, and famine ravage the world. This is the great tribulation Jesus spoke of."

"I see," the pope said carefully as if mentally cataloguing the information. "So then how are we to know when the time clock will again begin to tick for Israel?"

"The consensus is that the clock will begin to tick again when Israel signs a peace accord lasting seven years."

The pope sighed. “The world would jump at the prospect of true peace in the Middle East.”

“And they will, sir,” Gabe continued. “The world will fall at the feet of the man who brings peace to the Middle East. He will first be considered a hero, but ultimately a god.”

“The Antichrist,” Chris said somberly, “the beast of revelation.”

“And the blasphemous little horn described by Daniel,” Gabe added.

The pope summed his concern. “It seems so much hinges on the proper interpretation of Daniel’s prophecy. If only we could know we are reading it correctly.”

“We can know that, sir,” Gabe said with conviction. “I’ve brought a chart you may find enlightening.” Gabe reached into his briefcase to pull out a briefing packet he intended to leave with the Holy Father.

“I am indebted to an American scholar named Chuck Missler for this analysis and to the Scottish scholar from the turn of the twentieth century, Sir Robert Anderson. I’ve included a bibliography of their work at the end of this briefing packet if you would care to see more of their views.”

Gabe flipped through the briefing packet to find the appropriate page. He then handed it to the pope and continued. “Notice that the text of Daniel 9:25 reads as follows: ‘Know therefore and understand, that from the going forth of the commandment to restore and to build Jerusalem unto the Messiah the King shall be seven weeks and threescore and two weeks; the street shall be built again, and the wall, even in troublous times.’ Sixty-nine weeks of years equates to 483 years. As you may well know, in Old Testament times the year was measured as 360 days. If you do the math, you will see the prophecy predicts the presentation of the Messiah 173,880 days following the commandment to restore Jerusalem. Artaxerxes Longimanus issued that commandment on May 14, 445 BC. If you add the days to this date, it leaves you with April 6, 32 AD, which happens to be the presumed date of Jesus’ triumphal entry into Jerusalem.”

“Palm Sunday,” Chris interjected. “And this is why, before that date, Jesus asked people not to declare him King or Messiah because ‘My hour has not yet come.’ But on Palm Sunday, He allowed them to do it.”

"Because His exact day and hour had come, as predicted," the pontiff said softly, in awe at the precision of the prophecy.

"Exactly," Gabe said.

"But there is no such numbering of days to indicate when the last seven years will come upon us," the pope commented.

"No, Holiness," Chris said. "Remember, the Lord said no one knows the day or the hour."

"But in the same passages, we are commanded to know the *season* of His return," Gabe interjected.

"The parable of the fig tree." The pope nodded. "But if we are to take these scriptures literally—and I must admit the evidence you present is compelling—then we are in for a time of horrible plagues and disasters on Earth."

Gabe moved to sit next to the pope as he pointed to other sections of his briefing packet. "They will come to pass, sir, but there is also strong biblical evidence that the Lord may remove His people from the time of judgment to come on the world. In St. Jerome's Latin Vulgate, there is a word, *rapire*, from which we get the word 'rapture.' Rapture, or *harpazo* in the Greek, literally means to snatch away. Some believe the Lord will rapture His people to safety prior to the tragedies."

"I know of this belief," the pope said, "but even many American Protestants admit this belief only came into existence during the last century."

"With all due respect, sir, the briefing packet shows quotes from teachings and sermons of the early Church fathers who espoused this belief," Gabe commented as he flipped through the briefing packet to a page of quotes. "The idea became a matter of much public attention in the last century, but the belief is traceable the entire way back to St. Paul."

The pontiff continued the thought. "Which would bring us then to the letters written to the Thessalonians."

"Yes, Holiness," Chris added. "In those letters, St. Paul examines the mystery that at one point in time, we who are alive will be transformed to glorious bodies, and we will meet the resurrected dead in Christ in the air, on our way to Him."

"For centuries, some very capable scholars have indicated that this is to happen *just prior* to the final judgment," the pope said.

"From the ancient perspective of the prophets, looking forward in time, the rapture and final judgment may indeed seem to be one event because they are separated by a very short period of time ..."

"The tribulation," the pope said, finishing Gabe's thought.

"Precisely, Holiness," Chris commented.

"How can we know this?" the pope asked, looking over the top of his reading glasses.

"The Jewish scholars also saw prophecy in the patterns of the Scripture," Gabe said. "Looking to Noah, Lot, and others throughout Scripture, an argument can be made that the Lord removes His people out of harm's way when He is about to administer holy judgment."

The pope shook his head and paused for a moment as he flipped through the briefing packet. After a few moments, he asked, "Even among Protestants, the timing of the rapture is disputed, is it not?"

"Yes, sir," Gabe said. "There are those who believe it will occur in the midst of the seven-year period, just prior to the great tribulation that Jesus talks of, and others who believe it will occur at the end of the tribulation."

"For the sake of our sheep, I pray you are right and that He delivers us from the evil to come as an answer to countless men and women of God praying The Our Father through the centuries."

The meeting continued for hours as Gabe and Chris took the pontiff through the Scriptures to enforce their claims. Finally, Hans entered the room to advise the pope of an upcoming appointment. The pope warmly hugged his brothers in Christ, and Hans led them from the office.

After the door closed, the pope opened a golden box and removed a single sheet of paper. In 1917, three Portuguese children had received visions that they related as three "secrets." The first two involved the first and second world wars. The third secret was sealed—with the instruction that it was to be opened and publicly proclaimed by the reigning pope in 1960. Pope John XXIII read it, turned ashen, and decided not to reveal its contents. Since then, each pope maintained the secret before him in this golden box.

The pope wept silently as the words of the third secret of Fatima flooded over him, not refuting but confirming the scriptural points raised by Chris and Gabe. What tragedy awaited an unsuspecting world!

The limo ride from the airport was surprisingly quick. Rather than go straight to the hotel, Kim and Tina decided to surprise the guys at the papal offices. The Swiss Guard, who never forget a face, immediately sent the family, with an escort, to Chris's office.

As the family walked down the hallway, Chris and Gabe were exiting the pope's offices.

"Daddy!" both kids yelled. They ran to their surprised father, who went down to his knees to hug them.

"You are a sight for sore eyes," Gabe said to Tina as he kissed her.

The kids moved from Gabe to Grandpa Chris for hugs and kisses.

Gabe hugged Tina and Kim. "This has been the most amazing day," he said to them.

"It's about to get more amazing," Chris called from behind him. They turned to see the children staring up at the pontiff.

"I don't wish to interrupt a family time," the pope said with a smile, "merely to share it. It seems like a long while since I have been around children who see me as only a nice old man. Would you please come into my office for a few moments?"

The adults followed in stunned silence as the kids ran into the pope's office. The pope had candy and hot chocolate brought in for the children as he returned a small gold box to his desk. The adults were served espresso.

"So are you Grandpa Chris's boss?" young Chris asked.

"Yes." The pope smiled. "And I can assure you he is one of my most valuable employees."

"Sir, we don't want to take up your time," Gabe said apologetically.

"And you won't," the pope said with a slight wink to Tina. "*Signora*, I must tell you I accused Chris of bragging about your children, but I was remiss. They appear to be as wonderful as he claims."

"Thank you," Tina said awkwardly, not knowing how exactly to address the pope.

"Sir," Michele asked the pope, "what's your name?"

"You can just call me Papa; a lot of people do," the pontiff said with a Santa Claus grin, as the little girl crawled into his lap. She lay her head back against his chest and fell instantly asleep.

"Let me take her from you, Holiness," Kim said. "I'm afraid the children didn't sleep very well on the flight from the United States." She gently lifted the girl from the pope's arms and cuddled her. Young Chris settled on Grandpa Chris's lap to watch with heavy eyes.

"I think we should get these kids to the hotel for a nap," Gabe said with a smile.

"If you wait just a second," the pope said, "I've arranged for some assistance with the children."

"That is so thoughtful, but it really isn't necessary," Tina began.

Hans entered the room and whispered something in the pope's ear, to which he replied, "By all means, show him in."

Michael entered the room with obvious trepidation at being summoned to the papal offices. "Holiness, you sent for me?" he asked with confusion.

"Yes, Michael. I was hoping you could assist this fine family to their hotel," he said over the sounds of Michael hugging and kissing his mother and sister-in-law.

"You sure know how to scare a fellow away from his work!" he exclaimed to the pope with bemused exasperation.

In German, the pope said, "This is where you belong, my son. Don't follow in the ways of your uncle."

Michael froze for a second and looked at the pope with questioning eyes.

"One day you must show me what keeps you so busy, Father Michael," the pope said in English.

"Yes, Holiness," the young priest said with downcast eyes.

"But for now, you will enjoy this wonderful family the Lord has provided to you."

"Yes, Holiness," Michael answered with a crooked smile.

Young Chris scampered from Grandpa Chris's lap to hug his uncle

Michael. Michael swept the boy into his arms and kissed him. Gabe took Michele from Kim, and the family moved toward the door. The pope hugged each of them, thanked them for the visit, and asked them to visit again.

Michael and Gabe were on either side of their mother as the group left the pope's offices. Kim said, "We need to stop by Benny's office. He doesn't even know we're here."

Gabe rolled his eyes at Michael and Tina as they followed after Chris and Kim to Benny's office. Kim knocked softly on Benny's open office door.

He looked up with a smile and said, "Kim! What are you doing here?"

"Tina and the kids were really missing Gabe, so we decided to take a long weekend."

"What a great surprise!" he said as he made his way around the desk to hug his only sister.

"Hi, Benny," Tina said as she entered the room.

"You remember Tina," Gabe snapped. "She's your sister's ward's wife." Tina gave Gabe a "not now" stare before giving Benny a hug. Gabe shut up.

"She's got to teach me how to do that." Michael grinned at his brother.

"You wouldn't know what to do with me if I started weighing my words around you." Gabe chuckled.

"Excuse me," a young, handsome man said as he made his way through the group.

"Oh, Kim," Benny said. "You have to meet this most remarkable young man. Isa, come here please."

Isa pushed past the brothers. Michael caught the young man's eye for a second and lost control of his thoughts. For a moment, he was in the alien craft with the Lady, watching the birth of an infant.

His consciousness returned to the present as the young man grinned knowingly and said, "Excuse me, Father."

"Kim, this is Isa Kurtoglu. His father is the prime minister of Turkey. He will be my diplomatic intern for a couple months."

"It is a pleasure to meet you, Mrs. ..."

"You can just call me Kim."

Michael knew his mother well. He could see she was loath to offer him her hand. *She feels it too!*

"So what is my brother going to teach you?" she asked courteously.

Isa sighed and said in a studious manner, "The Vatican has tremendous diplomatic power despite its small size and theocratic form of government. I hope to learn how it manages this feat." Isa flashed a perfect smile that seemed to glow against his swarthy complexion. "And there is always the hope that I will make a good impression. My country would greatly enjoy Vatican support of its application to join the European Union."

"Are you sure you still want to join the EU, considering how its economies have been weakened by the subprime mortgage debacle?" Michael asked, looking closely into the eyes that were identical to his own.

Isa said reflectively, "The Western economies have been shaken to be sure, but not so much that my country would not act on an invitation to join the EU."

"That's very interesting," Michael commented absently. Could the Lady have been real after all? He shuddered at the thought.

"I am glad you think so. I hear you are involved in some very interesting archeological work from my area of the world. I would love to sit with you, to learn of your discoveries." Isa smiled again, and Michael's knees buckled ever so slightly. He had become very practiced at diversion when asked about his work. He was about to offer some offhanded comment about his schedule being too tight to accommodate an interview, but something prevented it. It was as if he wanted to please this young man, despite his conscious desire to do nothing of the sort.

"It would be an honor, Mr. Kurtoglu." Michael heard himself respond.

Throughout the brief conversation, Chris shifted his stance uncomfortably and coughed repeatedly. *He feels it too!* Michael thought.

Chris said, "Well, Benny, these kids aren't babies anymore. I'm sure they're getting heavy for Gabe and Michael. We really should get them to bed. We'll leave the two of you to carry on."

They said their good-byes. Michael bristled when Isa shook his hand and said, "It was nice to meet you, *Father*."

THIRTEEN

Fran sat on the couch as David pointed the remote and turned on the TV. She wondered why she put herself through the aggravation.

The show was winding down as Zach smiled broadly and looked into the camera for the final product pitch. "And be sure to get a copy of our new book, *Your Greatest Life Ever.* Gloria and I worked hard to bring you daily meditations to keep you strong in your faith." Stirring music began a crescendo in the background. "Once you release the power of these messages into your life, there will be no stopping you. You won't have to look for it; wealth will find you. Your illnesses will melt before your growing awareness of who you are in God. Isn't that right, Gloria?"

"Zack, I have to tell you, I think these words have a power in their own right." Gloria shook her head as if she couldn't believe the incredible blessings available for purchase. "I know you and I wrote them, but even *I am* blessed daily by meditating on them." She gushed, turning to the camera. "Ladies, if you want a happy home, a devoted husband, and loving children, you have to get this book. Each day opens a new treasure of insight and hope you can use to create the greatest life you can."

Zack put his arm around Gloria's waist and moved his face close to hers in the camera shot. "Gloria, I wish everyone could find the happiness we have. Why, there is no problem too big or too small that we can't overcome with a blessed attitude," Zack said through his broad smile.

"I'm even embarrassed to admit it, Zack, but one day last week I found a gray hair." She paused as Zack pulled away to ape a shocked expression, and then continued. "Now I know it's silly to worry about stuff like that, but I've learned to cast my cares on the Lord. I spoke to that nasty old gray hair and told it to get in line with all the others. I said, 'Don't you dare try to make me unattractive to my husband! I rebuke anything that would try to enter our home and make it less than perfect!'"

"Aww," Zack said, grinning to the camera, "you did that for me?"

"Turn it off," Fran said to David, referring to the program. "Tom would be mortified. His little girl has turned into a snake-oil salesman."

"I won't lie to you," David said. "It's not the most anointed preaching I've ever heard, but maybe there's still something redeemable in what they do."

"This beloved little girl of a missionary is on her way to becoming a billionaire by selling hackneyed formulas to curse gray hair—at worst, she's promoting witchcraft, at best she's *selling* the Gospel. What is redeemable about that?"

"Well, they have quite a following, so there must be something about their message that resonates with people. And they do believe in Jesus and salvation. Maybe we're the ones who are behind the times."

"Do you really believe that?" she asked with exasperation.

"Not really," he admitted softly. His eyes were downcast. "I'm trying to find some good there. To tell the truth, Zack has always annoyed me, but I think Gloria's a great kid. The girl we know isn't like the spokeswoman-model we see on television. She's much more genuine in real life."

"I agree on that point. When I'm with her, she doesn't seem like the glitzy-ditsy she portrays on television." Fran moved to the kitchen to pour a cup of coffee. David followed.

"Then concentrate on the girl we know and love," David said, "because I want to have a peaceful visit with them." They packed the car and drove off to Gloria's home.

Within a couple of hours, they were driving on the terra cotta pavers around the front fountain and came to a stop at the twenty-foot tall double doors at the entrance of Gloria and Zack's new mansion.

Gloria strolled through the double doors to greet them. "Mom, I feel really bad you and David drove all the way here when I could have sent one of our jets for you!" she exclaimed as they exited their car.

It was their first visit to the new "house"—a thirty-room mansion on the Gulf of Mexico. Done in pinkish-tan stucco with huge, white, wooden window frames and doors, it looked more Caribbean than Texan. There was every appointment, every modern convenience, and a private beach. Some of the funds for the striking edifice came from Mack and Sarah's life insurance policies. Zack had been devastated when letters to his parents were returned unopened. It was as if they had just disappeared from their retirement on Grand Cayman. After waiting the prescribed seven-year period, Zack had no alternative but to have them declared dead.

"Gloria, it's beautiful," Fran said over and over as they toured the home. Each room had been decorated as if it was from a previous time. The woodwork was ornate. The high ceilings had gold filigree and frescoes at their center. The huge staircase in the foyer reminded her of *The Sound of Music*. Fran was disappointed to see that, for all of the planning, there was no space set apart for the Lord, like the chapel on Kim's estate.

"Sweetheart, don't you think it's a bit much for just the two of you?" Fran asked gently as she felt David tug slightly at her sleeve.

"What's that supposed to mean, Mother?" Gloria snapped.

"Nothing, Gloria. It was a simple question," Fran responded tersely.

"Well, the answer is no. I *don't* think it's too much, if it's what the Lord wants to give me. Who am I to turn down His blessings?"

Fran stared briefly at David, silently conveying her fear that Gloria was actually becoming her TV persona, the Barbie to Zack's Ken. She tried to cover up her previous remark. "Actually, Gloria, you misunderstand me. I was wondering when I'll become a grandmother."

"I don't think I can have kids," Gloria said, letting down her defenses.

"But, Gloria," Fran offered, "Gabe and Tina are working with so many kids who need a good home. And you have so many resources. Imagine the life you could give a child!"

"I don't think I'll ever be able to talk Zack into an adoption," Gloria said sadly.

Fran could see she'd hit a nerve. In the final analysis, her girl was just a lonely prop used by a spoiled, selfish husband. She brushed away a tear forming in her eye and hugged Gloria tightly.

Zack was pouring Gloria a cup of coffee when David walked into the kitchen.

"Did you sleep well, David?"

"Like a rock." David smiled. "That bed is fantastic!"

"Hopefully not too comfortable. We have a bit of a surprise for Fran this morning." Zack grinned.

"What kind of a surprise?" David asked warily.

"Only the best kind," Gloria said. She was wearing a gold suit with an embroidered collar. With it she wore a simple white blouse and gold jewelry. The net effect was simple sophistication. Her hair and makeup were flawless, as they always were when she was on television.

"You look stunning, Gloria," David said, "but I thought the plan was for you and your mom to hang around the house today."

"It is," she said with a giggle as she pulled a bed tray out of the pantry closet. "Is breakfast ready yet?"

"The serving plates are empty," Zack said with a bit of a scowl. "I'm guessing Rosalita is running late again today."

"Hard to get good help these days," Zack said to David with a grin, as the harried Mexican woman rushed into the kitchen and fluttered about the chafing dishes. Within seconds, she had deposited scrambled eggs with cheese, espresso french toast that smelled heavenly, fruit compote, and hot cereal.

Gloria fixed a beautiful plate with french toast, one of Fran's favorites, eggs, and a fresh fruit salad. She deftly cut an orange as garnish, poured a glass of juice, and covered the plate.

"Everything's ready from my end," Gloria said to Zack.

"Just on time," Zack said as he peered out the window. "The camera crew is pulling up now."

The doorbell rang and Zack ran to open it. "Oh my goodness!" he said with surprise that sounded remarkably sincere. "I knew you guys were going to do this. I just didn't think it would start today!" Looking into the camera, he said, "Welcome, brothers and sisters, to a new project we've just initiated." He turned away from the camera to yell back into the house. "Gloria! Come here. We have company!"

Returning to the camera, he said, "Brothers and sisters, a lot of people write to us wondering what our lives are like off-camera. Some people have even accused us of hurting our parishioners by building a fairy-tale existence on TV that real people can't attain. So the other day Gloria had an idea."

"It was more of an inspiration," Gloria announced as she glided across the grand foyer. "I feel strongly in my heart that God wants us to show you what our day-to-day lives are like. So I presented this idea to Zack."

Zack continued the story. "She said, 'Darling, what if we told our film crew to visit us at home—whenever. We won't know when they're coming, and whatever they shoot, that's what we'll show everyone.'"

"Exactly," Gloria said. "We want our lives to be an open book, because we want you to know we are no different from anyone else. We just know how to appropriate the right spiritual principles to gain all the Lord has for us."

"And you can do anything we do," Zack said. "All you need is to know the spiritual principles that unleash the power of heaven into your lives. This isn't a commercial video, so I won't go into the details, but I have a seven-disc series called 'Unlocking Heaven's Gates' that you can get on our website, free to you, with a love gift of seventy dollars." Addressing the film crew, Zack asked, "So now what, guys?"

Off camera, the director said, "Go about what you were doing before we came."

"Okay," Gloria said, as she looked directly into the camera. "We're so blessed today because my dear old mama is visiting us. Her husband, David, is in the kitchen, and I was just preparing a breakfast tray to take to Mama."

David was enjoying his breakfast when the bright lights of the camera shined on him. Seated in shorts and T-shirt, hair uncombed, powdered sugar around his mouth, he made quite an impression. Caught by surprise, he quickly fled the kitchen as the camera followed.

"Oh, enough teasing, David!" Gloria laughed loudly. "He is such a hoot! Come over here, Mr. Cameraman. I want you to see the beautiful breakfast tray I made for my mama. She loves french toast, and I came across a wonderful recipe that uses espresso in the dip. It's delicious, especially when topped with toasted pecans. Oh, my goodness, the pecans!" She opened the oven door to find a cookie sheet filled with perfectly roasted pecans Rosalita had left there. "And let me tell you, they smell as good as they look!"

She sprinkled a few on the french toast, pulled a small pitcher of heated syrup from the microwave, and poured a cup of coffee for the breakfast tray, all while humming *Amazing Grace.*

"Cut," the director said. "Let's get to the actual breakfast-in-bed scene. No matter how much we shoot, this has to edit down to three minutes."

"Oh, right," Zack said as Gloria relaxed her facial muscles.

"I had a couple of the guards detain David," Zack added. "Just to make sure he doesn't spoil your mother's surprise."

The darkness of the bedroom gave way to a sudden burst of light from the camera. Fran awoke with a start to see Gloria in makeup and heels bringing a breakfast tray to her.

"Good morning, Mama!" she sang with a bit more drawl than usual.

"Gloria! What are you doing?" Fran demanded as she pulled the bed covers up to her chin. She had slept soundly but had awakened with a particularly bad case of bed-head. Brushing a stray lock from her face, she stared up at the camera in disbelief.

"I'm bringing breakfast in bed to the most wonderful mama in the world!" Gloria exclaimed.

Fran had to think fast. If she lashed out, it would all be on camera ... and only God knew how Zack and his cronies would edit it. Although she wanted to do nothing more than spank this wayward child of hers, she decided to play along for the camera. "Why, what a surprise, Gloria!" Then looking into the camera, she smiled and said, "It smells delicious. Rosalita must have really gone out of her way. I'll have to thank her."

The camera panned from her to Zack, leaning one shoulder on the doorway, arms crossed and staring lovingly at his mother-in-law. He said softly to the camera, "She's the only mother I have now. I love to spoil her."

Fran had the good sense to ignore the comment. She would play along for Gloria, but she would give nothing to Zack. "Mmmm," she said as she dug into the french toast.

There was an uncomfortable silence as the camera zoomed in on Fran, expecting her to say something. She responded only with taking another bite. Then a sip of coffee.

"So, Mama, it's been a long time since I last made you breakfast in bed!" Gloria squealed as she looked directly into the camera.

"Mmmm," Fran agreed, and smiled broadly. "In fact, I don't remember when you last did this for me. But I can tell you today's breakfast is delicious. My compliments to the chef."

The camera turned to Gloria, who looked at her mother adoringly. "I remember making you breakfast in bed when I was little. Then I'd crawl into the bed and snuggle up to you," Gloria said as she sat gingerly on the side of the bed, her legs crossed at the ankles. She leaned her head back to just touch her mother's shoulder, careful not to muss her hair.

"I remember," Fran said as she pretended to recall events that never happened. "And then I would stroke your hair, and tell you that you were my beautiful little girl." Fran reached up, her hand sticky with syrup and slowly petted her daughter's perfectly quaffed hair.

Gloria smiled at the camera and said lovingly, "Oh, Mama."

"Cut!" the director called.

"You knew you had syrup on your hands when you put them in my hair!" Gloria shrieked at her mother.

Zack hustled the cameraman and director out of the room.

"And you knew I would never want to be awakened with a camera glaring down on me, but you did it anyway, didn't you?" Fran answered in disgust. "Just how many people are you and Zack willing to throw under the bus for this pretense of a ministry, Gloria?"

"How dare you, Mom! When you and Daddy were preaching in Africa, how many were in your church? Fifty to a hundred? How many are in the church you pastor with David? Two hundred? Zack and I are reaching the world, Mom! The entire freaking world!" Gloria paced the room.

"So I'm a failure? Only you and Zack are preaching God's Word?" Fran asked indignantly.

"No. I didn't say that," Gloria said tensely. "But the world has changed a lot. We have to reach people where they are. God wants a lot more from his people. He wants a lot more *for* his people!" Gloria stomped out of the room.

"Oh, Tom," Fran said. "If you can hear me, I'm so sorry for the way she turned out. I must have done something very wrong."

"Don't blame yourself," David said as he entered the room. "If I were to blame anyone, it would be Zack."

"I don't believe what just happened," Fran said as she angrily got out of bed. "David, she used me as a prop for this farce of a ministry!"

"Keep your voice down," David said. "We need to look at this rationally and prayerfully. This is your only child, Fran. Don't let your anger push you into saying or doing something you'll regret later."

"Like going home?" Fran asked as she angrily filled their suitcase.

"Exactly like that," David said as he sat on the bed. "Sit down for a moment and talk to me."

Reluctantly, Fran sat beside him.

"In a perfect world, what would you want for Gloria? How do you see her?" he asked tenderly.

"A woman devoted to Christ, a beautiful mother and wife."

"And your relationship with her?"

"A supportive role, I guess. Sharing recipes, helping to care for her children. Making sure she had time for her husband."

"How would you describe your relationship with her now?"

"She just used me as a prop, David, and I'm upset!"

David said calmly, "Yes, and that was wrong of her. But on a more foundational level, could you also be angry that she doesn't *need* you enough?"

"What do you mean?" Fran asked a bit defensively. She bit her lip. She knew where David was going with this, and she knew he was right.

David continued. "No babysitting. No recipes. No motherly marriage advice. Fran, you have done a good job in raising a very independent, strong-willed woman. Her choices and actions don't line up with your expectations. The question is: Can you love her even though she's not who *you* want her to be?"

"Of course I can! I'm her mother!" She wiped at a tear of self-recrimination.

"Who is considering stomping out of here—out of her only child's life?" he asked softly.

"Okay. Fine. You're right. I'm acting emotionally, and I need to think this through. Do you really think I'm hard on Gloria for not living up to my expectations?"

"I think that's the emotional component. I also think you have some valid concerns about the Christianity she and Zack promote."

"Do you think?" she asked sarcastically.

"Sarcasm aside, Frannie, what would be the rational way to handle a problem like that?"

"Christian love and prayer."

He nodded and took her hand. "The Lord can touch them in ways we can't, Fran. We need to move into serious prayer for them, and we need to ask the Lord to share with us His love for them."

"You're so wise," Fran said, lying her head on his shoulder.

"Not really." David laughed. "I still want to go downstairs and wipe that smug smile off Zack's face."

"Well, I think your first plan will work better, but if you decide to go with the second one, I'll be your 'wing man,'" Fran said with a sad chuckle.

Zack grimaced as he signed off on the wire transfer to Benny's account. They had come up with a dummy charity, Children for Christ. Zack made regular monthly payments to CfC for 10 percent of the earnings of Riverside Ministries. That included donations, book sales, and DVD sales, the whole operation. In 2008, Zack crossed the five million dollar threshold for donations to CfC. But, he mused, there would be no income stream if he hadn't found a way to take control of the ministry. Benny was part of that, and he got a cut. It was that simple.

Benny's influence in the ministry's message was not a problem to Zack. At the outset, he had been concerned Benny would demand practices associated with Roman Catholicism. His concerns were completely unfounded. He soon found himself awash in a message that was barely Christian—but it was a message of hope, telling people how to find the best in their lives. The message fit Zack like a glove, and he wore it with pride. In fact, it had been years since Benny had any kind of corrective suggestions. All in all, Zack would have to say his association with the bloated cardinal had been pleasant. And it certainly was profitable.

There was a knock, followed by a brief pause and the opening of his office door. His secretary, Bonnie Anderson, swept into the room. She was a statuesque twenty-eight-year-old who clearly worshipped her spiritual leader. Today she wore a tight yellow pencil skirt and a ruffled white blouse that caught her lightly curled auburn hair at the shoulders.

"I have your mail, Pastor Zack." She smiled a perfect, dazzling white smile, her bronze skin accentuated by her white blouse. Her deep brown eyes looked adoringly at the pastor. She had known him since her parents first attended Riverside fifteen years earlier. Zack and Gloria had taken an immediate liking to her family and had been a sort of second set of parents to her.

"Thanks, Bonnie. And may I say you look particularly stunning today." He grinned at the young girl's lithe, athletic body as she strode around the desk and reached in front of him to place the mail on the desk. The smell of her perfume was intoxicating.

"Is that a new perfume?" Zack asked as she brushed past him. "It smells great."

"No. It's the same perfume I always wear. You just noticed it today," she said with a smile.

"I've noticed a lot today," Zack said with a sly grin.

The day had gone much better after Fran and David had their talk. Fran dressed, went downstairs, and spoke kindly to her daughter. She attributed her difficult attitude to not wanting to be on television with bed-head and a wish Gloria had given her some kind of warning. Gloria hugged her mother, and the two set about a day filled with memories and laughter.

David was glad to see Fran could put this behind her. There was only one way to reach Gloria, and that was with love. Zack, on the other hand, was a different story in David's view. He had been happy to see the younger man leave for a day at the church office. David made himself busy while Fran and Gloria visited. He read his Bible, had devotions, and polished up his sermon for the coming Sunday services.

In the early afternoon, Fran offered to cook some of Gloria's favorites for dinner. Gloria was happy to give Rosalita the night off after asking her to come in so early in the morning. Around four o'clock, Fran sent David to the local grocery store with a list of items she would need to make the lamb chop dinner Gloria had loved as a young girl. Fran wanted to have dinner on the table at seven, when Zack was scheduled to come home from the church. He always demanded dinner be eaten promptly at seven.

David was looking forward to dinner. Fran had a way with lamb, and it suddenly sounded even more appetizing when Zack's secretary called to say he wouldn't be home for dinner—something about wining and dining a major contributor to the ministry.

Purchases on the front seat beside him, David left the store parking lot for the quick drive to Gloria's house. He had no notion that the way home would be so clogged with rush-hour traffic. Not wanting to disappoint Fran with his tardiness, he took the first right turn down a smaller road, hoping it would be quicker.

David knew he would have to turn north soon and drove slowly to find a left-hand turn. Finally, he happened upon an intersection with a traffic light. As he approached the light, he could see the road to the left would merge with his original route. He moved to the left lane and waited for what seemed to be an eternity for a left-turn signal.

As he waited, he got a good look at the neighborhood. He hadn't realized Zack and Gloria built their estate so close to such a run-down area of the city. To his left was a Motel 6 that had seen better days. Just then something caught David's eye. It was Zack's car pulling into the motel parking lot. He stared with disbelief as he saw Zack exit the car with a woman he presumed to be Zack's secretary. They entered the lobby just as the car behind David beeped to signal the light had turned green.

David, badly shaken, continued the ride to Gloria's house. He had never particularly cared for Zack. In fact, as far as David was concerned, Zack's only redeeming quality was his love for Gloria. The remainder of the drive seemed too short as David frantically tried to decide what to do. In his heart of hearts, David believed he had caught Zack in the midst of adulterous activity, but he had no proof. Without some kind of proof, he couldn't tell Fran and Gloria what he had just seen—not when they were working so hard to get past the angry start to the day.

Gloria had called Zack several times throughout the evening. Each call went directly to voice mail. She said he often forwarded his calls to voice mail when he was in an important meeting.

The three of them watched a Lifetime TV movie about a man who "done his woman wrong." David could barely contain himself after what he had witnessed. When the movie was finally over, the girls decided to call it a night. David said he wanted to watch the news for a while before coming to bed.

He couldn't care less about the news that night. He wanted to be sitting there when Zack sauntered in. He didn't know what he was going to say. He might not say anything, just look at the younger man knowingly. He decided to play it by ear.

David had dozed slightly but came fully awake when he heard Zack's key in the door. He looked at his watch. One forty-five a.m. Some business meeting!

"Late night?" David asked, startling Zack.

"Sure was." Zack smiled disarmingly. "But it's part of the job. It's very important that I be there for our major benefactors."

"What did you do all this time?" David asked, arms crossed.

"This guy loves to talk over dinner. Dinner led to a cocktail, and then stories about our lives. You know how an evening can spin out of control." Zack took off his jacket and casually tossed it on a chair.

"I didn't know the Motel 6 down the road had a cocktail bar," David said curtly.

Zack grinned one last time, and then his face turned deadly serious. "I don't know what you're getting at, old fellow, but I don't *appreciate* your tone," he snarled.

"Of course you know what I'm getting at," David said tersely, standing to confront the younger man.

With nearly inhuman speed, Zack was in the older man's face. His nose barely touching David's, he growled, "You have no idea how far I'll go to protect my ministry from this type of salacious innuendo."

"Apparently you won't go so far as marital fidelity," David snapped.

Zack's hand went to David's throat, squeezing it firmly. "Don't push me, old man."

They heard footsteps in the stairwell. "Zack?" Gloria called down the stairs.

"I'm home, darling'," Zack purred. "I'm just trying to wake up David. He'll get an awful crook in his neck if I let him sleep in this chair."

"Aww, that's sweet. Are you hungry? Can I get you anything?" she asked.

"No, sweetheart. All I need is to lie down next to my loving, beautiful wife." He glared one last time at David and then met his wife on the stairs.

FOURTEEN

The screams from the five computer programmers could not be heard through the extensive sound baffling Kurt put in their chambers. He found it frustrating that he couldn't be there to see and hear in person the frantic cries as the men underwent total sensory deprivation. Thankfully he had thought to equip each chamber with a wireless transmitter so he could at least hear the men in his headset.

The programmers had been kidnapped in the night. They were immediately injected with a drug cocktail that caused them to lose spatial orientation and coherent thought—a concentrated form of LSD that came from the experiments of the US's CIA in the 1960s and '70s. Then they were fitted with earplugs to filter out even the sounds of their own voices and placed in individual soundproof chambers measuring four feet wide, four feet long, and three feet high. There was no opportunity to stand and little opportunity for comfort in the pitch-blackness.

For the first three hours, the chambers were cooled to 40 degrees Fahrenheit. Following that, they were suddenly warmed to 110 degrees. At other times, water cannons shot at them from the walls.

But this was just the warm-up. After the first twenty-four hours, they would be in a state of total confusion, and that would be the time to administer the physical punishment to break their personalities—and for Kurt, the psychosexual abuse to come was the main event. He grew excited at the mere thought of what would soon transpire.

"How's it going?" Michael startled Kurt, who quickly removed the headphones.

"Fine, Father. The personality is an amazingly fragile construct of the brain. The five programmers are in the chambers right now."

"It seems pretty quiet. I was afraid this process would be more brutal."

"Not at all, Father. Right now they're in a state of sensory deprivation. No light, sounds, or smells."

"Doesn't sound very good." Michael grimaced.

"As you can hear, they all are taking it very calmly. They are anesthetized for the most part ... in a sort of dream state, but the mind is allowed no external stimuli."

"And that's it?" Michael asked.

Kurt could see the release of tension in Michael's body. *Clearly he doesn't have the intestinal fortitude to run the project. Michael should never have been chosen to lead the team over me.*

"For the most part," Kurt lied. "We simply shut down stimuli to this personality. After a period of hours, the kernel of a new persona will begin to emerge. We reward this new persona with stimuli, such that the brain defaults to the new identity."

"Because the brain hungers for stimulation," Michael said.

"Exactly."

"But how do you get the new personality to emerge only when these men are at work?"

"A bit trickier," Kurt continued the ruse, "but basically it relies on the same techniques used in posthypnotic suggestion. Entering the work environment will become a sort of trigger that engages the new identity."

"So it is uncomfortable for these men, but not really torturous, right?" Michael asked hopefully.

"Absolutely no torture." Kurt smiled to placate Michael's nearly palpable guilt over the conditioning of the men. "It's not necessary. Like I said, personality is a very fragile mental construct. It can be modified and changed quite easily." Kurt paused and then played to Michael's deepest desires. "And besides, Father, the end result is unparalleled scientific advancement that will benefit the entire planet."

Michael smiled in an awkward attempt to wholeheartedly buy what Kurt was telling him. "My family is in town for a few days, so I will be spending time with them. If you need me, don't hesitate to call me on my cell phone."

"There will be no need, Father, but I have your cell phone number—just in case."

Gabe waited for Michael at the hotel restaurant. The others had gone to see the sights of Rome. He had stayed behind to talk to Michael, and he wasn't looking forward to the conversation. The family's financial advisers had informed him that Michael had withdrawn ten million dollars. Given the recent market crash, this sudden cash need required the sale of securities that would be worth twice as much once the market rebounded. Michael had told the financial advisors the withdrawal was an urgent and private matter. The entire transaction was inconsistent with the manner in which he and Michael had handled finances in the past. A withdrawal of more than two hundred fifty thousand dollars was a threshold beyond which each had agreed to seek the consent of the other and their mother. Given the unusual nature of the transaction, the family's advisors had naturally called Gabe to ensure that all was well.

Michael cut the figure of a dashing medieval man as he entered the restaurant in his full-length cassock and winter cape. Gabe always found amusement in the clerical garb worn by Chris and Michael. Although he was concerned about the money, one look at his brother brought a smile to his face. He rose to help Michael out of the cape.

"So what have you been up to, Caped Crusader?" Gabe chuckled.

"Same old, same old." Michael grinned broadly.

As Gabe took the cape, folded it, and draped it over a chair, Michael's grin froze to an uncomfortable smile. "Where are Mom, Tina, and the kids?"

"Taking in a bit of the town with Chris. I thought maybe you and I could get some brother time over breakfast." Gabe casually took his seat and motioned for Michael to do the same.

"I see," Michael said warily. "So what's this? You miss hanging out with me?"

Gabe's voice was quiet but intense. "Truthfully, I do, Michael. I feel like there is a gap between us that I never in my wildest dreams imagined would occur."

"I've been working hard, and it is stuff that would rock your boat."

"Is that why you didn't even attempt to notify Mom or me about the ten million dollars?" Gabe asked in a staccato tone, his clear sense of betrayal coming through.

Michael let out a slow sigh. "I was hoping I could do that without involving you and Mom. Who told on me?"

"The financial advisors were worried there was some kind of trouble. You have every legal right to the money, Michael, but they also know that all three of us usually sign off on large withdrawals."

"Yeah, I know." Michael nodded. He reached out to pat Gabe's shoulder. "Look, I'm sorry about that."

Gabe appreciated the apology but stayed focused on the matter at hand. "The question still stands. Are you in some kind of trouble?"

"No! We're in the middle of some incredible discoveries. We needed some equipment, fast. I didn't want to go through the Vatican approval process. They're still working on bills from the Crusades!"

Gabe grinned at the remark. "I was able to track the funds. They were all wired to the Italian account of a Dr. Kurt Waldenbaum."

"That's right," Michael said. "He used his own account as a dispersing account."

"Local laws prevent us from tracking any money he spent in Italy, but international law allows for tracking funds passed between countries. It might interest you to know that the day after receiving the funds, he sent five-and-a-half million dollars to his private account in Switzerland."

"So you think he ripped us off?" Michael asked incredulously. Clearly it hadn't even dawned on him that such a thing would occur.

"He ripped you off, Michael." Gabe's demeanor changed to one of support, a man looking out for his only brother. "What happened that you would abandon the financial principles you've espoused all your life? I'm not nearly so worried about the money as I am about you."

"It seems that we've reversed roles. Now you're the responsible one," Michael joked to relieve the tension.

"Michael," Gabe said sternly as he stabbed at the table with his index finger, "I want to know what's going on."

"It's a top-secret project," Michael said defensively.

"I don't care!" Gabe waved his arms. "For the entirety of our lives as brothers, we've told each other everything. I want to know."

"Even if it would rock the foundations of your faith?"

"You underestimate the underpinnings of my faith," Gabe said dismissively. He was sure Michael was overdramatizing the importance of some crusty old relic. The amazing thing about archeologists, he mused, was that they always took what they found to be absolutely true, as if telling tales, being misinformed, sarcastic, or writing with an agenda were all invented in the age of the Internet.

"Gabe, this is serious stuff. I've been working on it since shortly after I came to Rome. When it all comes to light, it will change society as we know it."

To Gabe, Michael seemed more lighthearted than he had been for years, as if he were relieved to finally share about his work. He grinned. "I'm a big boy, Michael. I'm sure I can handle it. Tell me about it."

"I want to, but I'd much rather show you." Michael smiled proudly.

"So let's go."

"There are too many people working during the day. Even though I now run the project, there's no way I could take you there during normal working hours."

"Tonight then," Gabe said. He felt the exhilaration of a late-night adventure. It was as if they were kids all over again.

"Fine. But it has to stay our secret. I don't want to put you in this position, but you can't even tell Tina. This has to stay between you and me."

"I'll have to tell her we're meeting tonight. She's bound to notice I'm not in bed," Gabe said as he rolled his eyes.

"Okay, tell her as much truth as you can. Tell her I want to show you what I'm working on, but it's very hush-hush and you won't be able to talk about it."

Gabe let out a hearty laugh. "Good thing you're not married, Michael! There's only one thing worse than keeping a secret from your wife, and that's *telling* her you're keeping a secret!"

"So what are you going to tell her?"

"Some of the truth: that you and I have to follow up on a few things that came up in our discussion of the family businesses today. She's made it a point to stay out of the family's finances, but she'll ask me if everything is all right. What should I tell her?"

"Everything is fine, Gabe, really. I'm fine! Okay, I admit I stupidly let Kurt rip me off to the tune of five and a half million dollars ..."

"Which you're going to get back, right?"

"It's probably not possible to get the money," Michael said quietly, eyes downcast.

"Because ..." Gabe led the conversation.

"Because the secrecy of this project takes priority over everything. If I tick this guy off and he runs to the press ..."

"Then ..." Gabe prodded.

"Then our cover would be blown, and the whole world would know—"

"What you intend to reveal to them at some future date anyway?" Gabe challenged. "Get the money."

"It's not only that," Michael hedged.

"Spill."

"There may have been some activity that could be considered criminal in certain jurisdictions."

"Did you commit the crimes?" Gabe asked cautiously.

"No," Michael said glumly, "but I kind of authorized them."

"In writing? Just how did you authorize them?"

"In about ten million ways," Michael said with trepidation.

"Oh man," Gabe said with his head in his hands. "Is this the way it felt all the times you stuck by me when I was screwing up?"

"Pretty much," Michael said softly.

After a day of touring Rome with the family, Chris had gotten back to his apartment to find a message from the cloister where Vinnie lived. The proctor there was threatening to move Vinnie to another location. This happened periodically. The new proctor, Father Ignatius, was a bit stuffy, a man married to formalities, the opposite of Vinnie. The cloister housed monks who had taken a vow of silence, also the opposite of Vinnie. It was only natural that friction should arise.

Since it was only eight o'clock, Chris decided to take the brief ride to the cloister on the outskirts of Rome. Upon arrival, he was ushered into the proctor's office by a silent monk. He smiled at the thought that this little fellow's hand gestures made him look a lot like one of those guys who directs an airplane to the terminal.

Chris extended his hand to Ignatius, who ignored it. Dispensing with pleasantries, he launched immediately into a litany of Vinnie's faults. "Father Chris, I don't appreciate Vinnie's insolence. Do you know what he told me today?"

"No." Chris winced.

"He told me I could stand to lose a couple hundred pounds when I went for a second helping of dessert. I'm his superior!"

Chris tried to hold back a grin. Age had allowed for some leakage in Vinnie's filter, but his wit was firmly intact.

Ignatius continued. "Dear Brother Marcel has been assigned to help Vinnie care for the plants. Imagine my surprise to overhear Vinnie yelling at him, 'Just because you've chosen to be dumb doesn't mean you gotta be stupid!'"

Chris was getting the gist of things. The previous proctor had appreciated Vinnie's unique charm. This one did not. Chris would have to play a bit of hardball. "I'll talk to him, Father," Chris said gently, "but first let me call something to your attention. When you spoke of Marcel, you referred to him as 'dear Brother.' You've always addressed me as 'Father.' Why is it that you call Vinnie by his first name? I'm assuming it's not out of endearment."

"Hardly," Ignatius snapped. "If he behaved like a priest, I'd treat him as a priest." He sat straighter in his chair in a subtle but noticeable act of defiance.

It was time for Chris to bring this matter to a close. Sensing that Vinnie would one day need help with this guy, he had done his homework. "I'm perfectly willing to give you a rundown of Vinnie's lifetime of service, but let me tell you in summary that you should hope to be half the priest he has been." Chris spoke more quickly as his adrenalin rose.

"How dare you!" Ignatius threw himself back in his chair as if slapped.

"This is how I dare," Chris snapped back. "I've reviewed your level of service. You're an alcoholic who we've had to send away to dry out on several occasions. In one of your alcoholic binges, you made unseemly advances to both women and men in your parish. You're here because, frankly, we don't know what else to do with you. In contrast, Vinnie is here to rest from a lifetime of unblemished service to the Lord. Do we understand one another?"

"I believe we do, Father," Ignatius said with barely controlled rage.

Chris didn't let up. "I'm having this conversation with you today as Vinnie's friend. The next time, I promise to bring the full weight of the Vatican."

Chris stomped out of the office, hoping he had intimidated Ignatius enough to encourage a more collegial attitude toward Vinnie. Now the hard part: telling Vinnie to tone it down a bit. He walked down the hallway to the recreation room, where Vinnie was playing cards with some of the monks.

"Well there's a sight for sore eyes!" Vinnie yelled when Chris entered the room. The others at the table with him waved to Chris and smiled.

Chris gingerly hugged the old man. Over the past ten years, Vinnie's frame had given in to the ravages of age. Each time Chris hugged the old man, he felt more fragile.

"Do you have a few moments to talk?"

"Time I got!" Vinnie exclaimed. "You got a problem?"

"Actually, I think you do."

"Let me guess. Ignati-ass called you to say I've been a bad boy." Vinnie rolled his eyes and offered a sharp wave of his hand.

"Come on, Vinnie. You know as well as I do that you have to maintain a level of respect with your superior. It's like when you were in the army."

"I had a still in the army! And my commanding officer was happy to share the booze with me. But with this guy, everything's an insult. Chris, the guy's a putz! Speaking of which, are you still hanging out with my murderer?"

"Shhhhh," Chris said nervously.

"What? They're gonna tell somebody?" Vinnie said, waving his arm toward the speechless cast of characters in the rec room. Those who were unashamedly listening to the conversation slowly shook their heads.

Chris chuckled at the absurdity of the situation. "Look, Vinnie, I told him to back off, and I'm telling you the same thing. I'm afraid I'll have to move you if you can't make it work with Ignatius."

"Oh, thank you for coming here to correct me, *Il Grande Signore del Vaticano*!" Vinnie raised his arms in disgust. The older Vinnie got, the more childlike he became.

Chris hated to come down on a man who had been a father figure to him since he arrived in Rome, but for Vinnie's own good, he had to get stern. "You know what, Vinnie? Let's go to your room and pack up your stuff," Chris barked, hoping the bluff would work. There was a tumult amongst the monks in the room. Marcel, the one who helped Vinnie with the plants, scribbled hastily on a sheet of paper and handed it to Chris.

Chris took a long look at the paper but couldn't quite make out what it said.

Vinnie snatched the paper from his hand and said, "Marcel! How many times I gotta tell you: a man who took a vow of silence shouldn't have such bad penmanship!" Vinnie chucked the note at Chris and translated. "It says he doesn't want me to go."

Marcel nodded in agreement.

Chris noted that Marcel was near tears, as were many of the others. Soon a flurry of notes was pushed in his face. All of them asked him to reconsider. Note after note spoke of how Vinnie made them laugh, brought joy to their lives, made life interesting. Clearly Vinnie had charmed the entire group.

"Fine." Chris pretended to relent. "You can stay, but only if you promise to try to get along with Ignatius."

"Promise is a strong word, but I'll do my best," Vinnie countered.

"That's good enough."

"Then again, I'm an old man. You know I have gout, right?"

"Oh yeah." Chris rolled his eyes. "What's your point?"

"Just that my best isn't as good as it used to be ..."

"Vinnie," Chris moaned.

"Fine. Don't worry your pretty face any more about it. I'll play nice with the boss. Is that what you want to hear?"

"Yes."

"So you heard it! Now tell me, what's going on at the Vatican? And if you have any jokes, I'd love to hear them." Vinnie spoke loudly and waved his arms toward the room. "You've never heard a bad joke until you've heard the ones these guys tell. They're like a bunch of stand-up comics with a busted microphone." Noiseless laughter filled the room.

Chris had laughed about the absurdity of the evening most of the way home from the cloister. He checked his watch as he entered the apartment building. Quarter till eleven. It had been a long day. He would be happy to crawl into bed and read a bit. He heard the doors to the building open and close just as he got into the elevator, and he held the open-door button to accommodate the person who had just entered the building.

"Chris!" Gabe said with a start as he headed into the elevator.

"Gabe? What are you doing here at this late hour?" Chris thought Gabe looked more than just startled to see him. He had the same guilty, sheepish look he wore most of his life until he met Tina.

"I have an appointment with Michael." Gabe pushed the button for the tenth floor, two floors below Chris's.

"What's going on with him? Your mother told me about the money today. This is so out of character for Michael."

"It's all tied to this crazy project of his," Gabe answered, shaking his head. "I coerced him to clue me in on what's going on. Of course I promised to keep it a secret."

"Of course." Chris chuckled. "We wouldn't want anyone to know that Michael discovered some ancient beer recipe!"

"I hear you," Gabe said. "But I'll tell you something. Michael stuck by me through some pretty bad antics. I want to be there for him on this thing."

"See if you can help him," Chris said as the elevator reached Michael's floor. Chris guessed Michael must have been waiting in the hallway. As the elevator doors closed, Chris heard him ask in an annoyed tone, "Who were you talking to?"

"I ran into Chris in the lobby," Gabe said defensively. "What's up with the cloak-and-dagger routine, dude? It's all in the family."

"No," Chris heard Michael say sternly. "I'm showing *you*. Nobody else."

Luciano Begliali woke with a start. For the past two nights, the dream came upon him every time he closed his eyes. It was always the same. He was riding in the elevator of the World Trade Center with a young woman, the one with the nametag "Mary Ellen." She looked at him and smiled. That was the extent of the dream, yet it terrified him each time. The smiling face haunted him. He had found her name and photo in a list of September 11 victims on the Internet earlier that day.

Her blood was on his hands to be sure, but so was the blood of countless thousands over his lifetime. For years now, Begliali had been in the business of fomenting conflict and then profiting from it. He had grown fantastically wealthy dealing in the death of others. Why did this one face haunt him? And why now, after nearly eight years?

He got out of bed and went to the bathroom. As he passed the large mirrors above his bathroom sinks, he glanced at a man he hardly recognized. His hair had gone gray! He stood in front of the mirror in disbelief as crow's feet formed around his eyes and mouth.

"No!" he screamed to his lord. He had done everything commanded of him over the years. In return he received eternal youth and amassed great wealth. They had formed the pact many, many years ago. Luciano had come to view himself as nearly immortal.

But now the rapid aging raged on unabated. Gray hair fell in clumps from his head. Wrinkles became furrows. Liver spots dotted veiny, arthritic hands. His body lost its stature, and his once-beautiful eyes clouded over as he screamed at the impossible image forming in the mirror before him. How could this be happening?

The doorbell rang. He heard his servant answer the door. Whoever it was would have to go away. Luciano couldn't receive any visitors looking like this.

There was a knock at his bedroom door. "Sir, Cardinal Cross is here with Mr. Isa Kurtoglu. They insist on seeing you."

Begliali's heart leapt with joy. If anyone could reverse the aging, it was the young man of light.

"Send them to my room—and quickly," Luciano yelled through the door. His voice was now weak and crackled with age. He couldn't stand any longer and nearly fell onto a plush lounge chair.

"Uncle Luciano," Isa said in a loud, happy voice. "We've brought a document for you to sign."

"First things first, my nephew," Luciano said weakly. "A horrible thing has befallen me. I need your help to be young again."

Benny was clearly overcome with Begliali's appearance, and he steadied himself by leaning on a dresser.

"I am afraid your time has run out, old friend," Isa said softly. "My father is calling you home."

"Why?" Luciano gurgled from a throat filling with phlegm. There was no answer. Isa stared at him in silence. Finally, he threatened, "I must be made young again, or I sign nothing."

Benny groaned at the sight of his fallen hero. "Please, Isa," he pleaded with his young intern, "If you can do anything to help him, please, please do it."

"Ah, you drive a hard bargain, my uncle," Isa said to Begliali, "and I really do not want to hurt the cardinal's feelings." With a mere grin, Isa worked his magic. A sharp burst of light enveloped the old man. When it dissipated, Luciano looked as he always had. In an instant, color was restored to Luciano's hair. Wrinkles vanished from his face, and his fit body sprang from the chair.

"Thank you, Isa!" he said jubilantly.

"You are most welcome, my uncle." Isa smiled. "Now if you will only sign this document, everything will be in order."

"What is the document?" Luciano asked. "Surely you know I cannot sign any legal document without first having it cleared by my attorneys."

"It's your last will and testament, Uncle. You will leave me the entirety of your estate upon your death."

"Isa!" Benny gasped, evidencing that he had no idea of the young man's plan to steal all the worldly assets of his friend and benefactor.

Good old Benny!

"Patience, Cardinal," Isa enjoined. "I promise you one of my first acts will be to make a sizable donation to your favorite charity—CfC, I believe you call it?"

Luciano looked at Benny with pleading eyes. For a moment, he thought he saw compassion there, but then Isa chuckled. When he did, Luciano was thrown back to the memory of a body hanging in the refrigerator of his restaurant. He knew Benny would be reliving that memory as well.

"I'm sure you know best, Isa," Benny said coldly as he folded his hands.

"What a friend!" Luciano yelled at the Benny.

"Forget the cardinal!" Isa shouted. "This is between you and me.

Here are your choices: you can die of old age tonight, or you can retain your youth and sign this document."

"I'll sign it!" Luciano snapped. "And I'm not stupid. I realize this puts me right where you want me. From now on, I have to follow your every order to retain my youth, right?"

"Something like that," Isa said dismissively as Luciano signed. "I'm guessing you weren't told that you were amassing this fortune and power for my eventual use. Pity." As he opened the bedroom door, he said to Benny over his shoulder, "Cardinal, if you would do us the honor of signing as a witness." Luciano's servant was standing at the ready. Without a word, the servant entered the room, signed as a second witness, and left.

"Remind me to fire him," Luciano said to Benny. They were his last words before he lost consciousness. As the world around him grew dark, he found himself in the elevator again. Mary Ellen smiled at him kindly. The doors opened to a great light, filled with love and the answer to any desire Luciano had ever known. She left the elevator and ran to the waiting arms of Jesus, her Savior. Luciano wanted more than anything to run into those arms with her. He tried to leave the elevator but was stopped by some invisible wall. Then Mary Ellen turned to offer a sad wave. The doors closed and the elevator plummeted to hell.

Benny ran to Luciano when he collapsed. The first surge of nausea overwhelmed him as he looked at the rotted flesh of what had moments before been his mentor. His knees buckled and his hands trembled as he looked at the corpse and then back to Isa. In that moment, he saw the real face of evil in the grinning hatred of the young star child.

Isa touched his shoulder, sending a shiver down Benny's spine. "Nothing you can do, Cardinal," Isa said softly. "I am afraid he is quite dead, but he did retain his youthful appearance to the end, did he not?" Isa chuckled.

Benny was terrified at the power and determination of this young man.

"Come now," Isa said with a grin, "this is a fitting end to a long-term contract. It's not as if I knocked him from the deck of a cruise ship, is it?" Isa caused Benny to vividly recall the deaths of Mack and Sarah as another wave of nausea overtook him.

"We are two of a kind, Cardinal," Isa said. "And that is why it should be so easy for you to worship me."

"What?" Benny asked incredulously as he felt the pressure of unseen hands forcing him to his knees.

"Don't worry, Cardinal. You are not alone. You are the first of many. As they say, every knee shall bow and every tongue confess that Isa is Lord!'"

Michael waved dismissively to the Swiss Guard in front of the building and then entered with Gabe. They strode down a long, dimmed hallway that came to an abrupt end at a floor-to-ceiling mural of somebody from the Middle Ages. They stood in front of the wall for a few seconds.

"Don't tell me this old fart is what you've been studying all this time." Gabe chuckled.

"Shhh." Michael grinned and then said, "Access for Father Michael Martin and guest." They heard a slight click, and then a scanning light came from the eyes of the painting. It examined Michael head to toe, and then a computerized voice said, "Access granted. Permission to scan guest.'"

"Agreed," Michael said to the wall and then advised Gabe to stand very still. The light started at Gabe's head and slowly moved down his body as the hidden computer stored information about his height and weight, as well as taking fingerprints and iris prints.

"Welcome Gabriel Marron Martin," the computer said. "Please be advised your movements will be monitored at all times, and you should never leave the company of Father Michael Martin during your visit."

"Thanks," Gabe said with a shrug. "I think."

Michael chuckled and led Gabe through a doorway appearing out of what Gabe had believed to be a solid wall to their left. They entered an elevator and descended for a full forty-five seconds. They were moving fast. Gabe's ears popped shortly before the elevator came to a stop.

"Let me guess," Gabe said with an impressed grin, "you've discovered the Bat Cave."

"Cool, isn't it?" Michael smiled. "I've wanted to show this to you for years. I get to live every day in a science fiction paradise; only it's for real, and I run the joint!"

Gabe smiled at Michael's glee. He hadn't seen his brother this happy in years. They exited the elevator and walked down a brightly lit hallway to a suite of offices at the end.

"These are my offices," Michael said.

Gabe paused to take in the immense space. Two full walls were lined with cherry bookcases filled with Michael's books on antiquities. The high ceilings revealed a beautiful cherry spiral staircase to a loft that was also lined with bookcases filled to the brim. The overall look of the space was one of a centuries-old library in a mansion on a Scottish moor. Gabe chuckled as he imagined his brother in an English smoking jacket with a pipe, pondering the books in his library.

"My desk," Michael said as he pointed behind them to an incongruently modern European-style desk made of polished chrome with a glass top. Behind it sat a large white leather chair, and before it two small, white, leather and chrome club chairs. To the right of the desk was a wall of monitors Michael used to keep track of virtually every aspect of the facility.

"It's beautiful, Michael," Gabe said.

"More than that. It is state of the art. Watch this." As Michael sat in the large chair behind the desk, a computerized voice droned, "Welcome, Father Martin. Shall we continue from where we were earlier?"

"Yes," Michael said absent-mindedly. The glass desktop revealed itself to be a sophisticated video screen. Before Michael, pages of ancient text appeared along with first-pass translations performed from the algorithms Michael had prepared years before.

"So this is what you're translating?"

"No." Michael grinned with pride as he stood up from the desk, which immediately darkened. He moved Gabe to a set of double doors at the opposite end of the room. As they approached, they were scanned and apparently approved because the doors opened.

Gabe gasped as he saw the spinning plate surrounded by laser scanners that flashed continually.

Michael explained. "This disc was found years ago in Iraq.

Thankfully we managed to procure it. It's made of an alloy of gold that is extremely rare ... and, get this, Gabe, it's digitally encoded."

"You found a huge CD?"

Michael nodded, unable to contain a slight giggle and an ear-to-ear grin. "Uh huh. And it's about twelve thousand years old! Do you know what this means?"

"Time travel?" Gabe asked with a shrug. He had endured a lot of sci-fi with his brother but hadn't really paid a lot of attention except to the battle scenes.

"No." Michael laughed. "Gabe, we aren't the first advanced civilization to inhabit Earth! The Ancients were far beyond us in their understanding of science and of the intrinsic quantum nature of the universe."

At first Gabe was intrigued, but something in his spirit felt threatened by the disc. It was as if the thing itself harbored some inherent evil. His mind flashed to the ugly feeling he encountered in Isa's presence. He forced himself to focus on what Michael was telling him. A previous advanced civilization on Earth? There were many men of the cloth, including Gabe, who believed the Bible hinted toward this in the book of Genesis. As translated, it looked as if there were two accounts of creation, but in the original language, there were even more evident hints at an initial creation, and then for some unknown reason the world became void of life. The Garden of Eden was the second creation account but could be viewed as God's restoration of Earth following a huge catastrophe. Adherents to this view were pretty much on the fringe of Bible scholarship, but they held that this first creation was destroyed in Satan's rebellion.

"Michael, you know the story of the two creations," Gabe began, but he felt lost in the power of the spinning disc. It assaulted his senses. His eyes rapidly started to involuntarily blink to stop a flow of tears.

"I sure do." Michael grinned. "Something happened to the previous civilization, and God started over. I think there is a less spiritual explanation, Gabe. It appears to me that humanity has a much richer and longer history than we have assumed. The technological advancements of this civilization are hundreds, maybe thousands of years beyond anything we have now. This disc literally unlocks the secrets of the universe!"

"You know about the nephilim stories, right?" Gabe asked, referring to the theory of some biblical scholars that fallen angels endeavored to corrupt humanity with angelic-human hybrids, and that the Lord had no choice but to wipe clean the face of the planet via the Great Flood. The dark, foreboding feeling had become oppressive. Gabe felt short of breath, and his ears rang. He could no longer be in the same room with the spinning, humming disc. He walked swiftly back through the doorway to the relative comfort of Michael's office.

Gabe's head was spinning. This was no dusty old cuneiform tablet. Either Michael had happened upon an object of incredible scientific import, or he had managed to resurrect the knowledge of a beastly group of half-humans that God had wiped off the face of Earth.

Michael followed Gabe back into the office. Gabe sat in one of the club chairs, and Michael sat in the one next to him.

"Challenges your faith, right?" Michael asked.

"No!" Gabe said, astounded. He wiped at a migraine that was beginning to form. "Why should it?"

"Gabe, the information on this disc completely upends the Judeo-Christian concepts of sinful man and redeemer god. Those are mental constructs, Gabe. They don't stand up to the science and faith of the Ancients."

"This disc also talks about the *faith* of the Ancients?" Gabe asked.

"In a manner of speaking. I've been able to decipher their language over the past decade. But the language was the easy part. Their manner of classifying and storing data has been difficult, and their viewpoint of faith and science was very different from ours. For them, faith and science merged. In fact, I have come to believe that our separation of faith and science is what prevents us from reaching the heights of the Ancients."

"Their 'heights' being what? The destruction of the world?" Gabe asked incredulously.

Michael ignored the comment. "Gabe, these guys believed—and projects assigned to some of our scientists will soon confirm—that we live in a digital universe. The quantum foam at the base of all existence is like the series of on-off pulses on a microchip. Once confirmed, it will prove that all life, all creation, is actually a single, cohesive piece of information."

"So now you're saying we live in the Matrix?" Gabe asked in disbelief. He wasn't buying it. Maybe he was too emotionally involved with Christian theology to be impartial, but none of Michael's statements had the ring of truth to them. What rang true, however, was a far more real, palpable presence of evil to which Michael seemed oblivious.

"No." Michael laughed. "But there is strong evidence pointing to the fact that the quantum foam can be changed, manipulated by consciousness. That is the very reason why viewing one of a pair of entangled photons automatically determines the nature of the other. The experiments have been done, Gabe. The communication between the linked photons is faster than the speed of light. Think of it! Conscious thought creating physical quantum effects!"

"Michael, you've come a long way from the antiquities. Do you really understand all this physics?" To Gabe's mind, this super-subatomic physics talk was little more than a cover for the original sin, "You will be as gods." And Michael was buying it hook, line, and sinker.

Michael laughed. "In ways modern physicists don't! In effect, the disc has schooled me. And let me tell you something, brother. We have greatly underestimated the power we have in the universe. By the mere fact that we are conscious, we can be like little gods."

There it was, the lie at the root of all sin. "The Big God isn't good enough for you?"

"The Big God is nothing more, nothing less than the universe itself, Gabe."

Gabe had heard enough. This was not the Michael he had known all his life. Something had changed him. More than anything, Gabe wanted to be back in his warm bed, snug in the comfort of his family. He knew that, at some time, he would have to deal more strongly with the issue of Michael's faith, but it wouldn't be in the middle of the night, and it wouldn't be in the presence of that horrible spinning disc.

"I can see what's been keeping you so busy, Michael." He grinned uncomfortably.

"You just want to get home, right?" Michael smiled. "Gabe, I understand. This information blew me away at first too. It forces you to rethink just about everything in life."

"You're right. I'm blown away, and I have to think." Gabe had the curious urge to cry for his brother, to hug him and tell him the love of God is so much more beautiful than his quantum quackery. But Michael was in no position to understand. To turn the conversation, Gabe pointed to the seamless rows of television monitors on the wall. "So can you get American football on those things?"

"No." Michael chuckled. "But I can see everything that's going on in the entire facility." With the push of a button, all the screens glowed. Most of the screens showed empty hallways and desks, but in the lower right hand corner was a very different scene.

"What the heck is that?" Gabe asked as he moved closer to the screen. Gabe's approach blocked Michael's view. On it, Gabe saw a naked man with a whip. He was lashing at several emaciated young men who were naked, bound, gagged, and blindfolded. Each was hanging from a meat hook/pulley system that raised their bound hands above their heads.

Michael came to his brother's side. Immediately when he saw the screen, he ran back to his desk to turn off the system. As the screen went blank, Gabe turned to him, flush with rage.

"Michael! What the hell was that!" he demanded.

Michael didn't answer his brother. Instead, he ran down the hallway in a fury. Gabe followed.

FIFTEEN

Michael burst into the room where Kurt was doing his "training." Kurt turned quickly and motioned for him to be quiet. Michael closed and locked the door just as Gabe caught up. He was furious at what he saw. These men were being beaten and raped as part of their training. Kurt moved them back to their chambers. Their motions were robotic, as if they were soulless. Once they were in their chambers, Kurt motioned to Michael that it was okay to speak.

"What do you think you're doing?" Michael demanded. "You call this training?"

"Lower your voice, Father," Kurt said smugly as he donned a robe. "The fact that I enjoy it does not change what I have been called upon to do. These men are ready to be reprogrammed. They have been broken."

Gabe pounded on the door. "Michael! Michael, are you all right? Open this door!"

Michael slowly opened the door, wiping his face. He made quick introductions. "Gabe, Kurt. Kurt, Gabe,"

"Are you telling me this is *the Kurt*? This is the jerk who stole five-and-a-half million dollars from us?"

"One and the same," Michael said with disgust.

"So you paid him all that money to abuse young men?"

"I ... I didn't know this part of it," Michael stammered. "I had no idea I was playing into his deviant fantasy."

"Then what did you *think* you had bought into, Michael?"

"A training program used by the intelligence community around the world. Basically, you bring about enough stress to create an alternate personality that can be triggered to switch on and off when they enter and exit the lab." Michael reached out to his brother. Gabe brushed his hand away. "Listen, Gabe, I think this disc is highly encoded. I think the Ancients may have designed it to be read in three dimensions. I can't finish learning all its secrets without a supercomputer." He waved broadly toward the holding chambers. "These guys are the programmers who can make this happen, but they're security risks."

"The ultimate secrecy," Gabe said with disgust. "So to protect that stupid disc, you hurt these men irreparably. You know, Michael, a while back you asked me to tell you if you ever turned into Benny. Guess what, brother? That time has come."

The words stung. Michael blinked hard to push back hot tears forming there. "Gabe, these guys will be okay. At some point in the future, when all of this is made public, we'll be able to reintegrate their personalities. Until then, they're just a bunch of guys for whom the workday goes incredibly fast. They'll receive good paychecks and have nice lives outside of here."

"Set them free, Michael. *Now*!"

"That would be highly inadvisable," Kurt pronounced in the flat tone of a scientist. "To release them now would be to injure their primary personalities. We are on the downside of this process. If we release them now, they are liable to hurt themselves or others."

"So if you release them they die?" Gabe asked incredulously.

"Most probably. On the other hand, if you will give me about twelve hours to detoxify them, they'll be fine. I can even arrange for you to meet them at a local restaurant if you wish," Kurt assured.

Gabe stomped out of the room clutching at his cell phone. He dialed quickly and got no answer. He dialed again. "Michael, I'm calling the police," he murmured.

First Michael and then Kurt followed after him. "Your phone won't work here, Gabe," Michael said.

When they caught up to him, Michael grabbed his arm to plead with him. "Gabe, think about it. If you bring the police into this, all this knowledge could fall into the wrong hands. The entire world could be affected—Tina, the kids, Mom, and Chris. Why do you think we enforce such secrecy? Can you imagine what the world would be like if one nation managed to catapult centuries beyond the rest of us technologically? We could all be hideous slaves of a monstrous dictator with very little opportunity to resist. On the other hand, if we control the release of this information through the marketplace, the entire world will gradually come to enjoy the benefits of this discovery."

Gabe stopped short and in an emotional burst grabbed his brother's shoulders. Looking at him intently, he said, "But, Michael, what he was doing to these guys—"

"I know," Michael said somberly. He turned, and his voice grew exceedingly stern. "Kurt, you can be assured I'll have to administer some sort of sanction for this."

"Some sort of sanction?" Gabe aped his brother incredulously. "Michael, he stole five and a half million dollars from our family, and now we've caught him in a ridiculous act of perversion at the *Vatican*! He needs to be locked up!"

"I assure you," Kurt said smugly, "your brother will go down with me. And, as Father Michael said, the threat to society is huge."

Gabe couldn't bear the thought of Michael going to jail along with this sick criminal. Nor could he suffer the idea of his children growing up in the world Michael described. He just wanted to be in bed in his hotel room. These thoughts plagued him as he made a decision sure to haunt his every day on Earth.

"Tomorrow," Gabe said sternly, "if I don't see happy, healthy, functioning young men, I'm calling the police. You have to make this right, Michael. And I expect you to return the money, Kurt."

"Thanks, Gabe," Michael said quietly. "You'll see. It'll all turn out fine. These guys will be okay, and humanity will benefit from these discoveries for years to come—"

"Just get me out of here, Michael," Gabe interrupted in a flat tone. "I can't talk to you any more tonight. I'm too upset, too tired, and too disappointed in you."

Kim awakened early the next morning to meet Benny for breakfast. She quickly dressed in a tunic sweater and tights, brushed her hair, and headed for the elevator. She seriously doubted Benny would make a seven thirty breakfast meeting. To her knowledge, Benny had never been out of bed at that hour. But when she went to the breakfast room of the hotel, she saw her brother sitting with a pot of rich Italian coffee.

"I honestly thought you would stand me up, seeing how early it is," she teased.

When Benny looked up at her, however, she saw he was disheveled and looked as if he had been through a horrible night.

"Benny, are you okay?" she asked softly.

"No," he answered as he choked back a sob. "I've been up all night." He wiped a silent, single tear from his eye.

"What happened?"

"My old friend, Luciano Begliali, died suddenly last night."

"Oh, Benny. I'm so sorry." Kim placed her hand on top of his. "What happened?"

"His heart just gave out. I was there when it happened. There was nothing I could do. One minute he was fine, the picture of health. The next moment, he was dead." Benny choked back a sob.

"I'm sorry for the loss of your friend, but at least we have the consolation of knowing he went to a better place."

"I hope so," Benny said weakly, a far-off look in his eye.

"Did he believe in Jesus?" Kim asked innocently.

"No," Benny managed to whisper.

Kim moved around the table to her brother's side. She kissed his cheek and hugged him, shedding dim light on memories of the little girl who would comfort him after one of his bouts with her father. He placed his head on her shoulder and let her comfort him.

"Kim, Luciano wasn't a good man. He was fierce and driven. I think he viewed me more as a tool than as a friend." Benny's voice broke.

"I'm sorry to hear that. I know you cared for him."

"Do you?" he asked. "Because I'm not so sure now. Kim, I've succeeded in surrounding myself with very powerful people, but I don't think there's any love lost between any of us."

"A cold circle of friends."

Benny sighed and shrugged. "Indeed they are. In the long run, I guess it doesn't bother me."

Kim thought he was trying to convince himself more than her.

He continued, speaking softly, "These are the people I have courted all my life. But every once in a while, I wonder what life would have been like if I had chosen to do it differently."

"I have good news for you, brother," Kim said with a slight grin. "Your life isn't over. You can make any changes you want to make. Decide who you want to be, Benny, and then become that person."

"No." He took a deep breath of resignation. "I'm in very deep, Kim. I've chosen my lot."

She patted the back of his hand. "Oh, Benny, that sounds like depression talking. Are you still taking your medication?"

"Yes." He smiled briefly. "This isn't a chemical imbalance, Kim. I've just come to a full realization of the fearful, dark, and powerful world I have courted, and it terrifies me. If I told you about my secret life ..."

"You can tell me anything, Benny. I'm your sister, and I'll *always* love you."

"What a stunning coincidence!" Isa exclaimed, startling Kim as he approached their table. Kim noticed that Benny trembled slightly at the sound of the younger man's voice. Immediately he fell silent and turned an ashen color.

"May I join you?" Isa asked politely, but he didn't wait for a reply. He pulled up a chair and motioned for the wait staff. Kim felt a chill as Isa took his seat. She knew nothing about this young man, but there was no doubt in her mind that he was the object of Benny's dread.

Her blood ran cold as he smiled at her. She offered a weak smile in return.

"I hope I'm not interrupting anything," he said politely. "I don't know if your brother told you, but we lost a close friend last night."

Kim nodded, taking note of the way Benny bristled at the mention of Luciano's death. "My condolences," she said gravely.

"Thank you," Isa said with manufactured sadness. "Your brother and I have much to do to plan his service. He requested to be buried immediately following his death."

"Yes," Benny said as if on cue. "Kim, it would probably be best if Isa and I spoke privately. I'll try to catch up with you later."

"Oh," Kim gasped, startled at being dismissed from the table. "Are you okay, Benny?"

"Yes," he replied breathlessly, eyes downcast. "Just go."

She left with the odd feeling that Benny sent her away to protect her from the young Turk.

Although it was a bitterly cold winter day in Rome, there was sunshine, and it felt wonderful to the pontiff as his back faced the large windows of his office.

"This is a hard stance for me to assume, my young friend," the pope said to Gabe with a slight grin. "For years, the Church has taught that we are now the heirs of promises made to Abraham."

"I'm familiar with those beliefs, sir," Gabe said tenuously, "but a more literal interpretation of Scripture would most likely lead to a dispensational viewpoint ... one that tells us the Age of Grace, also known as the Age of the Church, will at one point end. Then the Lord will resume with His plan for the nation of Israel."

"Again," said the pontiff, "this would imply that the new nation of Israel is the fulfillment of ancient prophecies rather than the fulfillment of men's desires."

"It doesn't have to be either-or, Holiness," Chris said. "The facts are clear. The prophets predicted it, and it has happened. The motivations of the individuals involved would seem to be secondary to the actual event, would they not?"

"Yes. They would," the pope said gravely. "But as an institution, we must show prudence, restraint, and reverence. It is not an easy task to abandon theologies held for centuries."

"I personally think abandoning something inappropriate would be the most appropriate course of action, sir," Gabe said. Even before he finished his sentence, he was reminded of Michael's situation and how he had agreed to wait to meet the programmers before deciding to call the police. Magnify that by the size and scope of the Catholic Church and consider the growing cleft between the pope and the Curia. Gabe had a sudden revelation of how grave these conversations were to the pontiff. "If I could rephrase my remark, I would like to, sir. What I meant to say is that while abandoning previous doctrine may be the best answer, it may not be the most efficient path to reach the rank and file of your denomination."

"Something has happened to you, my young friend." The pope smiled at Gabe. "You seem to have more understanding of my position."

"I had never really considered it prior to our last meeting." Gabe smiled back. "But I can definitely state that I have a new appreciation for the constraints of your position."

"Be content with that response, Holiness." Chris chuckled. "That is as close as I've ever heard Gabe come to saying he was wrong."

"I wasn't wrong," Gabe insisted with a grin. "I wasn't fully informed."

The three men chuckled, and then the pope spoke. "Chris, I wholeheartedly agree with your suggestions to add more weight in the liturgical readings to St. Paul's Letters to the Thessalonians and the books of Daniel and Isaiah."

"Thank you, Holiness."

"I also think we have some other opportunities to include thoughts of the Lord's return into the revised Mass we will soon issue."

"Such as?" Chris asked.

"I was thinking of adding something to the doxology about recognizing the times through the lens of Scripture, something to bring the layperson's attention to the fact that we may well be living in prophesied times."

"I think it should be a small matter to find the appropriate words," Chris said, accepting his assignment.

"Thank you. Now for a bigger problem. I need you to get back to me with some ideas on how we can back away from the precepts of supersessionism without an explicit adoption of dispensationalism."

"If I may," Gabe interjected, "you could continue your predecessor's outreach to Israel. Let the Vatican show itself to be more of a friend to Israel. Soften your rhetoric on the plight of the Palestinians. Come out strongly for Israel's right to exist."

"This will be quite an undertaking," the pope said. "Liberation theology runs deep in the veins of the Jesuits, but I will meet with the head of that order. And, of course, I'll see to it that I revisit our agenda toward Israel with the Secretary of State."

"Thank you, sir," Gabe said softly.

The pope offered a dismissive wave. "Gabe, I want to thank you for working with me on these issues, and again I ask for your complete secrecy as to the nature of our discussions."

"You have my strictest confidence, sir. Besides, who would believe me even if I told them?"

The three men laughed. "Well, if you're as secretive as your brother, I believe I can trust you. I have yet to get a report from him regarding his research."

"He may have opened the door just a bit, Holiness," Chris said innocently. "He gave Gabe a tour of his facility last night."

"And what did you learn?" the pontiff asked Gabe, whose expression was one of a deer caught in the headlights.

"Well, sir," Gabe stammered, "Michael is a scientist, and I'm not. It's very hard for me to understand the significance of his work."

"Were you impressed with his labs?" the pope asked.

"Very impressed. They appear to be state of the art."

"From the money he has spent, I should hope they are." The pontiff looked over the rims of his reading glasses into Gabe's eyes.

Gabe got the withering feeling of a child caught in a lie. "Well, they seem to be very nice." Gabe grinned sheepishly and made a brief plaintiff look to Chris for help.

Picking up on the gesture, Chris interceded. "When all is said and done, Holiness, we are probably asking the wrong brother. Would you like for me to arrange a meeting with Michael so he can take you through his findings?"

"Yes, please do that," the pope answered. Turning to Gabe, he said, "Did everything seem to be in order at that facility? Nothing seemed unusual?"

"I'm hardly one to say what qualifies as archeologically unusual," Gabe said with what he hoped was a disarming grin. "Michael seems to be excited about it, though."

As Gabe had hoped, the ignorance of his reply seemed to thwart any other questions the pope may have had. "Well, thank you again, Gabe. Will you do me the honor of meeting with me next month as well? I still have more to learn."

"Yes, sir," Gabe said. "In the meantime, I can send Chris some of the current literature on the subject. He can then bring it to you."

"That would be greatly appreciated. And now, gentlemen, if you will excuse me, I am afraid I have a full day ahead of me."

They said good-bye to the pope and left his office. As soon as they were in the hallway, Chris grabbed Gabe's arm. "What the hell did you see last night?" he asked in a staccato whisper.

"I can't tell you," Gabe answered, his eyes pleading with Chris not to push the issue any further.

"Is Michael in trouble?" Chris asked in resignation.

"He could be, but I think there may be a way out of it. I'm meeting him for lunch today to sort it all out."

"Let me know if there's anything I can do."

"Pray for Michael."

"Do you think he lost his faith?"

"I'm not sure he ever really had any," Gabe said sadly.

Gabe was late. Michael anxiously waited for him outside the restaurant Kurt had chosen. Finally, Michael caught sight of him sprinting down the street.

"Sorry I'm late, Michael," Gabe called as he made his way to his brother.

"This is Italy, Gabe." Michael smiled uneasily. "You're practically early."

"Is everyone else here?" Gabe asked briskly. Michael could sense Gabe's residual anger at what he had seen the night before.

"They're inside," Michael said. "Before we go in, I want to apologize again to you for what you saw."

"I hear you, Michael. Please tell me you understand that my seeing it isn't the problem. The problem is that you let your passion for this project overwhelm your sense of right and wrong."

"You're right," Michael said contritely.

"And," Gabe interjected, "you have lost your first love. This project is causing you to not believe in Jesus. You're on very dangerous ground."

"I haven't so much given up on Him as suspended my belief until I can learn what the Ancients have to say. Then I'll have to make a decision."

"Somehow that makes me feel no better," Gabe said drolly. "Let's go in and get this over with."

Michael carefully watched his brother in the restaurant. Gabe was noticeably relieved at the look and demeanor of the young programmers. As the meal progressed, they joked with Michael and Kurt and were fully engaged in their surroundings and the conversation.

"I trust you have received notification of payment by your bank," Kurt said cheerily as he took a sip of his wine.

"Yes," Gabe said, "thank you very much."

Turning to the young men, Gabe prodded, "So tell me about your jobs."

They all looked at him blankly for a second, and then one spoke. "It's computer programming. Hours and hours and lines and lines of code. By the end of the day, even I'm not sure what I did."

The others laughed heartily in agreement.

"Well, I'm happy you got the chance to get out of the lab and have a nice meal," Gabe said earnestly.

The talk eventually dwindled, and Michael said they really should be getting back to work. Kurt and the programmers said their good-byes and waited outside the restaurant.

"Are we okay now, Gabe?" Michael asked.

"We're always okay, Michael," Gabe said with an awkward grin. Turning somber, he lectured, "But what went on in those labs was beyond the pale. Kurt's a criminal and a pervert. And you aided and abetted him."

"Like when you aided and abetted prostitution?" Michael asked with a subtle grin.

Gabe winced. "Touché. But I'm serious, Michael. Don't give me any more heart attacks, all right?"

"I won't," Michael said as he hugged his brother good-bye.

After Gabe left, Michael paid the actors, and then he and Kurt went straight to the lab where the programmers were coming down from their last dose of hallucinogens.

SIXTEEN

Michael thought about the day before him as he overlooked early morning Rome from the window of his tiny apartment. The spring air was sweet, and there was just a touch of dew. It was shaping up to be a long one. The programmers had made amazing progress on the hologram matrix, which Michael had nicknamed Holomax.

The basic idea was that the information contained on the disc could be interpreted lineally, a literal reading of the text, which Michael and his team had exhausted. But Michael was convinced that it also contained messages in three-dimensional space. The Holomax program would access the database and then place the text within a cubic format. The predicted result was that the text also carried messages when read "through" the cube. Given the wealth of information they had obtained from the written text, Michael anticipated a flood of new data from Holomax.

Today was a test. Their current computer system had neither the capacity nor the program to hold the entire cube of information, but if the data structure was truly holographic, information about a portion of the cube would yield insights as to the whole. With a comparatively small information field, the programmers would be ready today to perform a "mock read." If the resultant information was decipherable as an intelligent message, then they would begin work on Holomax proper, the program that would unlock a plethora of heretofore-undiscovered scientific knowledge.

Of all days, the Holomax test would fall on the day he was scheduled to meet with the pope about the status of his research. Michael was a touch more concerned about this meeting than with the Holomax test. He had decided to explain the disc to the pope, ignoring its religious overtones while accentuating the scientific potential. He also planned to emphasize the careful manner in which he secured, in the Vatican's name, all the intellectual property rights related to the new sciences. Within a couple of years, the telecommunications implications alone could well net the Vatican a substantial slice of what was expected to become a multibillion-dollar smartphone application. And that was just the beginning.

From the papal meeting, it was off to a lunch with Isa Kurtoglu. He had been putting this off for a couple of months as well, but finally Benny had cornered him.

The key for Michael on this day was to keep his focus. He may be in meetings with the Turkish son of someone or with the Holy Father, but if he wasn't careful, his mind would wander to the results of the tests in his subterranean laboratory.

He made his way to the papal offices, where the Holy Father greeted him warmly. He was shocked at how easily the pope accepted the idea of the Iraqi disc and his attempts to decode it. Then he reminded himself that the Vatican had one of the foremost intelligence networks in the world. No doubt the pope knew at least the basics of his research.

"As you can see, Holiness, the information obtained from the Iraqi artifact is indeed proof of an advanced civilization predating recorded history."

The pope stared at the information Michael had provided in his briefing packet. "Is there any indication in their records as to how they perished?" he asked thoughtfully.

"None, Holiness."

The pope nodded and sighed heavily. "So now, Michael, we must consider the theological implications."

"I have taken the decision to put them on hold, Holiness, in favor of mining the technological implications of their knowledge. If you turn to the next section of your presentation, you will see I have procured patents on a worldwide basis for each of the technologies we have discovered. Once the intellectual property was secured, I engaged the most celebrated university and commercial laboratories in the development of the technologies."

Michael saw the pope's eyes light up as he surveyed the impressive list of technological advances hinted at by the information on the disc.

"If you turn to page fifty of your presentation, you will see that we will soon be ready to go to market with some of our communications, agricultural, and immunological advances. We will change society with the production of food crops even in the harshest environments. Our communications platform will result in instantaneous transfer of information on a worldwide basis. And, we are expecting approval in several countries for a recombinant DNA procedure that will literally allow our bodies to regenerate and heal themselves of a host of maladies, from the common cold to cancer." Michael's voice grew in volume as he spoke with a passion for this project that had heretofore only found voice in the secret whispers of his lab.

"And we have just released to several oil companies schematics that could result in the development of a very reliable and very cheap form of energy produced from the quantum foam at the base of all matter. They have been given five years to develop and announce plans to transform the energy economy. If they fail, we'll do it in their stead."

The pope grimaced. "There is so much potential to benefit humanity with these discoveries, Michael, but in the wrong hands?"

"There is a high potential for weaponization in each of these disciplines. That is precisely why I thought a benevolent organization like the Church should control the information. We can direct it to peaceful purposes that are uplifting to the human condition," Michael said proudly.

"This is all very interesting. And don't misunderstand me. I too am intrigued by the opportunity to benefit the world on such a grand scale, but—"

Michael interrupted, his exuberance getting the better of him. "If I may be so impertinent as to interject, Holiness. Please turn to the last section of the briefing packet. As you can see, our control of the technologies will also place us in the middle of new income streams. While this is obviously not our primary concern, if you look at the projected cash flows—and I would like to point out that we have employed very modest assumptions—you'll see that the Church will be able to meet almost any remaining need." Michael took a deep breath and a pause to imagine it all. "Think of it, Holiness! We will finally be able to feed and clothe the poor. We will be able to use our influence to mediate in world conflict. We can use this technology to usher in a golden age for humanity."

The pope was clearly caught up in Michael's dream to bring peace, health, and prosperity to every man, woman, and child on Earth. "Michael, I am overwhelmed by what you have accomplished. In fact, I applaud your work, with a serious reservation. You should have informed me well in advance of this meeting. Thankfully you have been prudent in controlling the information, and clearly you have the interests of the poor and of the Church in mind. However, going forward, I will require a weekly briefing from you."

"Yes, Holiness," Michael said with a slightly bowed head. He had imagined a much harsher reprimand.

"We also have to get the very basics of this information to our best theologians. We must have an answer for our people if news of this discovery finds coverage in the press. To that end, I would like you to prepare a brief, presumably hypothetical summary of the issues for me to pass by our theologians. There are many serious implications, Michael."

The pope's tone became more brittle. "There are issues that need to be thoroughly vetted. You should have come to us earlier, before the genie had left the bottle." The pope waved his hand in exasperation. "You have committed us to a course of action through your involvement of the world's scientific community. Now that we are bound by your efforts, we must examine their underpinnings."

Michael responded to the aggravation in the pope's voice by pleading his case. "Understood, Holiness, but may I ask you a question? If I had come to you earlier with the information, could you have suppressed it with the thought of all those children going to bed in hunger? Could you have watched, firmly convicted of your decision, as the lights throughout Europe and the rest of the developed world slowly twinkle out of existence?"

The pope sighed heavily. "I can't answer that, Michael, but I believe my instincts would have been to use the technology to aid the world."

Michael sighed as well, and a faint smile of satisfaction dawned on his face. "Thank you, Holiness. So you can understand my position."

"No, Michael, I understand your motivation," the pope said

sharply. "*You* are the one who doesn't understand your position. From now on, you *will* keep me thoroughly informed with regular briefings, and you *will* work with the Vatican bank, which I am now making responsible for the collection of royalties. And you *will* prepare the summary for our theologians. To be clear, Michael, I applaud your work, but not your methods. If you continue along this course, I'll make you the chaplain of a military base in Antarctica. Do you understand me?"

"Yes, Holiness," Michael said submissively as he made a mental note to establish a back-up computer facility he alone could access.

Chris had just come in from his morning run. He was covered in sweat and longed for a shower as the phone rang. He paused a moment, thinking he could let the call go to voice mail, but at the last minute grabbed it when he saw the caller ID said "United States."

"Hello," he panted.

"Chris?" asked a voice with drawl.

"Yes. Is this David?"

"Yes. I didn't wake you, did I?"

"No. Actually, I was just coming in from a morning run when I heard the phone ringing. What's up? Is everything okay?"

"I don't know," David said. "I have some horrible suspicions about Zack. If I talk to Fran about them, she'll go ballistic. If I try to talk to anyone else here in Texas, it could get back to Zack. I was hoping to bend your ear."

"Shoot," Chris said as he reached for a towel to wipe perspiration from his face. He had never cared for Zack himself, but the dire tone in David's voice led him to believe the forthcoming concerns would be serious.

"First of all, about a month ago I am pretty sure I saw him going into a seedy motel with his secretary, just after calling Gloria to say he had to work late."

Chris grimaced. "Aww, I hate to hear something like that, David. Do you think Gloria suspects infidelity?" Chris threw himself into a chair and undid the laces of his running shoes.

"No. In fact, I'd say she's clueless. If you could see their ersatz television shows ..."

"Their audience has gone global, David. I can get them on TV every day with Italian subtitles. It all seems a little contrived and show business for me, but then I come from a different tradition than those two."

"No need to be kind, Chris. Most of Christianity comes from a different tradition."

"Do you think Gloria is ignoring the signs of infidelity to maintain their image?"

"No. I think she's bought Zack's story and his faith hook, line, and sinker. I think she believes she is leading the blessed life they portray to their TV audience."

"So if you told Fran your concerns, she would go to Gloria," Chris began.

"And Gloria wouldn't believe her," David interjected. "It would just add more strain to a relationship that isn't great to begin with."

"I hate to hear that about Fran and Gloria." For a second, Chris pictured how close they had been when Gloria was a little girl. He regained his train of thought. "Have you tried to talk to Zack? You know, some fatherly advice?"

"I might not have been exactly fatherly, but I confronted him that same evening when he came home."

"And?"

"It's hard to explain, Chris. He was smug, belligerent, and threatening."

"No sense of remorse? Did he deny it?" Chris took a long drink of water.

"No. He told me I had no idea the lengths to which he would go to protect his ministry."

"What did you take *that* to mean?" Chris asked, pushing his still-wet hair from his face.

"This is where I'm having a major problem, Chris. It felt like a veiled threat on my life. That's just plain stupid on my part, isn't it?"

Chris didn't know what to say. Personally, he would have viewed it as a threat. He had seen people killed for less, but he didn't want his past to color his advice in this situation. "I wasn't there, David. But I know you to be a pretty rational man."

"Well, here's where my thoughts are torturing me. You know that none of us ever saw Mack or Sarah after the cruise."

"Right. They retired to one of the islands, but then mysteriously disappeared."

"Nobody ever heard from them, except Zack. Could he be lying?"

Chris groaned at the implications. "Do you honestly think he could have killed his parents?" Chris asked incredulously, and then winced as he thought of his own parents' deaths.

"I don't know! Do you think I'm nuts?" David asked tensely.

"No, I don't," Chris said, wiping the last bit of perspiration from his brow. "I can't even tell you the amount of evil I've seen in my time."

"Oh, right." David chuckled awkwardly. "You've worked with Benny all these years."

"That does give me an interesting perspective." Chris laughed. Then the idea hit him. It seemed too ludicrous to mention at first, but his mind wouldn't let it go.

"David, I have this crazy idea: let me run this by Benny to see if he thinks we're off base. He seemed to get along with Zack."

"Thinking of using your relationship with Hannibal Lecter to get into the mind of the killer?" David asked.

"Sort of." Chris chuckled.

"It's a better idea than any I've had," David admitted.

"Then consider it done," Chris said in a reassuring tone. "It can't hurt, and hopefully it will help ease your mind."

"Just be careful, Clarisse," David warned.

Both chuckled.

Later in the day, Benny was enjoying a gigantic pastry at his desk following an incredible encounter with the Lady. He was nursing an expectation that something great would happen today, when Chris strode nonchalantly into his office.

"To what do I owe this unexpected visit?" Benny asked lightheartedly. For some reason, even Chris didn't bother him today, and after all these years, the ageless former football star still held a certain appeal as office eye-candy.

Chris furrowed his brow. "My apologies, Benny. I should have called to see if you were available."

Benny laughed. "Even when I'm sincere, people think I'm being sarcastic. Let me start over. To what do I owe this unexpected, pleasant surprise?"

"I kind of wanted to get your appraisal of a situation," Chris said, clearly caught off guard by Benny's good mood. "I got a strange phone call from David today. He's pretty sure he saw Zack going into a motel with the church secretary." Chris went on to describe David's confrontation with Zack, and then he summed his concerns. "David felt threatened. He seems to think Zack could be dangerous, and he's begun to wonder if the guy had something to do with the disappearance of his parents."

"Wow," Benny said in mock surprise as he blanched at the implications of being found out. "Interesting story, Chris, but why did you want to tell it to me?"

"Two reasons. First of all, you and Zack seemed to hit it off. And the second reason is a little bit hard to put into words."

"You think that, from experience, I understand bad guys?" Benny cackled.

"I might not have chosen those exact words." Chris blushed.

"It's okay, Chris." Benny chuckled. "My ministry has put me in contact with some of the seedier side of life." His whitewashed version of his life drove a chuckle from Chris. Benny continued, "Let me give you my impression of Zack. I see him as very driven and full of purpose. I think it would be possible for him to behave badly if he thought he was protecting his ministry. But do I think he would hurt his parents? Not a snowball's chance in Aruba." Benny stared across the desk at Chris, giving his best attempt to look wise.

Chris sighed and shifted in his chair. "Well, that's a bit of a relief. I would hate to think of Gloria living in constant danger."

Benny then waved his hand dismissively. "As to the alleged affair? I think David is probably wrong about that too."

"Why do you say that?"

Benny shrugged and rolled his eyes. "Suffice it to say I'm a man who knows when guys are interested in other guys."

"You think Zack is gay?" Chris asked in disbelief.

"Probably bisexual. But the important thing in this instance is to realize that if Zack ever went looking for something different from what he's got at home, well, it wouldn't be another woman."

"So you don't think Zack is capable of the murders or the affair?" Chris asked.

"Anyone is capable of anything, Chris, but I honestly believe that neither is in his nature. Tell David to relax. I'm sure everything's fine. Zack is a very calculating young man, who knows he's riding at the top of his game. I don't believe he would risk everything and be so blatant as to do so in his backyard."

Chris chuckled with a sense of relief. "You know, Benny, you have actually eased my mind on this. I'm really thankful to you."

"It's what friends are for." Benny smiled. This would be a great day after all.

Zack's office door was closed as he practiced his next telecast in a full-length mirror, honing every nuance. He was interrupted when Bonnie knocked briefly and pushed the door open a crack. "Zack," she said quietly, "you have a phone call from the cardinal."

"Put it through." Zack winked devilishly at his secretary before closing his office door.

"Benny! What a pleasant surprise! What can I do for you?"

"You can keep your fly zipped," Benny said.

"I don't know what you're talking about." Zack grimaced.

Benny barked, "Don't even begin to play coy with me, Zack. I've got your number. Break off the affair with your secretary. Today. This enterprise is too big for you to risk it on a tawdry roll in the hay."

"How did you know?" Zack asked defensively.

"Let's just say your veiled threat to David wasn't so veiled. He called Chris because he's worried you may have had something to do with the disappearance of your parents."

"Sometimes I can't stand that guy," Zack said, trying to suppress a growing rage.

"Well, forget what you're feeling. You know the old adage: keep your friends close and your enemies closer. It's time you call your father-in-law to apologize for being difficult with him. You'll tell him some crap about why you were going into that motel with your secretary, and you'll make him believe it."

"I don't like your tone, Benny," Zack snarled.

Benny's voice became a low growl. "Let me explain something to you, Zack. Any evil you have ever contemplated, I've already done. I will take you down in a heartbeat if you *ever* speak to me like that again. Do you understand me?"

Zack remembered the murder of his parents. It hadn't even fazed the cardinal. Realizing he had pushed too hard, he summarily retreated. "I apologize, Benny. I'm just so angry at David for this—and more than a little disappointed in myself."

"For you to know," Benny said, ignoring the apology, "I told Chris you most likely were not having an affair with your secretary."

"Thank you."

"I told him you are interested in men, and that if you strayed, it wouldn't likely be with another woman."

"How dare you!" Zack spat before he could catch himself.

"Oh, but it's true, Zack. I have some meetings in New York next week. You will join me there for a night, and I'll make sure what I told Chris isn't a lie."

"You're out of your mind!" Zack spat into the phone.

"And you're out of a job unless you comply," Benny hissed.

"Benny, I don't think I can physically do what you're asking of me," Zack whined.

"I'm not asking, Zack. It's time you knew who was in charge here."

"I am so pleased you have finally found the opportunity to meet with me," Isa Kurtoglu said ceremoniously to Michael as he strode to their table at the restaurant.

"I apologize for taking so long in setting up this lunch," Michael said as he shook the Turk's hand. "My research keeps me pretty busy."

"Tell me about it." Isa smiled.

"About what? My research? It's all highly classified. I'm afraid I couldn't—"

"Of course you could." Isa smiled as he probed Michael's mind.

Michael felt, more than saw, a flash of light when Isa entered his mind. His first instinct was to panic, but then, as if a switch was flipped, he felt peaceful.

"That's right," Isa said in a soothing voice, eyes locked on Michael's. "No need to be concerned, Father. I have no intention to harm you. I just want to know what you have found from the disc left by our ancestors."

Michael felt a flood of information being pulled from his mind. At first he tried to stop it, but he could not. In his mind's eye, he saw flashes as if a high-speed film were playing.

"Excellent," Isa said with a smile. "You have come very far, Father. The Lady was right to choose you for this effort."

Michael grimaced at the mention of the Lady. He whimpered slightly as Isa brought to the fore the memories of Michael's encounters with her, forcing him to relive those experiences.

Behind the images of those memories, Michael heard Isa speaking to him in soft tones. "Millennia ago, the Lady's race succeeded in producing hybrids that combined the intellectual prowess of her species with the brute strength of Earth's hominids. They had a great society, but they forgot who had created them. Eventually, the Lady's race had to destroy them and start over. Many of the records of that time were lost in the destruction. For thousands of years, the aliens have been cultivating a safer strain of human to receive and interact with their DNA. I am the first of that new breed."

Michael squirmed uncomfortably in his chair. More than anything he wanted to be away from this power that invaded the very recesses of his mind.

"The disc you have was an attempt by our ancient ancestors to store their cumulative knowledge. The Lady's home world would love to have it, but she has other plans—plans to build the new humans into a species superior to her own. If her race knew of the existence of the disc, they would stop her plans. To that end, Father, you have been chosen to access the information for her. You have done very well."

Michael's breathing became labored as he used all of his will to break the bond with Isa. Sweat beads formed on his brow, and his color turned deathly pale. The video images on the wall of his mind moved to slow motion and eventually stopped at the point when the baby was taken from Gloria. At that moment, he knew with certainty they had used some of his DNA in the creation of the thing sitting before him.

Then, in a sudden burst of energy, his mind cleared. Isa had withdrawn, and Michael found himself at the end of the meal. Isa smiled and chatted excitedly about his internship with Benny. Not since his early encounters with the Lady had Michael experienced such a complete break with reality, such a contemptuous rape of his personality. He was deathly tired and experienced a primordial urge to burrow underneath the covers of his bed.

"Isa, would you think ill of me if I decided not to stay for coffee? Suddenly I am feeling very ill."

"Of course not, dear Father." Isa smirked. Michael bristled at the double entendre. "I've taken the liberty of having a taxi wait for you. I'm sure you will feel much better after a short nap and some time to get your thoughts in order."

"Thank you," Michael muttered weakly, his head bowed, not wanting to look into Isa's eyes, so much like his own. He softly offered a hasty good-bye, recoiling slightly when Isa shook his hand, and then hurried out of the restaurant.

Michael was barely awake through the cab ride to his apartment. He scarcely had time to take off his coat and make it to his bed before fatigue overtook him. Images swirled in chaotic order in Michael's mind as he slept fitfully on top of his covers. He slept there for the better part of three hours as his brain worked feverishly to return some sort of order to the jumbled mess of memories left by Isa. Each memory passed before his mind's eye as he slept.

Slowly he became conscious of his surroundings and eventually woke up. He couldn't remember much other than saying hello to Isa. Wiping his eyes, he looked at the clock to discover he had been out for hours. He sprang from the bed and fished inside his pocket for his cell phone. Seven missed calls, all from the programmers. They knew better than to leave a message about the secret project. He had to get to the lab.

He went into the bathroom and splashed some water on his face. Although he wondered what exactly had transpired at the lunch, he had an overall feeling of optimism and hope. Whatever had overtaken him was gone. In its place was a feeling of well-being.

It's time, Michael, he heard a voice say in his head. Like most people, he had always entertained an inner dialog, so the presence of the voice wasn't so startling—but somehow he knew he hadn't initiated this particular thought.

"Time for what?" he said into the mirror.

"Time to get the manuscript." He had salted it into a Vatican archeological dig in Turkey, the permit for which Michael had only to thank Uncle Benny and the elder Kurtoglu. The site was near ancient Antioch, the city that St. Paul used as a base for his missionary outreach. So far, findings at the site had been mundane. The crew on the ground, mostly college students looking for an exotic experience, dug according to a carefully laid out grid. Of course Michael had laid out the grid so he could dictate when the fake manuscript would be found.

His intent was to book a flight to Turkey after he returned from the lab, but the voice grew stronger, more insistent. Even as he tried to leave his apartment, his mind rebelled and sent him instead to the phone. He booked a flight to Turkey, scheduled to leave the next day.

Gabe and Tina pulled into the garage around six o'clock. This was a bit later than their usual time. Gabe was scheduled on a flight to Rome the next day for another session with the pope. That meant he and Tina had to get through the monthly orphanage budgets with their staff before he left. As usual, Kim had dinner ready. This night it was roasted pork served with risotto and butternut squash.

"Mommy! Daddy!" the kids screamed as their parents came through the door from the garage. Even at the ages of seven and eight, they grew excited every evening to see their parents and to tell them details of their day—the same details Kim could never get them to divulge.

"Hi, guys," Kim said to the couple, each of whom held a child.

"Wow, it smells wonderful in here," Tina said.

"Thanks." Kim smiled. "We went through their homework, but I think Chris is holding out on me." Chris had a habit of not being able to understand his homework when doing it with Kim, only to have a glorious "ah-ha" moment when his mother sat next to him later in the evening.

Gabe returned from the foyer with the mail. He looked uneasily at a manila envelope. The return address simply read, "Kurt. Rome." It was only a matter of time before Kurt got the idea that he could blackmail the brothers.

"Bad news?" Tina asked as they sat at the table.

"No. I think it's junk mail, but I'll have to go through it, just in case it's important."

"Look at it later then," Tina said in her "mother" tone. "Spend some quality time with your family before you head out to Rome. Read it on the plane."

"You're right." He grinned at her. "Besides, I'm tired tonight." He stashed the envelope in his briefcase.

Michael made his way to his office, the dark hallways lighting for him as his presence triggered their sensors. He sat down at his desk, the top of which lighted at his touch, and stared at the screen embedded in its surface.

He touched the Holomax icon on the screen and then sat back to analyze the results. Holomax had clearly detected a pattern to the information as it was read from different perspectives along the axis of the data cube. The patterns detected weren't recognizable as full phrases, but there were clear word fragments from the information used in the sample.

Michael was trying to decide what to make of the results. Looking at his desk screen again, he noticed another Holomax simulation run a few moments after the one he had just viewed. There was only supposed to be one simulation. It would seem that the programmers had some time on their hands and knew only to work until quitting time. They must have run the program again. *Well,* Michael thought, *we would have had to run confirmations anyway.*

He opened the new file. Again patterns emerged. Again he recognized word fragments. At least the second run had produced an identical result ... or had it? Michael stared at a subtle difference in the results. The patterns existed, but the letters within the patterns had shifted, and these new patterns looked as if they formed word fragments as well. He pulled up the results and laid them out side by side. The entire database had shifted by one character, as if the original was rotating!

Michael ran his hands through his hair with excitement. The disc not only contained information in a cubic format, but the cube rotated such that the message kept changing. The implications were staggering. Each rotation of the data cube produced a whole new set of information. The stored knowledge was voluminous beyond all telling. Such incredible compression of data could have enabled the Ancients to encode the very secrets of the universe!

Gabe was already tired and the day had just begun. He had gotten to the airport two hours before his early morning flight to allow time for the enhanced security check-in. While he waited for the plane to board, he studied his notes for the next papal presentation. Finally, he got to his seat in first class. After takeoff, there was a brief breakfast service.

As he drank coffee, he opened the package from Kurt. He had already decided he would try to scare Kurt physically if the man was demanding money or threatening Michael. He hated the decision, but he wouldn't back down from it. If Kurt was looking to give his family a rough time, he would quickly find the tables turned.

Inside the envelope were photos and a handwritten letter: "I am sure I am the last person you expected to hear from, but I feel compelled to warn you of a great evil about to be unleashed on the world. Why do I warn you? You can believe me; it is not out of a sense of duty or friendship. I do it to indict your brother in your eyes. He has indeed punished me for my previous actions. Aside from the return of the funds, I have been relegated to a position of minimal importance. And now I have the great pleasure of revenge."

Gabe put the letter down and took a drink of coffee. He was tempted to throw it away as a lunatic's ravings, but he knew he would have to read it in its entirety.

"Enclosed you will find photos of what appears to be a very ancient codex. Carefully written in Koine Greek of the first century, it is destined to be the oldest complete Gospel of John. Carbon dating and chemical analysis will put it to within a few decades of Christ's death."

Gabe looked at the photos. He had taken Greek in seminary but was not strong in languages. To top that off, the script of the era was hard for him to decipher. It was obviously Greek. He could make out enough of the text to see it was about Christ. He continued to read.

"This codex will place significant doubt about the life of Jesus, His supposed virgin birth, crucifixion, and resurrection. It has been carefully crafted to subtly deny claims of Christ's deity. It is, of course, a brilliant forgery executed by the only person in the world with the skill to fool the experts: your brother Michael. The manuscript was carefully crafted shortly after we began to study the disc. It was then chemically aged and seeded into an archeological dig outside Antioch. I seriously doubt much will be done to discredit the forgery, as it is masterfully executed and bears a message that is most desired in our times."

Gabe looked again at the photos. His mind was spinning. Would Michael actually do something so unethical? He knew in his heart the answer. Michael would not see it so much as unethical as clearing the decks to bring about the hope for society contained on the disc.

The letter concluded. "I could extract significant sums of money to protect your brother's secret, but I desire retribution instead. Your only courses of action are to expose him as a fraud, or stand idly by as he impugns your faith."

There was some more rambling, but Gabe just skimmed it. When he got to Rome, he would have to confront Michael. Maybe he could get his brother to abandon this reckless plot.

SEVENTEEN

Antakya, Turkey, is a small city sandwiched by mountains to its north and south. It lies in a fertile valley formed by the Orontes River and is home to lush olive trees and a vibrant Arab culture. The flight from Rome is surprisingly short, less than an hour, but distance can be measured in more than miles or kilometers. Antakya is centuries away from the bustle of Rome. At one point in its history, the Romans had tried to make the spot "the Rome of the East," but the Middle Ages, Crusades, and Ottoman rule allowed the archeological treasures of that era to be subsumed in the deep sediments deposited by the Orontes River. The northern edge of the town had undergone recent expansion, in which large portions of the ancient city were summarily bulldozed in the name of progress.

It is in this developing area that Michael had prepared the archeological dig currently attended by students. Their findings had been relatively nondescript up to this point, considering the area was purported to be the hub of St. Paul's ministry. The set-up was perfect in Michael's estimation. St. Paul lived a simple life. Where better to find a purported manuscript than the humble side of the ancient city?

The cab pulled up to the Anemon Antakya Hotel. Michael paid the driver and conversed in the bit of Turkish he knew. That bit would seem very exhaustive to the normal person, but Michael's innate abilities left him feeling insecure when he attained anything less than unaccented fluency in a language. He briefly unpacked and indulged in a thick, rich, Turkish coffee before heading out to the site.

A student picked him up in an open-air jeep. The heat of the day was harsh when they snaked through the downtown streets, but as they neared the dig site at the edge of town, they were able to drive fast enough to create a breeze. Once at the site, Michael exited the jeep and examined the roped-off grid in which students carefully dug spoonfuls of dirt at a time. The work was tedious, and many students learned from such an internship that archeology wasn't their calling. But others, like Michael, learned that they felt a slight thrill of excitement with each spoonful. What if this scoop of dirt contained something profound and untouched by human hands for thousands of years? He grinned at the students as they stole glances at him and then quickly returned to their work, lest they appear to be something less than diligent in his presence. From their midst, a lanky, strawberry-blond kid with a Howdy Doody smile made his way to Michael. The student, a hearty young man from Alabama, grinned broadly as he pumped Michael's hand.

"Hi. I'm Todd Fairborne. It is such a pleasure to finally meet you, Father. I've followed your work, and I have to say I think you're a genius."

"Thanks." Michael grinned. He never got used to the fawning of the students. "But you need to remember we are just two guys on a dig. The major difference between you and me is that my knees have begun to make creaking noises."

"Yes, sir." Todd beamed.

"So fill me in, Todd. What have you and your team been doing?"

"Excavation of the southeastern quadrant, as you prescribed."

Michael nodded, and then placed the bait. "And what have you found?"

"As I detailed in my last report, mostly some pottery and cooking utensils. The area appears to have been a poorer section of town." Todd shrugged and offered a slight frown. "The pottery is functional, not decorative. The finds have been unimpressive from the standpoint of unearthing anything artistic. Nonetheless, they should be very helpful in piecing together the day-to-day life of an average citizen."

"I was hoping for a bit more," Michael said with a groan. "No offense, Todd, but we already know a lot about the day-to-day existence for the normal folk in the Roman Empire. It wasn't that great. Subsistence-level food, work seven days a week."

"I was hoping for more myself," Todd agreed with a touch of despair.

"Maybe I'm at fault," Michael said. "I just had a feeling we were going to find something in that quarter. Let me take a look at the site again. Maybe we'll move the dig a bit to the north and west."

"I was hoping you'd say that," Todd said excitedly. "I was looking at a spot in that quadrant. There is what appears to be the tip of something—maybe an intact artifact very close to the surface."

Of course there is. I made sure of it when I buried the manuscript. "You know what, Todd?" Michael asked. "I'd like to see it. Let's check it out."

"That sounds great to me." Todd grinned.

Chris met Gabe at Fiumicino.

"Welcome!" Chris said with a smile. "Are you ready for your presentation?"

"Yes," Gabe said. "I have a briefing book for you in my briefcase. It is pretty much what we spoke about over the phone. I don't think you'll find any surprises there."

"Good. I'll go through it this afternoon so that I'm up to speed for tomorrow's meeting."

"And I want to try to meet up with Michael this afternoon."

"Sorry to tell you, Gabe, but Michael had to go out of town today. Something came up at a Vatican dig in Turkey. I saw him last night, and he sends his apologies. Actually, he said that if you stick around for a few days, he should be back in time to visit with you."

Gabe sighed. He hoped against hope the trip to Turkey wasn't meant to unearth the manuscript detailed in Kurt's letter. He silently prayed he wasn't too late.

The moment he got to his hotel room, he opened Kurt's letter and dialed the phone number listed there. He spoke without any pleasantries the moment Kurt answered. "Kurt, I received your envelope, and I'm in town. Let's talk."

"So talk," Kurt said flatly.

"No. I mean in person," Gabe countered.

"I don't think so. I find you to be a bit physically imposing for my taste. What is it you would like to say?"

Gabe felt flush with rising anger, but he knew he had to control it. He spoke carefully in a diplomatic tone. "I'm concerned for my brother's well-being. I know how easily he can fall prey to the passions of one of his projects."

"There is nothing more for me to do, Reverend. The ball is in your court."

This conversation was going nowhere fast. He needed more information if he was going to stop Michael. "Can you convince me the documents are fraudulent?"

"I have no idea what you're talking about," Kurt said in mock innocence, a clear pretense against the possibility the conversation was being recorded.

"Did you know that Michael left for the Antioch dig site this morning?" Gabe asked as he nervously paced the room.

Kurt said somberly, "Well, then, I guess your trip and this conversation are unnecessary, Reverend. It's too late for you to stop him." Kurt chuckled and the line went dead.

Gabe stabbed at the redial button, and the call predictably went straight to voice mail. He slammed down the phone in disgust and then immediately snatched it up again. He dialed Michael's cell phone another time, but either his brother was not within range of a cell tower, or he had turned off his phone.

There were only a few hotels in Antakya where Michael would stay. Within a few phone calls, Gabe was able to find the right one. The operator put him through to the room, but the phone rang and rang. Finally, Gabe left a message for Michael to call him as soon as he could. Seconds after he hung up, the phone rang, startling him a bit. Chris's caller ID dashed his hopes that it was Michael.

"The briefing packet looks fine to me, Gabe," Chris said cheerily.

"Good," Gabe said distractedly.

"Are you okay? Everything fine?"

"A little jetlagged, I guess."

"Wow, like I believe that answer." Chris chuckled. "I know you're bummed that Michael isn't here."

Gabe took a deep breath and then let go of his feelings. "Chris, I have a long and deep relationship with him. He's my brother and my friend, but we're growing apart. I could easily find myself in a place where I am actually at odds with Michael! It's unthinkable, and it makes me really unhappy."

"Well, you're catching me a little off guard here, Gabe. But let me say that Michael's going to Turkey wasn't some sort of slap in the face. He didn't do it to avoid you."

"I know that. It's his stupid research. By the time he's done, he'll be telling the world that Jesus isn't the Son of God."

"You don't know that," Chris said gravely. "And there's always the Church's ability to keep things under a tight lid. If Michael ever released such a statement to the outside world, he would never again be permitted to work on his project. In short, if he wants to keep doing what he loves, he'll keep his crisis of faith to himself."

"I hope you're right, Chris. But if his message is subtle enough, the Curia may even herald it for its usefulness in uniting humanity."

"Well, I still have a measure of faith in the system and in this pope's ability to see through whatever Michael is doing. They finally had their meeting, and His Holiness was very impressed with Michael's findings. Maybe you're overreacting."

"I don't know. I have a feeling Michael didn't fully brief the pope," Gabe said with despair.

Zack smiled at his secretary but felt an instant twinge of despair. The affair had continued, despite Benny's strong admonition to end it.

In truth, he hadn't tried much to stop it. There was a week of abstinence immediately after Benny's call. And there had always been a sinking feeling in his soul after the horrible encounter with Benny in New York. But those times faded into memory when he looked at Bonnie's smile.

His feelings for her were complex. He still believed he loved his wife. Gloria was his partner in life, in this ministry, and in bringing forth the child who would save humanity. But with all that history, sometimes he just wanted the freedom of unbridled lust and instant gratification. He mulled it over in his mind. Why was he continuing this affair? His only answer: because he could. It was as simple as that.

His chief concerns now were to keep Gloria from finding out and to ensure that Bonnie didn't get too emotionally involved. He loved her body, loved using her body, but he didn't and never could love the vacuous girl who did his filing. She was, in the end, administrative staff. Some of her administrations were more personal than others, but that was about the extent of it.

"Are we on for tonight?" Bonnie asked seductively.

"Not tonight, darlin'," Zack drawled. "Gloria and I have plans."

Bonnie slammed his mail on the desk and began to huff out of the room.

"Well, look here." Zack grinned. "It looks like I have some time on my calendar right now. I could probably squeeze you in."

"Ditto." Bonnie grinned as she closed and locked the office door.

Immediately after Michael addressed the students at the dig site, he and Todd walked to the northwest quadrant, putting them out of sight and earshot of the rest of the group.

"So show me what you were talking about," Michael said. Todd led him directly to the site where the codex was buried.

"I see your point," Michael said. "This could easily be some sort of containment vessel."

"You mean like a jar?"

"Yes, something like that." If he had not been so interested in perpetrating his own deceit, Michael would have been flabbergasted by this young man's lack of knowledge. He dropped to his knees and carefully loosened the dirt around the vessel.

Todd joined him, mimicking his actions. The vessel, actually a large vase, was unearthed quickly, as Michael had planned. Even though he had salted this mine, Michael got the thrill that comes from an archeological discovery. The notion of finding a buried treasure was never far in the back of an archeologist's mind.

"Do you feel the excitement, Todd?" Michael asked. "You and I may have happened on something big."

"So far I just see a vase, Father. I don't want to get my hopes up."

"I've been doing this for a long time. After a while you sort of get a sixth sense about these things, and my sixth sense tells me we have found something significant."

With one last effort, the men freed the large, sealed vessel from the soil. The top of it had a ceramic lid that had been fitted with wax. "See what I mean, Todd? The wax seal could have preserved the contents of this vase by keeping the air out for centuries."

"What now?" Todd asked as Michael brushed dirt off the face of the vase.

"We take it to a lab, and open the wax seal in a chamber where we can control the atmosphere, but until then we may have a hint at the contents. Do you see this faint etching?" Michael grinned broadly, tracing it with his finger. "It seems to say Paulus. This could well be a stash of manuscripts owned by the apostle Paul."

"That's very interesting, Father," Todd said emotionlessly as he removed a handgun from his pocket.

"It really is," Michael said before he heard the click of Todd's gun. "Todd, what are you doing?" he asked, as the grin froze on his face.

"Open it, Father." Todd pointed at the wax seal with the barrel of the handgun.

"Todd, it should be opened in pristine conditions, not here," Michael gently protested.

"I could easily kill you and open it myself. Is that what you want?" Todd asked, his nervousness bringing about a high-pitched whine.

"No," Michael said gravely, looking deeply into the face of the troubled young man. He had been so focused on retrieving the fake manuscript that he had not noticed anything out of the ordinary in Todd's demeanor, other than his lack of archeological experience.

"Talk to me, Todd," Michael said calmly. "I'll open it, but while I do, why don't you tell me why you're holding a gun on me?"

"Because I think you are about to make a great discovery ..."

"And you want to take the credit?" Michael interrupted incredulously. "You can have it!"

"Just open it." Todd waved the gun.

Michael grimaced to indicate that opening the container outside a lab would be a terrible mistake. Todd just waved his gun.

"I'm going to gently remove the wax," Michael said, working slowly.

"I have very good sources who tell me you expect to find a priceless manuscript, possibly the earliest account of Christ's life," Todd said sharply.

For a second, Michael wondered how the young man could know such a thing. Michael had told nobody, other than Kurt. Kurt! So this was to be Kurt's revenge. Michael had a new appreciation of the situation's danger.

Speaking with deliberate calm, Michael said, "If it is as I suspect, Todd, this manuscript will rewrite the history books. It doesn't matter which of us is known as its discoverer. What matters is that it makes its way into the world."

"Not going to happen, Father. Allah is tired of the Christian offense of worshipping his prophet, Jesus."

"Allah?" Michael asked the fair-haired man from Alabama, unable to hide his skepticism.

"Yes. I'm what the American press would call a homegrown radical Islamist, Father. Does that surprise you?" Todd asked with a sneer.

"Frankly, yes. I didn't see this coming. So how do you know Kurt?"

"We kind of connected online. Like minds and all."

Michael laughed derisively. "You're not like minds, Todd. Believe me, Kurt is playing you."

"Open the container, Father, and very carefully hand its contents to me."

Michael removed the last of the wax seal and slowly opened the vessel.

"Aaaaaagh!" A shrill scream pierced the air. A young woman from the dig site had come looking for them. At the sight of the gun and Michael on his knees before the gunman, she screamed and ran back over the hill.

"They'll be coming for us very soon," Michael urged. "Are you sure you want to do this, Todd? If you holster the gun, we can both walk away from here. We'll tell her she misunderstood what she saw. We can say you were showing me that pistol."

"Grab the stuff and stand up slowly, Father," Todd said briskly. From the other direction, a jeep sped to the scene.

"Get in!" Todd demanded.

At the Vatican, Gabe's discussion with the pope continued down the path of the theoretical. "I have to admit, sir, that this is on the fringe of Protestant scholarship, but it may bear a bit of examination."

"I have come to enjoy your visits, my son," the pope said with a smile. "What will it hurt if we visit and pass the time with a bit of fancy?"

"The Bible says in Genesis that the sons of God cohabitated with the daughters of men, the result being ungodly hybrids who were totally rejected by the Lord."

"Yes," the pontiff said.

"This takes the thought a bit further. There are also times in the Old Testament where God seems to be very harsh, particularly when He wanted Israel to totally exterminate the people they had conquered."

"God's ways are not our ways, Gabe. Who would we be to question Him?" the pope asked.

"But what if we could understand Him a bit better?" Chris asked gently.

"In what way?" the pope asked.

"If you take the verse about the nephilim literally," Gabe began, "you will see it all in a different light. Scripture notes that Noah was saved from the flood because he was pure 'in his generations.' Yet even after the flood, the fallen angel strain resurfaced."

"And the result was the enemies of Israel?" the pope asked.

"Yes," Gabe answered. "The giants of the land."

"Think of Goliath," Chris said. "These giant men with six fingers were some sort of genetic aberration."

"If the writings are actual accounts and not just legend," the pope said judiciously.

"Turn the page of your briefing packet, Holiness," Chris said.

The pope turned the page to find photos of giant hominid skeletons unearthed in Saudi Arabia. In one photo, an averaged-sized man looked like a small child as he lay on the ground next to the recently unearthed, intact skeleton.

"Are these real?" the pope asked.

"I'm not sure if we'll ever know," Chris said. "It seems the Saudi government has secreted them away. These photos were leaked to the Internet. Of course there are those who claim the photos are faked."

"Fascinating!" the pope exclaimed as his intercom buzzed. He picked up the receiver and listened carefully. "Fine. Send him in," he said, placing the receiver in its cradle.

"It would appear your uncle Benny has urgent news from Turkey.

"Cardinal Cross, what is this urgent matter?" the pope asked as Benny rushed into the room.

"Isa Kurtoglu called me. Someone pulled a gun on Michael at the dig site in Turkey. They forced him into a jeep and sped away. Isa said his father is doing everything he can to find them."

Gabe's reaction was immediate and abrupt. He jumped up and demanded, "We've got to go to Turkey, now."

Chris stood beside Gabe. "It's a big country, Gabe. We need a plan, and we'll need help."

Gabe prayed silently for wisdom.

"There are little-known Vatican resources," the pope said quietly. "Our secret service is among the most secretive and best trained in the world."

Gabe had a burst of insight. He chose his words carefully so as not to incriminate his brother. "Holiness, there is a scientist who works with Michael named Kurt Waldenbaum. Michael disciplined him for some infraction, and the man has sought vengeance. He may know something about this."

The pontiff picked up his phone, dialed quickly, and spoke softly. In very short order, they were joined by a very powerfully built man in a black suit, white shirt, and thin, black tie. He looked the quintessential secret serviceman. He did not introduce himself, and the pope made no attempt at introductions.

"You requested to see me, Holiness?"

"Yes. We have an issue. One of our priests has been taken hostage in Antakya, Turkey."

"Father Michael left for Turkey yesterday," the agent said.

"In fact, it is Father Michael who was taken at gunpoint from our dig site," the pope confirmed. "This is his brother."

The man in black said, "I know all present, Holiness."

The pope nodded. "Of course. Gabe believes a scientist named Kurt Waldenbaum may have some information."

"A most unpleasant individual. I will question him immediately," the agent said briskly.

"I'm going with you," Gabe said forcefully.

"It would be better if you waited here."

"Sir, please tell him to take me along with him," Gabe pleaded with the pope, who looked at the secret serviceman knowingly.

"Come with me," said the man in black, looking at Gabe dispassionately.

"I'll call your mother," Chris called after Gabe. "She'll want to make some funds liquid in case there is a ransom call."

"Good idea," Gabe called back to him as he rushed to keep up with the agent. He hoped this situation could be resolved with something as simple as a ransom payment, but somehow he doubted it.

The jeep sped into the mountains. Michael got a good look at his captors, two young Arab men and Todd. He quickly assessed the situation. This was not a well-organized group. He doubted this was a very high-level operation.

"What do we do with him?" one of the Arabs asked the other. Michael's Arabic was rusty, but he understood enough of the conversation. "I say we kill him, but only after the other American. He annoys me."

"Hey, guys?" Todd asked with concern. "What do we do with this guy now?"

Well, it's pretty clear the Toddster doesn't speak Arabic. Michael didn't want anyone to know he understood. "Todd, why not just let me go? I promise not to go to the police. No harm, no foul."

"Shut up!" Todd yelled as he backhanded Michael in a show of strength for the other two.

The second said in Arabic, "We should kill the young one before he makes another stupid mistake."

Seeming to ignore him, the first one stopped the jeep. "Todd," he said in a thick accent, "you in front."

Todd protested as the one from the passenger side exited the jeep. He grabbed Todd by the neck, pulled him from the jeep, and knocked him to the ground with a swift punch to the stomach. He offered no explanation, and the winded Todd demanded none. Rather, he picked himself up and scurried to the front seat.

The young Arab sat next to Michael and, taking a handkerchief, wiped the blood from his mouth.

"Thank you," Michael said quietly in Arabic.

"You know what we were saying?" the young man asked.

"Yes," Michael replied, "but you don't need to kill us. You can let us go."

"Perhaps you," said the young man softly, "but he must die," referring to Todd.

They pulled the jeep to the opening of a cave. Todd, far less "large-and-in-charge," jumped from the passenger seat to pull aside some branches so the jeep could be parked inside. Then he pulled the branches back over the mouth of the cave. Some sunlight filtered through the leaves of the branches, bathing the cave in a constantly changing pattern of light and shadow.

"There has been a big error in judgment," Michael said cautiously in Arabic.

"You speak A-rab?" Todd asked incredulously.

"Shut up, Todd," Michael said tersely.

"What kind of error in judgment?" the driver asked derisively.

"I expect this manuscript will prove that Jesus was a prophet, but not the Son of God. If you let me bring these words to the Christian world, you will be doing Allah's will."

"Is this true?" He left the jeep and motioned for Michael to do the same.

"I am a priest. It would be an offense if I lied to you," Michael said as he joined his captors.

"But we were told the opposite."

"There are many who do not want this news to be exposed," Michael said. "Todd is the victim of one of those men. A very evil man who does not want the world to know the truth."

The driver pulled the manuscript from the jeep. "Show me," he said sharply.

"Do you understand ancient Greek?" Michael asked.

"Modern Greek," the would-be terrorist answered.

"Two thousand years of usage have changed the language quite a bit," Michael said, "but you should be able to follow along."

"We have plenty of time. We will wait here until they tire of looking for you."

They moved closer to the mouth of the cave to take advantage of the filtered sunlight. Michael read the document aloud as his captor followed along. Periodically he would pause to explain what he had just read, but his captor would stop him with an extended hand to indicate he had understood the meaning.

"You surprise me," Michael said to his lead captor. "You have very strong language skills."

"It's a gift." The young man smiled almost bashfully. "I have always found languages easy to learn."

"Me too." Michael grinned. "We haven't been introduced," he ventured, "and since it looks like we may be here for a while, what's your name?"

"My friends call me Hanny." The young man smiled awkwardly. "He is called Abdul."

These were obviously not their real names, but Michael saw hope in the very fact that the young man had ventured any names at all. From different things he had read over the years, he knew his best chance for survival was to befriend the hostage-takers.

Michael looked through the manuscript, careful not to tear the artificially aged document. He found the verse he wanted and pointed to it. "Can you read this sentence?" Michael asked Hanny.

"To me it looks as if it says, 'I am a way, a truth, a life. Any man can know the God like me,'" Hanny said.

"Very good!" Michael complimented. "The importance of the phrase is in its use of an indefinite article. There is no 'the' written or implied in this statement."

Hanny stared at him blankly, trying to understand the importance of what Michael was saying.

"Later manuscripts," Michael added, "have changed the emphasis. They say 'I am *the* way, *the* truth, and *the* life. No man can come to the Father but through me.'"

"So using the definite article makes it sound as if Jesus was calling himself God."

"Yes," Michael said, "when in the earliest manuscript, He seemed to be more about espousing a way of life than a theology."

"This is very interesting, Father. Our faiths may not be so different after all."

"At least not in their origins," Michael said, hoping the rest of the world could be as easily swayed as Hanny.

The agent was given immediate passage into Michael's facility. Even the computer system seemed to move more quickly for this guy.

"Kurt was doing experiments on some of his employees," Gabe explained to the agent. "Mind control stuff, and he tried to steal money from our bank accounts. I got the money back, and Michael chastised him. Michael didn't want to go to the police because of the secrecy of his project."

"And his complicity in any crimes committed," the agent said matter-of-factly.

"Or at least what would be taken as his authorization for Kurt to abuse these men," Gabe said cautiously. "But that's not important. What *is* important is that Kurt sent a note threatening retribution."

"What was the nature of the abuse you spoke of?"

"Something about creating an alternate personality for the computer programmers, one that would only be active when they were working in this facility."

"I know of such processes," the agent said, making Gabe wonder if he hadn't graduated from such an education as well.

"Well, does your knowledge include being naked with an erection while beating the pupils?"

"No, it doesn't," the agent said with the slightest inflection. The agent strode confidently into Kurt's office and shut the door, barely leaving enough time for Gabe to enter the room. "Herr Waldenbaum," he said sharply, "time is of the essence. You will tell me everything you know about the abduction of Father Michael."

"Who are you?" Kurt asked incredulously. He looked at Gabe with contempt.

"*Servizio Informazzioni del Vaticano*," the agent said in a clipped tone. Kurt blanched. Only the KGB would be a worse intruder.

"I don't know what you're talking about," Kurt offered weakly.

"Maybe I can assist you in remembering," the agent said nonchalantly as he fingered his smartphone. Within seconds, he had dialed up a file on Kurt.

"*Oh, mein Herr,* it seems you have been a naughty boy while working in the Vatican. Very naughty indeed!" He turned his phone around so that Kurt could see surveillance video of his exploits with the programmers. Kurt sat back in his chair and rubbed his forehead.

Gabe was indignant. The Vatican's Secret Service knew all about the crimes that had been committed. Yet they did nothing about it!

As if reading his mind, the agent turned to Gabe and said, "Knowledge is power, my friend. Storing knowledge allows the greatest leverage when it is needed. You may not agree with the method, but the results may well save your brother's life."

Gabe nodded in understanding, if not agreement.

"So, *mein Herr,* what do you know about this kidnapping?"

"It wasn't supposed to be a kidnapping," Kurt said softly. "I got in touch with a kid from Alabama, Todd Fairborne, who fashions himself a would-be Islamic terrorist. I managed to get him into online chats with two Arab kids: Hanny Fatima and Abdul Quadesh, who are looking to impress the real terrorists of the Middle East. Basically, they are all three midrash dropouts with delusions of grandeur."

"Doesn't sound like a particularly formidable group," the agent said. "What were they supposed to do, if not abduct the good Father Michael?"

"He was in Antakya for the unearthing of a manuscript that may prove to be an archeological treasure. I wanted the boys to steal the manuscript from him. Nothing more. I intended to sell it to Father Michael for five-and-a-half-million dollars." He glared at Gabe as he stated the amount.

"It would appear that a girl happened upon them and they panicked," the agent said. "Have they made contact with you since the abduction?"

"No," Kurt said. "I wasn't even aware there had been an abduction. I was hoping to hear from them about the manuscript."

"So you have no idea where they have gone?"

"No," Kurt said, "I swear."

"You will do more than swear, my friend," the agent said, motioning for Kurt to stand. He placed the man in handcuffs and phoned for the Swiss Guard to arrest him.

A few minutes with Kurt's cell phone was all it took. The agent easily identified the only American number in the system. He made a few phone calls to friends in the intelligence community around Antakya. The last ping from that phone had been near Michael's hotel.

"Did you learn anything?" Gabe asked the agent, who scowled. He was not accustomed to giving a detailed account of his phone conversations.

"The last time this phone had contact with a cell tower was yesterday, near your brother's hotel."

"Nothing since then?" Gabe asked, despair creeping into his voice.

"Relax. They've obviously gone into hiding, but they can't hide forever. The American will not be able to live long without his smartphone."

"So what do we do?" Gabe asked.

"We go to Antakya and wait."

It had been a tough night for the group trying to get comfortable in the jeep. Each of the three captors took a shift watching over their prisoner as he slept. For Michael, sleep came mercifully early. It was as if his only escape was to drift off to the solitude of sleep, leaving his captors far behind.

"This really sucks!" Michael heard Todd say to himself in the early morning hours.

"What's the matter?" Michael asked quietly, noting that the two Arab captors were asleep.

"I can't get a cell signal out here. I really need to stay in touch with people in the states, especially my girlfriend and my mom. I need to touch base with them to maintain an alibi."

"Deception," Michael said sleepily. "Not as easy as it looks, huh?"

"You don't like me very much, do you, Father?" Todd asked in dismay. "We're both American, yet you seem to be palling around with Hanny. Why is that?"

"Well, Todd, I think you need to come to terms with a few things. First of all, I'm not the one who dislikes you in this group," Michael said, sowing the seeds of distrust.

"What have they been saying about me?" Todd asked nervously.

"Like I'm going to jeopardize my already tenuous position by telling you that," Michael whispered. Todd grimaced.

"Second," Michael continued, "you're not exactly a Yankee Doodle Dandy. I can't see how your actions would lead me to believe you and I love the same nation.

"Third, if you are going to build an alibi, you'll need to find an excuse to get out of this cave to find a cell signal. If you and I really are bound by our nationality, then you'll try to take me with you."

"Fat chance!" Todd smirked. "Like I'd fall for that one."

"Why are you whispering?" Hanny said sleepily in English.

"We didn't want to awaken you," Michael said. "There's not so much to do here in this cave. We might as well all catch up on our sleep."

"I wasn't talking to you, Father. I was wondering why Todd felt the need to converse with you in a whisper."

"It's like he said," Todd responded defensively. "We were both awake, but we didn't want to awaken you guys. To pass the time, I thought maybe we could talk a little about baseball."

Michael stared hard at Hanny to let him know Todd was lying.

"Watch your step, Todd, or soon there will be two prisoners," Hanny said as he lay back in the driver's seat again.

Michael shrugged slightly as if to say to Todd, "What did I tell you?" Then he closed his eyes to see if sleep would rescue him again. His face broke into a slight grin at how well his plan was working. Hanny was beginning to see him as more than a prisoner, possibly even a compatriot.

Gabe, Chris, and the agent boarded the flight to Antakya.

"This is like a stupid joke," Gabe said with a wry grin. "A priest, a minister, and a spy ... ooof," he yelped as the agent elbowed him sharply in the stomach.

Chris chuckled and the agent broke his hardboiled veneer long enough to crack a smile.

"Point well taken," Gabe said, rubbing his stomach. "So what's our cover?"

"Tourists," the agent said softly.

"Oh," Gabe said seriously. "Anything else I should know?"

"Yes," the agent whispered in mock sincerity. "You and the good father here are a gay couple. I'm your heterosexual friend."

"What?" Gabe asked sharply.

"He's teasing!" Chris said as they took their seats. "Will you take it easy?"

"Just what I need. I was hoping for 007; I get Maxwell Smart," Gabe said tersely. He was more nervous than Chris, who placed a lot of trust in the agent and the Vatican Secret Service. Unlike Chris, he knew the incredible nature of the work in Michael's lab. What would nefarious individuals or governments do to gain access to that information? Each possibility was more heinous than the last.

The flight was uneventful. A car waited for them at the airport to take them to their hotel, the one that had been used by Michael.

"So now what?" Gabe asked.

"We wait. Eventually one of their cell phones will ping a tower. Most probably the American's. My people will know immediately when it does," the agent said.

"That's it?" Gabe asked.

The agent rolled his eyes as if it would be painful to explain everything else that had been going on behind the scenes. "Our agents on the ground have thoroughly examined the dig site and interviewed the students. We have been through the contents of your brother's room. I'm afraid there isn't much to report. The captors have no criminal history and no criminal contacts." He paused to order three Turkish coffees from the hospitality waitress. "Our only prudent course of action is the most difficult job in law enforcement—we wait."

"That's all we can do," Chris said in an effort to calm Gabe.

The agent sat straight in his chair. "The key is to not be lulled into a false sense of relaxation. You must remain ready to pounce at a moment's notice."

"Patience has never been his strong suit," Chris said with a smirk.

"I can't even joke about it, Chris," Gabe said sternly. "What if Michael's hurt—lying out there waiting for someone to help him?"

"If your brother was dead, or left to die, there would be cell phone activity. Since there is none, we can assume these people are holding him prisoner," the agent said to reassure Gabe.

"And that they haven't changed cell phones," Gabe said somberly.

"That too," the agent answered gravely.

Michael woke to a growling stomach. He was hungry and sure his reluctant captors were as well. They still had some water, which Hanny metered out judiciously while they waited. And waited. They had hoped the situation would soon calm down, but the jeep's radio carried reports of the involvement of Isa Kurtoglu. It sounded as if Isa had turned the situation into an international incident. Michael was no fool. These boys had neither the intellect nor the fortitude to go against whatever the hell Isa was. Michael had to find a way to break the stalemate, and in a way that kept them all alive. For now, though, he had to continue to build the trust of his captors.

"You seem to be a man of the times," Michael said to Hanny in Arabic. "No desire to be a martyr?"

"We are Muslims, but practical Muslims," Hanny answered. "If it falls to us to die for Allah, so be it. But we do not seek the experience."

"Good for you." Michael grinned slightly. "Eternity is a long time."

"And you, Father? Would you shy away from martyrdom?" Abdul asked.

"I'm afraid I would," Michael answered gingerly. "I have made some remarkable archeological discoveries that have changed my view of my faith."

"Such as this manuscript?"

"Yes, and so much more, Abdul. What if I were to tell you there is irrefutable evidence that Earth once was home to a society far more technologically advanced than our own?"

"Like Atlantis?" Hanny asked with a derisive wave of his hand.

"No." Michael smiled. "I'm not talking about an island nation, but a worldwide community that was in contact with other sentient life in our galaxy."

"I would say you are mistaken at best, insane at worst, and most probably an incompetent archeologist," Hanny said, prompting a chuckle from Abdul.

"Ah, but remember, in my example I said it was irrefutable evidence. Not my opinion but a vast source of electronic data chronicling the exploits of this society."

"Did this society believe in Allah?"

"In my example, let's assume they definitely believed in a creator-force that permeates the universe, but not a personal, knowable God."

"They would then deny that Mohammed is Allah's prophet."

"Maybe not," Michael said. "Maybe their religious teachings would say some men are more attuned to this creator-force than others. Maybe Mohammed was one of them."

"It would be hard for us to accept such a thing," Abdul said.

"But if the information also came with great technological advances to eliminate illness and ensure food and energy for every man, woman, and child on Earth?"

"If such a thing were to exist, I think we would have to reassess our faith," Abdul said tentatively.

"Do you think you are typical of Islam's response?" Michael asked.

"No," Hanny said. "There are those who would rather die than entertain even a conversation such as this."

"I think that is true of some Christians as well," Michael mused. "The only way to ensure world peace would be to withhold the benefits of the new technologies from those who resist its theological implications."

The agent took Chris and Gabe to the dig site at dawn the next day, before the morning traffic and arrival of more news teams. Beyond all else, the agent guarded his secrecy, but Chris and Gabe had demanded to see the site despite the worldwide attention Isa Kurtoglu had brought to the situation. The uniform grid pattern of roped off sections confirmed to Gabe that he would find archeology to be mind-numbingly tedious work. But the site felt homey on that morning, just because it was something close to Michael. He longed to see his brother again.

He would hug him, thankful for his safety—and then he would try to make him understand the horrible price of his actions. *All of this for a lie, Michael. What were you thinking!*

They arrived back at the hotel as Antakya was coming to life. Barely managing to avoid the ubiquitous reporters outside, they entered through the service entrance. Hotel security had been very adept at keeping the reporters at bay. Gabe and Chris had grown beards and donned hats and dark sunglasses any time they were in public. News of the kidnapping ran around the clock, and Isa Kurtoglu's handsome face had attained instant worldwide recognition. The guys made their way to a secure hospitality suite and ordered coffee.

"Another day of strong, Turkish coffee," Gabe said dryly as he turned down the volume of the television.

"I think I've become addicted to the stuff," Chris concurred. "Have you gotten hold of Tina or your mother?"

"They're both out of cell phone range. I've left them messages, though."

"It's unlike them not to check their messages," Chris said. "You don't suppose they're on their way to Rome, do you?"

"It's pretty unlikely," Tina said from behind them. The surprised men stood with a start and rushed to hug them.

At the sight of Gabe and Chris, Kim's emotions got the better of her. She buried her head in Chris's chest and cried uncontrollably. Gabe and Tina ended their embrace to help with her.

"He'll be okay, Kim," Chris said softly. "I have a feeling we'll be bringing him home real soon." Tina explained that Fran and David had flown to Georgia to stay with the kids.

"We have a ping," the agent said sternly as he walked up to the group.

Gabe and the agent took off in their car, followed by Chris and the women.

"I can't believe you talked me into this," Chris barked. "You two should have stayed behind."

"I'm his *mother*!" Kim screamed as they sped out of town.

"And," Tina continued, "this is the twenty-first century, Chris. Women don't need to stay behind and wait to be protected by the men-folk."

"This isn't a women's rights issue," Chris barked as he tried to keep up with the agent. "There are two beautiful kids at home. How does it help them to place all of us in danger?"

Silence filled the car.

Sprites of early morning light filtered through the leaves of the branches covering the cave's opening. Michael worried about transpiring events. Hanny and Abdul were livid, having awakened to find that Todd had abandoned his watch to leave the cave. No doubt to make a phone call to the states.

"Where were you?" Hanny demanded when Todd returned.

"Taking a leak," Todd said defensively.

"Liar!" Hanny screamed as he lashed out at the American boy, slamming him against the side of the jeep. "You used your cell phone, didn't you?"

"No!" Todd spat back. "I didn't!"

Michael ran to the men and placed his hand on Hanny's shoulder. "Don't hurt him, Hanny. Please."

"He has compromised our position, Father."

"You don't know that. He said he didn't use his cell phone."

"He lies, Father."

"Todd," Michael said calmly, "tell these guys the truth. Did you use your phone?"

"Just a bit," Todd said as Hanny placed his hands around the boy's throat.

"Pack up our stuff!" Hanny yelled to Abdul. "We have to run!"

Time spent with these young men had given Michael a pretty good appraisal of their ineptitude and their patent lack of fundamentalist fervor. He had planned to create in them a sort of reverse Stockholm syndrome, but he had come to identify with them as well. In the final analysis, they were just kids. If he didn't find a way to take hold of this situation, it could mushroom out of control, leaving them to be the latest in a list of Kurt's victims.

On the other hand, the boys' lack of expertise made them dangerous in their own right. They still had guns and were holding Michael captive. He had to be judicious and diplomatic with them, moving carefully along the bridge of trust he had slowly built with the would-be terrorists.

"Hanny," Michael pleaded. "I don't want any of us to get hurt. How about a back-up plan?"

"I'm listening, Father."

EIGHTEEN

The agent parked his car at the dig site. Chris pulled in just as Gabe and the agent were exiting their car. Kim and Tina jumped out before Chris could turn off the motor.

"Tina, Mom," Gabe said sternly, "you should have stayed at the hotel with Chris."

"Not happening," Kim said sharply to her son.

He knew better than to argue this point with her. "Well, at least stay here at the dig site. Please. Think of the kids!"

"Fine," Tina said as she pulled Gabe closer. "But the kids need their daddy too."

"She's right," Chris said as he strode toward the agent. "I should go."

"I'll take only one of you," the agent said. "And it will be Gabe. He's younger and faster."

Chris and Gabe somberly nodded their assent. Tina hugged her husband as tears flooded their eyes.

"Don't worry," said the agent to the family. "One of you I can protect, but there's no way for me to extricate Father Michael if I have to babysit his entire family."

"Point well taken," Kim said gravely as she nestled against Chris. "Gabe, do everything he tells you. No heroics. I want to be with both of my boys this afternoon."

"No problem, Mom. I want to be here too." Turning to the agent, he said, "I'm ready."

"Good," the agent said as he flipped the safety on his gun. "Let's go. The Turkish forces should be joining us any moment."

"What's your plan?" Hanny asked Michael.

"I can say you are students working on the dig. I'll say you two first found the manuscript's container sticking out of the soil. You alerted Todd, and the four of us went to check it out."

"But the girl who saw the gun ..." Todd offered anxiously.

"You were just showing me the gun while these guys went to get the jeep. She must have misunderstood."

"And why did we sleep in a cave?" Hanny asked.

"I like to dig early in the morning before it gets too hot. I didn't want to waste the time to go back to the hotel," Michael offered.

It was certainly more common to camp at a dig site than stay at a hotel. There was a simple elegance to the plan that even these guys could pull off. But the wildcard was Isa. He had turned the kidnapping into a media event for a reason. Finding Michael and the boys happily digging in the dirt could render him more of an international fool than a hero. He would never abide by that.

"It is the best plan, Father," Hanny said. "I will do it."

Abdul nodded in agreement.

"Todd?" Hanny asked.

"It's not really what I set out to do, but I guess I could. Father, shouldn't there be some kind of financial reward for us discovering the document?" Todd asked smugly.

"It's a Vatican dig," Michael said in exasperation with this fool who couldn't possibly imagine his very life was at stake. "You signed forms waiving any personal claims."

"This one will need to die," Hanny said.

"No!" Michael spat as he heard the click of Hanny's gun.

Hanny pointed the gun at Todd's forehead. "This is your last chance, Todd. If you agree to the plan, I will not shoot you. But if I ever hear you have violated our trust, I will find you and kill you. Do you understand me?"

"Yes," Todd said quietly as a wet spot appeared on the front of his jeans.

Hanny holstered his gun, and Abdul laughed.

In fewer than two minutes, they were exiting the cave and heading toward the dig site. Michael furiously scanned the surroundings. He didn't know how long it took to trace a cell signal and mount a rescue, but he guessed it wasn't long. His eyes fell on a relatively flat area in a clearing surrounded by trees.

"Pull over at that smooth patch of ground," Michael said to Hanny.

As the jeep slowed, Michael jumped out. "Come on, Todd," he said, "we have but a little time to make it look like we've been digging here."

Todd brought a small trowel, some rope, and stakes from his dig pack. The two of them rushed to stake and rope off a small area, while Hanny and Abdul dug haphazardly in the dirt.

"I think I found something!" Hanny said in Arabic.

Michael peered into the hole he and Abdul had dug. To his relief, the young man had actually found a pottery shard. This would go a long way in building their alibi.

"Hey, Todd, look at this," Michael said with a grin.

"Pottery shard," Todd said. "Looks like it's pretty common. Maybe not even ancient."

"Not the point, Todd," Michael said, shaking his head.

The agent walked swiftly, deliberately. Gabe strode beside him.

"Let me give you the rules," the agent said. "At all times, you are to stay behind me. Out of the line of fire. GPS shows the phone call was made within a quarter of a mile from here. I'm thinking they are holed up in one of the caves on the hillside. Kurtoglu's extraction team should be nearby. If we find your brother before they do, we'll monitor the situation and report back to them. No heroics."

"Understood," Gabe said. "There's only one thing. Why did you agree to bring me along?"

"If we are too late, I will need you to identify your brother's body," the agent answered in a clinical monotone.

They walked briskly through the foreign countryside in silence. Before long, the agent motioned for Gabe to stop. He placed a finger to his lips and then motioned toward some movement in a clearing beyond a nearby grove of trees. He motioned for Gabe to follow him as he walked quietly, making sure to use the trees as cover.

From the grove, Gabe and the agent could hear their voices but not make out the words they were saying. As the agent tried to call in the position to the Turkish military, his signal was cut off. He had been around long enough to know it was being jammed. Clearly the Turks knew where to find Michael and his captors ... and clearly they didn't want any interference from the Vatican Secret Service. That much was understandable, but jamming their signal was not standard procedure. The agent was beginning to feel as if this was a set up. He didn't trust Kurtoglu.

It didn't look to Gabe like Michael was in any immediate danger. The voices sounded congenial as the three younger men gathered around something Michael held in his hand.

Gabe raised his eyebrows toward the agent as if to say, "He's not in any trouble." Relief at finding such a benign situation overtook him, and he failed to heed the agent's previous advice. He stepped away from the cover of the trees and called out, "Michael, are you all right?"

Behind him, the agent cursed in Italian, raised his gun, and came from behind the tree.

"Everyone, put your hands up where I can see them," he said in English. Michael, Todd, and Hanny immediately raised their hands. Michael explained to Abdul in Arabic, and he followed suit.

"Gabe?" Michael said with surprise. Gabe heard a clear longing in his voice. The situation was not as benign as he had assumed.

"Yeah, buddy, it's me. Have these guys hurt you?"

"Only in that I'm too old to stay out at a dig site," Michael said with studied nonchalance and a forced chuckle. "I need a hotel bed and a hot shower."

The agent slowly began to lower his gun. Gabe shook his head ever so slightly, encouraging him not to drop his weapon. He didn't like something in the tone of Michael's voice.

"Cover me," Gabe whispered cautiously to the agent, who cussed again, this time in English.

Gabe stepped a few paces closer to the group of men. "Michael," he said cautiously, "you don't even hug your own brother?"

"Sure," Michael said, stepping cautiously away from his captors. He knew fully well they would be watching him carefully for any sign of betrayal.

"Gabe," Michael said in a scolding tone as he walked toward his brother. "Can we put our hands down? This is a ridiculous way to greet your brother."

"When you're over here with us," Gabe said as the droning of a helicopter first made itself known behind them.

The drone turned into a roar as Michael finally made his way to Gabe. Sensing there was no protection, no alibi, if Michael didn't honor his end of the deal, Hanny watched the agent closely, waiting for a moment of distraction, during which he would kill the man.

A credit to his training, the agent didn't blink, didn't take his eyes from his target. The helicopter circled the group of men. From an open side door, Isa appeared behind a soldier with a machine gun. At Isa's command the soldier began to shoot.

"No!" Michael screamed as he heard the gunfire, instantly realizing the tragic flaw of his plan. Isa wanted a media event, and he would have one. The young Turk wanted to reveal himself on the world stage as a Putin-esque hero who rescued the young priest. By moving the boys to the mock dig site, Michael had succeeded in doing little more than making them easy targets.

He pulled away from Gabe and ran toward the young men. He saw them, one after another, explode as the fifty-caliber rounds ravaged their bodies and sent them crumbling to the ground. Turning to the helicopter, he waved his hands over his head, screaming, "Stop!"

His eyes zeroed in on Isa behind the young soldier at the machine gun. He saw a brief smile on the young ruler's face as he pulled out a revolver and shot the agent without a second thought.

As the agent fell, Gabe threw Michael to the ground and lay on top of him. Michael felt Gabe jerk and then lose consciousness as bullets from Isa's gun tore at his flesh.

A man with a video camera jumped from the helicopter to film as Isa jumped out and ran to Michael.

"Father, are you all right?" he called with manufactured compassion.

"Isa!" Michael screamed, a now-familiar chill going down his spine as the young man approached. "You shot my brother!" he yelled as his hands fought to contain the sticky, warm blood gushing from Gabe's leg and chest.

In a quick move of exasperation, Isa motioned for the videographer to stop the film.

"The important thing is that you are safe, my friend," Isa said to Michael, who lay clutching his brother.

"The important thing is that you use this chopper to get my brother to the nearest hospital!" Michael spat.

"Of course," Isa said, motioning to the pilot to make the necessary calls. "You can thank me later." The soldier, who had previously manned the machine gun, helped Michael with Gabe. At the last moment, with the tape rolling, Isa helped as well.

En route to the hospital, Isa stared at Michael as he cradled Gabe. To Michael, it looked as if the younger man was at once confused and disgusted by the pain he saw.

Michael yelled at him through his tears. "He's your uncle, for God's sake!"

"Hardly." Isa chuckled. "You and I may share a gene or two, but that doesn't make your adopted brother my uncle."

Michael spied the chopper's first-aid kit and tore it open. Finding gauze, he frantically unwound it and shoved it at the bleeding wound in Gabe's chest, applying pressure. He estimated that Gabe's lung had to have been punctured based on the horrible rattling and sucking noises he made with each breath. *Oh God, Gabe, how do I help you?* His mind raced until it found a nearly banished memory.

"Isa," he screamed with wild rage. "If he dies, I swear to you that the Lady will never know the contents of the disc. I swear it!"

"And if he lives?" Isa asked with deliberate calm and the hint of a smile.

"*What*?" Michael screamed. He involuntarily raked his blood-soaked hand through his hair.

"What will you offer if he lives?" Isa asked as a delicate smile played on his lips. He silently motioned to the soldier to help Michael with the first-aid efforts. The soldier opened an expansive medical kit and knowledgably taped over the chest wound, allowing Gabe less labored breathing.

"What do you want?" Michael asked more quietly. For the first time, he realized Gabe's shooting hadn't been an accident. Isa shot him to create a bargaining chip. Michael's shoulders fell and hot tears filled his eyes when he realized he had been brought to heel.

"Your complete allegiance. I will need your support, and the knowledge from the disc, when I begin my reign."

"Of Turkey?"

"The world." Isa grinned.

Michael swallowed hard, staring at the madman before him. If only he were a mad *man*, he wouldn't be so fearful. But this was no man. Michael's mind raced. The Faustian nature of the agreement was not lost on him. If he believed as Gabe did, then Isa would be the embodiment of evil. But Michael knew Isa was merely a scientific oddity at the very worst. In the long run, there was only one way to ensure Gabe's safety.

"Fine," Michael said. "I agree to your terms."

"Do you have the manuscript, Father?" Isa asked.

"Yes," Michael said, pointing to his backpack. He was amazed at the progress made by the soldier. Gabe's bleeding had subsided, and an IV was flowing into his arm. The man was obviously well trained in medicine. For the first time, Michael felt confident Gabe would make it.

"Good. It is very important to me that you show your findings to the world."

"I understand," Michael said grimly as he held Gabe's hand. "How long until we get to the hospital?"

"We're there," Isa said mischievously. "I only have to order our landing."

"Michael," Gabe said weakly, finding consciousness for the first time since he had been shot.

"Gabe. Hang on, buddy," Michael said. "You're in a chopper. We're getting you to a hospital." Michael's eyes flashed with gratitude at the genetic monstrosity who had agreed to save his brother.

"Michael," Gabe spoke in a raspy whisper, "burn the fake manuscript. Don't let anyone see it."

Michael kissed his brother's forehead, knowing he couldn't accede to Gabe's wishes. He handed the backpack to Isa, who verified its contents and then ordered the chopper to land. As orderlies were getting Gabe onto a stretcher, Isa shoved the backpack to Michael and commanded, "Make sure the manuscript gets to Rome. Our people in the Vatican will know what to do with it."

Tina, Chris, and Kim burst into the emergency room at the hospital. None of them was sure what they would do next; none of them spoke Turkish. Thankfully, Michael was waiting for them. Kim and Chris ran to hug him.

"Where is he?" Tina asked nervously. Even though she was sure the Lord had told her he would be fine, she was apprehensive.

"They rushed him to surgery," Michael said. "He took a bullet to the torso and a couple to his right leg."

"Oh," Tina said softly as she steadied herself against a chair and fought the need to faint.

"What do they think the damage is?" Chris asked as he put his arm around Tina to support her.

"We don't know, Chris. They say they'll get a better idea of the damage once they've taken a look from the inside."

"Do they know what they're doing here?" Kim demanded, once again the lioness looking out for her cub. She placed her arm around Michael and pulled him close.

"It has a good reputation from what I can tell, Mom," Michael said. "For this type of damage, I would imagine treatment is the same the world over. Remove the bullet, stop the bleeding."

"How did he seem?" Tina asked, taking particular note of the bloodstains on Michael's pants and shirt.

"He regained consciousness, briefly. The doctors say that's a very good sign."

"Did he say anything?" she asked.

"It was a bit of nonsense at first," Michael said. Then seeing the desperation in her eyes, he spoke Gabe's heart to her, words he knew Gabe would have said. "Then he said he loves you and the kids more than life itself, and he asked me to give you a kiss." He bent forward and gently kissed her on the cheek as her tears flowed uncontrollably. Kim and Chris guided her to a nearby chair.

Kim stroked Tina's hair. "Don't you even think what you're thinking," Kim said anxiously. "Gabe's going to pull through!"

Tina's cell phone rang. Looking at the incoming number, she said, "It's the kids. How am I going to tell them what has happened?" Setting the phone to speaker, she swallowed hard and answered the call with a pleasant voice. "Hello."

"Mom, it's us, Michele and Chris," Michele said.

"I know, sweetheart. What are you guys up to?"

Michael and Chris paced anxiously at the thought of the kids having to hear such news over the phone. Kim drew a sharp breath and swallowed a sob.

"Mom. Let's get to the point," Chris said like one of the characters in his superhero comic books. "We know Dad is hurt, but God told us he's going to be all right." Tina's shoulders heaved and she lost her voice to tears.

Kim picked up the conversation. "Honey, Mom's having a little bit of a problem right now."

"Mimi," Michele said with confidence. "Dad's going to be all right. God told us he was hurt. We went to the chapel and prayed for a long time. Then he told us Dad would be fine."

"What great kids!" Chris beamed, wiping at tears in his eyes.

"Kim?" Fran said into the phone.

"Yes, Fran?" Kim barely managed to speak.

"It's just like Michele said. We were eating breakfast and both kids started to cry, saying their dad had been hurt. Chris grabbed the keys and ran to the chapel. We all prayed in silence for about half an hour, and then there was a strong reassuring presence of the Lord."

"I felt it too," David yelled into the phone. "Gabe is going to be fine."

"Oh, thank you, Jesus!" Tina said as she got herself under control.

Or Isa, Michael thought.

The bullet to Gabe's torso had done surprisingly little damage, passing through some muscle tissue and out of his body. Other than the collapsed lung, no major organs, bones, or arteries were hurt. Nonetheless, there was a pretty nasty-looking exit wound in his back.

The surgeons easily stopped the bleeding and sanitized the wound. His right leg, however, had suffered significant structural damage. When he got back to the United States, he would need a knee replacement and lots of surgery. For now, though, the goal was to allow the muscle damage to heal in a sanitary place.

For two weeks, he was in an isolation room, where all visitors had to wear masks, sterilized gowns, and head covers. There was a large portion of muscle missing in his upper thigh. The open wound was dressed and bathed periodically in a sterile, iodine solution. He was given significant doses of medication, both to ward off the pain and to calm him so as to prevent any undue flexing of the leg muscles.

Most of those days, Gabe slept. Tina stayed in the hospital, grabbing an occasional catnap in the waiting room. Michael was there with her every step of the way. Kim had flown back to the states to care for the kids and to line up the best doctors she could find for her son's return. Chris had been called back to Rome, and Michael sent the manuscript with him.

Ten days after his return to Rome, Chris was called to a meeting with the pope.

"We are at a serious juncture, Chris," the pope said gravely.

"In what way?"

"Our best scholars have been looking at the manuscript found by Michael. It appears to be the earliest intact Gospel of John. For millennia, St. John's Gospel was thought to be the last-written book of the New Testament. Now it looks as though it was actually the first."

"That's fascinating," Chris said. "At least there was a significant discovery to ameliorate all the pain we've been through."

"I fear more pain is to come," the pontiff said. "This document is different than others that followed it. In this gospel, Jesus makes no claims to be the Son of God, the Jewish Messiah. In fact, He makes statements that carry significant inferences to the contrary."

"How could the Church have missed such a thing for two thousand years?" Chris asked. "Surely Michael found a forgery."

"Would that it were so," the pope said in disbelief. "If it is a forgery, it is exceedingly masterful. My experts believe only one man would have a chance at producing such a perfect forgery: Father Michael himself."

The implications rocked Chris. His choices were to believe that the manuscript was a genuine challenge to Christ's deity or that Michael had conspired to defraud the world. The Michael he knew would never do such a thing. "Holiness, Michael is so dedicated to archeology. I find it hard to believe he would ever compromise his science with a forged document. To what end?"

"The Great Apostasy, as Gabe would call it."

"Holiness, on occasion I worry about the level of Michael's commitment to his faith. But I have never doubted his scientific integrity, and I know beyond a shadow of a doubt that he wouldn't have put himself in danger and risked his brother's life for a document he knew to be a forgery. Michael loves his brother too much to even consider such an action." Chris said resolutely.

"If that is the case, then we have quite a dilemma on our hands," the pope said.

"Holiness, couldn't we suppress this knowledge until we are *very* sure of its origin? The world doesn't need a Vatican release questioning the very foundation of Christianity."

"My sentiments exactly," the pope moaned as he pointed a remote control toward a television screen. A beautiful African American reporter spoke from St. Peter's Square. "In a stunning revelation," the reporter began, "Vatican sources have leaked news of the discovery of what is possibly the oldest intact Gospel of John. Our sources indicate that preliminary dating of the document places its origin as early as a mere ten years after Christ lived. The document purportedly differs from later versions and indicates that Jesus did not consider himself to be the Son of God. The Vatican has officially denied such claims, but photos of the document have been provided to this news organization. We have given them to leading scholars for examination. Although verifying a discovery of this significance will take years, their initial assessment is that the language, structure and formation of Greek letters are all consistent with existing manuscripts of the period."

The image cut away to an older man with long, stringy gray hair and a salt-and-pepper beard. The news crawl identified him as an ancient manuscript scholar from Union Theological Seminary in New York City. The professor explained that the codex could be a pivotal find for Christianity."

"Benny!" Chris said through clenched teeth. "He had to have leaked it."

"That would be my guess," the pope responded. "To make matters worse, Turkey is demanding the return of the manuscript, even though there was a prior agreement that the Vatican would retain the results of the dig, at least until they could be properly examined and catalogued."

"You won't consider returning it, will you?" Chris asked with the realization that the Turkish government would stifle any further study to disprove the veracity of the document.

The pope sighed. "This younger Kurtoglu has become an international hero. We may be powerless to resist his request based on international antiquities laws and media pressure."

"Great!" Chris said sarcastically.

Gabe had been given heavy sedatives for the ride home. He grinned passively as Michael helped the crew load his wheelchair onto the private plane Kim had sent. "You take care of yourself, and do everything they tell you to do for your recovery," he said as he kissed his brother's cheek.

Gabe grinned even more broadly at his brother. "Will do. I just want to get home and hug my kids."

"I hear you," Michael said. His voice faltered. "Gabe, again I want to tell you how sorry I am that you got in the middle of this. If I had it to do over—"

Gabe rolled his eyes. "So you've had two screw-ups that I've covered you on. By my reckoning, I only owe you about a million more." He chuckled as Michael ruffled his hair.

Tina hugged Michael tightly. "Thanks so much for staying with me. I couldn't have done it without you. You're very special to me."

He returned her embrace. "And you're my sister. I love you a lot. Make sure you give those kids a hug and kiss from their uncle Michael."

Early on, Michael had tired of television coverage of Isa's

grandstanding. He, Gabe, and Tina stopped watching any news reports while in the Turkish hospital, leaving Gabe totally unprepared for the news team that greeted his plane in Atlanta. He hugged his mother and children from his wheelchair as a reporter ran up to him, followed by her cameraman.

"Reverend Martin, your books on end-time prophecies have become major sellers in the Christian press. Do you have any comment about your brother's recent discovery in Turkey? Couldn't his discovery disprove your contention that the world is headed toward what you claim to be the prophesied return of Christ?"

"No comment," Gabe said with a confused look. "I just want to focus on being with my family and getting better right now," he offered weakly.

"You heard him," Kim interrupted. "No further comments," she said briskly to the reporter as she hustled the wheelchair toward their car. Security at the private landing field ushered the reporter away as Gabe wiped at a tear in his eye.

Benny leaned back in his chair and put his feet on the desk. His smug smile betrayed the Lady's pleasure at his release of the manuscript. He spoke nearly gleefully into the secured phone. "We have managed to release copies of the manuscript to academics, but I thought we could use a more popular way to disperse the message."

"And that's where I come in?" Zack asked scornfully.

"Now, now. No need to be so testy with me." Benny smiled. His last encounter with Zack had been their tryst in New York. "As I recall, you weren't unexcited when last we met."

"I won't discuss it with you, Benny. I was humiliated."

The response brought an unexpected chuckle from Benny. Zack's humiliation had only heightened the pleasure. "Fair enough, but look at what it has gained for you. You will be the first to promote the new message to the masses. Think of it! We are embarking on a new world where religion is no longer a barrier to unity. " Benny's voice grew animated. "And you, my young friend, will be a vanguard of this new society. Can you imagine the incredible wealth, power, and prestige about to come your way?"

"When you put it that way, I don't feel so bad," Zack said more cheerily.

"Good man," Benny said. "Expect an international package in the mail—unmarked, of course."

"Thank you, Cardinal Cross," Zack said deliberately.

"I'm sorry?" Benny asked, fearing Zack would be stupid enough to try to tape the conversation.

"I said, 'Thank you, Cardinal Cross,'" Zack repeated.

"I'm afraid we must have had a miscommunication, sir. I'm not who you think me to be. I'm just calling to tell you that you are among the few people in the world to receive our newest offer. If you like the manuscript we send you, then you will have the opportunity to invest. But our offer expires in five days."

"Benny ..." Zack tried to recover.

"I'm sorry, sir. I have another call. Have a nice day." Benny hung up and immediately used a burner phone to dial Zack's cell. "You'll pay for trying to tape that conversation," Benny hissed. "Get in line, kid, or you'll be living out Earth's golden years as a murderer on death row. Do you understand me?"

"Yes," Zack said tersely as Benny slammed down the phone.

Chris met Michael's flight from Turkey at the Vatican's private terminal at Fiumicino. "Michael!" he called at the airport gate. Michael grinned softly. "Have you been keeping up with the press?" Chris asked as they hugged.

"Well, I know Isa wants the manuscript back. He found me in Turkey to see if I could petition the Holy Father."

"Great!" Chris spat. "And have you heard what's going on in the states?"

"No," Michael said warily, concerned that something had happened to his family. "What's going on?"

Chris said with disgust, "Now Zack, the religious hack, is claiming he has been sent a secret copy of the manuscript. He has promised to present new insights into Christianity."

"*What?*" Michael shrieked with genuine surprise. "Who would send *him* such a thing?"

"Well, I figured it was either you or your uncle," Chris said in a harsh tone. "Now I know it wasn't you."

Michael colored at Chris's indignation. "Chris, there's no reason to take this out on me. I was kidnapped and then spent every day at the hospital with Gabe, remember? Why do you suddenly lump me into Benny's category?"

A porter came with Michael's luggage. Michael and Chris each took a bag.

"I'll ask you straight out, Michael. Did you forge that document?"

"No," Michael lied. "But thanks for the vote of confidence, Chris," he said with dripping sarcasm.

The two men walked to their car in silence.

Finally Michael spoke. "Listen to me, Chris. I got a good look at that manuscript while those guys were holding me captive. There are some startling discoveries, if the document is legit."

Chris spoke quietly as he stared into Michael's eyes, "Preliminary findings are that it is either authentic or a masterful forgery. The Vatican's people know of only one person in the world with the talent to pull off such a forgery."

"Me?" Michael asked in genuine distress. Surely the forgery couldn't be detected so quickly.

"You," Chris said sternly.

"Well, at least now I understand why you asked me if I faked it."

"But you didn't, Michael. So that means it may very well be real."

"Chris, this document could be the new standard on which the New Testament is translated. It will change things a lot," Michael said gravely. "Christianity will survive this. It just won't retain the preeminent status it has claimed. If you think about it, it's really an idea whose time has come."

"I can never accept any Christianity but the one I currently embrace," Chris said through clenched teeth.

"I understand," Michael said somberly. It hurt to see Chris rocked like this, but the forgery highlighted a broader *truth* that the world needed to hear. "Look, Chris, these revelations aren't so much for your generation, or even mine. But a new generation will grow up in a world free of religious tension. It could be great!"

Chris spoke sullenly. "That's not my eschatology, Michael."

"Well, we'll have to agree to disagree, but I don't want our differences to come between us." Even the thought of losing Chris was tragic to Michael. He felt tears forming as he said, "You're the only father I've ever known. I want you in my life."

Chris put his arm around the younger man's shoulders and responded warmly, "It won't come between us. You're my son, and you always will be."

"Thanks," Michael said, placing his arm around Chris's shoulders. He winced at the thought of what it would be like if Chris ever found out about the lie he had told. Then he pushed the thought aside. The die was cast. They were rushing headlong into a future world that would be dramatically changed by Michael's discoveries. He looked forward to that new world, convinced that the disc had given him the keys to solving the major problems facing humanity.

PRESENT DAY

NINETEEN

Zack gazed out at the twenty thousand people who applauded him in the near stadium-sized auditorium that had become his church. His television audience included tens of millions of regular viewers, all of whom gratefully accepted his Christ-less version of Christianity. The manuscript found by Michael enabled his church to push past the exclusive claims of Christ as the only way to heaven. Today's message centered on "Chrislam," the joining of Christians and Muslims to celebrate the wisdom of prophets Jesus and Mohammed. The message resonated with a broader donor base. Even more important to Zack, it was an attempt to reach out to the Turkish leader, Isa Kurtoglu, who had resisted all of Zack's previous attempts to meet him.

"We are so proud to have our Muslim brothers with us at our service today," Zack intoned with a broad smile. "I believe the great Allah Himself would approve of this day. From a Christian perspective, I can tell you this has been a dream for the world since Jesus walked the Earth. He said, 'I pray they may be one.' Well, today we have taken the first steps toward the fulfillment of that prayer. Thank you for coming."

The choir began a rousing version of "Let There Be Peace on Earth" as Zack and Gloria waved good-bye to the television audience.

"I wish you would change your mind and come with me," Gloria said, barely disrupting the smile on her face.

"I can't, darlin', someone has to stay here and man the fort."

"It's Kim's sixty-fifth birthday. Could you just fly in for the party and then head back here?" Her eyes pleaded.

"We'll see," Zack said patiently, meaning no. He loved Michael's discovery, but he didn't like the man—and he certainly preferred dealing at a distance with his buggering uncle.

"Well, after the service, I'm going to run out to get her a gift."

"Fine," Zack said, looking into his wife's eyes with great devotion for the camera. "I'll catch up on some work here." He gave her a slight kiss, and then continued to wave.

"In three, two, one," the director called. Michael was on a New York morning show discussing the manuscript findings. The academic community had arrived at the results Michael intended from the beginning. They confirmed the authenticity of the document, and more importantly its politically expedient implications. As discoverer of the document, Michael had gained a bit of international fame. The pope had tasked him with the job of calming fears of the faithful when confronted with the new findings.

"We're here today with Father Michael Martin, the Vatican archeologist who discovered the Antakya Codex that has been making so much news these past few years. Welcome, Father."

"Thank you, Steve. It's a pleasure to be here." Michael wore a black suit and clerical collar despite the movement of younger priests to adopt the use of street clothes in the wake of changing revelation.

"Father, there has been a lot of confusion about the implications of this document. Church attendance is down all over the world, while the attendance of non-Christian religions is on the rise. Some people are seeing this as the demise of Christianity, or at a minimum, the end of the Catholic Church."

Michael smiled warmly at the television host. It was his host's job to incite fear. It was Michael's job to dispel it. "That's not the case at all, Steve. The Antakya Codex isn't the death of Christianity but its rebirth." Michael shifted in his seat to look directly into the camera. "We fully expected a short-term drop in church attendance as people look at other paths, which we now know are as valid as Christianity in finding unity with our creator."

"So you expect them to return, Father? Are you keeping their seats warm?" The host couldn't contain a smirk.

Michael wanted more than anything to reach out and wipe that smirk off his face, to tell this talking fool that technology from the disc is what enabled him to post his endless selfies online. Instead Michael ignored it—as he did with all the others—preferring his standard overanimated response. "Absolutely! And when they come back, they will bring with them a number of rich traditions that will become incorporated into our faith. These new traditions will cause others to come and check us out. This is not about the death of one worldview and the birth of another. That would exclude too many wonderful souls. No, this is about the recreation of our existing faiths in the light of superior revelation."

"But, Father, there are a lot of people out there who don't see it that way. They say that once you take away the claim that Christ was uniquely the Son of God, you strip the Christian faith of its purpose and power."

"That's a bit of a narrow view in my opinion," Michael said, taking a sip of water. "To think that way would be to deny the self-sacrifice and generosity that have been the hallmark of Christianity for the past two millennia. Even to this day, Christian charitable organizations are unmatched in their effectiveness in the battle against hunger and strife the world over. I expect this to continue, and even to flourish, in the coming years."

"So you don't see any downside, Father?" the interviewer asked with a carefully measured inflection of doubt.

"No. In fact, I see incredible potential." Michael abandoned the camera to stare directly at his inquisitor, who only seemed interested when he was on camera. "Look, Steve, this has been shocking news for the Church, and we don't have a history of responding quickly to new developments. Ask Galileo. Having said that, I am proud of the work being done by Vatican theologians to find new meaning in Scripture."

The camera panned to Steve, catching him as he looked at notes for the next interview.

Michael's voice took a lecturing tone. "And may I add they are working hand in hand with the World Council of Churches so that the new theology will be consistent across Christendom. And more importantly, the new Christian theology will place a high value on other spiritual traditions. When all is said and done, we will look upon these exciting days as the dawning of a new Age of Enlightenment."

"I'm afraid that's all the time we have, Father. Thanks for stopping by to calm the waters a bit."

"My pleasure, Steve." Michael smiled into the camera.

"Next up. Has the Arab spring given way to a new caliphate? How will Iran react to a revived Ottoman Empire?"

Gabe turned off the TV. He hadn't spoken much with Michael in the years since the manuscript went public, and he didn't want to. The brothers exchanged pleasantries, but there was a wall between them.

"I know you don't agree with him," Tina said, "but he's your brother. You can't just hold him at arm's length for the rest of your lives."

"I know," Gabe said with resignation, "but I can't accept what he's doing. Tina, biblical prophecies are falling in line, and Michael and I are on opposite sides of that line. It disgusts me."

"And it shows," she said gently. "I miss the old Gabe who was always happy. This is eating you up inside. If not for Michael or for yourself, think of the kids and me. Find a way to make some kind of peace with him, Gabe."

"He's wrong, and he's responsible for a lot of damage. How do I just overlook that?"

"You don't. Jesus didn't overlook our sins. He died to make us whole. Would you embrace your only brother to bring him back to the fold?" She didn't wait for an answer. She strode out of the room to let him think about what she had said.

The kids left for school, and the house was abuzz with activity. Kim had hired a cleaning crew to bring the estate to its shiny best condition. Landscapers were paying extra attention to the gardens, and the exterior of the chapel had been power washed.

Gabe and Tina had taken the day off to help with preparations and greet guests as they arrived.

"Are you going to the airport to pick up your brother?" Kim asked.

"No, he's going to rent a car and wait for Chris's flight. They'll drive here together," Gabe said.

"I thought you would want to spend some time with him."

"I'll see him when he gets here, Mom," Gabe said defensively. He took his coffee to the formal dining room in a pretense at checking the preparations. Tina looked on a bit sadly, watching the limp that characterized her husband's walk since he had been shot.

"One of the main reasons I'm throwing this party is to get those two together again," Kim said.

"I know, and I want that too. But you know Gabe. The more you push, the more he'll resist," Tina replied.

"That's the thing with kids," Kim said with a wry smile. "It's all downhill once they go through puberty."

Tina smiled, thinking of her own two teenagers. "Just give them some time and don't push things too much," Tina said. "It may all work out yet."

Chris spotted Michael as he came out of the jetway.

"How did the interview go?" he asked as he hugged the younger priest.

"Shop talk, huh?" Michael asked.

"His Holiness will want to know," Chris said with a shrug.

"I think it went well, Chris. His Holiness wants damage control, and that's what I'm trying to do for him. But between you and me, I don't think there is a lot of damage to be controlled. If the Church seizes the tremendous opportunity before it, it could define Christianity for generations to come."

"I wish I had your optimism, Michael. But all I see is a people confused and hurt because their religious institutions are now questioning their belief in a Savior."

They walked straight to the car. Each had clothes and toiletries in his quarters at the estate. There was never a need to pack when they came home to Georgia. In days past, the family butler and friend, Joseph, would have been waiting for them. He was a throwback to the elaborate lifestyle of Michael's grandfather. Kim and the boys opted for a much more "normal" lifestyle, even though the family fortune had grown significantly since the days of Stan Martin.

Michael rented a car. As they settled in, he tried to ease Chris's discomfort over the changing times. "Chris, all kids are hurt when they find out there is no Santa Claus. But as time goes by, they realize they never really needed him. Christianity is at the 'mourning for Santa' stage, but they'll come out of this with a stronger, more resilient spirituality that they can celebrate freely with the rest of the people on this planet. After this brief bit of pain, there will be a lot of great times."

"Everything in my spirit tells me you're wrong, Michael. You haven't witnessed the deliberate acts to hurt the Church that I have. I've spent my life combating some very evil men … and to be honest, I'm afraid you are unwittingly playing to their hand."

Michael resented the implications but reminded himself that Chris had yet to see the full extent of the technology offered by the disc. He took stock of the older man. By anyone's standards, Chris had aged incredibly well. His body was still toned, and the gray hair at his temples accentuated his light eyes. Crow's feet and laugh lines made him look distinguished in his older years. But to Michael's mind, Chris's opinions hadn't aged nearly so well.

"There is bound to be a generation that puts out cookies and milk on Christmas Eve," he said with what he hoped to be taken for loving condescension. "But don't expect the world to eat them and leave you a nice little note in Santa's name. We're moving on, Chris."

Chris colored. "Michael, you have no idea how offensive you sound when you talk like this. Do me a favor. Keep it on the down low this weekend. Spare your mother, and don't aggravate your brother."

In a flash, Michael grew angry at the comment. He didn't like the idea of having his speech restricted in his own home. "So what are you telling me? Stand in the corner with Benny? I don't think so, Chris. It's my home too, you know, and it *always* was."

Chris turned in his seat to stare at the younger man. "Come on, Michael. Stop the charade. You put up a big front, but the truth is you blame yourself for Gabe's disability. You 'stand in the corner with Benny' to punish yourself. Nobody puts you there."

Michael drew a sharp breath. Chris's words hit him like a hammer.

His eyes reddened as he said quietly, "I hate that limp, Chris. I hate that Gabe was such a physical, vital man before he was shot and that I'm responsible for everything he lost. I took his vigor and his optimism. His kids have no idea what a fun guy their dad used to be."

Chris rested an arm on Michael's shoulder. "The old Gabe is in there somewhere, Michael. And the old Michael is somewhere in here," Chris said, pointing his finger at Michael's chest. "We need to find both of them."

The door to Zack's office opened silently. Bonnie always entered the room as if she were interrupting some sacred ritual. It had long ago gotten on Zack's nerves. Their entire affair had, but Zack knew what a spurned lover could do to a church. He wasn't about to risk a blackmail attempt or a press report if Bonnie became unhappy. Zack realized his only choice was to feign interest in her, and while he was at it—what the heck—he might as well enjoy the sex. And it was enjoyable. Bonnie bought into Riverside's marketing campaign. She saw Zack as something more than the usual man. In a word, she idolized him, and that made her accepting of sexual experiments Zack would never attempt to bring into his marriage bed. He pretended to be working, but behind his desk he had already undone his pants.

"Zack," Bonnie said softly.

Zack looked up with a grin, only to see her tear-streaked face. "Bonnie. What's the matter?" he asked with a start.

"I'm pregnant," she cried. It wasn't her first child. She had two with her husband.

"Is Quentin happy about it?" Zack asked with nonchalance.

"He was away on business last month. Remember?"

"Looks like you're going to have a premature birth," Zack said callously.

"He's suspicious. I don't think he'll buy it."

"Are you sure it's mine?" he asked defensively.

"You're the only man for me. I sleep with Quentin just enough to keep him from suspecting. Trust me. You're the father."

"What about birth control? You told me you had taken care of it," Zack accused sharply.

"Sometimes birth control fails," Bonnie said somberly.

He wondered if she hadn't gone off birth control in some silly attempt to force his hand. She was the type to entertain the ridiculous delusion she could replace Gloria. Well, he certainly wasn't about to ruin his ministry. He reached for his checkbook in the upper right drawer. "All right. Here's some money for an abortion," he said tersely. "But don't go someplace in town. In fact, if you can go out of state, it would even be better."

Bonnie gasped at the suggestion. "I want to keep the baby. I could never kill the result of our love." She put her head in her hands and cried convulsively.

Zack moved around the desk to comfort her in the only way he knew. When the lovemaking ended, he reassured Bonnie of his love for her and their baby. In reality, he could not stop thinking about how much a threat Bonnie had become to the ministry. What was he supposed to do? He couldn't force her to get an abortion. He couldn't very well take her on a cruise and lose her at sea. Been there. Done that. Besides, he had been pathetic in removing his parents. If it hadn't been for Benny finishing them off …

Benny! Zack could get Benny's help to make Bonnie disappear. Zack's hands would be clean in the sight of any observer. After all, Benny was the one with the taste for murder. But he would require a payment. After their tryst in New York, Zack knew exactly what that payment would entail. He winced at the thought. The time in New York had been painful and humiliating. Repeating it would be difficult, but in the long run, it would be less humiliating than living through the publicity of having a child out of wedlock. Zack had made his hard choice. He jumped up and quickly dressed.

"What are you doing?" Bonnie asked.

"I've got to leave, darlin'," Zack said with a disarming smile. "I have to attend the birthday party of a dear family friend in Georgia."

Kim, Tina, and Gabe spilled out to the rambling front porch as Michael and Chris exited the car.

"Well, hello, strangers!" Kim said excitedly.

"Hello to you," Chris said with a grin as he bounded up the stairs to hug his family.

Michael moved more deliberately. Despite any awkwardness he felt, something inside him breathed a sigh of relief to be home. He had spent such wonderful times on this estate. "Hi, guys," he said with a grin as Kim and Tina rushed to hug him. Gabe moved closer as well, but in a more measured manner.

"Hi, Michael," Gabe said with a smile, "welcome home." He held his arms open.

"It's great to be here," Michael said as he hugged his brother tightly.

"Where are the kids?" Chris asked.

"Both had big tests in school this morning," Tina answered. "I've arranged for them to leave shortly after lunch. They should be home soon."

"I miss them," Michael said. "You guys raised great kids."

"Puberty has its challenges," Tina said with a shrug, "but if you can get past the bravado and emotionalism, they're good kids."

"Ah. The teen years." Michael grinned. "I pray they're more like their uncle Michael than their dad."

"You and me both." Gabe laughed.

They started into the house. Michael winced at the sight of his brother limping through the doorway.

They made their way to the breakfast room off the informal kitchen, where they ate lunch: Kim's barbequed beef sandwiches, a favorite for Chris, and homemade chicken tortellini soup to welcome Michael.

When the back door opened and closed, Michael ran to greet his nephew and niece.

"Uncle Michael!" Michele grinned as she ran to hug the man after whom she was named.

"What a beautiful young woman you've become!" Michael exclaimed with a wide grin.

"Everyone says I look like my father," she said, pointing to her piercing green eyes.

"Just the good parts of him." Michael laughed. "I see plenty of your mom's beauty there too."

"Please!" young Chris moaned as he came through the back door. "She already thinks too much of her looks."

"Shut up, Chris," Michele said.

Michael hugged his nephew, who was already a couple inches taller than he. Chris looked a lot like Tina's departed father. He was tall and thin with a fine nose and brooding brown eyes.

"I can't believe how big you are," Michael said.

"And handsome," Chris added with a grin.

"And handsome," Michael conceded.

"More importantly," Gabe said as he limped to Michael's side, "they're both nice kids who love the Lord."

Michele rolled her eyes, but Chris put his arm around his father's shoulders. The elder Chris then joined the group to get his share of hugs and kisses from the kids.

Isa Kurtoglu was fascinated. Could the Western world not see the amassing of Russian troops in Iran? Most probably they chose to ignore the build-up. True enough, Iran's ties to Russia and the subsequent build-up had occurred over the course of many years. Israel had complained repeatedly to the United Nations, but the world was focused on Syria, Iraq, and Ukraine. When push came to shove, the weak American president was unable to stand against the fierce Russian leader. Instead, he caved and chose a rhetoric that disavowed America's role of policeman to the world. He chose instead to follow the poles and focus on the struggling domestic economy, leaving the EU to do the same as its constituent economies fell like dominos. Both seemed happy to believe the popular myth that Russia's presence was actually a stabilizing factor in the Middle East.

Isa knew differently. Soon he would be given a sign, and he would play both sides against each other. *A wise man knows how to bide his time.* Yet he waited impatiently for the sign.

The sign! The sign! He strode around the Turkish presidential office in disgust. It was no longer enough to be the head of only one nation. When would it be time for his ascendance to worldwide authority? When would they be given *the sign*?

In a flash of light, the Lady appeared. "Patience, young one, your time will come," she cautioned.

"Yes, but how much longer must I wait?" His frustration was palpable. He strode to the bar, poured himself a drink, and quickly downed it.

"You know as well as I that the sign is the only part of the plan not in our control," she said in her breathless monotone. With insect-like, lightning-quick speed, she knocked the glass from his hand. "You have to control your human nature," she spat at him. "Your impatience is our only potential enemy."

Collecting himself, he apologized. "You're right of course, my Lady." Inwardly, he had grown to hate her. He longed for the day when that toothless slit of a mouth gasped in a singular "Oh" as she realized that all along he had been the one in control. He smiled at her disarmingly—and waited.

In order to enjoy herself fully, Kim hired an agency to cook the meals and keep the estate in order during the birthday visits. They ran the house with the charm and unobtrusive efficiency of a five-star resort. The guests merely had to enjoy the food, the company, and the diversions offered by the grounds, from the indoor and outdoor pools, to the tennis courts, to the chapel.

Dinner had been an accommodation to her boys from Rome. While the food in Rome was unsurpassable, there were some things that just couldn't be beat in the United States. For an appetizer, she served peanut soup. For the main course, she served filet mignon with lobster and stuffed baked potatoes. The wagyu beef was the best she could find, and it fairly melted in the mouth. Homemade rolls, a salad, and asparagus rounded out the meal. She finished with individual baked Alaska.

Michael complimented, stretching backward in his chair, "Mom, that was fantastic!" The rest of the guests joined him in praising the meal.

"Thanks," Kim said with a disparaging laugh, "I worked all day on that meal!" Then looking at an empty chair at the other end of the table, she said, "I really thought your uncle Benny would be here in time for dinner."

"I'm sure he just got a bit hung up at the airport," Chris said reassuringly. He placed his hand on hers. The evening had a soft, relaxed air about it. Tina snuggled closer to Gabe. David kissed Fran softly on the cheek. Michael extended his arm behind Gloria's chair, and she leaned into his shoulder.

"So tell us about your time in Africa," young Chris said. "I want to hear how Grandpa Chris got beat up but managed to save you guys."

"Some stories are hard to tell," Chris said. "How about I tell you another story. One about your father and your uncle Michael in Germany."

"Ouch!" Gabe said. "Make sure you tell the PG version, please."

"I promise the only R-rated stuff will be about Michael," Chris said with a grin.

"Great!" Michael said as he caught a warm glow in his brother's eye.

"Cardinal!" Zack yelled out to Benny at the Atlanta airport. He had been waiting in line at a car rental desk when Benny went past.

"Reverend Jolean," Benny said with a smile and a slight leer. "I heard you weren't going to attend Kim's party."

"Well, there's been a bit of a change in plans." Zack smiled with a gaze that lingered slightly. He consciously used the tools he normally reserved to woo the opposite sex. If he played his cards right, he might not only accomplish Bonnie's elimination, but a power shift in his relationship with Benny as well.

"I have a limo waiting," Benny said. "You won't need to rent a car."

Once they were settled in the limo, Benny raised the privacy screen to thwart any attempt by the driver to eavesdrop; although by the sound of it, the driver's inability to understand English would have been enough. "I have to commend you, Zack. Your ministry has become far more profitable than I would have imagined."

"Thanks, Benny." Zack flashed a winning smile. "And not just for the compliment. When you sent me the Antakya Codex, you effectively put me at the forefront of the greatest thing to happen in Christianity since the Reformation!" The smile froze on his face as he realized that he and Benny would have been on opposite sides of the Reformation.

"Benny, I'm sorry," he recovered, placing his hand on Benny's knee. He let it rest there.

Benny placed his hand on top of Zack's and rubbed it lightly. "No need to apologize," Benny said sweetly. "You of all people should know I am a proponent of Christian unity."

"I can't believe you got stoned and wanted to go to the bathroom off the Berlin Wall," young Chris said in awe at his uncle Michael.

"Grandpa Chris might have taken some liberty with the story," Michael protested, which brought a huge grin to Gabe's face.

"I like the part where Daddy was studying, and you made him go to the wall with you and your drug-addict friends." Michele chuckled. "Now I understand why he always tells us to choose our friends carefully."

Gabe couldn't contain a giggle. Tina laughed just to see him enjoy himself so much. She caught Kim's eye and winked.

"Now it's time to let your poor uncle Michael off the hook," Gabe said. "Grandpa Chris got the story right, but he switched the names. I was the one who was running amuck. Uncle Michael was the studious, upstanding one."

The kids burst into laughter. "No street cred with that one, Dad!" Young Chris smiled. "We've known you all our lives. You probably took your books with you to study while you were at the wall."

Now it was Michael's turn to chuckle. "It's true," Michael assured them. "Every day I used to wonder what new trouble your dad would get us into."

"No way!" Michele exclaimed. The kids looked eagerly toward their father, understanding him in a new way.

"Way!" Gabe smirked. "That was before Jesus."

"What made you sober up and find the Lord?" young Chris asked.

"A beautiful young girl." Michael beamed. "I knew the moment your father saw your mother that she was something different. Their souls connected the moment they met." Michael took a sip of wine and winked at the kids. "Your dad was a glorified aerobics instructor on a cruise ship by then and—"

"Ah!" Michele screamed. "I don't believe it!"

Young Chris giggled at the thought.

"Well, let me tell you the story," Michael said with a twinkle in his eye, his arm still around Gloria.

"Look who I found," Benny said to the surprised group as he and Zack entered the dining room. Zack stared at Michael. Michael saw the fire in his eyes.

Gloria quickly pulled away from Michael. "Zack," she said, running to her husband. "What a surprise!"

"Guys, take a seat," Gabe said, rising to shake their hands. "We just finished a great meal. I'm sure Mom has extra for you."

"You bet I do," Kim said, warmly kissing her brother. She then hugged Zack and said, "Welcome."

Michael left his seat so that the staff could put out a clean place setting for Zack. He moved to the other side of the table by Gabe and Tina.

"I expected you earlier," Kim said to Benny. "Was the flight delayed?"

"These new security screenings take so much time!" Benny exclaimed. "And they're intrusive. Don't get me wrong, if I were a younger man, I would enjoy them, but now they're just awkward."

Young Chris cracked up at his great-uncle's joke. The kids knew him as an eccentric older man who said goofy things. They had no notion of the dangerous aspects of Benny's character.

"There are a lot of family stories they don't know," Michael said quietly to Gabe.

"Unfortunately, none of them are PG," Gabe said softly. "Pretty soon they'll be old enough to know everything."

"If I can help give it some 'street cred,'" Michael offered, mocking his nephew, "I'd be glad to help."

"I just may take you up on that," Gabe responded, placing his arm around his brother's shoulder.

Michael got up early the next day, just to enjoy the home of his youth. He wandered from room to room, remembering happy days with his mother and Gabe. Every room brought a flood of memories and smiles as he remembered their lives together.

Entering the kitchen, he saw that coffee had already been made, an indication that Chris was already up and about. No doubt he was on a morning run.

"Michael," Benny said drearily as he entered the kitchen. "What are you doing up so early?"

"Mostly remembering how happy I was growing up here." Michael smiled. "Forget me—why are *you* up so early?"

"Zack and I are going to take a walk. He wants to get my thoughts on the scrolls you found. And may I say I'm happy at least *you* had a great childhood in this house. There are times when I'd like to bulldoze it along with the memories of my formative years."

Michael shrugged at the melodrama. "I'm sorry to hear that, Benny. This was like the Fortress of Solitude for Gabe and me." Michael saw that Benny didn't get the Superman reference, but he didn't have one that involved Barbie and Skipper. "Why doesn't Zack just talk to *me* about the manuscript?" Michael asked.

"He doesn't like you all that much, Michael, and what does he see when he walks through the door last night? You with your arm around his wife, and her leaning into you like you're a couple. It looked seamy. Like your mother and Chris."

Michael huffed. "I'm not too inclined to take a moral lesson from you this morning, Benny. As far as I'm concerned, you and Zack are both welcome in my home, and if either or both of you choose not to be here, I understand." Michael took his coffee out to the back patio to enjoy what was left of the sunrise. He only nodded briefly at Benny and Zack when they passed.

It wasn't long afterward that Michele joined him. "Good morning," she said quietly as she nuzzled next to him on the patio couch.

"Good morning yourself," Michael said, giving the girl a hug. "Why are you up so early?"

"Creaky old floors." Michele grinned. "I heard people walking down the stairs, and it woke me. Then I just couldn't go back to sleep. What about you?"

"In some ways it was the creaky old floors for me too. They didn't wake me up, but I just wanted to spend some time in the house by myself, remembering good times when your dad and I were growing up."

"It's a great place," Michele said in agreement. "Sometimes I wish it was closer to town so I could spend more time with my friends, but in the long run, I love the old place."

"Me too." Michael grinned.

"I thought maybe it would be too traditional for you," Michele said.

"Michele," Michael corrected, "I live in the Vatican, for crying out loud!"

Michele chuckled. "I know, but your beliefs are anything but traditional. I thought maybe you had more modern tastes as well."

"No." He sighed contentedly. "This place is just great for me."

"But what about your beliefs?" she asked, and then she said with a quiet, nearly conspiratorial tone, "My dad thinks they're dangerous."

"Michele, your dad is a wonderful man of God, a great dad, a wonderful husband, and the best brother I could ever ask for. He's a good man—a great man—but he may have trouble acclimating to some new revelations about Christianity. Do you understand what I'm saying?"

"Yeah," Michele said, leaning into her uncle. "You don't have to worry about me. I love my parents very much. I just don't happen to share their beliefs. That's why I wanted to talk to you. Is the Antakya Codex real? My dad thinks it's a hoax."

"I've held it in my hands," Michael hedged, "read it myself in the original language."

"So we've gotten it wrong all these years?"

"Not so much." Michael grinned. "We're just learning now that Jesus' message was far less restrictive and far more inclusive than we ever thought. In the long run, it's a beautiful new message that enables Christians of good will to embrace their non-Christian brothers and sisters. I'm telling you, this discovery will revolutionize the world."

"Tell me more," Michele said enthusiastically.

"Okay," Michael agreed, "but let's take a walk. I don't want your father to hear us. I'm afraid it would upset him, and this weekend is about us being together in peace as a family."

"Works for me."

"So you need to talk?" Benny asked warily once he and Zack were out of Michael's earshot. Zack heard a slight panting in Benny's voice and slowed his pace for the aging, out-of-shape cardinal.

"Yes," Zack said, "and it's an uncomfortable topic, Benny. Remember years ago when you told me to end it with my secretary?"

"Let me guess. You never did," Benny said drolly.

Zack found his tone annoying, but he needed Benny's help. He responded with a shrug and a halfhearted smile. "Actually, I did. I tried to stay away from her, Benny, but in the end I couldn't."

Benny arched one eyebrow. "Well, I'm sure you aren't looking to me for absolution, Zack. So why are you telling me this?"

"She's pregnant," Zack said with a sigh, "and I would bet my last dollar she did it on purpose." He paused a second. Hearing it said out loud drove home feelings of self-recrimination. "If she turns this into a scandal, then my whole ministry will come crashing down around me. And I don't need to remind you that you have a lot to lose if it all hits the fan."

"And what do you want from me?" Benny asked cautiously.

Zack answered the question with a question. "Do you remember my parents?"

"You want a lot from me," Benny said dispassionately, but Zack could tell he was considering the opportunity before him.

"Think of how much we have to lose," Zack said conspiratorially.

"But then I think of all the great sex you enjoyed. Why should it be my job to pay for it?" Benny asked to start the negotiations.

"I know where you're going with this," Zack said, trying to sound coy. The New York experience was distasteful, but he surely could repeat it to save his ministry. "I'm willing to repeat the weekend in New York in payment."

"Do you still have those tight abs?" Benny leered.

"Work them every day." Zack grinned seductively.

"Well." Benny grinned in return as he lowered the boom, "I'm afraid a weekend won't do."

Zack's grin froze as Benny's dramatic pause hung in the air.

"I'm in the mood for a more permanent relationship, perhaps a paramour who could meet me when I come to the United States. Someone to keep me so happy that I wouldn't want to share with the world the conversation I've just recorded ... edited, of course, to remove my words." Benny pulled the pen-sized recording device from his pocket.

Zack colored. He always knew the day would come when he would regret the pact he had made with this devil. Now that day had come, in spades.

Zack stammered, "I ... I don't know if I can do that, Benny."

Benny shrugged. "Then live publicly as a disgraced minister who tried to contract the murder of his pregnant girlfriend."

"I've already explained that you'll lose all your income from the ministry," Zack protested.

"I have a lot of wealthy friends, Zack. I'll survive quite nicely, but thanks for your concern."

Zack faltered. "I don't know what to say."

"The choices seem pretty simple to me," Benny said haughtily. "March back to the house and confess all to your wife and her family, or succumb—I love that word—to my charms."

Benny's haughty smile birthed hatred in the core of Zack's being. "So it appears I've traded one psychotic, possessive witch for another," he spat.

"With one difference." Benny smiled. "I'm not going anywhere."

"I have no choice," Zack moaned.

"Well, then," Benny said, motioning to the chapel, "why don't we seal our deal with a kiss, so to speak?"

Zack felt hot bile burn the back of his throat.

Michael enjoyed walking with his niece. He found her to be a spirited and passionate girl filled with intellectual curiosity. She easily grasped the basics of his multi-dimensional view of faith, forged during years of wrestling with the information contained on the disc. He looked at his watch. Their conversation had lasted the better part of an hour—time had flown. Soon they would need to join the others for breakfast, but first he wanted to visit the chapel. Warm memories washed over him as he relived the expectant joy of gifting it to Chris on a Christmas Eve long ago.

Michele bent to tie her shoe as Michael opened the chapel door.

His eyes fell immediately upon Benny, who was naked as Zack knelt before him. He quickly closed the door.

"Uncle Benny is having devotions," Michael said tersely. "We can't go in there."

"Okay," Michele said casually.

Michael smiled. "I'll race you back to the house. Take a head start. I'll catch up to you."

Competitive like her father, Michele was off in a flash. Michael grabbed his phone.

"Chris," Michael said quickly into his phone, "get to the chapel right away. Bad stuff is going on there. I'm trying to get Michele back to the house so she doesn't see anything."

Michael hung up and ran to catch his niece.

Curious about Michael's call, Chris picked up his pace and ran full speed to the chapel. What could be going on in there that Michele couldn't see?

In no time, he bounded up the stairs and threw open the chapel doors. He was so instantly shocked and repulsed that he couldn't quite comprehend what was going on. All he remembered seeing was naked activity. In a heartbeat, he knew he had seen enough. It was the last straw. Regardless of the personal consequences, he would see that Benny was removed from power for this desecration. He raised his cell phone and clicked a few hasty photos before interrupting the men.

"Get out!" he screamed in a fury as he grabbed the pile of clothes and threw them at the men.

Startled, both Benny and Zack grabbed quickly at the clothing and struggled to dress.

"Benny! This is a new low even for you!" Chris shrieked. He grabbed a handful of Zack's dark curly hair and yanked the younger man's face to within an inch of his own. "Gloria deserves better than this, Zack! How dare you treat her this way!"

Zack looked at him, speechless.

"Chris, I think you need to calm down," Benny said sternly, once he had pulled on his pants. "You're right. This shouldn't have happened, and certainly not here. But we have some decisions to make. Do we ruin Kim's birthday by making this an issue for the broader group, or do we just move on from here?"

Chris hated that Benny would again try to use Kim as his shield, yet he knew Benny was right. There was no way Chris would ruin this weekend for Kim. "For Kim's sake, we won't mention this here," Chris consented, "but this isn't over, Benny." His voice lowered with gritty resolve as he stared at Benny and growled, "I'll deal with you in Rome, and I'm probably going to bring the pope into it. Hopefully it can be brought up at the consistory meeting of the cardinals next week. With the grace of God, you'll be asked to resign."

"We'll see about that, Chris," Benny snapped. "We'll just see about that!"

Chris lost it. His voice cracked as he screamed, "There's nothing to debate here, Benny! *Get out*!"

After they left, Chris closed the door and locked it. He wasn't even sure of the procedure to reclaim this holy space. He pulled out his cell phone and called the Holy Father.

TWENTY

The service had begun to cook breakfast while Michael and Michele were out walking. As they raced to the house, they smelled bacon, eggs, toast, and assorted other breakfast foods.

"One of the best smells in the world," Michael said to his niece as he looked over his shoulder to see Benny and Zack walking down the road toward the house. He and Michele made their way to the dining room, where Kim, Fran, and David had begun to eat with young Chris, Tina, and Gabe.

"You're up early," Gabe said with a grin to his brother.

"Rome time," Michael said. "My body is still six hours ahead."

"And what about you, my princess?" Gabe smiled at his beautiful daughter.

"Creaky floorboards," Michele said, shaking her head. "Once I heard people walking around, I couldn't go back to sleep."

"That's because you're *nosey*," young Chris teased. Michele rolled her eyes.

Gloria entered the room and said good morning to everyone. She took a seat next to Fran at the table. Michael sat next to her, feeling protective.

"Did you sleep well?" he asked Gloria.

"Like a log! I didn't even hear Zack get out of bed. Has anyone seen him?"

"Right here, darlin'," Zack said as he and Benny entered the room.

Zack looked at Michael, clearly expecting him to once again relinquish his seat. Michael stared at him defiantly and noticed that Gabe had seen the unspoken confrontation. He arched an eyebrow at his brother.

"Where have you been?" Gloria asked her husband, who was now forced to sit beside Benny.

"The cardinal and I took a walk. Sometimes it's good for the denominations to spend time with each other."

"Indeed," Benny said smugly. "I think we have come to a new understanding of one another, and I, for one, am appreciative."

Zack colored slightly.

Gabe stared at Michael for an explanation. Michael briefly waved his hand in dismissal, indicating he would tell Gabe later.

Chris came into the dining room as the others were finishing breakfast. His hair was hanging in his eyes, and his demeanor was tense. He had obviously been distressed about something. Gabe saw it on his face the moment he walked in the room.

"Whoa, cowboy," he said softly, "looks like you just fell off your horse."

"Something like that," Chris said to him with a knowing look that told Gabe not to push it in front of the group. He ran his hands through his hair and put on a smile for the room.

"Good mornin', Chris," Zack drawled with his characteristic smile. "I feel bad leaving the table just as you're arrivin', but the shower is calling me."

"Actually, Chris," Kim said sweetly, "I was about to take Fran, David, and Gloria to town on a quick shopping run. So you'll have to eat without us as well."

"And I have some devotions to attend to," Benny said.

"Not in the chapel," Chris snarled.

"Not to worry, Chris," Benny said cheerily. "I'm going to my room."

As everyone else left the table, Chris ate silently. Gabe caught Tina's eye as she poured more coffee for him. His look was enough to tell her the men of the family needed to have a conference.

"Kids," she said with a raised eyebrow, "I need you guys to help me with a few things before the day gets going."

"Come on, Mom," Michele droned, "I thought today was about hanging out and having fun."

Young Chris rolled his eyes. "Michele, she's just getting us out of the room so these three can talk—as if the talk between a preacher and two priests would be so riveting that we would want to stay."

"Who says that kid's dumb?" Michael asked, ruffling young Chris's hair.

"Actually, that would be Michele," old Chris joined in. It was his first real attempt at conversation since he sat down.

"I never said you're dumb, Chris," Michele answered. "You're a lot of things, but you're not dumb."

"I don't know how to handle the compliment, Michele," young Chris said, pretending to wipe a tear from his eye.

"Come on, guys, let's take this comedy routine on the road," Tina said, rolling her eyes.

"Thanks, babe," Gabe said as he lightly patted her hand.

When they had gone, Michael and Chris remained quiet. Gabe's curiosity took control of him. "Come on, guys. Out with it. Did Benny pee in the rose bushes or something?"

"I think this was the last straw, Michael," Chris said. "I called the pope about it and asked him to bring it up in consistory."

"Great," Gabe muttered. "What the heck is that?"

"A worldwide meeting of the cardinals in Rome next week," Michael answered quickly. Turning to Chris, he said, "Do you think they'll take action, Chris? He's got a lot of powerful connections. Everyone I know in the Vatican is afraid of him."

"This isn't some banking fraud, Michael. It's a sick and disgusting violation of a holy place. It shows a total lack of regard for the Lord and the Church."

"So," Gabe stammered, "he peed on the chapel?"

Chris put down his fork and stared at the young preacher for a moment. "I caught him having sex in the chapel."

Gabe's mouth formed a silent "oh" of shock before giving way to speech. "Ewww," he moaned in disgust, "by himself, right? I mean, who would have the bad taste to have sex with Benny?"

"Zack," Michael said as he put his head in his hands. "Poor Gloria."

Gabe was speechless. He opened his mouth in surprise but then covered it with his hand. "How did you find out about it?" he finally asked Michael.

"Michele and I were taking a walk this morning, and we headed toward the chapel."

"Don't tell me my daughter saw that!" Gabe paled.

"No, she didn't. She bent to tie her shoe and I opened the door. I saw them, quickly closed the door, and challenged her to a run back to the house."

"She's at that age," Gabe said. "She won't ignore a challenge."

"Not so unlike her dad at that age."

"Which worries me," Gabe said, "but that's an entirely different conversation. How did Chris find out?"

"I gave Michele a head start, called Chris's cell, and told him to get to the chapel right away."

"And I did. When I opened the door, there they were. My head just exploded. I kicked them out and told Benny I would end his career."

"You *told* him that?" Michael exploded.

"Yes," Chris said defensively.

"He's so devious, Chris," Gabe added. "I think it's a bad idea to let him see your hand."

"I don't care," Chris said sternly. "I'm done."

"What about Gloria?" Gabe asked. "Are you guys going to tell her?"

"I would like to," Michael said, "but if it comes from me, Zack will just say I'm trying to ruin their marriage for selfish reasons. I think it has to be Chris."

"Oh, of course it has to be *me*!" Chris said, pounding the table in a brief burst of temper.

"Don't stress over it, Chris," Gabe comforted. He had never seen Chris this angry. "Maybe I could talk to David about it, and he and I can decide what to do."

"I'm sorry, boys," Chris said. "I didn't mean to sound like I did, but challenging Benny like this is a big deal. I don't want to have to divide my attention between Rome and here. I have to stay focused."

"Well, that settles it," Gabe said as he slapped the older man's shoulder. "I'll talk to David."

"But not here," Chris said. "Not on your mother's birthday. I want her to have a nice day. You can pick a time to call David after everyone leaves tomorrow."

"Agreed," Gabe said.

"Sounds good to me," Michael added. "On the brighter side, it feels kind of good, like the old days. The three of us figuring out how to save the world from the ravages of Ben-zilla."

"I missed you guys too," Gabe said as he winked at his brother.

The chapel looked beautiful, lit only by candlelight. Chris said Mass, which was concelebrated by Michael. During the sermon, Chris, Gabe, and Michael all took turns paying tribute to Kim, each by showing how she had shown the light of Christ in his life. During his part of the sermon, Gabe mentioned his belief that these were the days prophesied of old—the days when Jesus would return to take believers with Him to heaven. At the end of the service, everyone applauded Kim, who promptly announced that dinner was being served back at the estate.

The meal was sumptuous. The menu was primarily a collection of Kim's favorites: arugula salad with mango and a pomegranate vinaigrette, stuffed salmon, aged Angus filets sliced and served in a white truffle sauce over whipped potatoes, fresh green beans in a butter-almond sauce, eggplant parmesan, and macaroni and cheese for Michele and young Chris.

During dinner, Zack turned to Gabe and asked, "Do you really believe all of that second coming and tribulation stuff?"

"Well, yes, Zack. If I didn't believe it, I wouldn't have said it," Gabe answered. He smiled as he spoke, but his tone was terse. He had never cared for Zack, but after the affairs of the day, he could barely look at the man.

"I thought most of the sane Christian world had become preterist by now." Zack grinned. Gabe blanched.

"What's preterist?" young Chris asked.

"Basically, it means someone who believes all of those prophecies were actually fulfilled in the first century," old Chris answered.

To Zack, Gabe said, "There's just no basis to believe that without assuming the Bible is filled with allegory. When in the first century did a fifteen-hundred-mile by fifteen-hundred-mile city called 'New Jerusalem' land on Earth? When was the entire world governed by a dictator so evil that Christ himself had to come to Earth to stop him before he destroyed the entire planet? When in the first century did mankind have the ability to destroy the entire world?"

"Wow! You're one of those!" Zack gasped in the Hollywood fashion typical of his preaching. "I apologize. I didn't mean to upset you. I just figured since it was your brother who discovered the Antakya Codex, you would have a more modern view of Christianity."

"In Gabe's defense," Michael interjected, "a lot of men and women of God still hold to the more traditional aspects of Christianity. He's not as anachronistic as you make him sound."

"*As* anachronistic?" Gabe demanded.

"Well, if anachronistic is what you call it, count me in," David said in a lighthearted enough way to bring a chuckle.

"What's anachronistic?" young Chris asked.

"Kind of fuddy-duddy. Out of step with the times," Michele answered. "Sounds like Dad to me."

"You don't believe we're coming close to the rapture?" young Chris asked his sister.

"Well, since you asked. I don't. Uncle Michael and I had a great talk today, and I realized I never really believed that Jesus is the only way to heaven. It just seems so prejudiced that billions of people are damned to hell if they don't believe one old Jew."

Tina stared a hole into her daughter. "Michele. Eat or leave the table," she said softly but sternly.

Michele dropped her eyes and picked up her fork. Gabe felt betrayed that Michael would try to indoctrinate his daughter into a ridiculous religion arising from the fraudulent discovery of a manufactured antiquity.

"Let's change the subject," Kim said. "Come on, guys, it's a party. We're not going to resolve such a theological debate over dinner. Let's just enjoy each other's company."

"I agree with Kim," Benny said, staring in a menacing way at Zack.

"Me too," Fran said as she left the table. "We came here to have a good time with each other."

Michael said remorsefully, "I apologize for the ill-chosen word, anachronistic, Gabe. You know I think the world of you."

Gabe was still smarting from Michele's comment, and he was livid with Michael. "Apology accepted, Michael," he said with forced graciousness, "but you and I need to have a talk before we turn in tonight. I think some boundaries have been crossed."

"Fine," Michael said with a frown.

Mercifully, Fran brought an end to the conversation when she entered the dining room with Kim's cake. Candles blazing, she began to sing "Happy Birthday" as young Chris scrambled to turn out the lights.

The rest of the evening went well. Emotions stayed under the surface as Kim, Chris, and Fran told stories of the old days. As the night proceeded, Michael was lost in thought, at one moment fearing Gloria's pain when she heard of Zack's betrayal, at another moment worried about the upcoming talk with Gabe.

Finally, as the evening wound down and people started to say good night, Gabe asked Michael to join him in the library. After Michael entered, Gabe closed the huge doors, the shelves on which blended seamlessly with the library shelves when the doors were shut. Although he had always found the library to be beautiful, to Michael it felt that night like a room without an exit.

"Michael, I don't know that there is a nice way to say this," Gabe began. "Don't you *ever* pollute my kids with this fraud of yours."

"Fraud?" Michael said, fully taken aback. "Gabe, I have a greater handle on the ultimate truth than anyone you know. And let me tell you something, what you preach will leave your kids ill-prepared to live in the coming new world."

"You listen to me," Gabe hissed. "I gave a leg to your cause. To your stupid, fraudulent scroll!"

"They're two different things, Gabe," Michael shouted back. "I would do anything, *anything* to take back that day! Every day I feel the shame and guilt about what happened to you! But I don't regret what I did with the Antakya Codex. It will serve humanity for generations to come." Michael lay his hand on Gabe's shoulder. Gabe brushed it away.

"A lie! A lie, Michael? How will a lie benefit the world for generations to come?" Gabe shot back.

"Gabe, if you could see the things I've seen!" Michael said excitedly. He motioned with his thumb and forefinger. "We are this close to fully decoding the alien message, but even what we've learned so far is amazing. Gabe, we actually have instructions on how to use retroviruses to change our DNA to bring out our latent, inherent psychic abilities."

"Great. A globe with seven billion demigods. Tell me that doesn't scare you, Michael!"

"Humanity won't be the same, Gabe. We'll evolve to a new species. I'm telling you, in twenty years the world will be at peace, one united planet, trading with our galactic counterparts."

Gabe pulled a book from the shelf. "Read this, Michael. It's a leaked report of a governmental group called The Collins Elite. They've been studying the UFO phenomenon for years, and do you know what they've concluded?" He chucked the book at his brother. "That UFOs are not extraterrestrial; they're extra-dimensional. This group, a US government think-tank, has concluded that these aliens are actually the same entities we called demons years ago. What if you're cavorting with demons, Michael?"

"I'm not!" Michael yelled in exasperation. "I'm building a glorious future for mankind!"

"Just take the book and read it. Will you do that much for me?" Gabe shrieked.

"Of course I will," Michael answered with deliberate calm.

"Good. Maybe at least if you read the book, you'll see where I'm coming from when I tell you I've decided I don't want you around my kids. As long as I can't trust you not to tear down their faith, you're not welcome here."

The words hit Michael like a punch to the gut. He lost his breath for a moment, staring at his beloved brother in disbelief. Then he ran from the library, book in hand.

Gabe exited the library to find his mother in stunned silence and Tina chasing out the front door after Michael.

In less than a minute, Michael was speeding out of the driveway.

The cell phone rang through the car's audio system. Michael saw that the caller was Tina. He wanted to ignore it and just get the hell out of

Dodge, but he loved and respected her too much. He pushed the button on the steering wheel to connect the call.

"Michael," Tina sobbed, "come back. Don't leave like this. Let's just all get a good night's sleep and figure it out in the morning."

"I can't stay right now, Tina," Michael said as tears flooded his eyes. "Gabe told me he doesn't want me around the kids." His voice broke. Banned from the kids! Shunned by his own family! He wiped furiously at tears streaming down his cheeks.

"Michael, he was angry, and he said angry things," she pleaded.

"He blames me for his leg," Michael said. "I can't deal with that right now."

Tina didn't deny it, confirming Michael's worst suspicions. "Okay, Michael, but that's not an excuse to leave. It's an opportunity to work through it."

"Not now, Tina. I have important work back in Rome. I would have to fly out tomorrow morning anyway. We wouldn't be able to resolve this in such a short amount of time."

"Fine, but hear me on this. I may be Gabe's wife, but I'm not the only love of his life. He's as tied to you as a man can be to another man. He's not the guy I married without you in his life. And he's not the only one that loves you. The kids and I adore you. Give me some time to work on him. Please!"

Michael felt his love for his family overpower the anger he was feeling toward his brother. He tried to speak, but the words caught in his throat. "Okay," he finally squeaked.

"And, Michael," Tina continued, "In every way that matters, you're *my* brother too. If there's anything ... *anything* I can do to make this right between you and Gabe, let me know, okay?"

"I'll do that, Tina." Michael sobbed.

"Just one more thing before I hang up," she said cautiously. "Gabe might not be the only one who blames you for his leg. You may have to forgive yourself, Michael. Sometimes things happen. Not everything is someone's fault."

Fresh, hot tears coursed down Michael's cheeks. "Ah-hum," was all he could mutter.

"Just remember that we love you, Michael, all of us. This is your home, and we want to see you here *very soon*. Okay?"

"Yes," Michael said with a cracked voice.

"I love you, Michael."

"And I love you too. Hug Mom and the kids good-bye for me."

Gabe sat elbows to knees with his head in his hands. He looked up in tears as Tina entered the house to find Kim standing over him in the middle of a lecture.

"In my heart, you're my son, and I love you more than life itself, Gabe. But here are some stark facts. If it weren't for Michael, you wouldn't be my son." She made a sweeping gesture toward the estate. "You, Tina, and the kids would have none of this if Michael hadn't chosen to bring you into the family all those years ago. He's the reason for all of this. He gave it to you, and you sent him away." Her voice broke. "I won't have it." She sat next to Gabe, wiping her eyes.

"I was angry, Mom. And I was protecting my kids." Gabe's eyes were red from crying.

"Well, I hope you never have to protect your kids from each other, because let me tell you, it breaks your heart." She cried openly.

"You think I was wrong?" Gabe asked more like a child than a man.

"Gabe," Kim said in a softer tone as she took his hand in hers. "You were poor, alone, and frightened. Then the son of a wealthy family pulled you in. He gave everything he had for you. It's the gospel story, honey. Your first real taste of Jesus' love came through Michael's actions. How can it be right that you reject him? Turn him away?"

Gabe lost control of his emotions at that point. His mother was right. He had a commitment to work it out with Michael, not spurn him. Michael! Of all people! His brother, his best friend—the one who had saved him from a horrible fate when his birthmother died! The one who stood up to Benny on his behalf when he was only nine years old!

"There's something else," Tina said as she sat down next to him and rubbed his heaving shoulders. "Gabe, you and Michael are both suffering because both of you blame him for your leg. You both have to let it go."

"I know," Gabe said resolutely.

"Follow him," Kim said.

"Maybe give him a day or two," Tina urged. "I spoke with him on the phone. He's hurting right now and so is Gabe. If they each take a day or so to cool off, pray, and think it through, they may be able to patch this up."

"I think you're right," Kim said soberly. "But no more than a couple of days, Gabe. I won't rest until I know my boys have stopped hurting each other."

TWENTY-ONE

It was a small matter for Michael to catch an earlier flight. As he waited, he checked in with his lab to find out what progress had been made. The original Holomax program had yielded significant genetic information that could truly transform the human race, but it also hinted at something more … a projectable holographic interface to the disc itself. The programmers had been working years on Holomax 2.0. Within days, it would be ready to test.

As he waited to board the flight, he reluctantly began to read the book Gabe had given him. Within a few moments, he found himself engrossed in its tale. It was an expose of a secret governmental group that had been examining the UFO phenomenon since the 1940s. This group's conclusion, which was presumably shared by many in power in the United States, was that UFOs might well be the twenty-first-century iteration of demonic activity.

The idea sounded preposterous to Michael at first, but then the author developed his thesis. Many of the events that had been communicated to him by whistleblowers were independently verifiable. Further, the impact on people who have had contact with UFOs bore incredible similarity to the historically documented effects of demon activity.

A flight attendant called to board the first-class section. Michael looked down at the book, astonished he had been through the first one hundred pages. It was an easy read, and while he hadn't bought into the hypothesis, he found it compelling.

Once seated in the plane, Michael read again. His mind wondered about the UFO incidents in his life. The Lady was a frightening creature. He could easily see her as demonic. His mind flashed to his encounter with her and to the manner in which fear of her had ring-fenced him, tied him to the disc. He thought of Isa's eyes—his own eyes, stolen from him. He shivered when he thought of the palpable evil exuded by Isa. Could the lure of intellectual achievement and technological advance have blinded him to what now seemed ridiculously obvious?

What if Gabe was right? If the Lady was an evil apparition, then what about the information on the disc? What are its effects? It led me to lie to the entire world! These were the thoughts that weighed heavily on Michael's mind as the flight crew served a small meal. Shortly after, he drifted off to sleep, the questions still bouncing around in his mind.

Michael's sleep was fitful. In dreams he relived the nightmare in Amsterdam when the Lady first took him. Every second, every detail was etched into his brain. He also relived the incidents with Gloria and Zack onboard the alien craft.

Then he dreamt with startling clarity of a future filled with the ancient technology. The family estate had been retrofitted to include a transportation chamber, and a voice-activated computer system controlled nearly all operations of the household. He made his way through the formal part of the house to the family area in the back. There he saw his mother, no older than thirty, looking out the windows to the backyard.

As he joined her, she turned a tear-stained face toward him. "Oh, Michael, it's horrible," she cried. She leaned her head on his shoulder and continued to peer out the window.

He put his arm around her, drawing her close to offer some comfort, and followed her gaze to the backyard, where a craft hovered above the chapel. A bright light pulsed from the craft.

Everything turned white and he heard his mother say, "Michael, only Jesus can save you from the evil you brought on the world." Then he felt her body dissolve into nothingness as the light faded.

Tears burned his eyes as he contemplated her words. He ran throughout the yard to find her. The chapel was gone. In its place stood the Lady and Isa, who held the Antakya Codex tightly in his hands. Standing in front of them were Michele and a young man with long, dark hair. He looked so much like a younger Gabe, but with ice-blue eyes. Dressed in a black medieval tunic and wearing black leather strips on each powerful forearm, he pulled an arrow from a quiver on his back, placed it in a crossbow, took aim, and fired on Isa. His arrow grazed the young Turk. Thunder rumbled as an invisible force knocked the young man to the ground, shattering the crossbow.

Michele screamed in horror and bent to help him. She was knocked to the ground by the same invisible force, and Isa grinned at her with delight as her body twisted in pain. Michael's heart was in his throat as he ran to help his niece.

"Worship me!" Isa screamed in a voice like thunder. The Lady's toothless mouth broke into a full grin as a sea of people appeared behind Michele, all writhing in agony.

"Stop it!" Michael screamed with anguish as he approached the pair. When he got within striking distance, Isa's eyes locked on his. The monster's gaze held him transfixed for a moment. In that second, everything turned silent.

Isa spoke very softly, barely a whisper, "Worship me."

Unable to speak, Michael shook his head while his mouth formed a silent *no*.

"Yes, Father." Isa grinned. The silence gave way to the unending shrill shouts of horror from the oppressed crowd. Michael felt himself being forced to the ground, joining them in a position of worship. Every nerve of his body pulsed simultaneously, sending a barrage of pain signals to his brain. In an instant, the only focus of his life, the only purpose to his existence was to alleviate the pain. Putting aside all pretense at understanding or thwarting his persecutor, he mindlessly joined the crowd in worshipping the beast before him.

Isa again caught his gaze, a sneer forming on his lips as he mocked, "Father ..."

"Father?" The stewardess nudged him awake. "Are you all right? You seem to be having some difficulty." For a second, Michael had forgotten where he was. He stared blankly at the stewardess.

"Father, are you all right?" she repeated.

"I'm fine," Michael said awkwardly as awareness returned to him. *Father! What a joke! I became a priest to keep the Lady at bay!*

The flight crew served dinner about an hour and a half before landing. Michael had some wine with dinner and came to some resolution for the questions in his mind. He decided the book might be right. The fruits of Michael's interaction with these beings were his lifelong fear of intimacy; a lie perpetrated on the entire world; and the crippling of his brother ... all indicators that a malevolent force was at work.

But what to do if Gabe and the book were right? Obviously he would have to destroy the disc and expose the Antakya Codex as a forgery. Then he would get on his knees and ask Jesus' forgiveness—ask Him to be the Master of his life—and then truly, with his whole heart and soul, live up to the vows he had taken. The very thought of this lifestyle filled him with longing. It would be wonderful to feel clean and free of secrets.

But what if the book was wrong? Then he owed it to himself, his colleagues, and to the civilized world to make known the alien technologies and philosophies.

He would soon have to make a decision as to which path he would choose. He decided to see the result of Holomax 2.0. Perhaps he could discern the truth from the information they would unlock this coming week.

Chris headed to the kitchen for some coffee before his morning run. He was surprised to see Kim having a cup at the kitchen table.

"You're up early, birthday girl." he grinned. As she looked up, he saw the sleepless worry in her eyes. In a concerned tone, he asked, "What's wrong?"

Her voice cracked and a tear streamed down her cheek as she formed the words. "Gabe and Michael had a confrontation last night, Chris. Gabe told Michael he's not welcome here as long as he's a bad influence on the kids' spirituality. Michael left immediately." She began to cry. Chris hugged her.

"They both have their points," Chris said. "I didn't like what I heard Michele say at dinner last night. I'm guessing it got Gabe pretty upset."

"This is Michael's home too, Chris!" Kim blurted through her tears.

"Of course it is," Chris comforted. "Let me tell you something. I've never seen a friendship like those two guys have. They won't stay angry at each other for long. I know it."

"Tina spoke with Michael. I think she's made some headway. She told him that this is his home and that we all love him."

"What did he say?" Chris asked.

"Well, he didn't turn around and come home. He said that there wouldn't be enough time to work things out with Gabe before he had to return to Rome. I spoke to Gabe. He's going to Rome to make it right with Michael."

"There you have it, Kim," Chris encouraged. "They both know they have to work it out. It doesn't sound like their relationship is broken beyond repair."

"Some of this is my fault. One of the major reasons Tina and I pushed this birthday thing was to get Gabe and Michael to spend some time together."

"You don't say," Chris wisecracked.

Kim playfully slapped his arm. "I can't stand to see them at each other. I thought they would spend some time together and enjoy it so much that they could drop their religious differences and just be brothers."

Chris gave up his run to sit with Kim. They talked about their lives with the boys. It was an odd family, but they had given the boys lots of love and good role models. They had to trust them now to do the right thing. All the while, the service was setting up to give everyone a sturdy breakfast before they departed.

At the first scent of bacon, Benny found his way to the kitchen. "Good morning, Kim," he said, ignoring Chris. "Is breakfast ready yet?"

"Another fifteen minutes," she said, patting a chair as an invitation for him to sit down.

"I think I'll shave," he said icily, staring at Chris. "Michael and I will have to leave shortly after we eat if we want to make our flight."

"Oh," Kim said, "Michael went back to Rome last night. He said something came up in his lab. If you can get rescheduled on the later flight, you could fly with Chris. Then we'll all go down to the airport together."

"I'll call a car service," Benny said as he huffed out of the room.

Kim rested her forehead in her hand. "I'm sure I don't want to know, but I have to ask, Chris. What's going on with Benny?"

Chris took her hand. "In a nutshell, he was caught with another man *in flagrante delecto*—in a church no less."

"I was always afraid something like that might happen. He's my brother and I love him, but sometimes he lacks self-control."

Chris smiled incredulously for a moment at the understatement. "The pope will probably dismiss him at the meeting of cardinals next week."

"So why is he mad at you?" Kim asked.

Chris fiddled nervously with his spoon and sighed. "I was the one who found him."

"And you told the pope?"

"Yes." Chris cleared his throat. "I don't want to hurt you, Kim, but it was more than I could take. He has to be reprimanded."

"When did this happen?" she asked.

"Yesterday."

"You mean it happened *here*! In our chapel?" She quickly covered her mouth as if subconsciously desiring to stop the words from exiting.

"Yeah," Chris said, looking down at the table. "Before you ask, it was with Zack."

Kim moaned. "What was I thinking bringing this group together? Remind me not to plan any more parties."

"I promise," Chris said with a smirk. He first chuckled and then laughed. He tossed the spoon casually on the table.

"What?" Kim asked.

"It's like we live in a TV show ... or some cheap novel."

"Nah," she said with a chuckle. "If this were a cheap novel or a TV show, we would've had sex."

They laughed as she laid her head on his shoulder.

David picked up the phone on the first ring. Caller ID showed it was from Gabe. "Hello."

"Hi, David. It's Gabe. How was the trip home?"

"Good, Gabe," David said cheerily, "and we want to thank you again for a great time."

"Don't thank me yet," Gabe said with hesitation. "I have to lay a really tough bit of news on you."

"That sounds ominous," David said. "Might as well get it over with, Gabe. Just say it."

"Chris happened upon Zack and Benny in the chapel this past weekend. He found them in an intimate situation."

"*What?*" David shrieked, drawing Fran's immediate attention.

"I know," Gabe said apologetically, "it's hard news to hear."

Fran came to David's side with a questioning look. He mouthed, "I'll tell you in a minute," as he raised his index finger. "It's flat-out disgusting!" David said fiercely. "I've always found that to be a strange combination … but to violate the chapel like that! To have such disrespect for God and your family! I'm appalled, Gabe. That's all I can say." Fran's eyes grew wide as she stared at him.

Gabe continued. "Well, for Chris, it was the last straw. He was livid. He's spending his time in Rome right now trying to get Benny defrocked, so he asked me to tell you the news."

"Because you want Fran and me to tell Gloria," David said with a sigh. At the mention of Gloria, Fran grabbed David's arm. He held out the palm of his hand in a "stop" motion to indicate it would just be a few more moments.

"That's up to you and Fran. If Benny is dismissed, it will make the press. It's doubtful that the details will be forthcoming from the Vatican. But a displaced Benny, mad as a hornet … who knows what he's likely to say or do?"

"Wow, what a bit of news," David said, more to himself than Gabe.

"I didn't want to say anything while you were here," Gabe said. "There were other … tensions."

"We know," David said. "We're light sleepers and sound carries at the estate. If you'll take some fatherly advice, Gabe?"

"Shoot."

"Your brother may be in some real trouble spiritually. Cutting him off will push him to the very place you want him to avoid. Show him Jesus in you. Give him something to come home to."

"I'm on it, David. I have a flight to Rome tomorrow. I'm not coming home until I've patched things up with Michael."

"Good man," David said. "The Lord could use your trip to restore Michael to us, Gabe. What better witness to Michele?"

"I'm with you 100 percent, David. If I could take back what I've said to him, I would, but I can't. With the Lord's help, though, it may all come to a good outcome." Despite Gabe's confident words, David could hear the underlying despair in his voice.

"It will," David reassured. "Fran is staring at me, wanting to know what's going on. I'd better hang up."

"I'll say a prayer for you guys," Gabe said.

"Back at you, buddy."

David explained to Fran after he hung up. She cried and punched the sofa in anger as he related the story.

"I've never really trusted Zack," Fran said in astonished pain, "but I never imagined something like this."

"The question is: Do we tell Gloria?" David asked. He sat next to her, pulling her close. Fran wrung her hands, reminding him briefly of Sarah and resurrecting old fears about Zack.

She said, "I don't know if she'll hear it from us, David. She's likely to believe we're slandering him. And she'll be immediately concerned about their viewing audience."

"But if it comes out in the press and she finds out we knew all along?"

"It would kill her," Fran muttered. "It would be like we were part of a conspiracy to keep her in the dark."

"Then we've got to tell her," David said.

"*I've* got to tell her," Fran corrected. She stared at David with fierce determination. "You have to let Zack know I'm talking to Gloria about it."

"I'll trade you," David said with resignation. He thought of how threatening Zack had become when confronted years before. This would not go well. He just knew it.

"I wish I could," Fran said. "I'd rather wipe the smile off his smug face than break my little girl's heart."

There was a brief knock at Chris's apartment door, followed by Gabe's voice as he let himself in. "Chris?"

"Hey," Chris said, looking up from his computer. He was disheveled and hadn't shaved for days.

"You look like hell," Gabe said.

"My incident report of what happened at the chapel wasn't enough for the pope. His Holiness wants me to sum up my suspicions of Benny's unacceptable activity since the time I met him."

Gabe whistled. "That's quite a tale."

"I decided to break it into sections: suspected malfeasance, other suspected criminal activity, and noncriminal activity that amounts to breaching the vows of priesthood." Chris pointed to the hundred-page document. "I have to give it to His Holiness this afternoon. It will be entered into the minutes of the meeting tomorrow."

"Too bad you couldn't add a section called, 'In General, Pain in the Butt.'"

"Trust me. There's enough here." Chris threw himself against the back of his chair and pushed a hand through his ramshackle hair. He paused a second and then spoke softly. "Gabe, I feel horrible about this. Not because of Benny, but because I feel like I'm betraying your mother's friendship. She still sees something redeemable in Benny."

"Maybe this will help him find that small part of himself—and I mean miniscule—that wants to change," Gabe offered as he patted the older man's shoulder.

Chris frowned. "I hope so, for your mother's sake. Have you seen Michael yet?"

"No." Gabe shrugged. "He doesn't even know I'm in town. I was afraid he would bolt if he knew I was coming."

"I don't think so. You two have a strong bond. I'm sure he wants to patch things up with you too." Chris placed the document in a manila envelope and sealed it.

"I hope you're right, Chris. I really do."

There was a knock at the door, the Swiss Guardsman who had been sent to retrieve the finished report for the pope. Chris dutifully handed it to the young man.

"So that's it," Gabe said. "Maybe you can get some rest now. You look spent."

"You said it. How about I take you to a quick lunch first? Then I'm going to hit the sack."

"Do you have to present anything to the cardinals tomorrow?"

"No. His Holiness will do it. In fact, I'm getting out of town. There's a cloistered monastery not far from here. I have a friend there. I thought I'd visit him for the day. Kind of stay under wraps until your uncle cools down."

It was past ten o'clock at night when Michael got home from the lab. He was shocked to find Gabe asleep on his couch when he entered the apartment. There was a catch in his throat. He knew Gabe was there to make peace between them. He wanted that as well.

"Hey," he said softly as he nudged his brother awake.

"Hey." Gabe woke with a start and then launched into the talk he had rehearsed in his mind over and over. "Michael. I was wrong to say what I did. I don't deserve your forgiveness, but I'm asking for it anyway. I don't want to live my life without you in it. Neither do Tina and the kids—"

"Slow down, buddy," Michael said with a grin. "It's done. It's over and forgotten. Go back to sleep. I'm going to hit the hay as well. We'll talk in the morning."

"Okay," a jetlagged Gabe said with a smile. "I love you, Michael."

"I know. I love you too, brother," Michael said as he brought a blanket and pillow to the couch.

Benny was up early. He hated to be up before sunrise, but today he had no choice. He had one opportunity to make his stand, and he intended to keep his job. In fact, he intended to have Chris defrocked for filing a false report about him.

First things first. He walked silently along the pre-dawn streets to an alley behind the building where the cardinals would meet. He looked around to be sure nobody was watching and knocked quickly on a nondescript door, which was answered by a bearded man dressed all in white. He hurried inside.

If I had known the kitchen staff could be bought so cheaply, I would have done this years ago. He handed an envelope of cash to the man, who bid him entrance. Once inside, the man counted the money, much to Benny's consternation. *How crass!*

The man led him to a simmering pot of chicken that would become the soup course of the day's lunch. He poured out the vial of potion Isa had sent and then motioned for the chef to stir the pot. He stared at the chef contemptuously, "Was that so hard? Did I really need to wake up early to do the pouring? You couldn't have done it yourself?"

"No, Signore. Non la potrei fare."

Benny just shook his head at the man's weakness and left the building. So the wheels were set in motion. It would now be a small matter for him to influence the pope and cardinals to take a more favorable view of him. After all, he had the only antidote.

Bonnie returned from the ladies room just after Zack had emptied the small vial from Benny into her Diet Coke. "So you still haven't told me why you're taking me out to this gorgeous dinner." She smiled lovingly.

"I just wanted to take the opportunity to spend some quality time with you," Zack said. "And I wanted to let you know I'm very happy about the baby—our baby."

"Oh Zack!" Bonnie exclaimed. "I'm so happy to hear you say that. I know it will be hard on the ministry, but we can find a way to raise this child of ours."

"Indeed we can, darlin'." Zack smiled broadly.

As the meal progressed, his lies became more and more bold as he expressed his love for her and the fact that he couldn't live without her. It had all been rehearsed, of course. It came out of him as effortlessly as a Sunday-morning sermon. But as he spoke, his mind could not help but wander and wonder about the child she was carrying. His child. How nice it would be to hold a baby! To teach his son or daughter about life. To leave a legacy of flesh, not just the cold stone and glass of the ever-expanding Riverside complex.

As the meal drew to a close, Bonnie excused herself again to go to the ladies' room. "It seems like Little Zack wants to rest on mama's bladder today." She grinned.

"Little Zack?"

"That's what I call him." She smiled down at him as she walked away from the table. It was the last straw. He couldn't kill "Little Zack." He dumped the antidote vial into her drink and made sure she finished it before they left.

Gabe woke to the smell of coffee—or more precisely, a homemade café au lait.

"I figured I could lure you awake with this," Michael said as he placed the cup in front of Gabe.

"Michael, again, I want to tell you how sorry I am about what I said."

Michael raised a hand to silence him. "I'm sorry for everything, Gabe. I blame myself for what happened to you. If I could do anything to change it, trust me, I would."

"I know," Gabe said. "And I think I blamed you too, or at least that crazy disc of yours."

Michael drew a sharp breath. "About that, Gabe. I read the book you gave me. All the stuff that's happened to me with the Lady—"

"The psychotic breaks?" Gabe chuckled at the thought. Michael was anything but psychotic.

Michael grinned. "Yeah. I probably mislabeled them. I now think I was having alien encounters, but the fear and the pain and the changes to my personality were all bad, Gabe. So I started thinking. What if there's something to this idea of it being demonic?"

This was more than Gabe could ever have hoped for, but he wanted to tread carefully. If he pushed too hard, he could run the risk of pushing Michael away from the right decision. "And what did you decide?" he asked cautiously.

"Basically, I want to find a relationship with Christ, but the potential for scientific discovery from the disc is tremendous. I think we may have finally cracked the code to get to the full amount of the information on the disc. We'll turn on our new program today. If I'm correct, we'll have an interactive interface with the disc. I should be able to ask it some pointed questions. Then I'll decide whether to destroy it or not."

"Destroy it?" Gabe gasped. He never thought he would hear those words escape his brother's lips.

"I only ever wanted to bring good to the world, Gabe." A look of anguish passed over him. He opened his mouth to continue, but his voice broke. He took a deep breath and started again. "But I lost my soul in the process. If the contents of that disc turn out to be pure science, then I'll have to find a way to accommodate what it says to

Christian belief ... *real* Christian belief. If it is patently unchristian, and I suspect it is, then I'll destroy it. When it all comes down to it, Gabe, I want what you and Chris have ... and Mom and Tina." Tears coursed down his cheeks, seemingly incongruent with the joyful grin at having finally come to terms with this conflict.

"You can have that right now, Michael. We can invite Jesus into your heart right now."

"Not right now, Gabe. Maybe tomorrow, okay? I need to see what's on that disc first."

"Sure. Okay." Gabe grinned.

"Of course, at some point I'll have to announce that the Antakya Codex was a forgery."

"Yes!" Gabe fist-pumped.

Michael grinned and went off to shower for work.

A grim foreboding overtook Gabe. To what lengths would the powers-that-be go to prevent Michael from making such an announcement?

"You can lead a horse to water, but you can't make her drink," Tina said to herself. She had awakened the kids early even though there was no school. She knew she couldn't force her daughter to make a commitment to Christ, but she could surely try to undo the damage Michael had done in supporting her alternate viewpoint.

She heard footsteps on the creaky stairs.

"Good morning, Mom!" Chris said, always in a happy mood when he woke.

"Good morning." Michele yawned with a look of disdain at being awakened so early.

"Hey, guys," Tina said with a smile. "I have a bit of a surprise today."

"Yeah?" a leery Chris asked.

"Whatever it is, I'm not interested, " Michele said drolly.

"Well, actually, I guess it is more of a surprise for Chris then. Mimi wants to take him fishing."

"Awesome!" Chris yelled. "Mimi? Where are you?" He left the kitchen to search for Kim.

"I thought it would be a mother-daughter day for us," Tina said.

"Why do I feel like a bird caught in a snare?" Michele asked ruefully.

Zack and Gloria had worked together in the kitchen to prepare an early breakfast for Fran and David. Their rapport had never been better. Gloria caught him looking at her and smiled in return. The night before she had seen such intense passion from her husband that it reminded her of their college days.

However, breakfast was stilted. Zack and Gloria wondered why Fran and David had invited themselves the night before. After they had finished eating, David asked Zack if the two of them could speak privately. Gloria raised an eyebrow toward her husband as if to say, "Well, at least we'll know why they're here."

"What was that all about?" Gloria asked her mother once the guys had left.

"David is telling Zack about the conversation we're having right now."

"Don't hold me in suspense, Mother. Just tell me what you came to say."

"Last weekend, Chris came across Zack and Benny in the Chapel. They were being … intimate."

"Oh praise God," Tina said into the phone. "Gabe, that's better than I could have ever wished for. Please stay the extra day, and make sure he's firmly planted in the Lord."

"Shouldn't be hard," Gabe said. "He knows more theology than any of us. He just needs to open his heart, and I think he's ready. What about Michele?"

"She and I are having a girls' day. Your mom took Chris fishing."

"My *mom* went fishing? I smell a plot."

"Yeah, well, so does your daughter."

"Don't push her away. Maybe just tell her where Michael now stands."

"Zack, the jig is up," David said seriously. "We know what happened in the chapel last weekend. Fran is telling Gloria right now."

Zack burst past David and ran to the dining room. "Gloria! It's not true. I can explain it, but you're not going to like what I have to say."

"Well, you tell me your side," Gloria demanded, her tear-filled eyes downcast to avoid contact with either her husband or her mother.

"I was the one who found Chris and Benny in the chapel," Zack said waving his arms dramatically. When I saw them, I lost it. I mean, it was God's sanctuary and they were violating it!" His voice continued to grow with the story as if it were a parody of his own Sunday morning broadcasts.

"They told me to just forget what I saw, or they would ruin me. But I just couldn't forget it. I guess this is Chris's way of warning me to keep quiet."

Kim and young Chris were speeding down the interstate. The car stereo played a new song by TMV called *Come Away* about Jesus calling His church home. They sang along: "We will be together. We will never part. We will be together. Come on home and share my heart."

In an instant, the sky lighted brighter than a million suns in a single, explosive crack of lightning. Kim's car careened off the road, where it crashed violently into the guardrail.

The thunder dissipated, leaving only the sound of the car stereo: "The dark spell they have chosen has led them all astray. They won't even notice; I've carried you away. Now we are together. Now we'll never part. Let's start our lives together. Come on home and share my heart."

"So you mean, just like that, Uncle Michael has changed his mind about all of his research?" Michele asked incredulously.

"Yes." Tina beamed. "Your dad thinks he'll give his heart to Jesus soon."

"That just makes no sense to me," Michele said. "Like he would turn his back on his life's work. Like he's going to renounce everything he's said on those TV shows. I don't believe you." She crossed her arms and stared defiantly at her mother.

"But it's the truth. Your dad will tell you himself," Tina protested.

"Come on, Mom. The most Dad accomplished in Rome was to get Uncle Michael not to talk to Chris and me about this stuff."

"And what?" Tina asked incredulously. "Dad and I are lying to you?"

"Not in a malicious way, Mom. I just think you and Dad are so entrenched in an old-fashioned belief that you're deluding even yourselves."

Tina's first reaction would have been to deal sternly with the girl in the wake of her accusation, but she remembered Gabe's admonition not to push too hard, lest she push her away. "I just wanted to tell you what your dad told me. You'll have time to talk to Uncle Michael himself about it."

Tina's measured response spoke louder than any frontal assault could have. In a softer tone Michele said, "I'm really happy Dad and Uncle Michael ironed things out. I wouldn't like it too much around here if Mimi and Daddy sulked all day, every day. Plus, I love Uncle Michael too."

"Me too," Tina said as the sky turned a blistering white. The lightning was sharp and bright, like a nuclear detonation. As the brilliance faded, a deafening roar of thunder shook the old estate.

Michele dropped to the floor and covered her head until the thunder slowly subsided in distant rumbling echoes. Carefully she stood to survey the damage. "Mom?" she called to no one there.

The time had come for the pope to discuss the matter of Benny's deportment. Before the pontiff could proceed, Benny stood to announce his offer of the antidote to any who would choose not to hear the charges brought against him. Gasps of shock and dismay rang out among the cardinals as they learned to their horror they had been poisoned. He stared malevolently at the pope as he clearly laid out their choices and waved the antidote before them. Suddenly he was knocked off his feet by a burst of light, followed by a thunderous rumble that shook the ancient building to its core, sending dusty mortar flying through the air.

Benny quickly stood to see through the dust that many, maybe half the cardinals had disappeared, along with the pope.

"It's time," he heard the Lady say in his mind.

"Gentlemen!" he said as the old men slowly rose to their feet. "It would appear that an era of greatness has come upon us! See for yourselves—the Lord has removed this recalcitrant pope and those who stood with him. It is time for us to choose his successor.

"I think I can bring the deliberations to a short close. By now I'm sure the poison has left you with a bit of nausea, dryness in your throat, and an overwhelming sense of fatigue." He waved the vial of antidote before them and grinned. "Fear not, friends. I'll be happy to share the antidote with you as we toast my ascendancy to the papacy."

He picked the pope's mitre out of the ruble, blew dust from it, and placed it precariously on his head. "You see, friends, with your votes or with your deaths, I will leave this convocation as Pope Peter Romanus. It has a nice ring to it. St. Malachy would approve. Don't you think?"

"Why would Chris lie about such a thing?" Fran asked.

Gloria, who had rushed to her husband's side, said bitterly, "Who knows? Who cares? The important thing is that you had such little faith in Zack that you believed it without question!"

Then the lightning struck. The suddenness of it sent Gloria into Zack's arms. They held each other closely until the light faded and the thunder subsided.

"What could that have been?" Gloria asked, looking around the dining room. "And where did Mom and David go?"

As the bright light dissipated and thunder echoed for long moments, Isa stared out the window. First he grinned, and then he laughed with wild abandon. "The sign!" he screamed. "*The sign!*"

The brothers had just eaten in the fresh air of a local piazza. Nothing in the states could compare to a European pizza. They laughed, talked, and enjoyed each other's company in a way that had eluded them for years.

"I've dilly-dallied enough, today," Michael said. "By now the program should be ready to run, and I'll have the answers to my questions."

"Before you go, I should tell you I got a text from Tina. Michele doesn't buy it that you've changed your position. She thinks her mother and I are lying to her." Gabe frowned and shook his head.

"I promise to talk some sense to her," Michael offered. "In fact, maybe I'll go home with you. God knows I won't have any work to do here once I trash the disc."

Gabe grinned at Michael's forgone conclusion that he would abandon the research and finally give his heart to Jesus.

The two men stood, and Michael hugged Gabe tightly. When the lightning struck, he felt his brother evaporate in his arms. In an instant, he knew it was the rapture. Even as the Earth shook and the thunder pealed, he ran to his laboratory, screaming, "No!"

He stormed into the lab to destroy the disc. He may have missed the rapture, but he was determined he would no longer aid the cause of evil.

"You're a bit late, Michael," the voice of the interface purred as he entered the lab. He knew the voice in an instant. Before him stood the Lady.

"Thank you for opening the portal, Michael," she purred.

Michael ran screaming from the lab into an uncertain future.

EPILOGUE

As Chris sat next to Vinnie's bed, the sharp, shrill sound of a trumpet blast filled his ears. Every molecule of his body seemed to vibrate with the sound, and then he instantly felt light and free. His body rose through the ceiling of the building and into the sky. In the few nanoseconds that followed, his knowledge and consciousness expanded exponentially. To his right was a young, vibrant, and healthy man. Chris's newly modified intellect immediately recognized him as his old friend Vinnie. The pain of illness and the ravages of age had been wiped away, and Vinnie's face glowed with the grace of the Lord.

"You look great, kid!" Vinnie said to his friend.

"You're looking pretty good yourself." Chris laughed.

"So this is it!" Vinnie grinned. "I was beginning to think I wouldn't live long enough to see it."

"I always thought we would see Jesus right away," Chris said. "But now I understand. We'll meet him above Earth. Looks like we're going to be astronauts, Vinnie."

As they rose higher and higher, they could see multitudes of Christians coming together in the sky. The sheer number was astounding. Over the years, many biblical scholars developed dogmatic restrictions about who would be chosen to join Him in the air. They had great arguments, but they had forgotten the inclusive nature of Love that had bought salvation. It wasn't meted out meagerly.

Chris wondered if he would see Kim in the crowd. With the speed of his thought, he was with her and young Chris, who now had the appearance of a grown man. In no time, Gabe and Tina joined them.

To his left, Chris heard a shriek of joy. He turned to see Fran hugging Tom and his parents. The four of them then reached out to embrace Chris. Fran and Tom looked young and happy, as they had in Africa years before. David and his first wife joined them, and everyone hugged everyone else. The scene was repeated a million times as people from all over the globe met with their formerly dead friends and relatives. In a very touching moment, Gabe introduced his birth mother to Tina and Kim. She hugged them both but was especially warm with Kim as she thanked her for being a mother to Gabe. Joseph, the combination butler and friend who had helped raise Gabe and Michael, found his way to young Chris.

Fran and Tom hugged Sarah, Mack, and Sandy.

All along, the group rose higher and higher. The blue sky of the atmosphere was giving way to the darkness of space. In the distance, a bright Light beckoned. It grew exponentially as the crowd sped toward it. Everyone knew the Light was none other than their Lord and Savior, Jesus.

As if prompted by an invisible hand, the group turned to see the full sphere of Earth below them.

"We have to pray for Michele and Michael," Tina said with sadness.

"And Gloria," Tom said.

For a brief second, Kim thought to add Benny's name to the list, but her newly enhanced intellect showed her that Benny was now fully a product of evil. Nor did anyone mention Zack.

They turned back to see that the Light was no longer distant. It was upon them. Bathed by the brilliance stood Jesus. Although glorified, His body bore the scars of His death ... far more brutal than anything depicted in artwork or movies. All gasped at the horror He had endured for them. Finally they knew the full extent of the price He paid. And then He smiled broadly, and all they could see was the *love.*

The multitude disappeared into the Light, which had appeared as a stroke of lightning to those on Earth. With one final crack, the Light disappeared, leaving Earth reeling in the thunderous aftershock.

AFTERWORD

This story is based on the viewpoint that Jesus will come to remove His faithful followers prior to a series of horrible judgments on the world. This is by no means the only viewpoint when it comes to the interpretation of Bible prophecy. Many scholars believe the rapture will take place during the tribulation, or even after it. I have chosen the pre-tribulation rapture because it is the most hopeful scenario. Nonetheless, I have been cautioned by some friends, who are very learned men of God, that we must always be careful to place our faith in Jesus and not in any one particular view of prophecy's fulfillment. Their concern is that we will lose faith if it is indeed our lot to be present for the tribulation.

I pray to God we will be spared that horrible time, but we may not be. In any event, the only secure hope in these turbulent times is the firm belief that Jesus has died for your sins. Accept His extended hand and remember that we are asked to carry on until He comes. That means we should keep one eye on the sky, but be steadfast in the individual ministries He has given on Earth.

I hope you have enjoyed this novel and, more importantly, have found it affirming to your faith. As the story continues, we will learn through the eyes of Michael, Benny, and the rest those things that will surely come ... those things from which we pray to be spared. The journey continues. Keep looking up, and keep looking for the chance to do His will in this day.

TC Joseph
August 2014

Keep your eye on the sky—but don't forget to look out for **Penance** to discover how Michael, Gloria, and Michele contend with the horrors that Benny and Isa bring upon the world!

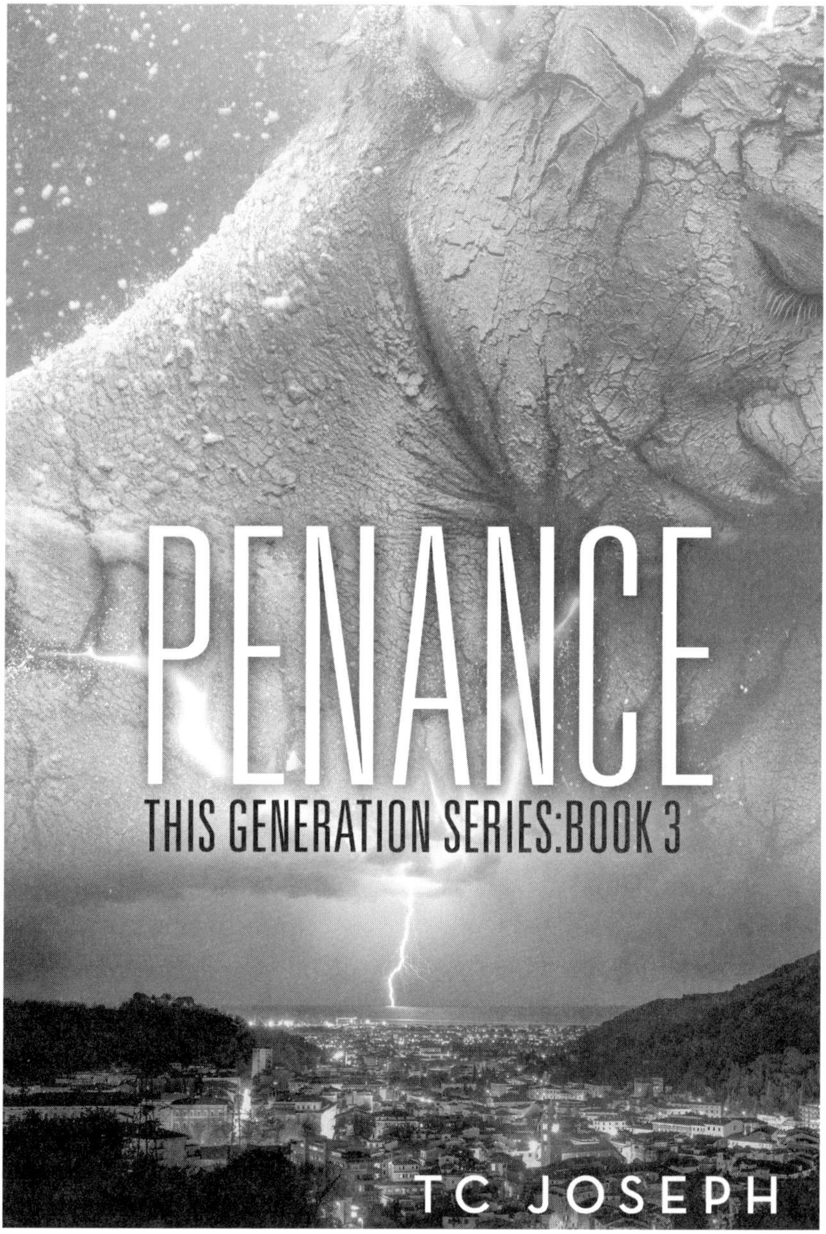

SELECTED BIBLIOGRAPHY

Anderson, R. *The Coming Prince*. Three Rivers, UK: Diggory Press Ltd., 2008.

Berliner, D. with Marie Galbrath, and Antonio Huneeus. *UFO Briefing Document*. New York: Dell Publishing, a Division of Random House, 1995.

Colman, J. *The Conspirators' Hierarchy: The Committee of 300,* 4th Edition. Las Vegas, NV: World Intelligence Review, 1997.

Dolan, R. and Bryce Zabel. *A.D. After Disclosure: The People's Guide to Life After Contact*. Rochester, NY: Keyhole Publishing Company, 2010.

Dolan, RM. *UFOs and the National Security State, Chronology of a Cover-up 1941–73*. Charlottesville, VA: Hampton Roads Publishing Company, Inc., 2000.

_______. *UFOs and the National Security State, The Cover-up Exposed*. Rochester, NY: Keyhole Publishing Company, 2009.

Estulin, D. *The True Story of the Bilderberg Group*. Walterville, OR: TrineDay, LLC, 2007.

Flynn, D. *Temple at the Center of Time, Newton's Bible Codex Deciphered and the Year 2012*. Crane, OR: Official Disclosure, a Division of Anomalos Publishing House, 2008.

Foden, G. *The Last King of Scotland*. New York: Vintage Books, 1998.

Fowler, RE. *The Andreasson Affair: The Documented Investigation of a Woman's Abduction Aboard a UFO.* Newberg, OR: Wild Flower Press, 1979.

______. *The Andreasson Affair, Phase Two.* Newberg, OR: Wild Flower Press, 1982.

Grant, JR. *The Signature of God: Astonishing Bible Codes.* Colorado Springs, CO: Waterbrook Press, 2002.

Griffin, GE. *The Creature from Jekyll Island: A Second Look at the Federal Reserve.* Appleton, WI: American Opinion Publishing, 1994.

Hamilton III, WF. *Project Aquarius: The Story of an Aquarian Scientist.* Bloomington, IN: AuthorHouse, 2005.

Hitchcock, M. *The Complete Book of Bible Prophecy.* Wheaton, IL: Tyndale House Publishers, Inc., 1999.

Hogue, J. *The Last Pope: The Prophecies of St. Malachy for the New Millennium.* Boston: Element Books Limited, 2000.

Horn, T. *Apollyon Rising 2012: The Lost Symbol Found and the Final Mystery of the Great Seal Revealed.* Crane, MO: Defender, 2009.

______. *Nephilim Stargates: The Year 2012 and the Return of the Watchers.* Crane, MO: Anomalos Publishing, 2007.

Horn, T. and Nita Horn. *Forbidden Gates: The Dawn of Techno-Dimensional Spiritual Warfare.* Crane, MO: Defender, 2010.

Horn, T. and Cris Putnam. *Petrus Romanus.* Crane, MO: Defender, 2012.

Horton, M., ed. *The Agony of Deceit: What Some TV Preachers Are Really Teaching.* Chicago: Moody Press, 1990.

Hunt, D. and TA McMahon. *America, the Sorcerer's New Apprentice: The Rise of New Age Shamanism.* Eugene, OR: Harvest House, 1988.

Imbrogno, PJ. *Interdimensional Universe, the New Science of UFOs, Paranormal Phenomena and Otherdimensional Beings.* Woodbury, MN: Llewellyn Publications, 2008.

______. *Ultraterrestrial Contact: A Paranormal Investigator's Explorations into the Hidden Abduction Epidemic.* Woodbury, MN: Llewellyn Publications, 2010.

Jeremiah, D., with CC Carlson. *The Handwriting on the Wall: Secrets from the Prophecies of Daniel.* Nashville, TN: W Publishing Group, 1992.

Knight, C. and Alan Butler. *Before the Pyramids: Cracking Archeology's Greatest Mystery.* London: Watkins Publishing, 2009.

Lindsey, H. *The Late Great Planet Earth.* Grand Rapids, MI. Zondervan. 1970.

______. *There's a New World Coming, an In-depth Analysis of the Book of Revelation.* Eugene, OR: Harvest House, 1973.

Marrs, J. *Alien Agenda,* New York: HarperCollins Publishers. 2008.

______. *The Rise of the Fourth Reich,* New York: HarperCollins Publishers, 2008.

______. *Rule by Secrecy,* New York. HarperCollins Publishers, 2000.

Martin, M. *Windswept House,* New York: Doubleday, 1996.

Milor, JW. *Aliens and the Antichrist: Unveiling the End-Times Deception,* Lincoln, NE: iUniverse, 2006.

Missler, C., Dr. *Prophecy 20/20: Profiling the Future Through the Lens of Scripture,* Nashville, TN: Thomas Nelson, Inc., 2006.

______. *Cosmic Codes: Hidden Messages from the Edge of Eternity,* Coeur d'Alene, ID: Koinonia House, 1999.

Picknett, L. and Clive Prince. *The Stargate Conspiracy: The Truth About Extraterrestrial Life and the Mysteries of Ancient Egypt,* New York: Berkley Books, 1999.

Redfern, N. *Final Events and the Secret Government Group on Demonic UFOs and the Afterlife*, San Antonio, TX: Anomalist Books, 2010.

______. *The NASA Conspiracies,* Pompton Plains, NJ: New Page Books, 2011.

Rice, Andrew. *The Teeth May Smile but the Heart Does Not Forget: Murder and Memory in Uganda,* New York: Metropolitan Books, 2009.

Richardson, J. *The Islamic Antichrist: The Shocking Truth about the Real Nature of the Beast,* Los Angeles: WND Books, 2006.

______. *Mideast Beast: The Scriptural Case for an Islamic Antichrist,* Washington, DC: WND Books, 2012.

Romanek, S. *Messages, The World's Most Documented Extraterrestrial Contact Story,* Woodberry MN: Llewellyn Publications, 2009.

Rothkopf, D. *Superclass: The Global Power Elite and the World They Are Making,* New York: Ferrar, Straus and Giroux, 2008.

Seftel, A. *Uganda, the Bloodstained Pearl of Africa and its Struggle for Peace, From the Pages of DRUM,* Lanseria, South Africa: Bailey's African Photo Archives, 1994.

Sherman, D. *Above Black: Project Preserve Destiny, A True Story,* Kearney, NE: Order Dept, LLC, 2008.

Sherman, ER. with Nathan Jacobi, PhD and Dave Swaney. *Bible Code Bombshell, Compelling Scientific Evidence that God Authored the Bible,* Green Forest, AR: New Leaf Press, 2005.

______. *Bible Code Bombshell: Compelling Scientific Evidence that God Authored the Bible,* Green Forest, AR: New Leaf Press, 2005.

Shoebat, W., with Joel Richardson. *God's War on Terror: Islam, Prophecy, and the Bible,* USA: Top Executive Media, 2010.

Shriner, S. *Bible Codes Revealed: The Coming UFO Invasion,* New York: iUniverse, 2005.

Smith, WB. *Deceived on Purpose: The New Age Implications of the Purpose-Driven Church*, Magalia, CA: Mountain Stream Press, 2004.

Strieber, W. *Breakthrough: The Next Step*, New York: Harper PaperBacks, a Division of HarperCollins Publishers, 1996.

______. *Communion: A True Story*, New York: Harper, 1988.

______. *Confirmation*. New York: St. Martin's Press, 1998.

______. *Transformation*. New York: Avon, 1998.

Vallee, J. *Messengers of Deception: UFO Contacts and Cults*, Brisbane, Australia: Daily Grail Publishing, 1979.

Ventura, J. with Dick Russell. *63 Documents the Government Doesn't Want You to Read*, New York: Skyhorse Publishing, 2011.

Yallop, D. *In God's Name: An Investigation into the Murder of Pope John Paul I*, New York: Basic Books, 2007.

Internet Sites

Apollo Moon Conversations and Pictures Show NASA Cover-Up. August 31, 2010. http://www.ufos-aliens.co.uk/cosmicphotos.html.

Air Force Advisory Panel Briefing January 12, 1967. http://www.cufos.org/1967 01 12 AF PanelBriefing.pdf.

Booth, Billy. 1959–The Papua, New Guinea UFOs. August 26, 2010. http://ufos.about.com/od/bestufocasefiles/p/papua.htm.

Coast to Coast. Full Interview with Father Malachi Martin. https://www.youtube.com/watch?v=DEDXYPgsp9M.